Praise for
Frederick Forsyth's
thundering achievement

NO COMEBACKS

"Quite possibly the most entertaining collection of short stories currently making the rounds. . . . Each tale offers generous helpings of mystery and suspense mingled with a wry sense of humor, philosophy, and real style. Not to mention some lovely twists and double crosses in the best O. Henry tradition."

—*Penthouse*

"Few writers do physical action any better than Forsyth. . . . These stories are very good value, creating an appetite for more."

—*Los Angeles Times*

"The 10 stories of Forsyth's collection vibrate with drama and the shock of the unexpected."

—*Publishers Weekly*

"A collection which will appeal to you whether you read for fun, for enrichment, or both. Forsyth has reestablished his position as an excellent teller of adventure stories. . . . Unadulterated pleasure."

—*Denver Post*

"Forsyth is a first-class narrator—instantly sketching in characters, tossing off perfect dialogue, creating mood and atmosphere. . . . A crisp, solid treat."

—*Kirkus Reviews*

"Forsyth is as adept at the short story as he is at the novel. He grabs the reader with his opening lines, swiftly embroils him in the plot, and then leads him in a merry dance to a highly surprising solution."

—*John Barkham Reviews*

FREDERICK FORSYTH

NO COMEBACKS

Collected Short Stories

BANTAM BOOKS
NEW YORK · TORONTO · LONDON · SYDNEY · AUCKLAND

NO COMEBACKS
A Bantam Book / published by arrangement with Viking Penguin.

PRINTING HISTORY
Viking edition published May 1982
A Selection of Literary Guild of America
*"No Comebacks," "Money with Menaces," and
"Used in Evidence" appeared originally in* PLAYBOY
Bantam edition / April 1988
12 printings through April 1990

ISBN 0-553-27673-5

Published simultaneously in the United States and Canada

PRINTED IN THE UNITED STATES OF AMERICA

RAD   20   19   18   17   16   15   14   13

For Carrie

Contents

No
Comebacks

No Comebacks

Mark Sanderson liked women. For that matter he also liked Aberdeen Angus fillet steaks, medium rare with tossed heart-of-lettuce salad, and he consumed both with equal if passing enjoyment. If he ever felt a little peckish, he rang up the appropriate supplier and ordered what he needed to be sent round to his penthouse. He could afford it, for he was a millionaire several times over, and that was in pounds sterling, which even in these troubled times are each worth about two U.S. dollars.

Like most rich and successful men, he had three lives: his public and professional life as the golden-boy tycoon of the City of London; his private life, which is not necessarily what it means, for some men like to lead a private life in a glare of publicity; and his secret life.

The first was regularly chronicled in the financial columns of the major newspapers and TV programmes. In the mid-sixties he had started work for a real-estate agent in the West End of London with little formal education but a brain like a razor for a lucrative property deal. Within two years he had learned the rules of the game and, more importantly, how to break them legally. At the age of twenty-three he clinched his first solo deal, a mere £10,000 profit inside twenty-four hours for a residential property in St. John's Wood, and founded Hamilton Hold-

1

ings which remained sixteen years later the pivot of his
wealth. He named it after the first deal he clinched, for
the house had been in Hamilton Terrace. It was the last
sentimental thing he ever did. By the early seventies he
was out of residential property with his first million
pounds and into office-block development. By the mid-
seventies he was worth close to £5 million and began to
diversify. His Midas touch was as shrewd in finance,
banking, chemicals and Mediterranean holiday resorts as
it had been in St. John's Wood. City editors reported it,
people believed it and the shares of the ten-division con-
glomerate grouped under Hamilton Holdings rose steadily.

His private life could be found in the same newspapers
a few pages earlier. A man with a Regent's Park penthouse, Elizabethan manor in Worcestershire, chateau in
the Loire Valley, villa at Cap d'Antibes, yacht, Lambor-
ghini, Rolls Royce, and a seemingly endless succession of
young and athletic starlets photographed in his company
or envisaged in his four-metre circular bed, tends to have
a compulsive fascination for the scribes of the William
Hickey column. A mention in dispatches at the divorce
hearing of a million-dollar film actress and a paternity suit
from a dusky Miss World contender would have ruined
him fifty years ago, but at the turn of this decade it merely
proved, if proof were needed and nowadays apparently
often is, that he could do it, which among the "In" people
of the West End of London is sufficiently remarkable to
excite admiration. He was a much chronicled man.

His secret life was something else again, and could be
summed up in one word—boredom. Mark Sanderson was
bored out of his mind with the whole shooting match. The
quip he had once coined—"Whatever Mark wants Mark
gets"—had become a sour joke. At thirty-nine he was not
bad-looking in a glowering, Brando sort of way, physi-

cally fit and lonely. He was aware he wanted someone, not hundreds of them, just someone, and children by her and a place in the country called home. He also knew he was extremely unlikely to find her, for he had a fair idea of what he wanted and he had not met one in a decade. Like most rich philanderers, he would be impressed only by a woman who quite genuinely was not impressed by him, or at least the public him, the him of money and power and reputation. Unlike most rich philanderers he still retained enough capacity for self-analysis to admit this, at least to himself. To do so publicly would mean death by ridicule.

He was quite certain he would never meet her, when in the early summer he did. It was at a party in aid of some charity, the sort of thing where a boring time is had by all and the tiny balance left from the ticket money is sent to provide a bowl of milk in Bangladesh. She was across the room listening to a small fat man with a large cigar to compensate. She was listening with a calm half-smile that gave no indication whether she found the anecdote amusing, or the antics of the short man, who was trying to get an eyeful of her cleavage.

Sanderson drifted across and on the strength of a nodding acquaintance with the short film producer had himself introduced. Her name was Angela Summers, and the hand that took his was cool and long, with perfect nails. The other, holding what looked like a gin and tonic but turned out to be just tonic, bore a slim band of gold on the third finger. Sanderson could not have cared less; married women were as easy as any others. He ousted the film producer and guided her elsewhere to talk. Physically she impressed him, which was unusual, and excited him, which was not.

Mrs. Summers was tall and straight-backed, with a calm and handsome if not fashionably beautiful face. Her figure certainly was unfashionable in the lath-thin eighties—deep-bosomed, small-waisted, with wide hips and long legs. Her gleaming chestnut hair was coiled behind her head, and seemed to be healthy rather than expensive. She wore a simple white dress which improved a medium-gold suntan, no jewellery and only a touch of make-up round the eyes, which alone set her off from the other socialite women in the room. He put her age at thirty, and later learned it was thirty-two.

He assumed the suntan came from the usual winter skiing holiday extended into April or from a spring Caribbean cruise, meaning she or her husband had to have the money to live that way, which the other women in the room also had. He was wrong on both counts. He learned that she and her husband lived in a chalet on the coast of Spain on the basis of her husband's tiny earnings from books about birds and her own from teaching English.

For a moment he thought the dark hair and eyes, the carriage and the golden skin might mean she was Spanish by birth, but she was as English as he was. She told him she had come to visit her parents in the Midlands and a former school friend had suggested she spend a week in London before returning. She was easy to talk to. She didn't flatter him, which suited his mood, nor did she burst into peals of laughter if he said something mildly amusing.

"What do you think of our West End society?" he asked as they stood with backs to the wall watching the party.

"Probably not what I'm supposed to," she replied thoughtfully.

"They're like a lot of parakeets in a jamjar," he muttered savagely.

She raised an eyebrow. "I thought Mark Sanderson was

one of the pillars of it." She was teasing him, quite gently but firmly.

"Do our doings penetrate down to Spain?" he asked.

"Even on the Costa Blanca we can get the *Daily Express*," she answered deadpan.

"Including the life and times of Mark Sanderson?"

"Even those," she said quietly.

"Are you impressed?"

"Should I be?"

"No."

"Then I'm not."

Her reply caused him a sense of relief. "I'm glad," he said, "but may I ask why?"

She thought for a few moments. "It's really rather phoney," she said.

"Including me?"

He was glancing down at the gentle rise and fall of her breasts under the simple white cotton when she looked round at him.

"I don't know," she said seriously. "I suspect that given half a chance you might be quite a nice person."

The reply caught him off balance.

"You could be wrong," he snapped, but she just smiled tolerantly as to a fractious small boy.

Her friends came to reclaim her a few minutes later, gushed to Sanderson and prepared to leave. On the way to the lobby he whispered a request to take her out to dinner the following night. He had not asked in that way for years. She made no arch rejoinder about the dangers of being seen out with him, assuming he would take her where there were no photographers. She considered the request for a moment, then said, "Yes, I think I'd like that."

He thought about her all that night, ignoring the bony and hopeful model he had found at Annabel's in the small

hours, lying awake, staring at the ceiling, his mind filled
with a fantasy vision of gleaming chestnut hair on the pillow beside him and soft, golden skin under his touch. He
was prepared to bet she slept calmly and quietly, as she
seemed to do everything else. He moved his hand across
the darkness to caress the model's bosom, but found only
a diet-starved puppy's ear and an exaggerated gasp of
feigned arousal. He went into the kitchen and brewed
coffee, drinking it in the darkened sitting room. He was
still sitting there looking out over the trees of the park
when the sun rose over distant Wanstead marshes.

A week is not long to have an affair, but it can be enough
to change a life, or two, or even three. The next evening
he called for her and she came down to the car. She wore
her hair piled high on top of her head, a white ruffled
blouse with leg-of-mutton sleeves ending in a froth of lace
at the wrists, a wide cinch belt and black maxi-skirt. The
outfit gave her an old-fashioned Edwardian air that he
found exciting because it was in contrast to his own private thoughts about her of the night before.

She talked simply but with intelligence and listened
well when he talked about his business, which he seldom
did with women. As the evening wore on he became
aware that what he already felt for her was not a passing
attraction, nor even simple lust. He admired her. She had
an inner calmness, a self-composure, a serenity that rested
and relaxed him.

He found himself talking to her more and more freely
about things he usually kept to himself—his financial affairs, his boredom with the permissive society that he at
once despised and used like a bird of prey. She seemed
not so much to know as to understand, which is far more
important in a woman than mere knowledge. They were

still talking quietly at the corner table after midnight when the restaurant wanted to close. She declined in the nicest possible way to come up to his penthouse for a nightcap, which had not happened to him in years.

By the midweek he was admitting to himself that he was smitten like a seventeen-year-old boy. He asked her what her favourite perfume was, and she told him it was Miss Dior, of which she sometimes permitted herself a quarter ounce duty free on the plane. He sent a minion to Bond Street and that evening gave her the largest bottle in London. She accepted it with unaffected pleasure, and then immediately protested at the size of it.

"It's far too extravagant," she told him.

He felt embarrassed. "I wanted to give you something special," he said.

"It must have cost a fortune," she said severely.

"I really can afford it, you know."

"That may be so, and it's very nice, but you mustn't go buying me things like that again. It's sheer extravagance," she told him with finality.

He rang up his Worcestershire manor before the weekend and had the heating in the pool turned on, and on the Saturday they motored down for the day and swam, despite the chill May wind that forced him to have the sliding glass screens wheeled round three sides of the pool. She appeared from the dressing rooms in a one-piece swimsuit of white towelling and the sight of her took his breath away. She was, he told himself, a magnificent woman, in every sense.

Their last evening out was on the eve of her departure for Spain. In the darkness of the Rolls parked in a side street round the block from where she was staying they kissed for a long time, but when he tried to slip his hand down her frock she gently and firmly removed it and put it back in his lap.

He proposed to her that she leave her husband, divorce him and that they marry. Because he was evidently very serious she took the suggestion seriously, and shook her head.

"I couldn't do that," she said.

"I love you. Not just passingly, but absolutely and completely. I'd do anything for you."

She gazed forward through the windscreen at the darkened street. "Yes, I think you do, Mark. We shouldn't have gone this far. I should have noticed earlier and stopped seeing you."

"Do you love me? Even a little?"

"It's too early to say. I can't be rushed like that."

"But could you love me? Now or ever?"

Again she had the womanly sense to take the question completely seriously.

"I think I could. Or rather, could *have* loved you. You're not anything like you and your reputation try to make you out to be. Underneath all the cynicism you're really rather vulnerable, and that's nice."

"Then leave him and marry me."

"I can't do that. I'm married to Archie and I can't leave him."

Sanderson felt a surge of anger at the faceless man in Spain who stood in his way. "What's he got that I can't offer you?"

She smiled a trifle ruefully. "Oh, nothing. He's really rather weak, and not very effectual . . ."

"Then why not leave him?"

"Because he needs me," she said simply.

"I need you."

She shook her head. "No, not really. You want me, but you can get by without me. He can't. He just hasn't the strength."

"It's not just that I want you, Angela. I love you, more

than anything else that's ever happened to me. I adore you, and I desire you."

"You don't understand," she said after a pause. "Women love to be loved and adore to be adored. They desire to be desired, but more than all these together a woman needs to be needed. And Archie needs me, like the air he breathes."

Sanderson ground his Sobranie into the ashtray.

"So, with him you stay . . . 'until death us do part'," he grated.

She didn't rise to the mockery but nodded and turned to stare at him. "Yes, that's about it. Till death us do part. I'm sorry, Mark, but that's the way I am. In another time and another place, and if I weren't married to Archie, it might have been different, probably would. But I am married to my husband, and that's the end of it."

The following day she was gone. He had his chauffeur drive her to the airport to catch the Valencia plane.

There are very fine gradations between love and need and desire and lust, and any one can turn into an obsession in a man's mind. In Mark Sanderson's all four did, and the obsession grew with the mounting loneliness as May turned into June. He had never been baulked in anything before, and like most men of power had developed over a decade into a moral cripple. For him there were logical and precise steps from desire to determination, to conception, to planning, to execution. And they inevitably ended in acquisition. In early June he decided to acquire Angela Summers, and the phrase that ran incessantly through his mind when he studied the stage of conception of the method was from the Book of Common Prayer. Till death us do part. Had she been a different woman, impressed by wealth, luxury, power, social standing, there would have been no problem. For one thing he could have dazzled her with wealth to get her; for another she would have been a different woman and he would not have been so obsessed by her. But he was going round in a circle, and the circle would lead to madness, and there was only one way to break it.

He rented a small flat in the name of Michael Johnson, contacting the letting agents by telephone and paying a month's rent and a month's deposit in cash by registered mail. Explaining he would be arriving in London in the small hours of the morning, he arranged for the key to be left under the doormat.

Using the flat as a base, he telephoned one of the no-questions-if-it's-legal private inquiry agencies in London and stated what he wanted. Hearing the client wished to remain anonymous, the bureau needed money in advance. He sent them £500 in cash by special delivery.

One week later a letter came to Mr. Johnson stating the commission had been completed and the account balance was another £250. He sent it by post, and three days later received the dossier he wanted. There was a potted biography, which he skimmed through, a portrait taken from the flyleaf of a book about birds of the Mediterranean, long since out of print after selling a few score of copies, and several photos taken with a telephoto lens. They showed a small, narrow-shouldered man with a toothbrush moustache and a weak chin. Major Archibald Clarence Summers—"He would have to keep the Major," thought Sanderson savagely—expatriate British officer living in a small villa half a mile back from the coast outside an undeveloped Spanish coastal village in Alicante province, halfway between Alicante and Valencia. There were several shots of the villa. There was finally a rundown on the way of life of the villa, the morning coffee on the tiny patio, the wife's morning visits to the Castillo to teach

English to the Condesa's three children, her inevitable afternoon's sunning and swimming on the beach between three and four while the major worked on his notes about birds of the Costa Blanca.

He started the next stage by informing the staff at his office that he would be staying at home until further notice, but that he would be in daily contact by phone. His next step was to change his appearance.

A small hairdresser advertising in *Gay News* was most helpful in this regard, cutting Sanderson's longish hair to a very "butch" crewcut and dyeing it from its natural dark chestnut to a pale blond. The operation took over an hour, would be good for a couple of weeks and was accompanied by much appreciative cooing from the hairdresser.

From then on Sanderson made a point of driving straight into the underground car park of his apartment block and taking the lift to the penthouse, avoiding the lobby porter. By telephone from his apartment he secured from a contact in Fleet Street the name and address of one of London's leading archive libraries specializing in contemporary affairs. It contained a superb section of works of reference and a copious collection of newspaper and magazine cuttings. After three days he had obtained a reading ticket in the name of Michael Johnson.

He began with the master heading of "Mercenaries." This file contained subfiles and cross-indexes bearing such titles as "Mike Hoare," "Robert Denard," "John Peters" and "Jacques Schramme." There were other subfiles on Katanga, Congo, Yemen, Nigeria/Biafra, Rhodesia and Angola. He ploughed through them all. There were news reports, magazine articles, commentaries, book reviews and interviews. Whenever a book was mentioned, he noted the name, went to the general library section, withdrew the volume and read it. These included such titles as

History of Mercenaries by Anthony Mockler, *Congo Mercenary* by Mike Hoare and *Firepower*, which dealt exclusively with Angola.

After a week a name began to emerge from this welter of snippets. The man had been in three campaigns and even the most notorious of the authors appeared to speak warily of him. He gave no interviews and there was no photograph of him on file. But he was English. Sanderson had to gamble that he was still somewhere in London.

Years earlier, when taking over a company whose main assets were in blue-chip property, Sanderson had acquired a small menu of other commercial firms which included a cigar merchant, a film-processing laboratory and a literary agency. He had never bothered to be shot of them. It was the literary agency which found the private address of the author of one of the memoirs that Sanderson had read in the library. The man's original publisher had no reason to be suspicious and the address was the same as the one to which the slim royalty cheques had once been sent.

When the property tycoon visited the mercenary/author, on the pretext of being from the man's own publishers, he found a man long gone to seed and drink, over the hill, living on his memories. The former mercenary hoped that the visit might herald a reprint and further royalties, and was plainly disappointed when he learned it did not. But he brightened at the mention of an introduction fee.

Sanderson, passing himself off as Mr. Johnson, explained his firm had heard a certain former colleague of the ex-mercenary might be thinking of publishing his own story. They would not want another firm to get the rights. The only problem was the man's whereabouts. . . .

When the ex-mercenary heard the name, he grunted.

"So, he's going to come clean, is he?" he said. "That surprises me."

He was unhelpful until his sixth large whiskey and the feel of a bundle of notes in his hand. He scribbled on a piece of paper and handed it to Sanderson.

"When the bastard's in town he always drinks there," he said.

Sanderson found the place that evening, a quiet club behind Earl's Court. On the second evening his man came in. Sanderson had seen no picture of him, but there was a description in one of the mercenary memoirs, including the scar on the jaw, and the barman greeted the man by a first name which also fitted. He was rangy, wide-shouldered and looked very fit. In the mirror behind the bar Sanderson caught a glimpse of brooding eyes and a sullen mouth over the pint of beer. He followed the man home to a block of flats 400 yards away.

When he knocked on the door ten minutes after watching the light go on from the street, the mercenary was in a singlet and dark slacks. Sanderson noted that before opening up, he had killed the light in his own hallway and left himself in shadow. The light in the corridor illuminated the visitor.

"Mr. Hughes?" asked Sanderson.

The man raised an eyebrow. "Who wants to know?"

"My name is Johnson, Michael Johnson," said Sanderson.

"Warrant card," said Hughes peremptorily.

"Not fuzz," said Sanderson. "Private citizen. May I come in?"

"Who told you where to find me?" asked Hughes, ignoring the question.

Sanderson gave him the name of his informant. "Not that he'll remember in twenty-four hours," he added. "He's too boozed up to remember his own name these days."

A hint of a smile appeared at the corner of Hughes's mouth, but there was no humour in it.

"Yeah," he said, "that fits," and jerked his head towards the interior. Sanderson moved past him into the living room. It was sparsely and shabbily furnished, in the manner of a thousand rented premises in that area of London. There was a table in the centre of the floor. Hughes, following behind, gestured him to sit at it. Sanderson sat down and Hughes took a chair opposite him.

"Well?"

"I want a job done. A contract. What I believe is called a hit."

Hughes stared at him without change of expression.

"Do you like music?" he asked at last. Sanderson was startled. He nodded.

"Let's have some music," said Hughes. He rose and went to a portable radio standing on a table near the bed in the corner. As he switched on the set he also fumbled under the pillow. When he turned round Sanderson was staring into the muzzle of a Colt .45 automatic. He swallowed and breathed deeply. The volume of the music swelled as Hughes turned the radio up. The mercenary reached into the bedside drawer, his eyes still on Sanderson above the muzzle. He withdrew a notepad and pencil and returned to the table. One-handed he scribbled a single word on the sheet and turned it to Sanderson. It just said: "Strip."

Sanderson's stomach turned over. He had heard men like this could be vicious. Hughes gestured with his gun that Sanderson should move away from the table, which he did. Sanderson dropped his jacket, tie and shirt on the floor. He wore no vest. The gun gestured again, downwards; Sanderson unzipped his fly and let his trousers fall. Hughes watched without a trace of expression. Then he spoke.

"All right, get dressed," he said. With the gun still in his hand, but pointing at the floor, he crossed the room and turned the music from the radio lower. Then he came back to the table.

"Toss me the jacket," he said. Sanderson, with his trousers and shirt back on, laid it on the table. Hughes patted the limp jacket.

"Put it on," he said. Sanderson did so. Then he sat down again. He felt he needed to. Hughes sat opposite him, laid his automatic on the table near his right hand and lit a French cigarette.

"What was all that about?" asked Sanderson. "Did you think I was armed?"

Hughes shook his head slowly.

"I could see you weren't," he said, "but if you had been wired for sound I'd have tied the mike flex round your balls and sent the recording to your employer."

"I see," said Sanderson. "No hardware, no tape-recorder, and no employer. I employ myself; sometimes others. And I'm serious. I need a job done, and I'm prepared to pay well. I'm also very discreet. I have to be."

"Not enough for me," said Hughes. "Parkhurst is full of hard men who trusted punters with more mouth than sense."

"I don't want you," said Sanderson evenly. Hughes raised an eyebrow again. "I don't want anybody who lives in Britain or has roots here. I live here myself; that's enough. I want a foreigner for a foreign job. I want a name. And I'm prepared to pay for that name."

From his inside pocket he drew a wad of fifty brand-new £20 notes and laid them on the table. Hughes watched, expressionless. Sanderson split the pile in two, pushed one pile towards Hughes and carefully tore the other pile in half. He put one sheaf of twenty-five half-notes in his pocket.

"The first five hundred is for trying," he said, "the second half is for succeeding. By which I mean the 'name' must meet me and agree to take the job. Don't worry; it's not complex. The target is no one famous, a complete nonentity."

Hughes eyed the £500 in front of him. He made no move to pick it up.

"I may know a man," he said. "Worked with me years ago. I don't know if he still works. I'd have to find out."

"You could call him," said Sanderson. Hughes shook his head.

"Don't like international phone lines," he said. "Too many are on tap. Especially in Europe these days. I'd have to go over and see him. That would cost two hundred more."

"Agreed," said Sanderson. "On delivery of the name."

"How do I know you won't cheat me?" asked Hughes.

"You don't," said Sanderson. "But if I did, I think you'd come after me. I really don't need that. Not for seven hundred."

"How do you know I won't cheat you?"

"Again, I don't," said Sanderson. "But I'll find my hard man eventually. And I'm rich enough to pay for two contracts as opposed to one. I don't like being conned. Point of principle, you see."

For ten seconds the two men stared at each other. Sanderson thought he might have gone too far. Then Hughes smiled again, broadly this time, with genuine appreciation. He scooped up the £500 in whole notes and the other sheaf of half-notes.

"I'll get you your name," he said, "and set up the rendezvous. When you've met the name and agreed the deal, you mail me the other half of the bundle, plus two hundred for expenses. Poste restante, Earl's Court post office, name of Hargreaves. Ordinary mail, well-sealed envelope. Not registered. If not within one week of the rendezvous, my mate will be alerted that you're a welsher, and he'll break off. OK?"

Sanderson nodded. "When do I get the name?"

"In a week," said Hughes. "Where can I contact you?"

"You don't," said Sanderson. "I contact you."

Hughes was not offended. "Call the bar I was in tonight," he said. "At ten p.m."

Sanderson made his call at the agreed hour one week later. The barman answered, and then Hughes came on the line.

"There's a café in the Rue Miollin in Paris where the kind of people you want get together," he said. "Be there next Monday at noon. The man will recognize you. Read that day's *Figaro*, with the headline facing towards the room. He will know you as Johnson. After that it's up to you. If you are not there on Monday he will be there at noon on Tuesday and Wednesday. After that it's blown. And take cash with you."

"How much?" asked Sanderson.

"About five thousand pounds, to be on the safe side."

"How do I know it won't be a straight stick-up?"

"You won't," said the voice, "but he won't know whether you have a bodyguard elsewhere in the bar." There was a click and the dead phone buzzed in his hand.

He was still reading the back page of the *Figaro* at five past twelve the following Monday in the café in the Rue Miollin, seated with his back to the wall, when the chair in front of him was drawn back and a man sat down. He was one of those who had been at the bar for the past hour.

"Monsieur Johnson?"

He lowered the paper, folded it and placed it by his side. The man was tall and lanky, black-haired and -eyed, a lantern-jawed Corsican. The pair talked for thirty minutes. The Corsican gave his name only as Calvi, which was in fact the town of his birth. After twenty minutes Sanderson passed across two photographs. One was of a man's face, and on the back was typewritten: "Major Archie Summers, Villa San Crispin, Playa Caldera, Ondara, Alicante." The other was of a small white-painted villa with canary-yellow shutters. The Corsican nodded slowly.

"It must be between three and four in the afternoon," said Sanderson.

The Corsican nodded. "No problem," he said.

They talked for a further ten minutes about money matters, and Sanderson handed over five wads of notes, £500 in each. Foreign jobs come more expensive, the Corsican explained, and the Spanish police can be extremely inhospitable to certain kinds of tourists. Finally Sanderson rose to leave.

"How long?" he asked.

The Corsican looked up and shrugged. "A week, two, maybe three."

"I want to know the moment it is done, you understand?"

"Then you have to give me some way of contacting you," said the gunman. For answer the Englishman wrote a number on a slip of paper.

"In one week's time, and for three weeks after that, you can ring me between seven-thirty and eight in the morning at this number in London. Don't try to trace it, and don't fail at the job."

The Corsican smiled thinly. "I shall not fail, because I want the other half of the money."

"One last thing," said the client. "I want not a trace left behind, nothing that links back to me. It must look like a local burglary that went wrong."

The Corsican was still smiling. "You have your reputa-

tion to consider, Monsieur Johnson. I have my life, or at
least thirty years in Toledo Penal. There will be no traces,
no comebacks."

When the Englishman had gone Calvi left the café,
checked to see he was not followed, and spent two hours
on the terrace of another café in the city centre, lost in
thought in the early July sunshine, his mind on the problems of his job. The contract itself presented little trouble,
a straight shooting of an unsuspecting pigeon. The problem was getting the gun safely into Spain. He could take it
on the train from Paris to Barcelona and risk the customs
check, but if he *were* caught it would be by the Spanish
police, not the French, and they have old-fashioned atti-
tudes towards professional gunmen. Airplanes were
out—thanks to international terrorism every flight out of
Orly was minutely checked for firearms. He still had contacts in Spain from his old OAS days, men who preferred
to live along the coast between Alicante and Valencia
rather than risk returning to France, and he reckoned he
could get a shooter on loan from one of them. But he decided to avoid them all, for with nothing to do in exile
they were too likely to gossip.

Finally the Corsican rose, paid his bill and went shopping. He spent half an hour at the inquiry desk in the
Spanish tourist office, and another ten minutes in the office of Iberia Airlines. He finished his shopping in a book-
shop and stationers in the Rue de Rivoli and went back to
his flat in the suburbs.

That evening he rang the Hotel Metropol, the best in
Valencia, and booked two single rooms for one night
only, a fortnight hence, in the name of Calvi and the
name on his own passport. Over the phone he introduced
himself as Calvi, and agreed to confirm the bookings in

writing at once. He also booked a return air ticket from Paris to Valencia, arriving on the evening for which he had made the hotel reservation, and returning to Paris the following evening.

While the telephone call to Valencia was coming through he had already written his letter of confirmation to the hotel. It was short and to the point. It confirmed the two bookings and added that as the signatory, M. Calvi, would be travelling constantly until his arrival in Valencia, he had ordered a book on the history of Spain to be sent forward to him, care of the Hotel Metropol, from Paris, and asked the hotel to be kind enough to hold it until his arrival.

Calvi estimated that if the book were intercepted and opened the moment he inquired for it under his real name the expression on the clerk's face would indicate there was something wrong and give him time to get away. Even if he were caught, he could claim to be an innocent party doing a favour for a friend and with no suspicion of any ulterior motive in the absent Calvi's request.

With the letter signed left-handed in the name of Calvi, sealed and stamped for posting, he went to work on the book he had bought that afternoon. It was indeed a history of Spain, expensive and heavy, on fine quality paper, with plenty of photographs which gave it added weight.

He bent back the two covers and held them together with an elastic band. The intervening 400 pages he secured as a block to the edge of the kitchen table with two carpenter's clamps.

Onto this block of paper he began to work with the thin, razor-sharp scalpel acquired the same afternoon. He sliced away for almost an hour until a square, set 1½ inches into the area of the page from each edge, had been cut out, forming a box 7 inches by 6 inches and 3 inches deep. The insides of this hollow square he daubed thickly with a tacky glue, and smoked two cigarettes while waiting for the glue to dry. When it was hard the 400 pages would never open again.

A cushion of foam rubber, cut to size, went into the hollow to replace the 1½ pounds of paper which had been cut out and which he had weighed on the kitchen scales. He dismantled the slim Browning 9-mm automatic he had acquired on a trip into Belgium two months earlier when he had used and thrown into the Albert Canal his previous gun, a Colt .38. He was a careful man, and never used the same shooter twice. The Browning had had the tip of its barrel exposed to half an inch, and the barrel's end tooled to take a silencer.

A silencer on an automatic is never truly quiet, despite the efforts of the sound-effects men in television thrillers to pretend it is. Automatics, unlike revolvers, do not have a closed breech. As the bullet leaves the barrel the automatic's jacket is forced backwards to expel the spent cartridge and inject a fresh one. That is why they are called automatics. But in that split second as the breech opens to expel the used shell, half the noise of the explosion comes out through the open breech, making a silencer on the end of the barrel only 50 per cent effective. Calvi would have preferred a revolver with its breech closed during firing, but he needed a flat gun to go into the cavity in the book.

The silencer he laid beside the parts of the Browning was the largest component, 6½ inches long. As a professional he knew the champagne-cork-sized silencers shown on television are as much use as a hand-held fire extinguisher to put out Mount Vesuvius.

Arranged side by side on top of the rubber cushion, the five parts, including silencer and magazine, would not quite fit, so he smacked the magazine into the automatic's handle to save space. He marked out the beds of the four components with a felt-nib pen and began to cut into the foam rubber with a fresh scalpel. By midnight the parts of the gun lay peacefully in their foam beds, the long silencer vertical, parallel to the book's spine, the barrel, butt and jacket breech in three horizontal rows from top to bottom of the page.

He covered the assembly with a thin sheet of foam rubber, daubed the insides of the front and back cover with more glue and closed the book. After an hour pressed between the floor and an upturned table, the book was a solid block that would need a knife to prise it open. He weighed it again. It was just half an ounce heavier than the original.

Finally he slid the history of Spain into an open-ended envelope of strong polythene, such as publishers of high-quality books use to protect the dust covers from dirt and scratching. It fitted snugly, and he bonded the open end of the envelope together with the blade of his switchknife, heated over the gas stove. Should his parcel be opened, he hoped and expected the examiner would be content to assure himself through the transparent polythene that the contents were indeed a harmless book, and reseal the parcel.

He placed the book inside a large padded envelope of the kind books are sent in, sealed only by a metal clip which can be opened by simply bending the soft metal lugs through the hole in the envelope's flap. With a do-it-yourself printing set he devised a stick-on label in the name of a well-known book store, and typed the name and address of the consignee—Monsieur Alfred Calvi, Hotel Metropol, Calle de Jativa, Valencia, Espagne. With the same printing set he made up a stamp and daubed the package with the words "LIBROS—IMPRESOS—LIVRES."

The following morning he mailed the letter by air and

the package by surface post, which meant the train and a ten-day delay.

The Iberia Caravelle drifted into Camp de Manises and touched down as the sun was setting. It was still furiously hot and the thirty passengers, mostly villa owners from Paris arriving for six weeks' vacation, grumbled at the usual baggage delays in the customs shed.

Calvi carried one medium-sized suitcase as hand baggage. It was opened and inspected carefully, then he was out of the airport building and into the open air. First he wandered over to the airport car park and was glad to see that a large area of it was screened by trees from the airport buildings. The cars stood in rows beneath the trees, waiting for their owners. He decided to return the next morning and take his transport from there. Then he took a taxi into town.

The clerk at the hotel was more than helpful. As soon as the Corsican presented himself and his passport, the desk clerk recalled the booking, the letter of confirmation written by M. Calvi, and dived into the back office to emerge with the package containing the book. The Corsican explained that unfortunately his friend Calvi would not be joining him, but that he would obviously settle both room bills when he left the following morning. He produced a letter from the absent Calvi authorizing him to take receipt of the book awaiting collection. The clerk glanced at the letter, thanked the Corsican for offering to settle both the room bills, and handed over the package.

In his room Calvi checked the padded envelope. It had been opened, the metal staples had been bent together to pass through the sealing aperture, and then bent back again. The blob of glue he had placed on one of the metal lugs was missing. But inside, the book was still untouched in its polythene wrapper, for it would have been impossible to open the polythene without tearing or distorting it.

He opened it, forced the book covers apart with the blade of his penknife and extracted the parts of the gun. These he assembled back together, screwed on the silencer and checked the shells in the magazine. They were all there—his special slugs, with half the explosive removed to cut down the noise to a low crack. Even with half the usual power behind it, a 9-mm slug still goes straight into a human head at 10-foot range, and Calvi never fired at more than 10 feet on a job.

He locked the gun into the bottom of the wardrobe, pocketed the key and smoked a cigarette on the balcony, gazing out at the bullring in front of the hotel and thinking of the day ahead. At nine he came down, still in his dark grey suit (from one of Paris's most exclusive tailors) that passed perfectly with the staid atmosphere of the old and expensive hotel. He dined at the Terrassa del Rialto and slept at midnight. From the hotel clerk he learned there was a plane to Madrid at eight in the morning, and he had himself called at six.

The next morning he checked out at seven and took a taxi to the airport. Standing at the gate he watched a dozen cars arrive, noting the make and number of the car and the appearance of the driver. Seven cars were driven by men without passengers, in what looked like business suits. From the observation terrace of the airport building he watched the passengers stream out to the plane for Madrid, and four of the car drivers were among them. He looked at the notes on the back of an envelope in his hand, and found he had a choice of a Simca, a Mercedes, a Jaguar and a small Spanish Seat, the local version of the Fiat 600.

After the plane had taken off he went to the men's

room and changed from his suit into cream jeans, pale blue sports shirt, and the blue zip-fronted nylon windbreaker. The gun he wrapped in a towel and stowed in the soft airline bag he took from his suitcase. The case he checked into left-luggage deposit, confirmed his evening booking for the Paris flight and walked back to the car park.

He picked the Seat because it is the most common car in Spain and has easy door handles for the car thief. Two men drove into the car park as he waited, and when they had gone he approached the small red beetle of a car. He slipped a metal pipe from his sleeve, slid it over the door handle and jerked downwards. The lock gave with a soft crack. From inside he opened the hood and clipped a wire jumper from the positive battery terminal to the starter motor. Behind the wheel the car started at the touch of a button, and he bowled out of the car park on the road to Valencia and the new seaboard highway N332 south to Alicante.

It is 92 kilometres or 55 miles from Valencia to Ondara, through the orange-growing centres of Gandia and Oliva, and he took it easy, making the trip in two hours. The whole coast was blistering in the morning sun, a long ribbon of golden sand dotted with brown bodies and splashing swimmers. Even the heat was ominous, without a breath of wind, and along the sea horizon lay a faint and misty haze.

As he entered Ondara he passed the Hotel Palmera, where he knew the former secretary of General Raoul Salan, once head of the OAS, still lived with his memories. In the town centre he had no trouble asking the way to Playa Caldera, which he was told by helpful townspeople lay two miles out of town. He drove into the residential sprawl of villas, mainly owned by expatriates, just before noon, and began to cruise, looking for the

Villa San Crispin familiar from the long-destroyed photograph. To ask directions to the beach was one thing, to
ask them to the villa might stick in someone's memory.

He found the yellow shutters and the white-painted
terra cotta walls just before one o'clock, checked the
name marked on a tile set into the pillar by the front gate
and parked the car 200 yards farther on. Walking idly,
his bag slung over one shoulder like a tourist heading for
the beach, he cased the back entrance. It was easy. From
farther up the earth road on which the villa stood, a small
footpath led away into a plantation of orange trees behind
the row of houses. From the cover of the trees he could
see that only a low fence separated the red earth of the
orange orchard from the garden and the unshaded patio
at the back of the villa with the yellow shutters, and he
could see his man pottering about the garden with a
watering can. There were french windows leading from
the back garden into the main ground-floor room, wide
open to allow a draught to blow through, if there should
be a breath of wind. He checked his watch—time for
lunch—and drove back to Ondara.

He sat till three in the Bar Valencia on Calle Doctor
Fleming, and had a large plate of enormous grilled
prawns and two glasses of the local light white wine. Then
he paid and left.

As he drove back to the Playa the rain clouds finally
moved in off the sea and there was a dull rumble of thunder across the oil-smooth water, very unusual for the
Costa Blanca in mid-July. He parked the car close to the
path into the orange grove, tucked the silenced Browning
into his belt, zipped the windbreaker up to the neck and
headed into the trees. It was very quiet when he came
back out of the grove and stepped across the low wall into
the garden of the villa. The locals were all taking a siesta
in the heat, and the rain began to patter onto the leaves

of the orange trees; a score of large drops hit his shoulders as he crossed the flagstones, and when he reached the french windows the shower broke at last, drumming onto the pink tiles of the roof. He was glad; no one would hear a thing.

From a room to the left of the sitting room he heard a typewriter clack several times. He eased the gun out, standing immobile in the centre of the lounge, and moved the safety catch to "Fire." Then he walked across the rush matting to the open study door.

Major Archie Summers never knew what happened or why. He saw a man standing in the doorway of his study and half rose to inquire what he wanted. Then he saw what was in the visitor's hand and half opened his mouth. There were two soft plops, drowned by the rain outside, and he took both bullets in the chest. The third was fired vertically downwards at 2-foot range into his temple, but he didn't even feel that one. The Corsican knelt by the body for a moment and put a forefinger where the pulse should have been. Still crouching he swivelled round to face the sitting-room door . . .

The two men met the next evening in the bar in the Rue Miollin, the killer and the client. Calvi had telephoned his message that morning after arriving back from Valencia the previous evening just before midnight, and Sanderson had flown over at once. The client seemed nervous as he handed over the rest of the £5000.

"No problems at all?" he asked again. The Corsican smiled quietly and shook his head.

"Very simple, and your major is very dead. Two bullets in the heart and one through the head."

"No one saw you?" asked the Englishman. "No witnesses?"

"No." The Corsican rose, patting the wads of notes into his breast pocket. "Though I'm afraid I was interrupted at the end. For some reason it was raining hard, and someone came in and saw me with the body."

The Englishman stared at him in horror. "Who?"

"A woman."

"Tall, dark-haired?"

"Yeah. A nice-looking piece too." He looked down at the expression of panic in the client's face, and patted the man on the shoulder.

"Don't worry, monsieur," he said reassuringly, "there will be no comebacks. I shot her, too."

There Are No Snakes in Ireland

❧

McQueen looked across his desk at the new applicant for a job with some scepticism. He had never employed such a one before. But he was not an unkind man, and if the job-seeker needed the money and was prepared to work, McQueen was not averse to giving him a chance.

"You know it's damn hard work?" he said in his broad Belfast accent.

"Yes, sir," said the applicant.

"It's a quick in-and-out job, ye know. No questions, no pack drill. You'll be working on the lump. Do you know what that means?"

"No, Mr. McQueen."

"Well, it means you'll be paid well but you'll be paid in cash. No red tape. Geddit?"

What he meant was there would be no income tax paid, no National Health contributions deducted at source. He might also have added that there would be no National Insurance cover and that the Health and Safety standards would be completely ignored. Quick profits for all were the order of the day, with a fat slice off the top for himself as the contractor. The job-seeker nodded his head to indicate he had "goddit" though in fact he had not. McQueen looked at him speculatively.

"You say you're a medical student, in your last year at

the Royal Victoria?" Another nod. "On the summer vacation?"

Another nod. The applicant was evidently one of those students who needed money over and above his grant to put himself through medical school. McQueen, sitting in his dingy Bangor office running a hole-and-corner business as a demolition contractor with assets consisting of a battered truck and a ton of second-hand sledgehammers, considered himself a self-made man and heartily approved of the Ulster Protestant work ethic. He was not one to put down another such thinker, whatever he looked like.

"All right," he said, "you'd better take lodgings here in Bangor. You'll never get from Belfast and back in time each day. We work from seven in the morning until sundown. It's work by the hour, hard but well paid. Mention one word to the authorities and you'll lose the job like shit off a shovel. OK?"

"Yes, sir. Please, when do I start and where?"

"The truck picks the gang up at the main station yard every morning at six-thirty. Be there Monday morning. The gang foreman is Big Billie Cameron. I'll tell him you'll be there."

"Yes, Mr. McQueen." The applicant turned to go.

"One last thing," said McQueen, pencil poised. "What's your name?"

"Harkishan Ram Lal," said the student. McQueen looked at his pencil, the list of names in front of him and the student.

"We'll call you Ram," he said, and that was the name he wrote down on the list.

The student walked out into the bright July sunshine of Bangor, on the north coast of County Down, Northern Ireland.

By that Saturday evening he had found himself cheap

lodgings in a dingy boarding house halfway up Railway View Street, the heart of Bangor's bed-and-breakfast land. At least it was convenient to the main station from which the works truck would depart every morning just after sun-up. From the grimy window of his room he could look straight at the side of the shored embankment that carried the trains from Belfast into the station.

It had taken him several tries to get a room. Most of those houses with a B-and-B notice in the window seemed to be fully booked when he presented himself on the doorstep. But then it was true that a lot of casual labour drifted into the town in the height of summer. True also that Mrs. McGurk was a Catholic and she still had rooms left.

He spent Sunday morning bringing his belongings over from Belfast, most of them medical textbooks. In the afternoon he lay on his bed and thought of the bright hard light on the brown hills of his native Punjab. In one more year he would be a qualified physician, and after another year of intern work he would return home to cope with the sicknesses of his own people. Such was his dream. He calculated he could make enough money this summer to tide himself through to his finals and after that he would have a salary of his own.

On the Monday morning he rose at a quarter to six at the bidding of his alarm clock, washed in cold water and was in the station yard just after six. There was time to spare. He found an early-opening café and took two cups of black tea. It was his only sustenance. The battered truck, driven by one of the demolition gang, was there at a quarter past six and a dozen men assembled near it. Harkishan Ram Lal did not know whether to approach them and introduce himself, or wait at a distance. He waited.

At twenty-five past the hour the foreman arrived in his

own car, parked it down a side road and strode up to the
truck. He had McQueen's list in his hand. He glanced
at the dozen men, recognized them all and nodded. The
Indian approached. The foreman glared at him.

"Is youse the darkie McQueen has put on the job?" he
demanded.

Ram Lal stopped in his tracks. "Harkishan Ram Lal,"
he said. "Yes."

There was no need to ask how Big Billie Cameron had
earned his name. He stood 6 feet and 3 inches in his
stockings but was wearing enormous nail-studded, steel-
toed boots. Arms like tree trunks hung from huge shoulders and his head was surmounted by a shock of ginger
hair. Two small, pale-lashed eyes stared down balefully at
the slight and wiry Indian. It was plain he was not best
pleased. He spat on the ground.

"Well, get in the fecking truck," he said.

On the journey out to the work site Cameron sat up in
the cab, which had no partition dividing it from the back
of the lorry, where the dozen labourers sat on two wooden
benches down the sides. Ram Lal was near the tailboard
next to a small, nut-hard man with bright blue eyes, whose
name turned out to be Tommy Burns. He seemed
friendly.

"Where are youse from?" he asked with genuine curiosity.

"India," said Ram Lal. "The Punjab."

"Well, which?" said Tommy Burns.

Ram Lal smiled. "The Punjab is a part of India," he
said.

Burns thought about this for a while. "You Protestant
or Catholic?" he asked at length.

"Neither," said Ram Lal patiently. "I am a Hindu."

"You mean you're not a Christian?" asked Burns in
amazement.

McQueen had even lined up a deal to sell the best timbers and the hundreds of tons of mature bricks to a jobbing builder. After all, the wealthy nowadays wanted their new houses to have "style" and that meant looking old. So there was a premium on antique sun-bleached old bricks and genuine ancient timber beams to adorn the new-look-old "manor" houses of the top executives. McQueen would do all right.

"Right lads," said Big Billie as the truck rumbled away back to Bangor. "There it is. We'll start with the roof tiles. You know what to do."

The group of men stood beside their pile of equipment. There were great sledgehammers with 7-pound heads; crowbars 6 feet long and over an inch thick; nailbars a yard long with curved split tips for extracting nails; short-handled, heavy-headed lump hammers and a variety of timber saws. The only concessions to human safety were a number of webbing belts with dogclips and hundreds of feet of rope. Ram Lal looked up at the building and swallowed. It was four storeys high and he hated heights. But scaffolding is expensive.

One of the men unbidden went to the building, prised off a plank door, tore it up like a playing card and started a fire. Soon a billycan of water from the river was boiling away and tea was made. They all had their enamel mugs except Ram Lal. He made a mental note to buy that also. It was going to be thirsty, dusty work. Tommy Burns finished his own mug and offered it, refilled, to Ram Lal.

"Do they have tea in India?" he asked.

Ram Lal took the proffered mug. The tea was ready-mixed, sweet and off-white. He hated it.

They worked through the first morning perched high on the roof. The tiles were not to be salvaged, so they tore them off manually and hurled them to the ground away from the river. There was an instruction not to block the river with falling rubble. So it all had to land on the other side of the building, in the long grass, weeds, broom and gorse which covered the area round the distillery. The men were roped together so that if one lost his grip and began to slither down the roof, the next man would take the strain. As the tiles disappeared, great yawning holes appeared between the rafters. Down below them was the floor of the top storey, the malt store.

At ten they came down the rickety internal stairs for breakfast on the grass, with another billycan of tea. Ram Lal ate no breakfast. At two they broke for lunch. The gang tucked into their piles of thick sandwiches. Ram Lal looked at his hands. They were nicked in several places and bleeding. His muscles ached and he was very hungry. He made another mental note about buying some heavy work gloves.

Tommy Burns held up a sandwich from his own box. "Are you not hungry, Ram?" he asked. "Sure, I have enough here."

"What do you think you're doing?" asked Big Billie from where he sat across the circle round the fire.

Burns looked defensive. "Just offering the lad a sandwich," he said.

"Let the darkie bring his own fecking sandwiches," said Cameron. "You look after yourself."

The men looked down at their lunch boxes and ate in silence. It was obvious no one argued the toss with Big Billie.

"Thank you, I am not hungry," said Ram Lal to Burns. He walked away and sat by the river where he bathed his burning hands.

By sundown when the truck came to collect them half the tiles on the great roof were gone. One more day and they would start on the rafters, work for saw and nailbar.

Throughout the week the work went on, and the once

proud building was stripped of its rafters, planks and beams until it stood hollow and open, its gaping windows like open eyes staring at the prospect of its imminent death. Ram Lal was unaccustomed to the arduousness of this kind of labour. His muscles ached endlessly, his hands were blistered, but he toiled on for the money he needed so badly.

He had acquired a tin lunch box, enamel mug, hard boots and a pair of heavy gloves. which no one else wore. Their hands were hard enough from years of manual work. Throughout the week Big Billie Cameron needled him without let-up, giving him the hardest work and positioning him on the highest points once he had learned Ram Lal hated heights. The Punjabi bit on his anger because he needed the money. The crunch came on the Saturday.

The timbers were gone and they were working on the masonry. The simplest way to bring the edifice down away from the river would have been to plant explosive charges in the corners of the side wall facing the open clearing. But dynamite was out of the question. It would have required special licences in Northern Ireland of all places, and that would have alerted the tax man. McQueen and all his gang would have been required to pay substantial sums in income tax, and McQueen in National Insurance contributions. So they were chipping the walls down in square-yard chunks, standing hazardously on sagging floors as the supporting walls splintered and cracked under the hammers.

During lunch Cameron walked round the building a couple of times and came back to the circle round the fire. He began to describe how they were going to bring down a sizable chunk of one outer wall at third-floor level. He turned to Ram Lal.

"I want you up on the top there," he said. "When it starts to go, kick it outwards."

Ram Lal looked up at the section of wall in question. A great crack ran along the bottom of it.

"That brickwork is going to fall at any moment," he said evenly. "Anyone sitting on top there is going to come down with it."

Cameron stared at him, his face suffusing, his eyes pink with rage where they should have been white. "Don't you tell me my job; you do as you're told, you stupid feckin' nigger." He turned and stalked away.

Ram Lal rose to his feet. When his voice came, it was in a hard-edged shout. *"Mister Cameron . . ."*

Cameron turned in amazement. The men sat open-mouthed. Ram Lal walked slowly up to the big ganger.

"Let us get one thing plain," said Ram Lal, and his voice carried clearly to everyone else in the clearing. "I am from the Punjab in northern India. I am also a Kshatria, member of the warrior caste. I may not have enough money to pay for my medical studies, but my ancestors were soldiers and princes, rulers and scholars, two thousand years ago when yours were crawling on all fours dressed in skins. Please do not insult me any further."

Big Billie Cameron stared down at the Indian student. The whites of his eyes had turned a bright red. The other labourers sat in stunned amazement.

"Is that so?" said Cameron quietly. "Is that so, now? Well, things are a bit different now, you black bastard. So what are you going to do about that?"

On the last word he swung his arm, open-palmed, and his hand crashed into the side of Ram Lal's face. The youth was thrown bodily to the ground several feet away. His head sang. He heard Tommy Burns call out, "Stay down, laddie. Big Billie will kill you if you get up."

Ram Lal looked up into the sunlight. The giant stood

over him, fists bunched. He realized he had not a chance in combat against the big Ulsterman. Feelings of shame and humiliation flooded over him. His ancestors had ridden, sword and lance in hand, across plains a hundred times bigger than these Six Counties, conquering all before them.

Ram Lal closed his eyes and lay still. After several seconds he heard the big man move away. A low conversation started among the others. He squeezed his eyes tighter shut to hold back the tears of shame. In the blackness he saw the baking plains of the Punjab and men riding over them; proud, fierce men, hook-nosed, bearded, turbaned, black-eyed, the warriors from the Land of Five Rivers.

Once, long ago in the world's morning, Iskander of Macedon had ridden over these plains with his hot and hungry eyes; Alexander, the young god, whom they called The Great, who at twenty-five had wept because there were no more worlds to conquer. These riders were the descendants of his captains, and the ancestors of Harkishan Ram Lal.

He was lying in the dust as they rode by, and they looked down at him in passing. As they rode each of them mouthed one single word to him. Vengeance.

Ram Lal picked himself up in silence. It was done, and what still had to be done had to be done. That was the way of his people. He spent the rest of the day working in complete silence. He spoke to no one and no one spoke to him.

That evening in his room he began his preparations as night was about to fall. He cleared away the brush and comb from the battered dressing table and removed also the soiled doily and the mirror from its stand. He took his book of the Hindu religion and from it cut a page-sized portrait of the great goddess Shakti, she of power and justice. This he pinned to the wall above the dressing table to convert it into a shrine.

He had bought a bunch of flowers from a seller in front of the main station, and these had been woven into a garland. To one side of the portrait of the goddess he placed a shallow bowl half-filled with sand, and in the sand stuck a candle which he lit. From his suitcase he took a cloth roll and extracted half a dozen joss sticks. Taking a cheap, narrow-necked vase from the bookshelf, he placed them in it and lit the ends. The sweet, heady odour of the incense began to fill the room. Outside, big thunderheads rolled up from the sea.

When his shrine was ready he stood before it, head bowed, the garland in his fingers, and began to pray for guidance. The first rumble of thunder rolled over Bangor. He used not the modern Punjabi but the ancient Sanskrit, language of prayer. *"Devi Shakti . . . Maa . . .* Goddess Shakti . . . great mother . . ."

The thunder crashed again and the first raindrops fell. He plucked the first flower and placed it in front of the portrait of Shakti.

"I have been grievously wronged. I ask vengeance upon the wrongdoer . . ." He plucked the second flower and put it beside the first.

He prayed for an hour while the rain came down. It drummed on the tiles above his head, streamed past the window behind him. He finished praying as the storm subsided. He needed to know what form the retribution should take. He needed the goddess to send him a sign.

When he had finished, the joss sticks had burned themselves out and the room was thick with their scent. The candle guttered low. The flowers all lay on the lacquered surface of the dressing table in front of the portrait. Shakti stared back at him unmoved.

He turned and walked to the window to look out. The

rain had stopped but everything beyond the panes dripped water. As he watched, a dribble of rain sprang from the guttering above the window and a trickle ran down the dusty glass, cutting a path through the grime. Because of the dirt it did not run straight but meandered sideways, drawing his eye farther and farther to the corner of the window as he followed its path. When it stopped he was staring at the corner of his room, where his dressing gown hung on a nail.

He noticed that during the storm the dressing-gown cord had slipped and fallen to the floor. It lay coiled upon itself, one knotted end hidden from view, the other lying visible on the carpet. Of the dozen tassels only two were exposed, like a forked tongue. The coiled dressing-gown cord resembled nothing so much as a snake in the corner. Ram Lal understood. The next day he took the train to Belfast to see the Sikh.

Ranjit Singh was also a medical student, but he was more fortunate. His parents were rich and sent him a handsome allowance. He received Ram Lal in his well-furnished room at the hostel.

"I have received word from home," said Ram Lal. "My father is dying."

"I am sorry," said Ranjit Singh, "you have my sympathies."

"He asks to see me. I am his first born. I should return."

"Of course," said Singh. The first-born son should always be by his father when he dies.

"It is a matter of the air fare," said Ram Lal. "I am working and making good money. But I do not have enough. If you will lend me the balance I will continue working when I return and repay you."

Sikhs are no strangers to moneylending if the interest is

right and repayment secure. Ranjit Singh promised to withdraw the money from the bank on Monday morning.

That Sunday evening Ram Lal visited Mr. McQueen at his home at Groomsport. The contractor was in front of his television set with a can of beer at his elbow. It was his favourite way to spend a Sunday evening. But he turned the sound down as Ram Lal was shown in by his wife.

"It is about my father," said Ram Lal. "He is dying."

"Oh, I'm sorry to hear that, laddie," said McQueen.

"I should go to him. The first-born son should be with his father at this time. It is the custom of our people."

McQueen had a son in Canada whom he had not seen for seven years.

"Aye," he said, "that seems right and proper."

"I have borrowed the money for the air fare," said Ram Lal. "If I went tomorrow I could be back by the end of the week. The point is, Mr. McQueen, I need the job more than ever now; to repay the loan and for my studies next term. If I am back by the weekend, will you keep the job open for me?"

"All right," said the contractor. "I can't pay you for the time you're away. Nor keep the job open for a further week. But if you're back by the weekend, you can go back to work. Same terms, mind."

"Thank you," said Ram, "you are very kind."

He retained his room in Railway View Street but spent the night at his hostel in Belfast. On the Monday morning he accompanied Ranjit Singh to the bank where the Sikh withdrew the necessary money and gave it to the Hindu. Ram took a taxi to Aldergrove airport and the shuttle to London where he bought an economy-class ticket on the next flight to India. Twenty-four hours later he touched down in the blistering heat of Bombay.

On the Wednesday he found what he sought in the

teeming bazaar at Grant Road Bridge. Mr. Chatterjee's Tropical Fish and Reptile Emporium was almost deserted when the young student, with his textbook on reptiles under his arm, wandered in. He found the old proprietor sitting near the back of his shop in half-darkness, surrounded by his tanks of fish and glass-fronted cases in which his snakes and lizards dozed through the hot day.

Mr. Chatterjee was no stranger to the academic world. He supplied several medical centres with samples for study and dissection, and occasionally filled a lucrative order from abroad. He nodded his white-bearded head knowledgeably as the student explained what he sought.

"Ah yes," said the old Gujerati merchant, "I know the snake. You are in luck. I have one, but a few days arrived from Rajputana."

He led Ram Lal into his private sanctum and the two men stared silently through the glass of the snake's new home.

Echis carinatus, said the textbook, but of course the book had been written by an Englishman, who had used the Latin nomenclature. In English, the saw-scaled viper, smallest and deadliest of all his lethal breed.

Wide distribution, said the textbook, being found from West Africa eastwards and northwards to Iran, and on to India and Pakistan. Very adaptable, able to acclimatize to almost any environment, from the moist bush of western Africa to the cold hills of Iran in winter to the baking hills of India.

Something stirred beneath the leaves in the box.

In size, said the textbook, between 9 and 13 inches long and very slim. Olive brown in colour with a few paler spots, sometimes hardly distinguishable, and a faint undulating darker line down the side of the body. Nocturnal in dry, hot weather, seeking cover during the heat of the day.

The leaves in the box rustled again and a tiny head appeared.

Exceptionally dangerous to handle, said the textbook, causing more deaths than even the more famous cobra, largely because of its size which makes it so easy to touch unwittingly with hand or foot. The author of the book had added a footnote to the effect that the small but lethal snake mentioned by Kipling in his marvellous story "Rikki-Tikki-Tavy" was almost certainly not the krait, which is about 2 feet long, but more probably the saw-scaled viper. The author was obviously pleased to have caught out the great Kipling in a matter of accuracy.

In the box, a little black forked tongue flickered towards the two Indians beyond the glass.

Very alert and irritable, the long-gone English naturalist had concluded his chapter on *Echis carinatus*. Strikes quickly without warning. The fangs are so small they make a virtually unnoticeable puncture, like two tiny thorns. There is no pain, but death is almost inevitable, usually taking between two and four hours, depending on the bodyweight of the victim and the level of his physical exertions at the time and afterwards. Cause of death is invariably a brain haemorrhage.

"How much do you want for him?" whispered Ram Lal.

The old Gujerati spread his hands helplessly. "Such a prime specimen," he said regretfully, "and so hard to come by. Five hundred rupees."

Ram Lal clinched the deal at 350 rupees and took the snake away in a jar.

For his journey back to London Ram Lal purchased a box of cigars, which he emptied of its contents and in whose lid he punctured twenty small holes for air. The tiny viper, he knew, would need no food for a week and no water for two or three days. It could breathe on an infinitesimal supply of air, so he wrapped the cigar box, resealed and with the viper inside it among his leaves, in several towels whose thick sponginess would contain enough air even inside a suitcase.

He had arrived with a handgrip, but he bought a cheap fibre suitcase and packed it with clothes from market stalls, the cigar box going in the centre. It was only minutes before he left his hotel for Bombay airport that he closed and locked the case. For the flight back to London he checked the suitcase into the hold of the Boeing airliner. His hand baggage was searched, but it contained nothing of interest.

The Air India jet landed at London Heathrow on Friday morning and Ram Lal joined the long queue of Indians trying to get into Britain. He was able to prove he was a medical student and not an immigrant, and was allowed through quite quickly. He even reached the luggage carousel as the first suitcases were tumbling onto it, and saw his own in the first two dozen. He took it to the toilet, where he extracted the cigar box and put it in his handgrip.

In the Nothing-to-Declare channel he was stopped all the same, but it was his suitcase that was ransacked. The customs officer glanced in his shoulder bag and let him pass. Ram Lal crossed Heathrow by courtesy bus to Number One Building and caught the midday shuttle to Belfast. He was in Bangor by teatime and able at last to examine his import.

He took a sheet of glass from the bedside table and slipped it carefully between the lid of the cigar box and its deadly contents before opening it wide. Through the glass he saw the viper going round and round inside. It paused and stared with angry black eyes back at him. He pulled the lid shut, withdrawing the pane of glass quickly as the box top came down.

"Sleep, little friend," he said, "if your breed ever sleep. In the morning you will do Shakti's bidding for her."

Before dark he bought a small screw-top jar of coffee and poured the contents into a china pot in his room. In the morning, using his heavy gloves, he transferred the viper from the box to the jar. The enraged snake bit his glove once, but he did not mind. It would have recovered its venom by midday. For a moment he studied the snake, coiled and cramped inside the glass coffee jar, before giving the top a last, hard twist and placing it in his lunch box. Then he went to catch the works truck.

Big Billie Cameron had a habit of taking off his jacket the moment he arrived at the work site, and hanging it on a convenient nail or twig. During the lunch break, as Ram Lal had observed, the giant foreman never failed to go to his jacket after eating, and from the right-hand pocket extract his pipe and tobacco pouch. The routine did not vary. After a satisfying pipe, he would knock out the dottle, rise and say, "Right, lads, back to work," as he dropped his pipe back into the pocket of his jacket. By the time he turned round everyone had to be on their feet.

Ram Lal's plan was simple but foolproof. During the morning he would slip the snake into the right-hand pocket of the hanging jacket. After his sandwiches the bullying Cameron would rise from the fire, go to his jacket and plunge his hand into the pocket. The snake would do what great Shakti had ordered that he be brought halfway across the world to do. It would be he, the viper, not Ram Lal, who would be the Ulsterman's executioner.

Cameron would withdraw his hand with an oath from the pocket, the viper hanging from his finger, its fangs deep in the flesh. Ram Lal would leap up, tear the snake away, throw it to the ground and stamp upon its head. It would by then be harmless, its venom expended. Finally,

with a gesture of disgust he, Ram Lal, would hurl the
dead viper far into the River Comber, which would carry
all evidence away to the sea. There might be suspicion,
but that was all there would ever be.

Shortly after eleven o'clock, on the excuse of fetching a
fresh sledgehammer, Harkishan Ram Lal opened his
lunch box, took out the coffee jar, unscrewed the lid and
shook the contents into the right-hand pocket of the hanging jacket. Within sixty seconds he was back at his work,
his act unnoticed.

During lunch he found it hard to eat. The men sat as
usual in a circle round the fire; the dry old timber baulks
crackled and spat, the billycan bubbled above them. The
men joshed and joked as ever, while Big Billie munched
his way through the pile of doorstep sandwiches his wife
had prepared for him. Ram Lal had made a point of
choosing a place in the circle near to the jacket. He
forced himself to eat. In his chest his heart was pounding
and the tension in him rose steadily.

Finally Big Billie crumpled the paper of his eaten sandwiches, threw it in the fire and belched. He rose with a
grunt and walked towards his jacket. Ram Lal turned his
head to watch. The other men took no notice. Billie
Cameron reached his jacket and plunged his hand into the
right-hand pocket. Ram Lal held his breath. Cameron's
hand rummaged for several seconds and then withdrew
his pipe and pouch. He began to fill the bowl with fresh
tobacco. As he did so he caught Ram Lal staring at him.

"What are youse looking at?" he demanded belliger-
ently.

"Nothing," said Ram Lal, and turned to face the fire.
But he could not stay still. He rose and stretched, contriv-
ing to half turn as he did so. From the corner of his eye
he saw Cameron replace the pouch in the pocket and
again withdraw his hand with a box of matches in it. The

foreman lit his pipe and pulled contentedly. He strolled back to the fire.

Ram Lal resumed his seat and stared at the flames in disbelief. Why, he asked himself, why had great Shakti done this to him? The snake had been her tool, her instrument brought at her command. But she had held it back, refused to use her own implement of retribution. He turned and sneaked another glance at the jacket. Deep down in the lining at the very hem, on the extreme left-hand side, something stirred and was still. Ram Lal closed his eyes in shock. A hole, a tiny hole in the lining, had undone all his planning. He worked the rest of the afternoon in a daze of indecision and worry.

On the truck ride back to Bangor, Big Billie Cameron sat up front as usual, but in view of the heat folded his jacket and put it on his knees. In front of the station Ram Lal saw him throw the still-folded jacket onto the back seat of his car and drive away. Ram Lal caught up with Tommy Burns as the little man waited for his bus.

"Tell me," he asked, "does Mr. Cameron have a family?"

"Sure," said the little labourer innocently, "a wife and two children."

"Does he live far from here?" said Ram Lal. "I mean, he drives a car."

"Not far," said Burns, "up on the Kilcooley estate. Ganaway Gardens, I think. Going visiting are you?"

"No, no," said Ram Lal, "see you Monday."

Back in his room Ram Lal stared at the impassive image of the goddess of justice.

"I did not mean to bring death to his wife and children," he told her. "They have done nothing to me."

The goddess from far away stared back and gave no reply.

Harkishan Ram Lal spent the rest of the weekend in an

agony of anxiety. That evening he walked to the Kilcooley housing estate on the ring road and found Ganaway Gardens. It lay just off Owenroe Gardens and opposite Woburn Walk. At the corner of Woburn Walk there was a telephone kiosk, and here he waited for an hour, pretending to make a call, while he watched the short street across the road. He thought he spotted Big Billie Cameron at one of the windows and noted the house.

He saw a teenage girl come out of it and walk away to join some friends. For a moment he was tempted to accost her and tell her what demon slept inside her father's jacket, but he dared not.

Shortly before dusk a woman came out of the house carrying a shopping basket. He followed her down to the Clandeboye shopping centre, which was open late for those who took their wage packets on a Saturday. The woman he thought to be Mrs. Cameron entered Stewarts supermarket and the Indian student trailed round the shelves behind her, trying to pluck up the courage to approach her and reveal the danger in her house. Again his nerve failed him. He might, after all, have the wrong woman, even be mistaken about the house. In that case they would take him away as a madman.

He slept ill that night, his mind racked by visions of the saw-scaled viper coming out of its hiding place in the jacket lining to slither, silent and deadly, through the sleeping council house.

On the Sunday he again haunted the Kilcooley estate, and firmly identified the house of the Cameron family. He saw Big Billie clearly in the back garden. By mid-afternoon he was attracting attention locally and knew he must either walk boldly up to the front door and admit what he had done, or depart and leave all in the hands of the goddess. The thought of facing the terrible Cameron with the news of what deadly danger had been brought so close to his children was too much. He walked back to Railway View Street.

On Monday morning the Cameron family rose at a quarter to six, a bright and sunny August morning. By six the four of them were at breakfast in the tiny kitchen at the back of the house, the son, daughter and wife in their dressing gowns, Big Billie dressed for work. His jacket was where it had spent the weekend, in a closet in the hallway.

Just after six his daughter, Jenny, rose, stuffing a piece of marmaladed toast into her mouth.

"I'm away to wash," she said.

"Before ye go, girl, get my jacket from the press," said her father, working his way through a plate of cereal. The girl reappeared a few seconds later with the jacket, held by the collar. She proffered it to her father. He hardly looked up.

"Hang it behind the door," he said. The girl did as she was bid, but the jacket had no hanging tab and the hook was no rusty nail but a smooth chrome affair. The jacket hung for a moment, then fell to the kitchen floor. Her father looked up as she left the room.

"Jenny," he shouted, "pick the damn thing up."

No one in the Cameron household argued with the head of the family. Jenny came back, picked up the jacket and hung it more firmly. As she did, something thin and dark slipped from its folds and slithered into the corner with a dry rustle across the linoleum. She stared at it in horror.

"Dad, what's that in your jacket?"

Big Billie Cameron paused, a spoonful of cereal halfway to his mouth. Mrs. Cameron turned from the cooker. Fourteen-year-old Bobby ceased buttering a piece of toast and stared. The small creature lay curled in the corner by the row of cabinets, tight-bunched, defensive, glaring back at the world, tiny tongue flickering fast.

"Lord save us, it's a snake," said Mrs. Cameron.

"Don't be a bloody fool, woman. Don't you know there are no snakes in Ireland? Everyone knows that," said her husband. He put down the spoon. "What is it, Bobby?"

Though a tyrant inside and outside his house, Big Billie had a grudging respect for the knowledge of his young son, who was good at school and was being taught many strange things. The boy stared at the snake through his owlish glasses.

"It must be a slowworm, Dad," he said. "They had some at school last term for the biology class. Brought them in for dissection. From across the water."

"It doesn't look like a worm to me," said his father.

"It isn't really a worm," said Bobby. "It's a lizard with no legs."

"Then why do they call it a worm?" asked his truculent father.

"I don't know," said Bobby.

"Then what the hell are you going to school for?"

"Will it bite?" asked Mrs. Cameron fearfully.

"Not at all," said Bobby. "It's harmless."

"Kill it," said Cameron senior, "and throw it in the dustbin."

His son rose from the table and removed one of his slippers, which he held like a flyswat in one hand. He was advancing, bare-ankled, towards the corner, when his father changed his mind. Big Billie looked up from his plate with a gleeful smile.

"Hold on a minute, just hold on there, Bobby," he said, "I have an idea. Woman, get me a jar."

"What kind of jar?" asked Mrs. Cameron.

"How should I know what kind of a jar? A jar with a lid on it."

Mrs. Cameron sighed, skirted the snake and opened a cupboard. She examined her store of jars.

"There's a jamjar, with dried peas in it," she said.

"Put the peas somewhere else and give me the jar," commanded Cameron. She passed him the jar.

"What are you going to do, Dad?" asked Bobby.

"There's a darkie we have at work. A heathen man. He comes from a land with a lot of snakes in it. I have in mind to have some fun with him. A wee joke, like. Pass me that oven glove, Jenny."

"You'll not need a glove," said Bobby. "He can't bite you."

"I'm not touching the dirty thing," said Cameron.

"He's not dirty," said Bobby. "They're very clean creatures."

"You're a fool, boy, for all your school learning. Does the Good Book not say: 'On thy belly shalt thou go, and dust shalt thou eat . . .'? Aye, and more than dust, no doubt. I'll not touch him with me hand."

Jenny passed her father the oven glove. Open jamjar in his left hand, right hand protected by the glove, Big Billie Cameron stood over the viper. Slowly his right hand descended. When it dropped, it was fast; but the small snake was faster. Its tiny fangs went harmlessly into the padding of the glove at the centre of the palm. Cameron did not notice, for the act was masked from his view by his own hands. In a trice the snake was inside the jamjar and the lid was on. Through the glass they watched it wriggle furiously.

"I hate them, harmless or not," said Mrs. Cameron. "I'll thank you to get it out of the house."

"I'll be doing that right now," said her husband, "for I'm late as it is."

He slipped the jamjar into his shoulder bag, already containing his lunch box, stuffed his pipe and pouch into the right-hand pocket of his jacket and took both out to the car. He arrived at the station yard five minutes late and was surprised to find the Indian student staring at him fixedly.

"I suppose he wouldn't have the second sight," thought Big Billie as they trundled south to Newtownards and Comber.

By mid-morning all the gang had been let into Big Billie's secret joke on pain of a thumping if they let on to "the darkie." There was no chance of that; assured that the slowworm was perfectly harmless, they too thought it a good leg-pull. Only Ram Lal worked on in ignorance, consumed by his private thoughts and worries.

At the lunch break he should have suspected something. The tension was palpable. The men sat in a circle around the fire as usual, but the conversation was stilted and had he not been so preoccupied he would have noticed the half-concealed grins and the looks darted in his direction. He did not notice. He placed his own lunch box between his knees and opened it. Coiled between the sandwiches and the apple, head back to strike, was the viper.

The Indian's scream echoed across the clearing, just ahead of the roar of laughter from the labourers. Simultaneously with the scream, the lunch box flew high in the air as he threw it away from himself with all his strength. All the contents of the box flew in a score of directions, landing in the long grass, the broom and gorse all around them.

Ram Lal was on his feet, shouting. The gangers rolled helplessly in their mirth, Big Billie most of all. He had not had such a laugh in months.

"It's a snake," screamed Ram Lal, "a poisonous snake. Get out of here, all of you. It's deadly."

The laughter redoubled; the men could not contain

themselves. The reaction of the joke's victim surpassed all their expectations.

"Please, believe me. It's a snake, a deadly snake."

Big Billie's face was suffused. He wiped tears from his eyes, seated across the clearing from Ram Lal, who was standing looking wildly round.

"You ignorant darkie," he gasped, "don't you know? There are no snakes in Ireland. Understand? There aren't any."

His sides ached with laughing and he leaned back in the grass, his hands behind him to support him. He failed to notice the two pricks, like tiny thorns, that went into the vein on the inside of the right wrist.

The joke was over and the hungry men tucked into their lunches. Harkishan Ram Lal reluctantly took his seat, constantly glancing round him, a mug of steaming tea held ready, eating only with his left hand, staying clear of the long grass. After lunch they returned to work. The old distillery was almost down, the mountains of rubble and savable timbers lying dusty under the August sun.

At half past three Big Billie Cameron stood up from his work, rested on his pick and passed a hand across his forehead. He licked at a slight swelling on the inside of his wrist, then started work again. Five minutes later he straightened up again.

"I'm not feeling so good," he told Patterson, who was next to him. "I'm going to take a spell in the shade."

He sat under a tree for a while and then held his head in his hands. At a quarter past four, still clutching his splitting head, he gave one convulsion and toppled sideways. It was several minutes before Tommy Burns noticed him. He walked across and called to Patterson.

"Big Billie's sick," he called. "He won't answer me."

The gang broke and came over to the tree in whose

shade the foreman lay. His sightless eyes were staring at the grass a few inches from his face. Patterson bent over him. He had been long enough in the labouring business to have seen a few dead ones.

"Ram," he said, "you have medical training. What do you think?"

Ram Lal did not need to make an examination, but he did. When he straightened up he said nothing, but Patterson understood.

"Stay here all of you," he said, taking command. "I'm going to phone an ambulance and call McQueen." He set off down the track to the main road.

The ambulance got there first, half an hour later. It reversed down the track and two men heaved Cameron onto a stretcher. They took him away to Newtownards General Hospital, which had the nearest casualty unit, and there the foreman was logged in as DOA—dead on arrival. An extremely worried McQueen arrived thirty minutes after that.

Because of the unknown circumstance of the death an autopsy had to be performed and it was, by the North Down area pathologist, in the Newtownards municipal mortuary to which the body had been transferred. That was on the Tuesday. By that evening the pathologist's report was on its way to the office of the coroner for North Down, in Belfast.

The report said nothing extraordinary. The deceased had been a man of forty-one years, big-built and immensely strong. There were upon the body various minor cuts and abrasions, mainly on the hands and wrists, quite consistent with the job of navvy, and none of these were in any way associated with the cause of death. The latter, beyond a doubt, had been a massive brain haemorrhage, itself probably caused by extreme exertion in conditions of great heat.

Possessed of this report, the coroner would normally not hold an inquest, being able to issue a certificate of death by natural causes to the registrar at Bangor. But there was something Harkishan Ram Lal did not know.

Big Billie Cameron had been a leading member of the Bangor council of the outlawed Ulster Volunteer Force, the hard-line Protestant paramilitary organization. The computer at Lurgan, into which all deaths in the province of Ulster, however innocent, are programmed, threw this out and someone in Lurgan picked up the phone to call the Royal Ulster Constabulary at Castlereagh.

Someone there called the coroner's office in Belfast, and a formal inquest was ordered. In Ulster death must not only be accidental; it must be seen to be accidental. For certain people, at least. The inquest was in the Town Hall at Bangor on the Wednesday. It meant a lot of trouble for McQueen, for the Inland Revenue attended. So did two quiet men of extreme Loyalist persuasion from the UVF council. They sat at the back. Most of the dead man's workmates sat near the front, a few feet from Mrs. Cameron.

Only Patterson was called to give evidence. He related the events of the Monday, prompted by the coroner, and as there was no dispute none of the other labourers was called, not even Ram Lal. The coroner read the pathologist's report aloud and it was clear enough. When he had finished, he summed up before giving his verdict.

"The pathologist's report is quite unequivocal. We have heard from Mr. Patterson of the events of that lunch break, of the perhaps rather foolish prank played by the deceased upon the Indian student. It would seem that Mr. Cameron was so amused that he laughed himself almost to the verge of apoplexy. The subsequent heavy labour with pick and shovel in the blazing sun did the rest, provoking the rupture of a large blood vessel in the brain or, as the pathologist puts it in more medical language, a cerebral haemorrhage. This court extends its sympathy to the widow and her children, and finds that Mr. William Cameron died of accidental causes."

Outside on the lawns that spread before Bangor Town Hall McQueen talked to his navvies.

"I'll stand fair by you, lads," he said. "The job's still on, but I can't afford not to deduct tax and all the rest, not with the Revenue breathing down my neck. The funeral's tomorrow, you can take the day off. Those who want to go on can report on Friday."

Harkishan Ram Lal did not attend the funeral. While it was in progress at the Bangor cemetery he took a taxi back to Comber and asked the driver to wait on the road while he walked down the track. The driver was a Bangor man and had heard about the death of Cameron.

"Going to pay your respects on the spot, are you?" he asked.

"In a way," said Ram Lal.

"That the manner of your people?" asked the driver.

"You could say so," said Ram Lal.

"Aye, well, I'd not say it's any better or worse than our way, by the graveside," said the driver, and prepared to read his paper while he waited.

Harkishan Ram Lal walked down the track to the clearing and stood where the camp fire had been. He looked around at the long grass, the broom and the gorse in its sandy soil.

"Visha serp," he called out to the hidden viper. "O venomous snake, can you hear me? You have done what I brought you so far from the hills of Rajputana to achieve. But you were supposed to die. I should have killed you myself, had it all gone as I planned, and thrown your foul carcass in the river.

"Are you listening, deadly one? Then hear this. You

may live a little longer but then you will die, as all things die. And you will die alone, without a female with which to mate, because there are no snakes in Ireland."

The saw-scaled viper did not hear him, or if it did, gave no hint of understanding. Deep in its hole in the warm sand beneath him, it was busy, totally absorbed in doing what nature commanded it must do.

At the base of a snake's tail are two overlapping plate-scales which obscure the cloaca. The viper's tail was erect, the body throbbed in ancient rhythm. The plates were parted, and from the cloaca, one by one, each an inch long in its transparent sac, each as deadly at birth as its parent, she was bringing her dozen babies into the world.

The Emperor

❧

"And there's another thing," said Mrs. Murgatroyd.

Beside her in the taxi her husband concealed a small sigh. With Mrs. Murgatroyd there was always another thing. No matter how well things were going, Edna Murgatroyd went through life to the accompaniment of a running commentary of complaints, an endless litany of dissatisfaction. In short, she nagged without cease.

In the seat beside the driver, Higgins, the young executive from head office who had been selected for the week's vacation at the expense of the bank on the grounds of being "most promising newcomer" of the year, sat silent. He was in foreign exchange, an eager young man whom they had only met at Heathrow airport twelve hours earlier and whose natural enthusiasm had gradually ebbed before the onslaught of Mrs. Murgatroyd.

The Creole driver, full of smiles and welcome when they selected his taxi for the run to the hotel a few minutes earlier, had also caught the mood of his female passenger in the back, and he too had lapsed into silence. Though his natural tongue was Creole French, he understood English perfectly well. Mauritius, after all, had once been a British colony for 150 years.

Edna Murgatroyd babbled on, an inexhaustible fountain of alternating self-pity and outrage. Murgatroyd

gazed out of the window as Plaisance airport fell away behind them and the road led on to Mahebourg, the old
French capital of the island, and the crumbling forts with
which they had sought to defend it against the British
fleet of 1810.

Murgatroyd stared out of the window, fascinated by
what he saw. He was determined he would enjoy to the
full this one-week holiday on a tropical island, the first
real adventure of his life. Before coming, he had read two
thick guidebooks on Mauritius and studied a large-scale
map of it from north to south.

They passed through a village as the sugar-cane country began. On the stoops of the roadside cottages he saw
Indians, Chinese and Negroes, along with *métis* Creoles,
living side by side. Hindu temples and Buddhist shrines
stood a few yards down the road from a Catholic chapel.
His books had told him Mauritius was a racial mix of half
a dozen main ethnic groups and four great religions, but
he had never seen such a thing before, at least, not living
in harmony.

There were more villages passing by, not rich and certainly not tidy, but the villagers smiled and waved. Murgatroyd waved back. Four scrawny chickens fluttered out
of the way of the taxi, defying death by inches, and when
he looked back they were in the road again, pecking a
seemingly impossible living from the dust. The car slowed
for a corner. A small Tamil boy in a shift came out of a
shack, stood at the kerb, and lifted the hem of his gar-
ment to the waist. Beneath it he was naked. He began to
pee in the road as the taxi passed. Holding his shift with
one hand he waved with the other. Mrs. Murgatroyd
snorted.

"Disgusting," she said. She leaned forward and rapped
the driver on the shoulder.

"Why doesn't he go to the toilet?" she asked.

The driver threw back his head and laughed. Then he turned his face to answer her. The car negotiated two bends by remote control.

"Pas de toilette, madame," he said.

"What's that?" she asked.

"It seems the road *is* the toilet," explained Higgins.

She sniffed.

"I say," said Higgins, "look, the sea."

To their right as they ran for a short while along a bluff, the Indian Ocean stretched away to the horizon, a limpid azure blue in the morning sun. Half a mile from the shore was a white line of breaking surf marking the great reef that encloses Mauritius from the wilder waters. Inside the reef they could see the lagoon, still water of palest green and so clear the coral clusters were easily visible 20 feet down. Then the taxi plunged back into the cane fields.

After fifty minutes they passed through the fishing village of Trou d'Eau Douce. The driver pointed ahead.

"Hôtel," he said, *"dix minutes."*

"Thank goodness," huffed Mrs. Murgatroyd. "I couldn't have taken much more of this rattletrap."

They turned into the driveway between manicured lawns set with palm trees. Higgins turned with a grin.

"A long way from Ponder's End," he said.

Murgatroyd smiled back. "Indeed it is," he said. Not that he had no reason to be grateful to the commuter suburb of Ponder's End, London, where he was branch manager. A light-industry factory had opened nearby six months previously and on a stroke of inspiration he had approached both management and workforce with the suggestion that they minimize the risk of a payroll robbery by paying their weekly wages like the executive salaries—by cheque. Somewhat to his surprise they had mostly agreed and several hundred new accounts had been opened at his branch. It was this coup which had come to the attention of head office and someone there had proposed the idea of an incentive scheme for provincial and junior staff. In the scheme's inaugural year he had won it, and the prize was a week in Mauritius entirely paid for by the bank.

The taxi finally halted in front of the great arched entrance of the Hôtel St. Geran, and two porters ran forward to take the luggage from the boot and the roof rack. Mrs. Murgatroyd descended from the rear seat at once. Although she had only twice ventured east of the Thames estuary—they usually holidayed with her sister at Bognor—she at once began to harangue the porters as if, in earlier life, she had had half the Raj at her personal disposition.

Followed by the porters and the luggage the three of them trailed through the arched doorway into the airy cool of the vaulted main hall, Mrs. Murgatroyd in the lead in her floral print dress, much crumpled by the flight and the drive, Higgins in his natty tropical cream seersucker, and Murgatroyd in his sober grey. To the left lay the reception desk, manned by an Indian clerk who smiled a welcome.

Higgins took charge. "Mr. and Mrs. Murgatroyd," he said, "and I am Mr. Higgins."

The clerk consulted his reservations list. "Yes, indeed," he said.

Murgatroyd stared about him. The main hall was made of rough-hewn local stone and was very lofty. High above him dark timber beams supported the roof. The hall stretched away towards colonnades at the far end, and other pillars supported the sides so that a cooling breeze wafted through. From the far end he saw the glare of tropical sunlight and heard the splash and shouts of a swimming pool in full use. Halfway down the hall, to the left, a stone staircase led upwards to what must be the upper floor of the bedroom wing. At ground level another arch led to the lower suites.

From a room behind reception a blond young Englishman emerged in a crisp shirt and pastel slacks.

"Good morning," he said with a smile. "I'm Paul Jones, the general manager."

"Higgins," said Higgins. "This is Mr. and Mrs. Murgatroyd."

"You're very welcome," said Jones. "Now, let me see about the rooms."

From down the hall a lanky figure strolled towards them. His lean shanks emerged from drill shorts and a flower-patterned beach shirt flapped about him. He wore no shoes but he had a beatific smile and clutched a can of lager in one large hand. He stopped several yards short of Murgatroyd and stared down at him.

"Hullo, new arrivals?" he said in a discernible Australian accent.

Murgatroyd was startled. "Er, yes," he said.

"What's your name?" asked the Australian without ceremony.

"Murgatroyd," said the bank manager. "Roger Murgatroyd."

The Australian nodded, taking the information in. "Where you from?" he asked.

Murgatroyd misunderstood. He thought the man said, "Who are you from."

"From the Midland," he said.

The Australian tilted the can to his lips and drained it. He burped. "Who's he?" he asked.

"That's Higgins," said Murgatroyd. "From head office."

The Australian smiled happily. He blinked several

times to focus his gaze. "I like it," he said, "Murgatroyd of the Midland, and Higgins from Head Office."

By this time Paul Jones had spotted the Australian and come round from behind the desk. He took the tall man's elbow and guided him back down the hall. "Now, now, Mr. Foster, if you'll just return to the bar so I can get our new guests comfortably settled in . . ."

Foster allowed himself to be propelled gently but firmly back down the hall. As he left he waved a friendly hand towards the reception. "Good on yer, Murgatroyd," he called.

Paul Jones rejoined them.

"That man," said Mrs. Murgatroyd with icy disapproval, "was drunk."

"He *is* on holiday, my dear," said Murgatroyd.

"That's no excuse," said Mrs. Murgatroyd. "Who is he?"

"Harry Foster," said Jones, "from Perth."

"He doesn't talk like a Scotsman," said Mrs. Murgatroyd.

"Perth, Australia," said Jones. "Allow me to show you to your rooms."

Murgatroyd gazed in delight from the balcony of the first-floor twin-bedded room. Below him a brief lawn ran down to a band of glittering white sand over which palm trees scattered shifting shoals of shadows as the breeze moved them. A dozen round straw-thatched paillots gave firmer protection. The warm lagoon, milky where it had stirred up the sand, lapped the edge of the beach. Farther out it turned translucent green and farther still it looked blue. Five hundred yards across the lagoon he could make out the creaming reef.

A young man, mahogany beneath a thatch of straw hair, was windsurfing a hundred yards out. Poised on his tiny board, he caught a puff of wind, leaned out against the pull of the sail and went skittering across the surface of the water with effortless ease. Two small brown children, black-haired and -eyed, splashed each other, screaming in the shallows. A middle-aged European, round-bellied, glittering sea-drops, trudged out of the water in frogman's flippers, trailing his face mask and snorkel.

"Christ," he called in a South African accent to a woman in the shade, "there's so many fish down there, it's unbelievable."

To Murgatroyd's right, up by the main building, men and women in wraparound pareus were heading to the pool bar for an iced drink before lunch.

"Let's go for a swim," said Murgatroyd.

"We'd be there all the sooner if you'd help me with the unpacking," said his wife.

"Let's leave that. We only need our swim things till after lunch."

"Certainly not," said Mrs. Murgatroyd. "I'm not having you going to lunch looking like a native. Here are your shorts and shirt."

In two days Murgatroyd had got into the rhythm of holiday life in the tropics, or as much as was allowed him. He rose early, as he always did anyway, but instead of being greeted as usual by the prospect through the curtains of rain-slick pavements, he sat on the balcony and watched the sun ride up from the Indian Ocean out beyond the reef, making the dark, quiet water glitter suddenly like shattered glass. At seven he went for a morning swim, leaving Edna Murgatroyd propped up in bed in her curlers, complaining of the slowness of breakfast service, which was in fact extremely fast.

He spent an hour in the warm water, swimming once nearly two hundred yards out and surprising himself with his daring. He was not a strong swimmer, but he was becoming a much better one. Fortunately his wife did not witness the exploit, for she was convinced sharks and barracuda infested the lagoon and nothing would persuade her that these predators could not cross the reef and that the lagoon was as safe as the pool.

He began to take his breakfast on the terrace by the pool, joining the other holidaymakers in selecting melon, mangoes and pawpaw with his cereal and forsaking eggs and bacon, even though these were available. Most of the men by this hour wore swim trunks and beach shirts, and the women light cotton shifts or wraparounds over their bikinis. Murgatroyd stuck with his knee-length drill shorts and tennis shirts brought out from England. His wife joined him beneath "their" thatch roof on the beach just before ten to begin a day-long series of demands for soft drinks and applications of sun oil, although she hardly ever exposed herself to the sun's rays.

Occasionally she would lower her pink bulk into the hotel pool which encircled the pool bar on its shaded island, her permanent wave protected by a frilly bathing cap, and swim slowly for several yards before climbing out again.

Higgins, being alone, was soon involved with another group of much younger English people and they hardly saw him. He saw himself as something of a swinger and equipped himself from the hotel boutique with a wide-brimmed straw hat such as he had once seen Hemingway wearing in a photograph. He too spent the day in trunks and shirt, appearing like the others for dinner in pastel slacks and safari shirt with breast pockets and epaulettes. After dinner he frequented the casino or the disco. Murgatroyd wondered what they were like.

Harry Foster unfortunately had not kept his sense of humour to himself. To the South Africans, Australians and British who made up the bulk of the clientele, Murgatroyd of the Midland became quite well known, though Higgins contrived to lose the Head Office tag by assimilating. Unwittingly, Murgatroyd became quite popular. As he padded onto the breakfast terrace in long shorts and plimsoles he evoked quite a few smiles and cheery greetings of "Morning, Murgatroyd."

Occasionally he met the inventor of his title. Several times Harry Foster weaved past him, holidaying on his personal cloud, his right hand seeming only to open in order to deposit one can of lager and envelop another. Each time the genial Aussie grinned warmly, raised his free hand in greeting and called out, "Good on yer, Murgatroyd."

On the third morning Murgatroyd came out of the sea from his after-breakfast swim, lay under the thatch with his back propped against the central support and surveyed himself. The sun was rising high now, and becoming very hot, even though it was only half past nine. He looked down at his body which, despite all his precautions and his wife's warnings, was turning a fetching shade of lobster. He envied people who could get a healthy tan in a short time. He knew the answer was to keep up the tan once acquired, and not to revert between holidays to marble white. Some hope of that at Bognor, he thought. Their past three holidays had entitled them to varying quantities of rain and grey cloud.

His legs protruded from his tartan swim trunks, thin and whiskered, like elongated gooseberries. They were surmounted by a round belly and the muscles of his chest sagged. Years at a desk had broadened his bottom and his hair was thinning. His teeth were all his own and he wore glasses only for reading, of which most of his diet concerned company reports and banking accounts.

There came across the water the roar of an engine and he glanced up to see a small speedboat gathering momen-

tum. Behind it trailed a cord at the end of which a head
bobbed on the water. As he watched the cord went suddenly taut and out of the lagoon, streaming spray, tim-
ber-brown, came the skier, a young guest at the hotel. He
rode a single ski, feet one in front of the other, and a
plume of foam rose behind him as he gathered speed after
the boat. The helmsman turned the wheel and the skier
described a great arc, passing close to the beach in front
of Murgatroyd. Muscles locked, thighs tensed against the
chop of the boat's wake, he seemed carved from oak. The
shout of his triumphant laughter echoed back across the
lagoon as he sped away again. Murgatroyd watched and
envied that young man.

He was, he conceded, fifty, short, plump and out of
condition, despite the summer afternoons at the tennis
club. Sunday was only four days away, and he would
climb into a plane to fly away, and never come back
again. He would probably stay at Ponder's End for another decade and then retire, most likely to Bognor.

He looked round to see a young girl walking along the
beach from his left. Politeness should have forbidden him
to stare at her, but he could not help it. She walked bare-
foot with the straight-backed grace of the island girls. Her
skin, without the aid of oils or lotions, was a deep gold.
She wore a white cotton pareu with a scarlet motif,
knotted under the left arm. It fell to just below her hips.
Murgatroyd supposed she must be wearing something underneath it. A puff of wind blew the cotton shift against
her, outlining for a second the firm young breasts and
small waist. Then the zephyr died and the cloth fell
straight again.

Murgatroyd saw she was a pale Creole, wide-set dark
eyes, high cheekbones and lustrous dark hair that fell in
waves down her back. As she came abreast of him she
turned and bestowed on someone a wide and happy smile.

Murgatroyd was caught by surprise. He did not know anyone else was near him. He looked round frantically to see whom the girl could have smiled at. There was no one else there. When he turned back to the sea the girl smiled again, white teeth gleaming in the morning sun. He was sure they had not been introduced. If not, the smile must be spontaneous. To a stranger. Murgatroyd pulled off his sunglasses and smiled back.

"Morning," he called.

"Bonjour, m'sieu," said the girl, and walked on. Murgatroyd watched her retreating back. Her dark hair hung down to her hips, which undulated slightly beneath the white cotton.

"You can just stop thinking that sort of thing for a start," said a voice behind him. Mrs. Murgatroyd had arrived to join him. She too gazed after the walking girl.

"Hussy," she said, and arranged herself in the shade.

Ten minutes later he looked across at her. She was engrossed in another historical romance by a popular authoress, of which she had brought a supply. He stared back at the lagoon and wondered as he had done so often before how she could have such an insatiable appetite for romantic fiction while disapproving with visceral intensity of the reality. Theirs had not been a marriage marked by loving affection, even in the early days before she had told him that she disapproved of "that sort of thing" and that he was mistaken if he thought there was any need for it to continue. Since then, for over twenty years, he had been locked into a loveless marriage, its suffocating tedium only occasionally enlivened by periods of acute dislike.

He had once overheard someone in the changing room at the tennis club tell another member that he should "have belted her years ago." At the time he had been angry, on the point of emerging round the cupboards to remonstrate. But he had held back, acknowledging that the fellow was probably right. The trouble was, he was not the sort of man to belt people and he doubted she was the sort of person whom it would improve. He had always been mild-mannered, even as a youngster, and though he could run a bank, at home his mildness had degenerated into passivity and thence into abjection. The burden of his private thoughts came out in the form of a gusty sigh.

Edna Murgatroyd looked at him over the top of her spectacles. "If you've got the wind, you can go and take a tablet," she said.

It was on the Friday evening that Higgins sidled up to him in the main hall as he waited for his wife to come out of the ladies.

"I've got to talk to you . . . alone," Higgins hissed from the corner of his mouth with enough secrecy to attract attention for miles around.

"I see," said Murgatroyd. "Can't you say it here?"

"No," grunted Higgins, examining a fern. "Your wife may come back at any minute. Follow me."

He strolled away with elaborate nonchalance, walked several yards into the garden and went behind a tree, against which he leaned and waited. Murgatroyd padded after him.

"What's the matter?" he asked when he caught up with Higgins in the darkness of the shrubbery. Higgins glanced back at the lighted hallway through the arches to ensure the distaff side of Murgatroyd was not following.

"Game fishing," he said. "Have you ever done it?"

"No, of course not," said Murgatroyd.

"Nor me. But I'd like to. Just once. Give it a try. Listen, there were three Johannesburg businessmen who booked a boat for tomorrow morning. Now it seems they can't make it. So the boat's available and half the cost is paid because they forfeited their deposits. What do you say? Shall we take it?"

Murgatroyd was surprised to be asked. "Why don't you go with a couple of mates from the group you're with?" he asked.

Higgins shrugged. "They all want to spend the last day with their girlfriends, and the girls don't want to go. Come on, Murgatroyd, let's give it a try."

"How much does it cost?" asked Murgatroyd.

"Normally, a hundred American dollars a head," said Higgins, "but with half paid, it's only fifty dollars each."

"For a few hours? That's twenty-five pounds."

"Twenty-six pounds seventy-five pence," said Higgins automatically. He was after all in foreign exchange.

Murgatroyd calculated. With the taxi back to the airport and the various extra charges to get him home to Ponder's End, he had little more than that left. The balance would be assigned by Mrs. Murgatroyd for duty-free purchases and gifts for her sister in Bognor. He shook his head.

"Edna would never agree," he said.

"Don't tell her."

"Not tell her?" He was aghast at the idea.

"That's right," urged Higgins. He leaned closer and Murgatroyd caught the whiff of planter's punch. "Just do it. She'll give you hell later, but she'll do that anyway. Think of it. We'll probably not come back here again. Probably not see the Indian Ocean again. So why not?"

"Well, I don't know . . ."

"Just one morning out there on the open sea in a small boat, man. Wind in your hair, lines out for bonito, tuna or kingfish. We might even catch one. At least it would be an adventure to remember back in London."

Murgatroyd stiffened. He thought of the young man on the ski, hammering his way across the lagoon.

"I'll do it," he said. "You're on. When do we leave?"

He took out his wallet, tore off three £10 traveller's cheques, leaving only two in the booklet, signed the bottom line and gave them to Higgins.

"Very early start," Higgins whispered, taking the cheques. "Four o'clock we get up. Leave here by car at four-thirty. At the harbour at five. Leave port at a quarter to six to be on the fishing grounds just before seven. That's the best time; around dawn. The activities manager will be coming as escort, and he knows the ropes. I'll see you in the main lobby at four-thirty."

He strode back to the main hall and headed for the bar. Murgatroyd followed in bemusement at his own fool-hardiness and found his wife testily waiting. He escorted her in to dinner.

Murgatroyd hardly slept at all that night. Although he had a small alarm clock he dared not set it for fear it would waken his wife when it went off. Nor could he afford to oversleep and have Higgins rapping on the door at half past four. He catnapped several times until he saw the illuminated hands approaching four o'clock. Beyond the curtains it was still pitch dark.

He slipped quietly out of bed and glanced at Mrs. Murgatroyd. She was on her back as usual, breathing stertorously, her arsenal of curlers held in place by a net. He dropped his pyjamas silently on the bed and pulled on his underpants. Taking plimsoles, shorts and shirt, he went quietly out by the door and closed it behind him. In the darkened corridor he pulled on the rest of his clothes and shivered in the unexpected chill.

In the hall he found Higgins and their guide, a tall, raw-boned South African called Andre Kilian, who was in charge of all sporting activities for the guests. Kilian glanced at his attire.

"It's cold on the water before dawn," he said, "and bloody hot afterwards. The sun can fry you out there. Haven't you got a pair of long trousers and a long-sleeved windcheater?"

"I didn't think," said Murgatroyd. "No, er, I haven't." He did not dare go back to his room now.

"I've got a spare," said Kilian and handed him a pullover. "Let's go."

They drove for fifteen minutes through the dark countryside, past shacks where a single glim indicated someone else was already awake. At length they wound their way down from the main road to the small harbour to Trou d'Eau Douce, Cove of Sweet Water, so called by some long-gone French captain who must have found a drinkable spring at that point. The houses of the village were battened and dark, but at the harbourside Murgatroyd could make out the shape of a moored boat and other shapes working on board it by the light of torches. They pulled up close to the wooden jetty and Kilian took a flask of hot coffee from the glove compartment and handed it round. It was very welcome.

The South African left the car and went along the jetty to the boat. Snatches of a low conversation in Creole French drifted back to the car. It is strange how people always speak quietly in the darkness before dawn.

After ten minutes he came back. There was by now a pale streak on the eastern horizon and a few low, ribbed clouds gleamed faintly out there. The water was discernible by its own glow, and the outlines of jetty, boat and men were becoming clearer.

"We can get the gear aboard now," said Kilian.

From the rear of the estate car he hauled a refrigerated vacuum box which was later to provide the cold beer, and he and Higgins carried it down the jetty. Murgatroyd took the lunch packs and two more coffee flasks.

The boat was not one of the new, luxurious fibreglass models, but an old and beamy lady of timber hull and marine-ply decking. She had a small cabin up forward which seemed to be crammed with assorted gear. To starboard of the cabin door was a single padded chair on a high stem, facing the wheel and the basic controls. This area was covered in. The after area was open and contained hard benches along each side. At the stern was a single swivel chair, as one sees in a city office, except that this one had harness straps hanging loose from it and was cleated to the deck.

From either side of the afterdeck two long rods stuck out at angles, like wasp aerials. Murgatroyd thought at first they were fishing rods, but later learned they were outriggers to hold the outer lines clear of the inboard lines and prevent tangling.

An old man sat on the skipper's chair, one hand on the wheel, and watched the last preparations in silence. Kilian heaved the beer chest under one of the benches and gestured the others to sit down. A young boat boy, hardly in his teens, unhitched the after painter and threw it on the deck. A villager on the planks beside them did the same up front and pushed the boat away from the quay. The old man started the engines and a dull rumble began beneath their feet. The boat turned its nose slowly towards the lagoon.

The sun was rising fast now, only just below the horizon, and its light was spreading westwards across the water. Murgatroyd could clearly see the houses of the village along the lagoon's edge and rising plumes of smoke as the women prepared the breakfast coffee. In a few minutes the last stars had faded, the sky turned robin's egg blue and swords of shimmering light thrust through the water. A catspaw, sudden, coming from nowhere, going nowhere, ruffled the surface of the lagoon and the light broke up into shards of silver. Then it was gone. The flat calm returned, broken only by the long wake of the boat from its stern to the receding jetty. Murgatroyd looked over the side and could make out clumps of coral already, and they were four fathoms down.

"By the way," said Kilian, "let me introduce you." With the growing light, his voice was louder. "This boat is the *Avant*, in French that means 'Forward.' She's old but sound as a rock, and she's caught a few fish in her time. The captain is Monsieur Patient, and this is his grandson Jean-Paul."

The old man turned and nodded a greeting at his guests. He said nothing. He was dressed in tough blue canvas shirt and trousers from which two gnarled bare feet hung downwards. His face was dark and wizened like an old walnut and topped by a battered chip hat. He gazed at the sea with eyes wreathed in wrinkles from a lifetime of looking at bright water.

"Monsieur Patient has been fishing these waters man and boy for sixty years at least," said Kilian. "Even he doesn't know just how long and no one else can remember. He knows the water and he knows the fish. That's the secret of catching them."

Higgins produced a camera from his shoulder bag. "I'd like to take a picture," he said.

"I'd wait a few minutes," said Kilian. "And hold on. We'll be going through the reef in a short while."

Murgatroyd stared ahead at the approaching reef. From his hotel balcony it looked feathery soft, the spray like splashing milk. Close up, he could hear the boom of the ocean breakers pounding themselves into the coral heads, tearing themselves apart on ranks of sharp knives just below the surface. He could see no break in the line.

Just short of the foam, old Patient spun the wheel hard right and the *Avant* positioned herself parallel to the white foaming line 20 yards away. Then he saw the channel. It occurred where two banks of coral ran side by side with a narrow gap between them. Five seconds later they were in the channel, with breakers left and right, running parallel to the shore half a mile to the east. As the surge caught them, the *Avant* bucked and swung.

Murgatroyd looked down. There were breakers now on both sides, but on his, as the foam withdrew, he could see the coral ten feet away, fragile feathery to the sight but razor sharp to the touch. One brush and it could peel boat or man with contemptuous ease. The skipper seemed not to be looking. He sat with one hand on the wheel, the other on the throttle, staring ahead through the windshield as if receiving signals from some beacon known only to him on that blank horizon. Occasionally he tweaked the wheel or surged the power and the *Avant* moved surely away from some new threat. Murgatroyd only saw the threats as they swept frustrated past his eyes.

In sixty seconds that seemed an age it was over. On the right side the reef continued, but on the left it ended and they were through the gap. The captain spun the wheel again and the *Avant* turned her nose towards the open sea. At once they hit the fearsome Indian Ocean swell. Murgatroyd realized this was no boating for the squeamish and he hoped he would not disgrace himself.

"I say, Murgatroyd, did you see that damned coral?" said Higgins.

Kilian grinned. "Quite something, isn't it? Coffee?"

"After that I could do with something stronger," said Higgins.

"We think of everything," said Kilian. "There's brandy in it." He unscrewed the second vacuum flask.

The boat boy began at once to prepare the rods. There

were four of them which he brought from the cabin, strong fibreglass rods about 8 feet long with the lower 2 feet wrapped in cork to aid the grip. Each was adorned with a huge reel containing 800 yards of monofilament nylon line. The butts were of solid brass and cut with a cleft to fit into the sockets in the boat to prevent twisting. He slotted each one into its socket and secured them with lanyard and dogclip lest they fall overboard.

The first arc of the sun's edge rose out of the ocean and flooded its rays across the heaving sea. Within minutes the dark water had turned to a deep indigo blue, becoming lighter and greener as the sun rose.

Murgatroyd braced himself against the pitch and roll of the boat as he tried to drink his coffee, and watched the preparations of the boat boy with fascination. From a large tackle box he took a variety of lengths of steel wire, called traces, and a selection of different lures. Some looked like brilliant pink or green baby squids in soft rubber; there were red and white cockerel feathers and glittering spoons or spinners, designed to flicker in the water and attract the attention of a hunting predator. There were also thick, cigar-shaped lead weights, each with a clip in the snout for attachment to the line.

The boy asked something in Creole of his grandfather and the old man grunted a reply. The boy selected two baby squids, a feather and a spoon. Each had a 10-inch steel trace protruding from one end and a single or triple hook at the other. The boy attached the clip on the lure to a longer trace and the other end of that to the line of a rod. Onto each also went a lead weight to keep the bait just under the surface as it ran through the water. Kilian noted the baits being used.

"That spinner," he said, "is good for the odd roving barracuda. The squid and the feather will bring in bonito, dorado or even a big tuna."

Monsieur Patient suddenly altered course and they craned to see why. There was nothing on the horizon ahead. Sixty seconds later they made out what the old man had already seen. On the far horizon a group of sea birds dived and wheeled above the sea, tiny specks at that distance.

"Terns," said Kilian. "The birds have spotted a shoal of small fry and are diving for them."

"Do we want small fry?" asked Higgins.

"No," said Kilian, "but other fish do. The birds act as our signal for the shoal. But bonito hunt the sprats and so do the tuna."

The captain turned and nodded to the boy, who began to cast the prepared lines into the wake. As each bobbed frantically on the foam he unlocked a catch on the reel to which it was attached and the reel spun free. The drag took the bait, lead and trace far away down the wake until it disappeared completely. The boy let the line run out until he was satisfied it was well over a hundred feet clear of the boat. Then he locked the reel again. The rod tip bent slightly, took the strain and began to tow the lure. Somewhere, far back in the green water, the bait and hook were running steady and true beneath the surface like a fast-swimming fish.

There were two rods slotted into the after edge of the boat, one in the left-hand corner, the other at the right. The other two rods were in sockets farther up each side of the afterdeck. Their lines were clipped into large clothespegs, the pegs attached to cords running up the outriggers. The boy threw the baits from these rods into the sea and then ran the pegs up to the top of the rigger. The spread of the riggers would keep the outer lines free of the inner ones and parallel to them. If a fish struck, it would pull the line free of the mouth of the peg, and the strain would revert direct from reel to rod to fish.

"Have either of you ever fished before?" asked Kilian. Murgatroyd and Higgins shook their heads. "Then I'd better show you what happens when we get a strike. It's a bit late after that. Come and have a look."

The South African sat in the fighting chair and took one of the rods. "What happens when a strike occurs is that the line is suddenly torn out through the reel which, in turning, emits a high-pitched scream. That's how you know. When that happens the person whose turn it is takes his place here and either Jean-Paul or I will hand him the rod. OK?"

The Englishmen nodded.

"Now, you take the rod and place the butt here in this socket between your thighs. Then you clip on this dogclip, with its lanyard secured to the seat frame. If it *is* torn from your grasp, we don't lose an expensive rod and all its tackle. Now, see this thing here . . ."

Kilian pointed to a brass wheel with spokes that jutted out from the side of the reel drum. Murgatroyd and Higgins nodded.

"That's the slipping clutch," said Kilian. "At the moment it is set for a very light strain, say five pounds, so that when the fish bites the line will run out, the reel will turn and the clicking noise of a turning reel is so fast it sounds like a scream. When you are settled—and be quick about it because the longer you spend getting ready the more line you have to pull in later—you turn the clutch control slowly forward, like this. The effect is to stiffen up the reel until the line stops going out. The fish is now being pulled by the boat, instead of the fish pulling out your line.

"After that, you reel him in. Grip the cork here with the left hand and reel in. If he's really heavy, grip with both hands and haul back till the rod is vertical. Then drop the right hand to the reel and reel in while lowering the rod towards the stern. That makes reeling easier. Then do it again. Double grip, haul back, ease forward while reeling in at the same time. Eventually you'll see your prize coming up in the foam beneath the stern. Then the boat boy will gaff him and bring him inboard."

"What are those marks for, on the slipping clutch and the brass casing of the drum?" asked Higgins.

"They mark the maximum permissible strain," said Kilian. "These lines have a one-hundred-and-thirty-pound breaking strain. With wet line, deduct ten per cent. To be on the safe side, this reel is marked so that when these marks are opposite each other, the slipping clutch will only concede line when there's a hundred pounds pulling on the other end. But to hold a hundred pounds for very long, let alone reel it in, will nearly pull your arms out, so I don't think we need bother about that."

"But what happens if we get a big one?" persisted Higgins.

"Then," said Kilian, "the only thing is to tire him out. That's when the battle begins. You have to let him have line, reel in, let him run again against the strain, reel in, and so forth, until he is so exhausted he can pull no more. But we'll handle that if we get to it."

Almost as he spoke the *Avant* was among the wheeling terns, having covered the three miles in thirty minutes. Monsieur Patient reduced power and they began to cruise through the unseen shoal beneath them. The tiny birds with tireless grace circled twenty feet above the sea, heads down, wings rigid, until their keen eyes spotted some glitter along the heaving hills of water. Then they would drop, wings back, needle beak forward, into the heart of the swell. A second later the same bird would emerge with a struggling silver matchstick in the mouth, which instantly went down the slim gullet. Their quest was as endless as their energy.

"I say, Murgatroyd," said Higgins, "we'd better decide who gets first strike. Toss you for it."

He produced a Mauritian rupee from his pocket. They tossed and Higgins won. A few seconds later one of the inner rods bucked violently and the line hissed out. The turning reel gave a sound that rose from a whine to a scream.

"Mine," shouted Higgins delightedly and leaped into the swivel chair. Jean-Paul passed him the rod, still unreeling but slower now, and Higgins slammed the butt downward into its socket. He attached the dogclip and lanyard, and began to close the slipping clutch. The unreeling line stopped almost at once. The rod bent at the tip. Holding with his left hand, Higgins reeled in with his right. The rod bent some more, but the winding went on.

"I can feel him thudding on the line," gasped Higgins. He went on winding. The line came in without objection and Jean-Paul leaned over the stern. Taking the line in his hand he swung a small, rigid silver fish over into the boat.

"Bonito, about four pounds," said Kilian.

The boat boy took a pair of pliers and unhooked the barb from the bonito's mouth. Murgatroyd saw that above its silver belly it was blue-black striped like a mackerel. Higgins looked disappointed. The cloud of terns dropped astern and they were through the shoal of sprats. It was just after eight o'clock and the fishing deck was becoming warm but only pleasantly so. Monsieur Patient turned the *Avant* in a slow circle to head back to the shoal and its marker of diving terns, while his grandson threw the hook and its baby-squid lure back into the sea for another run.

"Maybe we could have it for dinner," said Higgins. Kilian shook his head regretfully.

"Bonito are for bait fish," he said. "The locals eat them in soups, but they don't taste much good."

They made a second run through the shoal and there was a second strike. Murgatroyd took the rod with a thrill of excitement. This was the first time he had ever done this and the last he ever would again. When he gripped the cork he could feel the shuddering of the fish 200 feet down the line as if it were next to him. He turned the clutch slowly forward and eventually the running line was silent and still. The rod tip curved towards the sea. With his left arm tensed he took the strain and was surprised at the strength needed to haul back.

He locked his left arm muscles and began methodically to turn the reel handle with his right. It turned, but it took all his forearm to do it. The pulling power at the other end surprised him. Maybe it was big, he thought, even very big. That was the excitement, he realized. Never quite knowing what giant of the deep was fighting down there in the wake. And if it was nothing much, like Higgins's tiddler, well, the next one could be a monster. He continued turning slowly, feeling his chest heave with the effort. When the fish was 20 yards short of the boat it seemed to give up and the line came quite easily. He thought he had lost the fish, but it was there. It gave one last tug as it came under the stern, then it was over. Jean-Paul gaffed and swung it in. Another bonito, bigger, about 10 pounds.

"It's great, isn't it?" said Higgins, excitedly. Murgatroyd nodded and smiled. This would be something to tell them at Ponder's End. Up at the wheel old man Patient set a new course for a patch of deep blue water he could see several miles farther on. He watched his grandson extract the hook from the bonito's mouth and grunted something to the boy. The lad unclipped the trace and lure and put them back in the tackle box. He stowed the rod in its socket, the small steel swivel clip at the end of the line swinging free. Then he went forward and took the wheel.

His grandfather said something to him and pointed through the windshield. The boy nodded.

"Aren't we going to use that rod?" asked Higgins.

"Monsieur Patient must have another idea," said Kilian. "Leave it to him. He knows what he is doing."

The old man rolled easily down the heaving deck to where they stood and without a word sat crosslegged in the scuppers, selected the smaller bonito and began to prepare it as bait. The small fish lay hard as a board in death, crescent tail fins stiff up and down, mouth half open, tiny black eyes staring at nothing.

Monsieur Patient took from the tackle box a big single-barbed hook to whose shank was stoutly spliced a 20-inch steel wire, and a 12-inch pointed steel spike like a knitting needle. He pushed the point of the spike into the fish's anal orifice and kept pushing until the blood-tipped point emerged from its mouth. To the needle's other end he clipped the steel trace and with pliers drew needle and trace up through the bonito's body until the trace was hanging from its mouth.

The old man pushed the shank of the hook deep into the bonito's belly, so that all disappeared except the curve and the needle-sharp point with its barb. This jutted stiffly outwards and downwards from the base of the tail, the tip pointing forward. He drew the rest of the trace out of the fish's mouth until it was taut.

He produced a much smaller needle, no larger than a housewife would use for her husband's socks, and a yard of cotton twine thread. The bonito's single dorsal and two ventral fins were lying flat. The old man nicked his cotton through the leading spine of the dorsal fin, whipped it over several times and then pierced the needle through a fold of muscle behind the head. As he drew the thread tight, the dorsal fin erected, a series of spines and membranes that give vertical stability in the water. He did the same to both ventral fins, and finally sewed the mouth closed with neat and tiny stitches.

When he had finished the bonito looked much as it had in life. Its three body fins stuck out in perfect symmetry to prevent rolling or spinning. Its vertical tail would give direction at speed. The closed mouth would prevent turbulence and bubbles. Only the line of steel between its clenched lips and the vicious hook hanging from its tail root betrayed the fact that it was baited. Lastly the old fisherman clipped the few inches of trace from the bonito's mouth to the second trace hanging from the rod's tip with a small swivel, and consigned the new bait to the ocean. Still staring, the bonito bobbed twice in the wake until the leaden cigar pulled it down to begin its last journey beneath the sea. He let it run 200 feet out, behind the other baits, before he secured the rod again and went back to his command chair. The water beside them had turned from blue-grey to a bright blue-green.

Ten minutes later Higgins took another strike, on the spinner bait this time. He hauled and reeled for a full ten minutes. Whatever he had hooked was fighting with mad fury to be free. They all thought it might be a fair-sized tuna from the weight of its pull, but when it came inboard it was a yard-long, lean, narrow-bodied fish with a golden tint to its upper body and fins.

"Dorado," said Kilian. "Well done; these lads really fight. And they're good to eat. We'll ask the chef at the St. Geran to prepare it for supper."

Higgins was flushed and happy. "It felt like I was pulling a runaway truck," he gasped.

The boat boy readjusted the bait and consigned it again to the wake.

The seas were running higher now. Murgatroyd held one of the supports that sustained the timber awning over the front part of the deck in order to see better. The

Avant was plunging more wildly amid great rolling waves. In the troughs they were staring at great walls of water on all sides, running slopes whose sunlit sheen belied the terrible strength beneath. On the crests they could see for miles the plumed white caps of each great wave and westwards the smudged outline of Mauritius on the horizon.

The rollers were coming from the east, shoulder to shoulder, like serried ranks of great green guardsmen marching upon the island, only to die in the artillery of the reef. He was surprised that he was not feeling queasy for he had once felt ill on a ferry crossing from Dover to Boulogne. But that had been a bigger vessel, hammering and butting its way through the waves, its passengers breathing in the odours of oil, cooking fat, fast-food, bar fumes and each other. The smaller *Avant* did not contest the sea; she rode with it, yielding to rise again.

Murgatroyd stared at the water and felt the awe that dwells on the edge of fear, so much companion to men in small boats. A craft may be proud, majestic, expensive and strong in the calm water of a fashionable port, admired by the passing socialite throng, the showpiece of its rich possessor. Out on the ocean it is sister to the reeking trawler, the rusted tramp, a poor thing of welded seams and bolted joints, a frail cocoon pitting its puny strength against unimaginable power, a fragile toy on a giant's palm. Even with four others around him, Murgatroyd sensed the insignificance of himself and the impertinent smallness of the boat, the loneliness that the sea can inspire. Those alone who have journeyed on the sea and in the sky, or across the great snows or over desert sands, know the feeling. All are vast, merciless, but most awesome of all is the sea, because it *moves*.

Just after nine o'clock Monsieur Patient muttered something to no one in particular. " *'Ya quelque chose*," he said. *"Nous suit."*

"What did he say?" asked Higgins.

"He said there was something out there," said Kilian. "Something following us."

Higgins stared around him at the tumbling water. There was nothing but water. "How on earth can he know that?" he asked.

Kilian shrugged. "Same way you know there is something wrong with a column of figures. Instinct."

The old man reduced power by a touch and the *Avant* slowed until she seemed hardly to be making way. The pitching and tossing seemed to increase with the drop of engine power. Higgins swallowed several times as his mouth filled with spittle. At a quarter past the hour one of the rods bucked sharply and the line began to run out, not fast but briskly, the clicking of the reel like a football rattle.

"Yours," said Kilian to Murgatroyd and jerked the rod out of its socket in the transom to place it in the fishing seat. Murgatroyd came out from the shade and sat in the chair. He tagged the rod butt to the dogclip and gripped the cork handle firmly in the left hand. The reel, a big Penn Senator like a beer firkin, was still turning briskly. He began to close the control of the slipping clutch.

The strain on his arm grew and the rod arched. But the line went on running.

"Tighten up," said Kilian, "or he'll take all your line."

The bank manager locked the muscles of his biceps and tightened the clutch still further. The tip of the rod went down and down until it was level with his eyes. The running line slowed, recovered, and went on running. Kilian bent to look at the clutch. The marks on the inner and outer ring were almost opposite each other.

"That bugger's pulling eighty pounds," he said. "You'll have to tighten up some more."

Murgatroyd's arm was beginning to ache and his fin-

gers were stiffening round the cork grip. He turned the
clutch control until the twin marks were exactly opposite
each other.

"No more," said Kilian. "That's a hundred pounds.
The limit. Use both hands on the rod and hang on."

With relief Murgatroyd brought his other hand to the
rod, gripped hard with both, placed the soles of his plimsoles against the transom, braced his thighs and calves
and leaned back. Nothing happened. The butt of the rod
was vertical between his thighs, the tip pointing straight at
the wake. And the line kept on running out, slowly, steadily. The reserve on the drum was diminishing before his
eyes.

"Christ," said Kilian, "he's big. He's pulling a hundred
plus, like tissues from a box. Hang on, man."

His South African accent was becoming more pronounced in his excitement. Murgatroyd braced his legs
again, locked his fingers, wrists, forearms and biceps,
hunched his shoulders, bent his head and hung on. No
one had ever asked him to hold a 100-pound pull before.
After three minutes the reel finally stopped turning.
Whatever it was down there, it had taken 600 yards of
line.

"We'd better get you in the harness," said Kilian. One
arm after the other he slipped the webbing over Murgatroyd's shoulders. Two more straps went round the waist
and another broader one up from between the thighs. All
five locked into a central socket on the belly. Kilian
pulled the harness tight. It gave some relief to the legs,
but the webbing bit through the cotton tennis shirt in
front of the shoulders. For the first time Murgatroyd realized how hot the sun was out here. The tops of his bare
thighs began to prick.

Old Patient had turned round, steering one-handed. He

had watched the line running out from the start. Without warning he just said, "Marlin."

"You're lucky," said Kilian. "It seems you've hooked into a marlin."

"Is that good?" asked Higgins, who had gone pale.

"It's the king of all the game fish," said Kilian. "Rich men come down here year after year and spend thousands on the sport, and never get a marlin. But he'll fight you, like you've never seen anything fight in your life."

Although the line had stopped running out and the fish was swimming with the boat, he had not stopped pulling. The rod tip still arched down to the wake. The fish was still pulling between 70 and 90 pounds.

The four men watched in silence as Murgatroyd hung on. For five minutes he clung to the rod as the sweat burst from forehead and cheeks, running down in drops to his chin. Slowly the rod tip rose as the fish increased speed to ease the pull at his mouth. Kilian crouched beside Murgatroyd and began to coach him like a flying instructor to a pupil before his first solo flight.

"Reel in now," he said, "slowly and surely. Reduce the clutch strain to eighty pounds, for your sake not his. When he makes a break, and he will, let him go and tighten the clutch back to a hundred. Never try to reel in while he's fighting; he'll break your line like cotton. And if he runs towards the boat, reel in like mad. Never give him slack line; he'll try to spit out the hook."

Murgatroyd did as he was bid. He managed to reel in 50 yards before the fish made a break. When it did the force nearly tore the rod from the man's grasp. Murgatroyd just had time to swing his other hand to the grip and hold on with both arms. The fish took another 100 yards of line before he stopped his run and began to follow the boat again.

"He's taken six-fifty yards so far," said Kilian. "You've only got eight hundred."

"So what do I do?" asked Murgatroyd between his teeth. The rod slackened and he began winding again.

"Pray," said Kilian. "You can't hold him over a hundred-pound pull. So if he reaches the end of the line on the drum, he'll just break it."

"It's getting very hot," said Murgatroyd.

Kilian looked at his shorts and shirt. "You'll fry out here," he said. "Wait a minute."

He took off the trousers of his own track suit and slipped them over Murgatroyd's legs, one at a time. Then he pulled them up as far as he could. The webbing harness prevented them reaching Murgatroyd's waist, but at least the thighs and shins were covered. The relief from the sun was immediate. Kilian took a spare long-sleeved sweater from the cabin. It smelt of sweat and fish.

"I'm going to slip this over your head," he told Murgatroyd, "but the only way to get it farther is to undo the harness for a few seconds. Just hope the marlin doesn't break in those seconds."

They were lucky. Kilian slipped off the two shoulder straps and pulled the sweater down to Murgatroyd's waist, then reclipped the shoulder straps. The fish just ran with the boat, the line taut but without much strain. With the sweater on, Murgatroyd's arms ceased to hurt so much. Kilian turned round. From his seat old man Patient was holding out his broad-brimmed chip hat. Kilian placed it on Murgatroyd's head. The band of shadow shielded his eyes and gave more relief, but the skin of his face was already red and scorched. The sun's reflection from the sea can burn worse than the sun itself.

Murgatroyd took advantage of the marlin's passivity to reel in some more line. He had taken 100 yards, each yard making his fingers ache on the reel handle, for there was still a 40-pound strain on the line, when the fish broke again. He took his 100 yards back in thirty seconds, pulling a full 100 pounds against the slipping clutch. Murgatroyd just hunched himself and held on. The webbing bit into him wherever it touched. It was ten o'clock.

In the next hour he began to learn the meaning of pain. His fingers were stiff and throbbed. His wrists hurt and his forearms sent spasms up to his shoulders. The biceps were locked and shoulders screamed. Even beneath the track suit and pullover the merciless sun was beginning to scorch his skin again. Three times in that hour he won back 100 yards from the fish; three times the fish broke and clawed back his line.

"I don't think I can take much more," he said between gritted teeth.

Kilian stood beside him, an open can of iced beer in his hand. His own legs were bare, but darkened by years in the sun. He seemed not to burn.

"Hang on, man. That's what the battle's about. He has the strength, you have the tackle and the cunning. After that it's all stamina, yours against his."

Just after eleven the marlin tail-walked for the first time. Murgatroyd had brought him in to 500 yards. The boat was for a second on the crest of a roller. Down the wake the fish came surging out of the side of a wall of green water and Murgatroyd's mouth fell open. The sharp needle beak of the upper jaw lunged for the sky; below it the shorter lower mandible was hanging open. Above and behind the eye the crested dorsal fin, like a cock's comb, was extended and erect. The glittering bulk of his body followed and as the wave from which he had come ebbed from him, the marlin seemed to stand on his crescent tail. His great body shuddered as if he were walking on his tail. For one second he was there, staring at them across the waste of whitecaps. Then he crashed back into another moving wall and was gone, deep down to his own cold dark world. Old man Patient spoke first to break the silence.

"*C'est l'Empereur,*" he said.

Kilian spun round on him. "*Vous êtes sur?*" he asked.

The old man just nodded.

"What did he say?" asked Higgins.

Murgatroyd stared at the spot where the fish had gone. Then, slowly and steadily, he began to reel in again.

"They know this fish around here," said Kilian. "If it's the same one, and I've never known the old man be wrong, he's a blue marlin, estimated to be bigger than the world record of eleven hundred pounds, which means he must be old and cunning. They call him the Emperor. He's a legend to the fishermen."

"But how could they know one particular fish?" said Higgins. "They all look alike."

"This one's been hooked twice," said Kilian. "He broke the line twice. But the second time he was close to the boat, off Rivière Noire. They saw the first hook hanging from his mouth. Then he broke line at the last minute and took another hook with him. Each time he was hooked he tail-walked several times and they all got a good look at him. Someone took a photograph of him in mid-air, so he's well-known. I couldn't identify him at five hundred yards, but Patient for all his years has eyes like a gannet."

By midday Murgatroyd was looking old and sick. He sat hunched over his rod, in a world of his own, alone with his pain and some inner determination that he had never felt before. The palms of both hands were running water from the burst blisters, the sweat-damp webbing cut cruelly into sunflayed shoulders. He bowed his head and reeled in line.

Sometimes it came easy as if the fish too were taking a rest. When the strain came off the line the relief was a pleasure so exquisite that he could never later describe it. When the rod was bent and all his aching muscles locked again against the fish the pain was like nothing he could have imagined.

Just after noon Kilian crouched down beside him and offered him another beer. "Look, man, you're pretty crook. It's been three hours, and really you're not fit enough. There's no need to kill yourself. If you need any help, a short rest, just say."

Murgatroyd shook his head. His lips were split from sun and salt-spray.

"My fish," he said, "leave me alone."

The battle went on as the sun hammered down onto the deck. Old Patient perched like a wise brown cormorant on his high stool, one hand on the wheel, the engines set just above the idle, his head turned to scan the wake for a sign of the Emperor. Jean-Paul was crouched in the shade of the awning, having long since reeled in and stowed the other three rods. No one was after bonito now, and extra lines would only tangle. Higgins had finally succumbed to the swell and sat miserably head down over a bucket into which he had deposited the sandwiches he had taken for brunch and two bottles of beer. Kilian sat facing him and sucked at his fifth cold lager. Occasionally they looked at the hunched, scarecrow figure under his native hat in the swivel chair and listened to the tickety-tickety-tick of the incoming reel or the despairing ziiiiing as the line went back out again.

The marlin had come to 300 yards when he walked again. This time the boat was in a trough and the Emperor burst the surface pointing straight towards them. He came in a climbing leap, shaking spray from his back. The arc of his leap was down the wake and the line suddenly went completely slack. Kilian was on his feet.

"Take line," he screamed. "He'll spit the hook."

Murgatroyd's tired fingers worked in a blur on the handle of the drum to take up the slack. He managed just in time. The line went tight as the marlin dived back into the sea and he had gained 50 yards. Then the fish took it all back. Down in the still dark depths, fathoms beneath the waves and the sun, the great pelagic hunter with instincts honed by a million years of evolution turned against his enemy's pull, took the strain at the corner of his bony mouth and dived.

In his chair the small bank manager hunched himself again, squeezed aching fingers around the wet cork grip, felt the webbing sear into his shoulders like thin wires, and held on. He watched the still-wet nylon line running out, fathom after fathom, before his eyes. Fifty yards were gone and the fish was still diving.

"He'll have to turn and come up again," said Kilian, watching from over Murgatroyd's shoulder. "That will be the time to reel in."

He stooped and peered at the brick-red, peeling face. Two tears squeezed out of the half-closed eyes and ran down Murgatroyd's sagging cheeks. The South African put a kindly hand on his shoulder.

"Look," he said, "you can't take any more. Why don't I sit in, just for an hour, eh? Then you can take over for the last part, when he's close and ready to give up."

Murgatroyd watched the slowing line. He opened his mouth to speak. A split in his lip cracked wide and a trickle of blood ran onto his chin. The cork grip was becoming slick from the blood coming from his palms.

"My fish," he croaked. "My fish."

Kilian stood up. "All right, Engelsman, your fish," he said.

It was two in the afternoon. The sun was using the afterdeck of the *Avant* as its private anvil. The Emperor

stopped diving and the line-strain eased to 40 pounds.
Murgatroyd began again to haul in.

An hour later the marlin leapt out of the sea for the
last time. He was only a hundred yards away. His jump
brought Kilian and the boat boy to the transom to watch.
For two seconds he hung suspended above the foam,
snapping his head from side to side like a terrier to shake
the hook that drew him inexorably towards his enemies.
From one corner of his mouth a loose strand of steel wire
flickered in the sunlight as he shivered. Then with a boom
of meat on water he hit the sea and vanished.

"That's him," said Kilian in awe, "that's the Emperor.
He's twelve hundred pounds if he's an ounce, he's twenty
feet from tip to tail and that marlin-spike bill can go
through ten inches of timber when he's moving at his full
forty knots. What an animal."

He called back to Monsieur Patient. *"Vous avez vu?"*

The old man nodded.

"Que pensez vous? Il va venir vite?"

"Deux heures encore," said the old man. *"Mais il est
fatigué."*

Kilian crouched beside Murgatroyd. "The old man says
he's tired now," he said. "But he'll still fight for maybe
another couple of hours. Want to go on?"

Murgatroyd stared at where the fish had gone. His
vision was blurring with tiredness and all his body was
one searing ache. Shafts of sharper pain ran through his
right shoulder where he had torn a muscle. He had never
once had to call on his ultimate, last reserves of will, so
he did not know. He nodded. The line was still, the rod
arched. The Emperor was pulling, but not up to 100
pounds. The banker sat and held on.

For another ninety minutes they fought it out, the man
from Ponder's End and the great marlin. Four times the
fish lunged and took line, but his breaks were getting

shorter as the strain of pulling 100 pounds against the clutch drag sapped even his primal strength. Four times Murgatroyd agonizingly pulled him back and gained a few yards each time. His exhaustion was moving close to delirium. Muscles in his calves and thighs flickered crazily like light bulbs just before they fuse. His vision blurred more frequently. By half past four he had been fighting for seven and a half hours and no one should ask even a very fit man to do that. It was only a question of time, and not long. One of them had to break.

At twenty to five the line went slack. It caught Murgatroyd by surprise. Then he began to reel in. The line came more easily. The weight was still there, but it was passive. The shuddering had stopped. Kilian heard the rhythmic tickety-tickety-tick of the turning reel and came from the shade to the transom. He peered aft.

"He's coming," he shouted, "the Emperor's coming in."

The sea had calmed with the onset of evening. The whitecaps were gone, replaced by a quiet and easy swell. Jean-Paul and Higgins, who was still queasy but no longer vomiting. came to watch. Monsieur Patient cut the engines and locked the wheel. Then he descended from his perch and joined them. In the silence the group watched the water astern.

Something broke the surface of the swell, something that rolled and swayed, but which moved towards the boat at the bidding of the nylon line. The crested fin jutted up for a moment, then rolled sideways. The long bill pointed upwards, then sank beneath the surface.

At 20 yards they could make out the great bulk of the Emperor. Unless there was some last violent force left in his bones and sinews he would not break for freedom any more. He had conceded. At 20 feet the end of the steel wire trace came up to the tip of the rod. Kilian drew on a tough leather glove and seized it. He pulled it in manually. They all ignored Murgatroyd, slumped in his chair.

He let go of the rod for the first time in eight hours and it fell forward to the transom. Slowly and painfully he unbuckled his harness and the webbing fell away. He took the weight on his feet and tried to stand. His calves and thighs were too weak and he slumped in the scuppers beside the dead dorado. The other four were peering over the edge at what bobbed below the stern. As Kilian pulled slowly on the wire trace that passed through his glove, Jean-Paul leaped to stand on the transom, a great gaff hook held high above his head. Murgatroyd looked up to see the boy poised there, the spike and curved hook held high.

His voice came out more a raucous croak than a shout.

"No."

The boy froze and looked down. Murgatroyd was on his hands and knees looking down at the tackle box. On top lay a pair of wire cutters. He took them in the finger and thumb of his left hand and pressed them into the mashed meat of his right palm. Slowly the fingers closed over the handles. With his free hand he hauled himself upright and leaned across the stern.

The Emperor was lying just beneath him, exhausted almost to the point of death. The huge body lay athwart the boat's wake, on its side, mouth half open. Hanging from one corner was the steel trace of an earlier struggle with the game-fisherman, still bright in its newness. In the lower mandible another hook, long rusted, jutted out. From Kilian's hand the steel wire ran to the third hook, his own, which was deep in the gristle of the upper lip. Only part of the shank was showing.

Succeeding waves washed over the marlin's blue-black body. From 2 feet away the fish stared back at Murgatroyd with one marbled saucer eye. It was alive but had no strength left to fight. The line from its mouth to Kilian's hand was taut. Murgatroyd leaned slowly down, reaching out his right hand to the fish's mouth.

"You can pat him later, man," said Kilian, "let's get him home."

Deliberately Murgatroyd placed the jaws of the cutters either side of the steel trace where it was spliced to the shank of the hook. He squeezed. Blood came out of his palm and ran in the salt water over the marlin's head. He squeezed again and the steel wire parted.

"What are you doing? He'll get away," shouted Higgins.

The Emperor stared at Murgatroyd as another wave ran over him. He shook his tired old head and pushed the spike of his beak into the cool water. The next wave rolled him back onto his belly and he dropped his head deeper. Away to the left his great crescent tail rose and fell, driving wearily at the water. When it made contact it flicked twice and pushed the body forward and down. The tail was the last they saw, labourious in its fatigue, driving the marlin back beneath the waves to the cold darkness of its home.

"Bloody hell," said Kilian.

Murgatroyd tried to stand up, but too much blood had rushed to his head. He remembered the sky turning slowly once in a big circle and the dusk coming very fast. The decking rose up to hit him first in the knees and then in the face. He fainted. The sun hung suspended above the mountains of Mauritius in the west.

It had set by one hour when the *Avant* cruised home across the lagoon and Murgatroyd had come awake. On the journey Kilian had taken back the trousers and sweater, so the cool evening air could play on the scorched limbs. Now Murgatroyd had drunk three beers in a row and sat slumped on one of the benches, shoulders hunched, his hands in a bucket of cleansing salt water. He took no notice when the boat moored beside the timber jetty and Jean-Paul scampered off towards the village.

Old Monsieur Patient closed the engines down and made sure the painters were secure. He threw the large bonito and the dorado onto the pier and stowed the tackle and lures. Kilian heaved the cold-box onto the jetty and jumped back into the open well.

"Time to go," he said.

Murgatroyd pulled himself to his feet and Kilian helped him to the quay. The hem of his shorts had fallen to below his knees and his shirt flapped open about him, dark with dried sweat. His plimsoles squelched. A number of villagers were lining the narrow jetty, so they had to walk in single file. Higgins had gone ahead.

The first person in the line was Monsieur Patient. Murgatroyd would have shaken hands but they hurt too much. He nodded to the boatman and smiled.

"*Merci,*" he said.

The old man, who had recovered his chip hat, pulled it from his head. "*Salut, Maître,*" he replied.

Murgatroyd walked slowly up the jetty. Each of the villagers bobbed his head and said, "*Salut, Maître.*" They reached the end of the planking and stepped into the gravel of the village street. There was a large crowd of villagers grouped round the car. "*Salut, salut, salut, Maître,*" they said quietly.

Higgins was stowing the spare clothing and the empty brunch box. Kilian swung the cold-trunk over the tailboard and slammed the door. He came to the rear passenger side where Murgatroyd waited.

"What are they saying?" whispered Murgatroyd.

"They're greeting you," said Kilian. "They're calling you a master-fisherman."

"Because of the Emperor?"

"He's something of a legend around here."

"Because I caught the Emperor?"

Kilian laughed softly. "No, Engelsman, because you gave him his life back."

They climbed into the car, Murgatroyd in the back where he sank gratefully into the cushions, his hands cupped, palms burning, in his lap. Kilian took the wheel, Higgins next to him.

"I say, Murgatroyd," said Higgins, "these villagers seem to think you're the cat's whiskers."

Murgatroyd stared out of the window at the smiling brown faces and waving children.

"Before we go back to the hotel we'd better stop by the hospital at Flacq and let the doctor have a look at you," said Kilian.

The young Indian doctor asked Murgatroyd to strip down and clucked in concern at what he saw. The buttocks were blistered raw from the contact backwards and forwards with the seat of the fishing chair. Deep purple welts furrowed shoulders and back where the webbing had bitten in. Arms, thighs and shins were red and flaking from sunburn and the face was bloated from the heat. Both palms looked like raw steak.

"Oh, dear me," said the doctor, "it will take some time."

"Shall I call back for him in, say, a couple of hours?" asked Kilian.

"There is no need," said the doctor. "The Hôtel St. Geran is close to my journey home. I will drop the gentleman off on my way."

It was ten o'clock when Murgatroyd walked through the main doors of the St. Geran and into the light of the hallway. The doctor was still with him. One of the guests saw him enter and ran into the dining room to tell the late eaters. Word spread to the pool bar outside. There was a scraping of chairs and clatter of cutlery. A crowd of holidaymakers soon surged round the corner and came down the hall to meet him. They stopped halfway.

He looked a strange sight. His arms and legs were thickly smeared with calamine lotion, which had dried to a chalky white. Both hands were mummified in white bandages. His face was brick red and gleamed from the cream applied to it. His hair was a wild halo to his face and his khaki shorts were still at knee-length. He looked like a photographic negative. Slowly he began to walk towards the crowd, which parted for him.

"Well done, old man," said someone.

"Hear hear, absolutely," said someone else.

Shaking hands was out of the question. Some thought of patting him on the back as he passed through, but the doctor waved them away. Some held glasses and raised them in toast. Murgatroyd reached the base of the stone stairway to the upper rooms and began to climb.

At this point Mrs. Murgatroyd emerged from the hairdressing salon, brought by the hubbub of her husband's return. She had spent the day working herself into a towering rage since, in the mid-morning, puzzled by his absence from their usual spot on the beach, she had searched for him and learned where he had gone. She was red in the face, though from anger rather than sunburn. Her going-home perm had not been completed and rollers stuck out like Katyushka batteries from her scalp.

"Murgatroyd," she boomed—she always called him by his surname when she was angry—"where do you think *you're* going?"

At the midway landing Murgatroyd turned and looked down at the crowd and his wife. Kilian would tell colleagues later that he had a strange look in his eyes. The crowd fell silent.

"And what *do* you think you *look* like," Edna Murga-troyd called up to him in outrage.

The bank manager then did something he had not done in many years. He shouted.

"Quiet . . ."

Edna Murgatroyd's mouth dropped open, as wide as, but with less majesty than, that of the fish.

"For twenty-five years, Edna," said Murgatroyd qui-etly, "you have been threatening to go and live with your sister in Bognor. You will be happy to know that I shall not detain you any longer. I shall not be returning with you tomorrow. I am going to stay here, on this island."

The crowd stared up at him dumbfounded.

"You will not be destitute." said Murgatroyd. "I shall make over to you our house and my accrued savings. *I* shall take my accumulated pension funds and cash in my exorbitant life-assurance policy."

Harry Foster took a swig from his can of beer and burped.

Higgins quavered, "You can't leave London, old man. You'll have nothing to live on."

"Yes, I can," said the bank manager. "I have made my decision and I am not going to go back on it. I was think-ing all this out in hospital when Monsieur Patient came to see how I was. We agreed a deal. He will sell me his boat and I will have enough left over for a shack on the beach. He will stay on as captain and put his grandson through college. I will be his boat boy and for two years he will teach me the ways of the sea and the fish. After that, I shall take the tourists fishing and earn my living in that manner."

The crowd of holidaymakers continued to stare up at him in stunned amazement.

It was Higgins who broke the silence again. "But Murgatroyd, old man, what about the bank? What about Ponder's End?"

"And what about me?" wailed Edna Murgatroyd.

He considered each question judiciously.

"To hell with the bank," he said at length. "To hell with Ponder's End. And, madam, to hell with you."

With that he turned and mounted the last few steps. A burst of cheering broke out behind him. As he went down the corridor to his room he was pursued by a bibulous valediction.

"Good on yer, Murgatroyd."

There Are Some Days . . .

❧

The *St. Kilian* roll-on roll-off ferry from Le Havre buried her nose in another oncoming sea and pushed her blunt bulk a few yards nearer to Ireland. From somewhere on A deck driver Liam Clarke leaned over the rail and stared forward to make out the low hills of County Wexford coming closer.

In another twenty minutes the Irish Continental Line ferry would dock in the small port of Rosslare and another European run would be completed. Clarke glanced at his watch; it was twenty to two in the afternoon and he was looking forward to being with his family in Dublin in time for supper.

She was on time again. Clarke left the rail, returned to the passenger lounge and collected his grip. He saw no reason to wait any longer and descended to the car deck three levels down where his juggernaut transport waited with the others. Car passengers would not be called for another ten minutes, but he thought he might as well get settled in his cab. The novelty of watching the ferry dock had long worn off; the racing page of the Irish newspaper he had bought on board, though twenty-four hours old, was more interesting.

He hauled himself up into the warm comfort of his cab and settled down to wait until the big doors in the bow opened to let him out onto the quay of Rosslare. Above the sun visor in front of him his sheaf of customs documents was safely stacked, ready to be produced in the shed.

The *St. Kilian* passed the tip of the harbour mole at five minutes before the hour and the doors opened on the dot of two. Already the lower car deck was a-roar with noise as impatient tourists started up their engines well before necessary. They always did. Fumes belched from a hundred exhausts, but the heavy trucks were up front and they came off first. Time, after all, was money.

Clarke pressed the starter button and the engine of his big Volvo artic throbbed into life. He was third in line when the marshal waved them forward. The other two trucks breasted the clanking steel ramp to the quayside with a boom of exhausts and Clarke followed them. In the muted calm of his cab he heard the hiss of the hydraulic brakes being released, and then the steel planking was under him.

With the echoing thunder of the other engines and the clang of the steel plates beneath his wheels he failed to hear the sharp crack that came from his own truck, somewhere beneath and behind him. Up from the hold of the *St. Kilian* he came, down the 200 yards of cobbled quay and into the gloom again, this time of the great vaulted customs shed. Through the windscreen he made out one of the officers waving him into a bay beside the preceding trucks and he followed the gestures. When he was in position he shut down the engine, took his sheaf of papers from the sun visor and descended to the concrete floor. He knew most of the customs officers, being a regular, but not this one. The man nodded and held out his hand for the documents. He began to riffle through them.

It only took the officer ten minutes to satisfy himself that all was in order—licence, insurance, cargo manifest, duty paid, permits and so forth—the whole gamut of controls apparently required to move merchandise from one country to another even within the Common Market. He was about to hand them all back to Clarke when something caught his eye.

"Hello, what the hell's that?" he asked.

Clarke followed the line of his gaze and saw beneath the cab section of the truck a steadily spreading pool of oil. It was dripping from somewhere close to the rear axle of the section.

"Oh Jaysus," he said in despair, "it looks like the differential nose-piece."

The customs man beckoned over a senior colleague whom Clarke knew, and the two men bent down to see where the flow of oil was coming from. Over two pints were already on the shed floor and there would be another three to come. The senior customs man stood up.

"You'll not shift that far," he said, and to his junior colleague added, "We'll have to move the others round it."

Clarke crawled under the cab section to have a closer look. From the engine up front a thick strong drive shaft ran down to a huge boss of cast steel, the differential. Inside this casing the power of the turning drive shaft was transmitted sideways to the rear axle, thus propelling the cab forward. This was effected by a complex assembly of cogwheels inside the casing, and these wheels turned permanently in a bath of lubricating oil. Without this oil the cogs would seize solid in a very short distance, and the oil was pouring out. The steel nose-piece casing had cracked.

Above this axle was the articulated plate on which rested the trailer section of the artic which carried the cargo. Clarke came out from under.

"It's completely gone," he said. "I'll have to call the office. Can I use your phone?"

The senior customs man jerked his head at the glass-walled office and went on with his examination of the other trucks. A few drivers leaned from their cabs and called ribald remarks to Clarke as he went to phone.

Then there was no one in the office in Dublin. They were all out at lunch. Clarke hung around the customs shed morosely as the last of the tourist cars left the shed to head inland. At three he managed to contact the managing director of Tara Transportation and explained his problem. The man swore.

"I won't be carrying that in stock," he told Clarke. "I'll have to get on to the Volvo Trucks main agent for one. Call me back in an hour."

At four there was still no news and at five the customs men wanted to close down, the last ferry of the day having arrived from Fishguard. Clarke made a further call, to say he would spend the night in Rosslare and check back in yet another hour. One of the customs men kindly ran him into town and showed him a bed-and-breakfast lodging house. Clarke checked in for the night.

At six head office told him they would be picking up another differential nose-piece at nine the following morning and would send it down with a company engineer in a van. The man would be with him by twelve noon. Clarke called his wife to tell her he would be twenty-four hours late, ate his tea and went out to a pub. In the customs shed three miles away Tara's distinctive green and white artic stood silent and alone above its pool of oil.

Clarke allowed himself a lie-in the next day and rose at nine. He called head office at ten and they told him the van had got the replacement part and was leaving in five minutes. At eleven he hitch-hiked back to the harbour. The company was as good as its word and the little van, driven by the mechanic, rattled down the quay and into the customs shed at twelve. Clarke was waiting for it.

The chirpy engineer went under the truck like a ferret and Clarke could hear him tut-tutting. When he came out he was already smeared with oil.

"Nose-piece casing," he said unnecessarily. "Cracked right across."

"How long?" asked Clarke.

"If you give me a hand, I'll have you out of here in an hour and a half."

It took a little longer than that. First they had to mop up the pool of oil, and five pints goes a long way. Then the mechanic took a heavy wrench and carefully undid the ring of great bolts holding the nose-piece to the main casing. This done, he withdrew the two half-shafts and began to loosen the propeller shaft. Clarke sat on the floor and watched him, occasionally passing a tool as he was bidden. The customs men watched them both. Not much happens in a customs shed between berthings.

The broken casing came away in bits just before one. Clarke was getting hungry and would have liked to go up the road to the café and get some lunch, but the mechanic wanted to press on. Out at sea the *St. Patrick*, smaller sister ship of the *St. Kilian*, was moving over the horizon on her way home to Rosslare.

The mechanic started to perform the whole process in reverse. The new casing went on, the propeller shaft was fixed and the half-shafts slotted in. At half past one the *St. Patrick* was clearly visible out at sea to anyone who was watching.

Murphy was. He lay on his stomach in the sere grass atop the low line of rising ground behind the port, invisible to anyone a hundred yards away, and there was no such person. He held his field glasses to his eyes and monitored the approaching ship.

"Here she is," he said, "right on time."

Brendan, the strong man, lying in the long grass beside him, grunted.

"Do you think it'll work, Murphy?" he asked.

"Sure, I've planned it like a military operation," said Murphy. "It cannot fail."

A more professional criminal might have told Murphy, who traded as a scrap metal merchant with a sideline in "bent" cars, that he was a bit out of his league with such a caper, but Murphy had spent several thousand pounds of his own money setting it up and he was not to be discouraged. He kept watching the approaching ferry.

In the shed the mechanic tightened the last of the nuts around the new nose-piece, crawled out from under, stood up and stretched.

"Right," he said, "now, we'll put five pints of oil in and away you go."

He unscrewed a small flange nut in the side of the differential casing while Clarke fetched a gallon can of oil and a funnel from the van. Outside, the *St. Patrick*, with gentle care, slotted her nose into the mooring bay and the clamps went on. Her bow doors opened and the ramp came down.

Murphy held the glasses steady and stared at the dark hole in the bows of the *St. Patrick*. The first truck out was a dun brown, with French markings. The second to emerge into the afternoon sunlight gleamed in white and emerald green. On the side of her trailer the word TARA was written in large green letters. Murphy exhaled slowly.

"There it is," he breathed, "that's our baby."

"Will we go now?" asked Brendan, who could see very little without binoculars and was getting bored.

"No hurry," said Murphy. "We'll see her come out of the shed first."

The mechanic screwed the nut of the oil inlet tight and turned to Clarke.

"She's all yours," he said, "she's ready to go. As for me, I'm going to wash up. I'll probably pass you on the road to Dublin."

He replaced the can of oil and the rest of his tools in his van, selected a flask of detergent liquid and headed for the washroom. The Tara Transportation juggernaut rumbled through the entrance from the quay into the shed. A customs officer waved it to a bay next to its mate and the driver climbed down.

"What the hell happened to you, Liam?" he asked.

Clarke explained to him. A customs officer approached to examine the new man's papers.

"Am I OK to roll?" asked Clarke.

"Away with you," said the officer. "You've been making the place untidy for too long."

For the second time in twenty-four hours, Clarke pulled himself into his cab, punched the engine into life and let in the clutch. With a wave at his company colleague he moved into gear and the artic rolled out of the shed into the sunlight.

Murphy adjusted his grip on the binoculars as the juggernaut emerged on the landward side of the shed.

"He's through already," he told Brendan. "No complications. Do you see that?"

He passed the glasses to Brendan who wriggled to the top of the rise and stared down. Five hundred yards away the juggernaut was negotiating the bends leading away from the harbour to the road to Rosslare town.

"I do," he said.

"Seven hundred and fifty cases of finest French brandy in there," said Murphy. "That's nine thousand bottles. It markets at over ten pounds a bottle retail and I'll get four. What do you think of that?"

"It's a lot of drink," said Brendan wistfully.

"It's a lot of money, you fool," said Murphy. "Right, let's get going."

The two men wriggled off the skyline and ran at a crouch to where their car was parked on a sandy track below.

When they drove back to where the track joined the road from the docks to the town they had only a few seconds to wait and driver Clarke thundered by them. Murphy brought his black Ford Granada saloon, stolen two days earlier and now wearing false plates, in behind the artic and began to trail it.

It made no stops; Clarke was trying to get home. When he rolled over the bridge across the Slaney and headed north out of Wexford on the Dublin road Murphy decided he could make his phone call.

He had noted the phone booth earlier and removed the diaphragm from the earpiece to ensure that no one else would be using it when he came by. They were not. But someone, infuriated by the useless implement, had torn the flex from its base. Murphy swore and drove on. He found another booth beside a post office just north of Enniscorthy. As he braked, the juggernaut ahead of him roared out of sight.

The call he made was to another phone booth by the roadside north of Gorey where the other two members of his gang waited.

"Where the hell have you been?" asked Brady. "I've been waiting here with Keogh for over an hour."

"Don't worry," said Murphy. "He's on his way and he's on time. Just take up your positions behind the bushes in the lay-by and wait till he pulls up and jumps down."

He hung up and drove on. With his superior speed he caught up with the juggernaut before the village of Ferns and trailed the truck out onto the open road again. Before Camolin he turned to Brendan.

"Time to become guardians of law and order," he said and pulled off the road again, this time into a narrow country road he had examined on his earlier reconnaissance. It was deserted.

The two men jumped out and pulled a grip from the rear seat. They doffed their zip-fronted windbreakers and pulled two jackets from the grip. Both men already wore black shoes, socks and trousers. When the windbreakers were off they were wearing regulation police-style blue shirts and black ties. The jackets they pulled on completed the deception. Murphy's bore the three stripes of a sergeant. Brendan's was plain. Both carried the insignia of the Garda, the Irish police force. Two peaked caps from the same grip went onto their heads.

The last of the contents of the grip were two rolls of black, adhesive-backed sheet plastic. Murphy unrolled them, tore off the cloth backing and spread them carefully with his hands, one onto each of the Granada's front doors. The black plastic blended with the black paintwork. Each panel had the word GARDA in white letters. When he stole his car, Murphy had chosen a black Granada deliberately because that was the most common police patrol car.

From the locked boot Brendan took the final accoutrement, a block two feet long and triangular in crosssection. The base of the triangle was fitted with strong magnets which held the block firmly to the roof of the car. The other two sides, facing forwards and backwards, also had the word GARDA printed on the glass panels. There was no bulb inside to light it up, but who would notice that in daytime?

When the two men climbed back into the car and reversed out of the lane, they were to any casual observer a pair of highway patrolmen in every way. Brendan was driving now, with "Sergeant" Murphy beside him. They found the juggernaut waiting at a traffic light in the town of Gorey.

There is a new section of dual carriageway north of Gorey, between that ancient market town and Arklow. Halfway along it, on the northbound lane, is a lay-by, and this was the spot Murphy had chosen for his ambush. The moment the column of traffic blocked behind the artic entered the dual carriageway section, the other car drivers joyfully sped past the lorry and Murphy had it all to himself. He wound down his window and said "Now" to Brendan.

The Granada moved smoothly up beside the cab of the truck, and held station. Clarke looked down to see the police car beside him and a sergeant waving out of the passenger seat. He wound down his window.

"You're losing a rear tyre," roared Murphy above the wind. "Pull in to the lay-by."

Clarke looked ahead, saw the big P on a notice by the roadside indicating a lay-by, nodded and began to slow. The police car moved ahead, swerved into the lay-by at the appointed spot and stopped. The juggernaut followed and drew up behind the Granada. Clarke climbed down.

"It's down here at the back," said Murphy. "Follow me."

Clarke obediently followed him round the nose of his own truck and down its green and white length to the rear. He could see no flat tyre, but he hardly had a chance to look. The bushes parted and Brady and Keogh came bounding out in overalls and balaclavas. A gloved hand went over Clarke's mouth, a strong arm round his chest and another pair of arms round his legs. Like a sack he was swept off his feet and disappeared into the bushes.

Within a minute he had been divested of his company

overalls with the Tara logo on the breast pocket, his wrists, mouth and eyes were sticky-taped and, shielded from the gaze of passing motorists by the bulk of his own lorry, he was bundled into the rear seat of the "police" car. Here a gruff voice told him to lie on the floor and keep still. He did.

Two minutes later Keogh emerged from the bushes in the Tara overalls and joined Murphy by the door of the cab where the gang leader was examining the driving licence of the unfortunate Clarke.

"It's all in order," Murphy said. "Your name's Liam Clarke, and this load of documents must be in order. Did they not pass it all at Rosslare not two hours back?"

Keogh, who had been a truck driver before he served time as a guest of the Republic in Mountjoy, grunted and climbed into the truck. He surveyed the controls.

"No problem," he said, and replaced the sheaf of papers above the sun visor.

"See you at the farm in an hour," said Murphy.

He watched the hijacked juggernaut pull out of the lay-by and rejoin the northward stream on the Dublin road.

Murphy went back to the police car. Brady was in the back with his feet on the recumbent and blindfolded Clarke. He had lost his overalls and balaclava and was in a tweed jacket. Clarke might have seen Murphy's face, but only for a few seconds, and then with a police cap on top of it. He would not see the faces of the other three. That way, if he ever accused Murphy, the other three would give Murphy an unbreakable alibi.

Murphy glanced up and down the road. It was empty for the moment. He looked at Brendan and nodded. Both men tore the Garda signs from the doors, screwed them up and tossed them in the back. Another glance. A car sped by unheeding. Murphy yanked the illuminated sign off the roof and threw it to Brady. A further glance. Again, no traffic. Both uniform jackets came off and went to Brady in the back. The windbreakers went back on. When the Granada pulled out of the lay-by it was just another saloon car with three civilians visible in it.

They passed the juggernaut just north of Arklow. Murphy, driving again, gave a discreet toot of the horn. Keogh raised one hand as the Granada passed, thumb upward in the OK sign.

Murphy kept driving north as far as Kilmacanogue then pulled up the lane known as Rocky Valley towards Calary Bog. Not much happens up there, but he had located a deserted farm high on the moor which had the advantage of a great barn inside it, large enough to take the juggernaut unseen for a few hours. That was all that would be needed. The farm was reached by a muddy track and screened by a clump of conifers.

They arrived just before dusk, fifty minutes before the juggernaut and two hours before the rendezvous with the men from the North and their four vans.

Murphy reckoned he could be justifiably proud of the deal he had clinched. It would have been no easy task to dispose of those 9000 bottles of brandy in the South. They were bonded, each case and bottle numbered and sooner or later bound to be spotted. But up in Ulster, the war-torn North, it was different. The place was rife with shebeens, illegal drinking clubs that were unlicensed and outside the law anyway.

The shebeens were strictly segregated, Protestant and Catholic, with control of them firmly in the hands of the underworld, which itself had long been taken over by all those fine patriots they had up there. Murphy knew as well as any man that a fair proportion of the sectarian killings performed for the glory of Ireland had more to do with protection racketeering than patriotism.

So he had done his deal with one of the more powerful heroes, a main supplier to a whole string of shebeens into which the brandy could be filtered with no questions asked. The man, with his drivers, was due to meet him at the farm, unload the brandy into four vans, pay cash on the spot and have the stuff into the North by dawn through the maze of country lanes crossing the border between the lakes along the Fermanagh-Monaghan line.

He told Brendan and Brady to carry the hapless driver into the farm where Clarke was thrown on a pile of sacks in the corner of the derelict kitchen. The three hijackers settled down to wait. At seven the green and white juggernaut grunted up the track in the near darkness, lights out, and the three ran outside. By muffled flashlights they heaved open the old barn doors; Keogh ran the truck inside and the doors were closed. Keogh climbed down.

"I reckon I've earned my cut," he said, "and a drink."

"You've done well," said Murphy. "You'll not need to drive the truck again. It'll be unloaded by midnight and I'll drive it myself to a point ten miles away and abandon it. What will you drink?"

"How about a nip of brandy?" suggested Brady, and they all laughed. It was a good joke.

"I'll not break a case for a few cups," said Murphy, "and I'm a whiskey man myself. Will this do?"

He produced a flask from his pocket and they all agreed it would do nicely. At a quarter to eight it was completely dark and Murphy went to the end of the track with a flashlight to guide the men from the North. He had given them precise instructions, but they could still miss the track. At ten past eight he came back, guiding a convoy of four panel vans. When they stopped in the yard a big man in a camel overcoat descended from the passenger seat of the first. He carried an attaché case but no visible sense of humour.

"Murphy?" he said. Murphy nodded. "Have you got the stuff?"

"Fresh off the boat from France," said Murphy. "It's in the truck still, in the barn."

"If you've broken the truck open I'll want to examine every case," threatened the man. Murphy swallowed. He was glad he had resisted the temptation to look at his loot.

"The French customs seals are intact," he said. "You can examine them yourself."

The man from the North grunted and nodded to his acolytes who began to haul open the barn doors. Their torches shone on the twin locks that kept the rear doors closed upon the cargo, the customs seals still covering the locks unbroken. The Ulsterman grunted again and nodded his satisfaction. One of his men took a jemmy and approached the locks. The man from the North jerked his head.

"Let's go inside," he said. Murphy led the way, torch in hand, into what had been the sitting room of the old farm. The Northerner unclipped his attaché case, laid it on the table and opened the lid. Rows of bundles of sterling notes greeted Murphy's gaze. He had never seen so much money.

"Nine thousand bottles at four pounds each," he said. "Now that would make thirty-six thousand pounds, would it not?"

"Thirty-five," grunted the Northerner. "I like round numbers."

Murphy did not argue. He got the impression from this man that it would not be wise. Anyway, he was satisfied. With £3000 for each of his men and his outlay recouped, he would be well over £20,000 clear. "Agreed," he said.

One of the other Northerners appeared at the broken window. He spoke to his boss.

"You'd better come and have a look," was all he said.

Then he was gone. The big man snapped the case closed, gripped the handle and stalked outside. The four Ulstermen, along with Keogh, Brady and Brendan, were grouped round the open doors of the truck in the barn. Six torches illuminated the interior. Instead of neatly stacked columns of cases bearing the world-renowned name of the brandy producer, they were looking at something else.

There were rows of piled plastic sacks, each bearing the name of a famous manufacturer of flower-garden aids, and beneath the name the words "Rose Fertilizer." The man from the North stared at the cargo without change of expression.

"What the hell's this?" he grated.

Murphy had to pull his lower jaw back from somewhere near his throat. "I don't know," he croaked. "I swear I don't know."

He was telling the truth. His information had been impeccable—and costly. He had got the right ship, the right transporter. He knew there was only one such truck on that afternoon's arrival of the *St. Patrick.*

"Where's the driver?" snarled the big man.

"Inside," said Murphy.

"Let's go," said the big man. Murphy led the way. The unfortunate Liam Clarke was still trussed like a chicken upon his sacks.

"What the hell's this cargo of yours?" the big man asked without ceremony.

Clarke mumbled furiously behind his gag. The big man nodded to one of his accomplices who stepped forward and tore the medical plaster unceremoniously from

Clarke's mouth. The driver still had another band across his eyes.

"I said what the hell's this cargo of yours," the big man repeated. Clarke swallowed.

"Rose fertilizer," he said. "Sure, it's in the cargo manifest."

The big man flashed his torch over the sheaf of papers he had taken from Murphy. He stopped at the cargo manifest and thrust it under Murphy's nose.

"Did you not look at this, you fool?" he asked.

Murphy took out his growing panic on the driver. "Why didn't you tell me this?" he demanded.

Sheer outrage gave Clarke boldness in the face of his unseen persecutors. "Because I had a fecking gag over my mouth, that's why," he shouted back.

"That's true, Murphy," said Brendan, who was rather literal.

"Shut up," said Murphy, who was becoming desperate. He leaned closer to Clarke. "Is there not any brandy underneath it?" he asked.

Clarke's face gave away his utter ignorance. "Brandy?" he echoed. "Why should there be any brandy? They don't make brandy in Belgium."

"Belgium?" howled Murphy. "You drove into Le Havre from Cognac in France."

"I've never been to Cognac in my life," yelled Clarke. "I was driving a cargo of rose fertilizer. It's made of peat moss and dessicated cow manure. We export it from Ireland to Belgium. I took this cargo over last week. They opened it in Antwerp, examined it, said it was substandard and they wouldn't accept it. My bosses in Dublin told me to bring it back. It cost me three days in Antwerp sorting out the paperwork. Sure, it's all there in the papers."

The man from the North had been running his torch over the documents he held. They confirmed Clarke's story. He threw them to the floor with a grunt of disgust.

"Come with me," he said to Murphy and led the way outside. Murphy followed, protesting his innocence.

In the darkness of the yard the big man cut short Murphy's protestations. He dropped his attaché case, turned, gripped Murphy by the front of his windcheater, lifted him off his feet and slammed him into the barn door.

"Listen to me, you little Catholic bastard," said the big man.

Murphy had wondered which side of the Ulster racketeers he had been dealing with. Now he knew.

"You," said the big man in a whisper that froze Murphy's blood, "have hijacked a load of bullshit—literally. You have also wasted a lot of my time and my men's time and my money ..."

"I swear to you ..." croaked Murphy, who was having trouble with his air supply, "on my mother's grave ... it must be on the next ship, arriving at two p.m. tomorrow. I can start again ..."

"Not for me," whispered the big man, " 'cos the deal's off. And one last thing; if you ever try and pull a stroke like this on me again I'll have two of my lads come down here and redistribute your kneecaps. Do you understand me?"

Sweet Jesus, thought Murphy, they're animals these Northerners. The British are welcome to them. He knew it was more than his life was worth to voice the thought. He nodded. Five minutes later the man from the North and his four empty trucks were gone.

In the farmhouse by the light of a torch Murphy and his disconsolate gang finished the flask of whiskey.

"What do we do now?" asked Brady.

"Well," said Murphy, "we clear up the evidence. We have gained nothing but we have lost nothing, except me."

"What about our three thousand quid?" asked Keogh.

Murphy thought. He did not want another round of threats from his own people after the scare the Ulsterman had thrown into him.

"Lads, it will have to be fifteen hundred apiece," he said. "And you'll have to wait a while until I make it. I cleaned myself out setting up this stroke."

They appeared mollified if not happy.

"Brendan, you, Brady and Keogh should clear up here. Every scrap of evidence, every footprint and tyre track in the mud, wipe it out. When you're done, take his car and drop the driver somewhere south of here by the roadside in his stockings. With tape on his mouth, eyes and wrists, he'll be a while getting the alarm up. Then turn north and drive home.

"I'll stick by my word to you, Keogh. I'll take the truck and abandon it way up in the hills towards Kippure. I'll walk back down and maybe get a lift on the main road back to Dublin. Agreed?"

They agreed. They had no choice. The men from the North had done a good job of smashing the locks on the rear of the artic's trailer, so the gang hunted round for wooden pegs to secure the two hasps. Then they closed the doors on its disappointing cargo and pegged them shut. With Murphy at the wheel the juggernaut growled back down the track from the farm and turned left towards the Djouce Forest and the hills of Wicklow.

It was just after 9:30 and Murphy was past the forest on the Roundwood road when he met the tractor. One would think farmers would not be out on tractors with one faulty headlight, the other smeared with mud, and ten tons of straw bales on a trailer at that hour. But this one was.

Murphy was bombing along between two stone walls when he discerned the looming mass of the tractor and trailer coming the other way. He hit the brakes rather sharply.

One thing about articulated vehicles is that although they can manoeuvre round corners that a rigid-frame lorry of similar length could not get near, they are the very devil when it comes to braking. If the cab section which does the towing and the trailer section which carries the cargo are not almost in line, they tend to jack-knife. The heavy trailer tries to overtake the cab section, shoving it sideways into a skid as it does so. This is what happened to Murphy.

It was the stone walls, so common in those Wicklow hills, that stopped him rolling clean over. The farmer gunned his tractor clean through a handy farm gate, leaving the straw bales on the trailer to take any impact. Murphy's cab section began to slither as the trailer caught up with it. The load of fertilizer pushed him, brakes locked in panic, into the side of the bales, which fell happily all over his cab, almost burying it. The rear of the trailer behind him slammed into a stone wall and was thrown back onto the road, where it then hit the opposite stone wall as well.

When the screech of metal on stone stopped, the farm trailer was still upright, but had been moved ten feet, shearing its coupling to the tractor. The shock had thrown the farmer off his seat and into a pile of silage. He was having a noisy personal conversation with his creator. Murphy was sitting in the dim half-light of a cab covered in bales of straw.

The shock of hitting the stone walls had sheared the pegs holding the rear of the artic shut and both doors had flown open. Part of the rose fertilizer cargo was strewn on the road behind the truck. Murphy opened his cab door and fought his way through the bales of straw to the road. He had but one instinct, to get as far away from there as possible as fast as he could. The farmer would never recognize him in the darkness. Even as he climbed down, he recalled he had not had time to wipe the interior of the cab of all his fingerprints.

The farmer had squelched his way out of the silage and was standing on the road beside Murphy's cab reeking of an odour that will never really catch on with the after-shave industry. It was evident he wished for a few moments of Murphy's time. Murphy thought fast. He would appease the farmer and offer to help him reload his trailer. At the first opportunity he would wipe his prints off the inside of the cab, and at the second vanish into the darkness.

It was at this moment that the police patrol car arrived. It is a strange thing about police cars; when you need one they are like strawberries in Greenland. Scrape a few inches of paint off someone else's bodywork and they come out of the gratings. This one had escorted a minister from Dublin to his country home near Annamoe and was returning to the capital. When Murphy saw the headlights he thought it was just another motorist; as the lights doused he saw it was the real thing. It had a Garda sign on the roof, and this one *did* light up.

The sergeant and the constable walked slowly past the immobilized tractor-trailer and surveyed the tumbled bales. Murphy realized there was nothing for it but to bluff the whole thing out. In the darkness he could still get away with it.

"Yours?" asked the sergeant, nodding at the artic.

"Yes," said Murphy.

"A long way from the main roads," said the sergeant.

"Aye, and late too," said Murphy. "The ferry was late at Rosslare this afternoon and I wanted to deliver this lot and get home to my wee bed."

"Papers," said the sergeant.

Murphy reached into the cab and handed him Liam Clarke's sheaf of documents.

"Liam Clarke?" asked the sergeant.

Murphy nodded. The documents were in perfect order. The constable had been examining the tractor and came back to his sergeant.

"One of your man's headlights doesn't work," he said, nodding at the farmer, "and the other's covered with clay. You would not see this rig at ten yards."

The sergeant handed Murphy the documents back and transferred his attention to the farmer. The latter, all self-justification a few moments ago, began to look defensive. Murphy's spirits rose.

"I wouldn't want to make an issue of it," he said, "but the garda's right. The tractor and trailer were completely invisible."

"You have your licence?" the sergeant asked the farmer.

"It's at home," said the farmer.

"And the insurance with it, no doubt," said the sergeant. "I hope they're both in order. We'll see in a minute. Meanwhile you can't drive on with faulty headlights. Move the trailer into the field and clear the bales off the road. You can collect them all at first light. We'll run you home and look at the documents at the same time."

Murphy's spirits rose higher. They would be gone in a few minutes. The constable began to examine the lights of the artic. They were in perfect order. He moved to look at the rear lights.

"What's your cargo?" asked the sergeant.

"Fertilizer," said Murphy. "Part peat moss, part cow manure. Good for roses."

The sergeant burst out laughing. He turned to the farmer who had towed the trailer off the road into the field and was throwing the bales after it. The road was almost clear.

"This one's carrying a load of manure," he said, "but you're the one up to your neck in it." He was amused by his wit.

The constable came back from the rear of the artic's trailer section. "The doors have sprung open," he said. "Some of the sacks have fallen in the road and burst. I think you'd better have a look, sarge."

The three of them walked back down the side of the artic to the rear.

A dozen sacks had fallen out of the back of the open doors and four had split open. The moonlight shone on the heaps of brown fertilizer between the torn plastic. The constable had his torch out and played it over the mess. As Murphy told his cellmate later, there are some days when nothing, but absolutely nothing, goes right.

By moon and torchlight there was no mistaking the great maw of the bazooka jutting upwards, nor the shapes of the machine guns protruding from the torn sacks. Murphy's stomach turned.

The Irish police do not normally carry handguns, but when on escort duty for a minister, they do. The sergeant's automatic was pointing at Murphy's stomach.

Murphy sighed. It was just one of those days. He had not only failed signally to hijack 9000 bottles of brandy, but had managed to intercept someone's clandestine arms shipment and he had little doubt who that "someone" might be. He could think of several places he would like to be for the next two years, but the streets of Dublin were not the safest places on that list.

He raised his hands slowly.

"I have a little confession to make," he said.

Money with Menaces

If Samuel Nutkin had not dropped his glasses case between the cushions of his seat on the commuter train from Edenbridge to London that morning, none of this would ever have happened. But he did drop them, slipped his hand between the cushions to retrieve them, and the die was cast.

His fumbling fingers encountered not only his glasses case, but a slim magazine evidently stuffed there by the former occupant of the seat. Believing it to be a railway timetable, he idly withdrew it. Not that he needed a railway timetable. After twenty-five years of taking the same train at the same hour from the small and sinless commuter town of Edenbridge to Charing Cross station, and returning on the same train at the same time from Cannon Street station to Kent each evening, he had no need of railway timetables. It was just passing curiosity.

When he glanced at the front cover Mr. Nutkin's face coloured up red, and he hastily stuffed it back down the cushions. He looked round the compartment to see if anyone had noticed what he had found. Opposite him two *Financial Times*, a *Times* and a *Guardian* nodded back at him with the rhythm of the train, their readers invisible behind the city prices section. To his left old Fogarty pored over the crossword puzzle and to his right, outside

126

the window, Hither Green station flashed past uncaring. Samuel Nutkin breathed out in relief.

The magazine had been small with a glossy cover. Across the top were the words *New Circle*, evidently the title of the publication, and along the bottom of the cover page another phrase, "Singles, Couples, Groups—the contact magazine for the sexually aware." Between the two lines of print the centre of the cover page was occupied by a photograph of a large lady with a jutting chest, her face blocked out by a white square which announced her as "Advertiser H331." Mr. Nutkin had never seen such a magazine before, but he thought out the implications of his find all the way to Charing Cross.

As the doors down the train swung open in unison to decant their cargoes of commuters into the maelstrom of platform 6, Samuel Nutkin delayed his departure by fussing with his briefcase, rolled umbrella and bowler hat until he was last out of the compartment. Finally, aghast at his daring, he slipped the magazine from its place between the cushions into his briefcase, and joined the sea of other bowler hats moving towards the ticket barrier, season tickets extended.

It was an uncomfortable walk from the train to the subway, down the line to the Mansion House station, up the escalator to Great Trinity Lane and along Cannon Street to the office block of the insurance company where he worked as a clerk. He had heard once of a man who was knocked over by a car and when they emptied his pockets at the hospital they found a packet of pornographic pictures. The memory haunted Samuel Nutkin. How on earth could one ever explain such a thing? The shame, the embarrassment, would be unbearable. To lie there with a leg in traction, knowing that everyone knew one's secret tastes. He was especially careful crossing the road that morning until he reached the insurance company offices.

From all of which one may gather that Mr. Nutkin was
not used to this sort of thing. There was a man once who
reckoned that human beings tend to imitate the nicknames
given them in an idle moment. Call a man "Butch"
and he will swagger; call him "Killer" and he will walk
around with narrowed eyes and try to talk like Bogart.
Funny men have to go on telling jokes and clowning until
they crack up from the strain. Samuel Nutkin was just ten
years old when a boy at school who had read the tales of
Beatrix Potter called him Squirrel, and he was doomed.

He had worked in the City of London since, as a young
man of twenty-three, he came out of the army at the end
of the war with the rank of corporal. In those days he had
been lucky to get the job, a safe job with a pension at the
end of it, clerking for a giant insurance company with
worldwide ramifications, safe as the Bank of England that
stood not 500 yards away. Getting that job had marked
Samuel Nutkin's entry into the City, square-mile headquarters of a vast economic, commercial and banking octopus whose tentacles spread to every corner of the globe.

He had loved the City in those days of the late forties,
wandering round in the lunch hour looking at the timeless
streets—Bread Street, Cornhill, Poultry and London
Wall—dating back to the Middle Ages when they really
did sell bread and corn and poultry and mark the walled
city of London. He was impressed that it was out of these
sober stone piles that merchant adventurers had secured
financial backing to sail away to the lands of brown, black
and yellow men, to trade and dig and mine and scavenge,
sending the booty back to the City, to insure and bank
and invest until decisions taken in this square mile of
boardrooms and counting houses could affect whether a
million lesser breeds worked or starved. That these men

had really been the world's most successful looters never occurred to him. Samuel Nutkin was very loyal.

Time passed and after a quarter of a century the magic had faded; he became one of the trotting tide of clerical grey suits, rolled umbrellas, bowler hats and briefcases that flooded into the City each day to clerk for eight hours and return to the dormitory townships of the surrounding counties.

In the forest of the City he was, like his nickname, a friendly, harmless creature, grown with the passing years to fit a desk, a pleasant, round butterball of a man, just turned sixty, glasses ever on his nose for reading or looking at things closely, mild-mannered and polite to the secretaries who thought he was sweet and mothered him, and not at all accustomed to reading, let alone carrying on his person, dirty magazines. But that was what he did that morning. He crept away to the lavatories, slipped the bolt, and read every advertisement in *New Circle*.

It amazed him. Some of the adverts had accompanying pictures, mainly amateurish poses of what were evidently housewives in their underwear. Others had no picture, but a more explicit text, in some cases advertising services that made no sense, at least not to Samuel Nutkin. But most he understood, and the bulk of the adverts from ladies expressed the hope of meeting generous professional gentlemen. He read it through, stuffed the magazine into the deepest folds of his briefcase and hurried back to his desk. That evening he managed to get the magazine back home to Edenbridge without being stopped and searched by the police, and hid it under the carpet by the fireplace. It would never do for Lettice to discover it.

Lettice was Mrs. Nutkin. She was mainly confined to her bed, she claimed by severe arthritis and a weak heart, while Dr. Bulstrode opined it was a severe dose of hypochondria. She was a frail and peaky woman, with a sharp nose and a querulous voice, and it had been many years since she had given any physical joy to Samuel Nutkin, out of bed or in it. But he was a loyal and trustworthy man, and he would have done anything, just anything, to avoid distressing her. Fortunately she never did housework because of her back, so she had no occasion to delve under the carpet by the fireplace.

Mr. Nutkin spent three days absorbed in his private thoughts, which for the most part concerned a lady advertiser who, from the brief details she listed in her advert, was well above average height and possessed an ample figure. On the third day, plucking up all his nerve, he sat down and wrote his reply to her advert. He did it on a piece of plain paper from the office and it was short and to the point. He said "Dear Madam," and went on to explain that he had seen her advert and would very much like to meet her.

There was a centrefold in the magazine that explained how adverts should be answered. Write your letter of reply and place it, together with a self-addressed and stamped envelope, in a plain envelope and seal. Write the number of the advert to which you are replying on the back of the envelope in pencil. Enclose this plain envelope, together with the forwarding fee, in a third envelope and mail it to the magazine's office in London. Mr. Nutkin did all this, except that for the self-addressed envelope he used the name Henry Jones, c/o 27 Acacia Avenue, which was his real address.

For the next six days he was down on the hallway mat each morning the instant the mail arrived, and it was on the sixth that he spotted the envelope addressed to Henry Jones. He stuffed it into his pocket and went back upstairs to collect his wife's breakfast tray.

On the train to town that morning he slipped away to the toilet and opened the envelope with trembling fingers.

The contents were his own letter, and written on the back in longhand was the reply. It said, "Dear Henry, thank you for your reply to my ad. I'm sure we could have a lot of fun together. Why don't you ring me at ——? Love, Sally." The phone number was in Bayswater, in the West End of London.

There was nothing else in the envelope. Samuel Nutkin jotted the number on a piece of paper, stuffed it in his back pocket, and flushed the letter and envelope down the pan. When he returned to his seat there were butterflies in his stomach and he thought people would be staring, but old Fogarty had just worked out 15 across and no one looked up.

He rang the number at lunchtime from a call box in the nearest subway station. A husky woman's voice said, "Hello?"

Mr. Nutkin pushed the five-penny piece into the slot, cleared his throat and said, "Er . . . hello, is that Miss Sally?"

"That's right," said the voice, "and who is that?"

"Oh, er, my name is Jones. Henry Jones. I received a letter from you this morning, about a reply I made to your advert . . ."

There was a rustling of paper at the other end, and the woman's voice cut in. "Oh, yes, I remember, Henry. Well now, darling, would you like to come round and see me?"

Samuel Nutkin felt as if his tongue were of old leather. "Yes, please," he croaked.

"Lovely," purred the woman at the other end. "There is just one thing, Henry darling. I expect a little present from my men friends, you know, just to help out with the rent. It's twenty pounds, but there's no rush or hurry. Is that all right?"

Nutkin nodded, then said "Yes" down the phone.

"Fine," she said, "well now, when would you like to come?"

"It would have to be in the lunch hour. I work in the City, and I go home in the evening."

"All right then. Tomorrow suit you? Good. At twelve-thirty? I'll give you the address . . ."

He still had the butterflies in his stomach, except that they had turned into thrashing pigeons, when he turned up at the basement flat just off Westbourne Grove in Bayswater the following day at half past twelve. He tapped nervously and heard the clack of heels in the passage behind the door.

There was a pause as someone looked through the glass lens set into the centre panel of the door, and which commanded a view of the area in which he stood. Then the door opened and a voice said, "Come in." She was standing behind the door and closed it as he entered and turned to face her. "You must be Henry," she said softly. He nodded. "Well, come into the sitting room so we can talk," she said.

He followed her down the passage to the first room on the left, his heart beating like a tambour. She was older than he had expected, a much-used mid-thirties with heavy make-up. She was a good six inches taller than he was, but part of that could be explained by the high heels of her court shoes, and the breadth of her rear beneath the floor-length housecoat as she preceded him down the passage indicated her figure was heavy. When she turned to usher him into the sitting room the front of her house-coat swung open for a second to give a glimpse of black nylons and a red-trimmed corset. She left the door open.

The room was cheaply furnished and seemed to contain no more than a handful of personal possessions. The woman smiled at him encouragingly.

"Do you have my little present, Henry?" she asked him.

Samuel Nutkin nodded and proffered her the £20 he had been holding in his trouser pocket. She took it and stuffed it into a handbag on the dresser.

"Now sit down and make yourself comfortable," she said. "There's no need to be nervous. Now, what can I do for you?"

Mr. Nutkin had seated himself on the edge of an easy chair. He felt as if his mouth was full of quick-drying cement. "It's difficult to explain," he muttered.

She smiled again. "There's no need to be shy. What would you like to do?"

Hesitatingly he told her. She showed no surprise.

"That's all right," she said easily. "A lot of gentlemen like a bit of that sort of thing. Now take off your jacket, trousers and shoes, and come with me into the bedroom."

He did as she told him and followed her down the passage again to the bedroom which was surprisingly brightly lit. Once inside she closed the door, locked it, dropped the key into the pocket of her housecoat, slipped out of the latter and hung it behind the door.

When the plain buff envelope arrived at 27 Acacia Avenue three days later Samuel Nutkin collected it off the front door mat along with the rest of the morning mail and took it back to the breakfast table. There were three letters in all, one for Lettice from her sister, a bill from the nursery for some potted plants, and the buff envelope, postmarked in London and addressed to Samuel Nutkin. He opened it without suspicion, expecting it to be a commercial circular. It was not.

The six photographs that fell out lay for a few moments face up on the table while he stared at them in incomprehension. When understanding dawned, sheer horror took its place. The photos would not have won prizes for clarity or focus, but they were good enough. In all of them the face of the woman was clearly seen, and in at least two of them his own face was easily recognizable. Scrabbling furiously he scoured the inside of the envelope for anything else, but it was quite empty. He turned all six photographs, but the backs were unmarked by any message. The message was on the front in black and white, without words.

Samuel Nutkin was in the grip of a blind panic as he stuffed the photographs under the carpet by the fireplace where he found the magazine still lying. Then on a second impulse he took the lot outside and burned them all behind the garage, stamping the ashes into the moist earth with his heel. As he re-entered the house he thought of spending the day at home, claiming illness, but then realized that must attract Lettice's suspicion since he was perfectly well. He just had time to take her letter upstairs to her, remove her breakfast tray and run to catch the train to the City.

His mind was still whirling as he gazed out of the window from his corner seat and tried to work out the implications of the morning's shock. It took him till just past New Cross to realize how it had been done.

"My jacket," he breathed, "jacket and wallet."

Old Fogarty who was studying 7 down shook his head. "No," he said, "too many letters."

Samuel Nutkin gazed miserably out of the window as southeast London's suburbs trundled past the train. He was simply not used to this sort of thing. A cold horror gripped his stomach and he could no more concentrate on his work that morning than fly.

In the lunch hour he tried to ring the number Sally had given him, but it had been disconnected.

He took a taxi straight to the basement flat in Bayswater but it was locked and barred, with a For Rent notice attached to the railings at pavement level. By mid-afternoon Mr. Nutkin had worked out that even going to the police would serve little purpose. Almost certainly the magazine had sent replies for that advertisement to an address which would turn out to be an accommodation, long since vacated without trace. The basement flat in Bayswater had probably been rented by the week for the week in a false name and vacated. The telephone number would probably belong to a man who would say he had been away for the past month and had found the door latch forced on his return. Since then there had been a number of calls asking for Sally, which had completely mystified him. A day later he too would be gone.

On his arrival home Lettice was in a more complaining mood than usual. There had been three calls, all asking for him by name, which had disturbed her afternoon rest. It was really not good enough.

The fourth call came just after eight. Samuel Nutkin shot out of his chair, left Lettice watching the television, and went into the hallway to take it. The voice was that of a man, but could it be the one he had spoken to in the lunch hour? Impossible to say. The voice was fogged as if by a handkerchief held to the mouthpiece.

"Mr. Nutkin?"

"Yes."

"Mr. Samuel Nutkin?"

"Yes."

"Or should I call you Henry Jones?"

Samuel Nutkin's stomach turned over.

"Who is that?" he queried.

"Never mind the name, friend. Did you get my little present in the morning's post?"

"What do you want?"

"I asked you a question, friend. Did you get the photos?"

"Yes."

"Have a good look at them, did you?"

Samuel Nutkin swallowed hard with the horror of the memory. "Yes."

"Well, then, you've been a naughty lad, haven't you? I really can't see how I can avoid sending the same set to your boss at the office. Oh yes, I know about your office, and the managing director's name. And then I might send another set to Mrs. Nutkin. Or to the secretary of the tennis club. You really do carry a lot in your wallet, Mr. Nutkin . . ."

"Look, please don't do that," burst out Mr. Nutkin, but the voice cut through his protests.

"I'm not staying on this line any longer. Don't bother to go to the police. They couldn't even begin to find me. So just play it cool, friend, and you can have the whole lot back, negatives and all. Think it over. What time do you leave for work in the morning?"

"Eight-twenty."

"I'll ring you again at eight tomorrow morning. Have a good night."

The phone clicked dead, and Mr. Nutkin was left listening to the dialling tone.

He did not have a good night. He had a horrible night. After Lettice had gone to bed he made the excuse of banking up the fire, and item by item went through the contents of his wallet. Railway season ticket, cheque book, tennis club membership card, two letters addressed to him, two photographs of Lettice and himself, driving licence, membership card for the insurance company's social club, more than enough to identify him and his place of work.

In the half light of the street lamp shining from Acacia

Avenue through the curtains he looked across the room at Lettice's disapproving face in the other twin bed—she had always insisted on twin beds—and tried to imagine her opening a buff envelope that had arrived, addressed to her, by second postal delivery while he was at the office. He tried to visualize Mr. Benson up on the directors' floor receiving the same set of photos. Or the membership committee of the tennis club passing them round at a special meeting convened to "reconsider" Samuel Nutkin's membership. He couldn't. It baffled his imagination. But of one thing he was quite certain; the shock would kill poor Lettice . . . it would simply kill her, and that must not be allowed to happen.

Before he dropped into a fitful doze just before dawn, he told himself for the hundredth time that he was simply not used to this sort of thing.

The phone call came on the dot of eight. Samuel Nutkin was waiting in the hallway, as ever in dark grey suit, white shirt and collar, bowler hat, rolled umbrella and briefcase, before setting off on his punctual morning trot to the station.

"Thought it over, have you?" said the voice.

"Yes," quavered Samuel Nutkin.

"Want those photo negatives back, do you?"

"Yes, please."

"Well, I'm afraid you'll have to buy 'em, friend. Just to cover our expenses and perhaps to teach you a little lesson."

Mr. Nutkin swallowed several times. "I'm not a rich man," he pleaded. "How much do you want?"

"One thousand quid," replied the man down the phone, without hesitation.

Samuel Nutkin was appalled. "But I haven't got one thousand pounds," he protested.

"Well, then, you'd better raise it," sneered the voice on

the phone. "You can raise a loan against your house, your car or whatever you like. But get it, and quick. By tonight. I'll ring you at eight this evening."

And again the man was gone, and the dialling tone buzzed in Samuel Nutkin's ear. He went upstairs, gave Lettice a peck on the cheek, and left for work. But that day he did not board the 8:31 to Charing Cross. Instead, he went and sat in the park, alone on a bench, a strange solitary figure dressed for the office and the City, but sitting gnome-like amid the trees and flowers, in a bowler hat and dark grey suit. He felt he had to think, and that he could not think properly sitting next to old Fogarty and his endless crossword puzzles.

He supposed he could borrow £1000 if he tried, but it would raise a few eyebrows at the bank. Even that would be as nothing compared with the bank manager's reaction when he asked for it all in used notes. He could say he needed it to pay a gambling debt, but no one would believe it. They knew he didn't gamble. He didn't drink much beyond a glass of wine now and again, and did not smoke either, except a cigar at Christmas. They would think it was a woman, he surmised, then dismissed that too. They would know he would not keep a mistress. What to do, what to do, he asked himself over and over, rocking backwards and forwards in his mental turmoil.

He could go to the police. Surely they could trace these people, even through false names and rented flats. Then there would be a court case and he would have to give evidence. They always referred to the blackmailed person as Mr. X, he had read in the paper, but the man's own circle usually discovered who it was. One could not keep going to court day after day and no one notice, not if one had led a life of unvarying routine for thirty-five years.

At 9:30 he left the park bench and went to a telephone kiosk where he rang his office and told the chief of his department that he was indisposed but would be at his desk that afternoon. From there he walked to the bank. On the way he racked his brains for a solution, recalling all the court cases he had read about in which blackmail was concerned. What did the law call it? Demanding money with menaces, that was the phrase. A nice legal phrase, he thought bitterly, but not much use to the victim.

If he were a single man, he thought, and younger, he would tell them where to go. But he was too old to change his job, and then there was Lettice, poor fragile Lettice. The shock would kill her, he had no doubt. Above all, he must protect Lettice, of that he was determined.

At the door of the bank his nerve failed him. He could never confront his bank manager with such a strange and inexplicable request. It would be tantamount to saying, "I am being blackmailed and I want a loan of a thousand pounds." Besides, after the first £1000, would they not come back for more? Bleed him white, then send the pictures? It could happen. But at any rate he could not raise the money at his local bank. The answer, he decided reluctantly, for he was an honest and gentle man, lay in London. It was thither he went on the 10:31 train.

He arrived in the City too early to present himself at his office, so to fill in the time he went shopping. Being a careful man he could not conceive of carrying a sum as large as £1000 around unprotected in his pocket. It would not be natural. So he went to an emporium for office equipment and bought a small steel cashbox with key. At a variety of other shops he bought a pound of icing sugar (for his wife's birthday cake, he explained), a tin of fertilizer for his roses, a mousetrap for the kitchen, some fuse wire for the electrical box under the stairs, two torch batteries, a soldering iron to mend the kettle, and a number of other harmless items such as every law-abiding householder might be expected to have about the house.

At two in the afternoon he was at his desk, assured his department head he was feeling much better, and got on with his work on the company accounts. Fortunately the idea that Mr. Samuel Nutkin might even think of making an unauthorized withdrawal on the company's account was not to be entertained.

At eight that evening he was once again in front of the television with Lettice when the phone rang in the hallway. When he answered, it was Foggy Voice again.

"You got the money, Mr. Nutkin?" he said without preamble.

"Er . . . yes," said Mr. Nutkin, and before the other could continue he went on, "Look, please why don't you send the negatives to me and we'll forget the whole thing?"

There was a silence as of stunned amazement from the other end.

"You out of your mind?" queried Foggy Voice at last.

"No," said Mr. Nutkin seriously. "No, but I just wish you could understand the distress this is all going to cause if you insist on going ahead."

"Now you listen to me, Nutcase," said the voice, harsh with anger. "You must do as you're bloody well told, or I might even send those photos to your wife and boss, just for the hell of it."

Mr. Nutkin sighed deeply. "That was what I feared," he said. "Go on."

"Tomorrow during the lunch hour take a taxi to Albert Bridge Road. Turn into Battersea Park and walk down West Drive heading away from the river. Halfway down turn left into Central Drive. Keep walking down there till you come to the halfway point. There are two benches. There won't be nobody about, not at this time of year. Put the stuff, wrapped in a brown paper parcel, under the first bench. Then keep walking till you come out the other side of the park. Got it?"

"Yes, I've got it," said Mr. Nutkin.

"Right," said the voice. "One last thing. You'll be watched from the moment you enter the park. You'll be watched as you place the parcel. Don't think the cops can help you. We know what you look like, but you don't know me. One hint of trouble, or the fuzz keeping a watch, and we'll be gone. You know what will happen then, don't you, Nutkin?"

"Yes," said Mr. Nutkin feebly.

"Right. Well, do what you've been told, and don't make mistakes."

Then the man hung up.

A few minutes later Samuel Nutkin made an excuse to his wife and went into the garage at the side of the house. He wanted to be alone for a while.

Samuel Nutkin did exactly as he was told the following day. He was walking down West Drive on the western side of the park and had reached the left turn into Central Drive when he was hailed by a motorcyclist sitting astride his machine a few feet away, studying a road map. The man wore a crash helmet, goggles and a scarf wrapped round his face. He called through the scarf, "Hey, mate, can you help me?"

Mr. Nutkin paused in his stride but being a polite man he covered the two yards to where the motorcycle stood by the kerb and bent to peer at the map. A voice hissed in his ear, "I'll take the parcel, Nutkin."

He felt the parcel wrenched from his grip, heard the roar of the engine kick-started, saw the parcel drop into an open basket on the handlebars of the motorbike, and in seconds the machine was away, weaving back into the lunchtime traffic of the Albert Bridge Road. It was over in seconds, and even if the police had been watching, they could hardly have caught the man, so quickly did he move. Mr. Nutkin shook his head sadly and went back to his office in the City.

The man with the theory about names and nicknames was quite wrong in the case of Detective Sergeant Smiley of the Criminal Investigation Department. When he called to see Mr. Nutkin the following week, his long horse face and sad brown eyes looked very sombre. He stood on the doorstep in the winter darkness in a long black coat like an undertaker.

"Mr. Nutkin?"

"Yes."

"Mr. Samuel Nutkin?"

"Yes, . . . er, yes, that's me."

"Detective Sergeant Smiley, sir. I wonder if I might have a few moments with you." He proffered his warrant card, but Mr. Nutkin bobbed his head in acceptance, and said, "Won't you come in?"

Detective Sergeant Smiley was ill at ease.

"Er . . . what I have to discuss, Mr. Nutkin, is somewhat of a private nature, perhaps even somewhat embarrassing," he began.

"Good Lord," said Nutkin, "there's no need to be embarrassed, Sergeant."

Smiley stared at him. "No need . . . ?"

"Good gracious me, no. Some tickets for the police ball no doubt. We in the tennis club always send a few along. As secretary this year I quite expected . . ."

Smiley swallowed hard. "I'm afraid it's not about the police ball, sir. I am here in the course of inquiries."

"Well, there's still no need to be embarrassed," said Mr. Nutkin.

The muscles in the sergeant's jaw worked spasmodically. "I was thinking, sir, of your embarrassment, not my own," he said patiently. "Is your wife at home, sir?"

"Well, yes, but she's in bed. She retires early, you know. Her health . . ."

As if on cue a petulant voice came floating from the upper floor down to the hallway. "Who is it, Samuel?"

"It's a gentleman from the police, my dear."

"From the police?"

"Now do not fret yourself, my dear," Samuel Nutkin called back. "Er . . . it simply has to do with the forthcoming tennis tournament with the police sports club."

Sergeant Smiley nodded in grim approval of the subterfuge and followed Mr. Nutkin into the sitting room.

"Now, perhaps you can tell me what this is all about, and why I should be embarrassed," said the latter as the door closed.

"Some days ago," began Sergeant Smiley, "my colleagues in the Metropolitan Police Force had occasion to visit a flat in the West End of London. While searching the premises, they came across a series of envelopes in a locked drawer."

Samuel Nutkin gazed at him with benign interest.

"Each of these envelopes, some thirty in all, contained a postcard on which had been written the name of a man, all different, along with home address and in some cases address of place of employment. The envelopes also contained up to a dozen photographic negatives, and in each case these proved to be pictures of men, usually mature men, in what one might only describe as an extremely compromising situation with a woman."

Samuel Nutkin had gone pale and he moistened his lips nervously. Sergeant Smiley looked disapproving.

"In each case," he went on, "the woman in the photographs was the same, a person known to the police as a convicted prostitute. I'm afraid to have to tell you, sir, that one of the envelopes contained your name and address, and a series of six negatives in which you featured engaged in a certain activity in company with this woman. We have established that this woman, along with a certain man, was one of the occupants of the flat visited by the Metropolitan Police. The man in the case was the other occupant. Do you begin to follow me?"

Samuel Nutkin held his head in his hands in shame. He gazed with haggard eyes at the carpet. Finally he sighed a deep sigh.

"Oh, my God," he said. "Photographs. Someone must have taken photographs. Oh, the shame of it, when it all comes out. I swear to you, Sergeant, I had no idea it was illegal."

Sergeant Smiley blinked rapidly. "Mr. Nutkin, let me make one thing quite plain. Whatever you did was not illegal. Your private life is your own affair as far as the police are concerned, providing it breaks no laws. And visiting a prostitute does not break the law."

"But I don't understand," quavered Nutkin. "You said you were making inquiries . . ."

"But not into your private life, Mr. Nutkin," said Sergeant Smiley firmly. "May I continue? Thank you. It is the view of the Metropolitan Police that men were lured to this woman's apartment either by personal contact or by contact through advertisements, and then secretly photographed and identified, with a view to subjecting them to blackmail at a later date."

Samuel Nutkin stared up at the detective round-eyed. He was simply not used to this sort of thing.

"Blackmail," he whispered. "Oh, my God, that's even worse."

"Precisely, Mr. Nutkin. Now . . ." The detective produced a photograph from his coat pocket. "Do you recognize this woman?"

Samuel Nutkin found himself staring at a good likeness of the woman he knew as Sally. He nodded dumbly.

"I see," said the sergeant and put the photograph away. "Now, sir, would you tell me in your own words how you came to make the acquaintance of this lady. I will not need to make any notes at this stage, and anything you say will be treated as confidential unless it now or later proves to have a bearing on the case."

Haltingly, ashamed and mortified, Samuel Nutkin related the affair from the start, the chance finding of the magazine, the reading of it in the office toilet, the three-day tussle with himself over whether to write a letter back or not, the succumbing to temptation and the writing of his letter under the name of Henry Jones. He told of the letter that came back, of noting the telephone number and destroying the letter, of making the telephone call that same lunch hour and being given an appointment for the following day at 12:30. He narrated the meeting with the woman in the basement flat, how she had persuaded him to leave his jacket in the sitting room while taking him into the bedroom, how it was the first time in his life he had ever done such a thing, and how on returning home that evening he had burned the magazine in which he had found the original advert and vowed never to behave in that way again.

"Now, sir," said Sergeant Smiley when he had finished, "this is very important. At any time since that afternoon have you received any phone call, or had knowledge of a phone call being made in your absence, that might have been connected with a demand for payment in blackmail as a result of these photographs being taken?"

Samuel Nutkin shook his head. "No," he said, "nothing

at all like that. It seems they haven't got round to me yet."

Sergeant Smiley smiled at last, a grim smile. "They haven't got round to you yet, sir, and they won't. After all, the police have the photographs."

Samuel Nutkin looked up with hope in his eyes. "Of course," he said. "Your investigation. They must have been detected before they could get round to me. Tell me, Sergeant, what will happen to these . . . dreadful photographs now?"

"As soon as I inform Scotland Yard that those pertaining to you personally are not connected with our inquiries, they will be burnt."

"Oh, I'm so glad, so relieved. But tell me, of the various men against whom this couple had evidence that could substantiate blackmail, they must have tried it on someone."

"No doubt they have," said the sergeant, rising to leave. "And no doubt various police officers, at the request of Scotland Yard, are interviewing the score or more of gentlemen who figure in those photographs. Doubtless these inquiries will elicit the names of all those who had already been approached for money by the time our investigation started."

"But how would you know who had, and who hadn't?" asked Mr. Nutkin. "After all, a man might have been approached, and have paid, but might be too frightened to let on, even to the police."

Sergeant Smiley nodded down at the insurance clerk. "Bank statements, sir. Most men in a small way only have the one or two bank accounts. To raise a large sum, a man would have to go to his bank, or sell something of value. There's always a trace left."

By now they had reached the front door.

"Well, I must say," said Mr. Nutkin, "I admire the

man who went to the police and exposed these scoundrels. I only hope that if they had approached me for money, as doubtless they would sooner or later, I would have had the courage to do the same. By the way, I won't have to give evidence, will I? I know it's all supposed to be anonymous, but people can find out, you know."

"You won't have to give evidence, Mr. Nutkin."

"Then I pity the poor man who exposed them, and who will have to," said Samuel Nutkin.

"Nobody on that list of compromised gentlemen will have to give evidence, sir."

"But I don't understand. You have exposed them both, with the evidence. Surely you will make an arrest. Your investigations . . ."

"Mr. Nutkin," said Sergeant Smiley, framed in the door, "we are not investigating blackmail either. We are investigating murder."

Samuel Nutkin's face was a picture. "Murder?" he squeaked. "You mean they have killed somebody as well?"

"Who?"

"The blackmailers."

"No, sir, they haven't killed anybody. Some joker has killed them. The question is: who? But that's the trouble with blackmailers. They may have blackmailed hundreds by now, and eventually one of their victims traced them to their hideout. All their business was probably by telephone from public booths. No records are kept except the incriminating evidence against the present victims. The problem is: Where to start?"

"Where indeed?" murmured Samuel Nutkin. "Were they . . . shot?"

"No, sir. Whoever did it simply delivered a parcel to their door. That's why whoever it was must have known their address. The parcel contained a cashbox with a key apparently taped to the lid. When the key was used the lid flicked open from the pressure of what the lab boys have established was a mousetrap spring, a brilliantly clever anti-handling device was activated and the bomb blew them both to bits."

Mr. Nutkin gazed at him as though he had descended from Mount Olympus. "Incredible," he breathed, "but where on earth would a respectable citizen get a bomb?"

Sergeant Smiley shook his head.

"Nowadays, sir, there's far too much of it about, what with the Irish and the Arabs and all them foreigners. And there's books about it. Not like in my day. Nowadays, given the right materials, almost any sixth-form chemistry student could make a bomb. Well, good night, Mr. Nutkin. I don't think I shall be troubling you again."

The following day in the City Mr. Nutkin dropped in at Gusset's the frame-makers and collected the photograph that had been in their hands for the past fortnight. He had arranged for them to keep it until he called, and to fit a new frame to replace the old. That evening it was back in its pride of place on the table beside the fire.

It was an old photograph depicting two young men in the uniform of the Royal Army Engineers bomb disposal unit. They were sitting astride the casing of a German "Big Fritz" five-ton bomb. In front of them on a blanket lay the scores of components that had once made up the six separate anti-handling devices fitted to the bomb. In the background was a village church. One of the young men was lean and lantern-jawed, with a major's crowns on his shoulders. The other was plump and round, with spectacles on the end of his nose. Beneath the photograph was the inscription: "To the Bomb Wizards, Major Mike

Halloran and Corporal Sam Nutkin, with grateful thanks
from the villagers of Steeple Norton, July 1943."

Mr. Nutkin gazed at it proudly. Then he snorted.
"Sixth-formers indeed."

Used in Evidence

❦

"You are not obliged to say anything, but anything you say will be taken down and may be used in evidence."

Part of the wording of the official caution used in the British and Irish police forces by the cautioning officer to the suspect.

The big police car slid to a halt by the kerb some fifty feet from where the cordon spanned the street to keep the bystanders back. The driver kept the engine running, the wipers flicking rhythmically across the screen to push away the insistent drizzle. From the rear seat Chief Superintendent William J. Hanley looked forward through the glass to the groups of watchers outside the cordon and the knots of irresolute officials beyond it.

"Stay here," he told the driver, and prepared to get out. The driver was pleased; the inside of the car was snug and warm and, he reasoned, this was no morning to be walking up and down a slum street in the drifting rain. He nodded and cut the engine.

The precinct police chief slammed the door after him, hunched himself deeper into his dark blue overcoat, and walked purposefully towards the gap in the crowd barrier where a damp police officer watched over those who en-

tered and left the cordoned area. Seeing Hanley he
brought up a salute, stepped aside and let him pass
through.

Big Bill Hanley had been twenty-seven years a policeman, starting by pounding the cobbled alleys of the Liber-
ties and rising through the ranks to his present status. He
had the build for it, over 6 feet and 1 inch of him and
built like a truck. Thirty years before, he was rated the
best lock forward that ever came out of Athlone County;
in his green Irish jersey he had been part of the best
rugby football team the country had ever produced, the
team that Karl Mullen led to victory three years running
in the Triple Crown and that wiped the floor with the English, the Welsh, the Scots and the French. That had not
done his promotion chances any harm either, when he
joined the force.

He liked the job; he got satisfaction from it, despite the
poor pay and the long hours. But every job has its tasks
that no one can enjoy, and this morning had brought one
of them. An eviction.

For two years, the Dublin city council had been steadily demolishing the rash of tiny, back-to-back, one room
up and one room down houses that formed the area
known as the Gloucester Diamond.

Why it had ever been called that was a mystery. It had
none of the wealth and privilege of the English royal
house of Gloucester, nor any of the expensive brilliance of
the diamond. Just an industrial slum lying behind the
dockland zone on the north shore of the Liffey. Now most
of it was flat, its dwellers rehoused in cubic council apartment blocks whose soul-numbing shapes could be seen
half a mile away through the drizzle.

But it lay in the heart of Bill Hanley's precinct, so this
morning's business was his responsibility, much as he
hated it.

The scene between the twin chains of crowd barriers that cordoned the centre section of what had once been Mayo Road was as bleak that morning as the November weather. One side of the street was just a field of rubble, where soon the earth-movers would be at work, gouging out fresh foundations for the new shopping complex. The other side was the center of attention. Up and down for hundreds of feet not a building stood. The whole area was flat as a pancake, the rain gleaming off the slick black tarmac of the new two-acre car park destined to house the vehicles of those who would one day work in the intended office blocks nearby. The entire two acres was fenced off by a 9-foot-high chain-link fence; that is to say, almost the whole two acres.

Right in the centre, facing onto Mayo Road, was one single remaining house, like an old broken stump of tooth in a nice smooth gum. Either side of it the houses had been torn down, and each side of the remaining home was propped up with thick timber beams. All the houses that had once backed onto the sole survivor had also gone and the tarmac tide lapped round the house on three sides like the sea round a lone sandcastle on the beach. It was this house and the frightened old man who sheltered within it that were to be the centre of the morning's action; the focus of entertainment for the expectant groups from the new apartment blocks, who had come to see the last of their former neighbours being evicted.

Bill Hanley walked forward to where, directly opposite the front gate of the lone house, stood the main group of officials. They were all staring at the hovel as if, now that the moment had finally come, they did not know how to go about it. There was not much to look at. Fronting the pavement was a low brick wall, separating pavement and what purported to be the front garden: no garden at all, just a few feet of tangled weeds. The front door stood to one side of the house, chipped and dented by the numerous stones that had been flung at it. Hanley knew that behind the door would be a yard-square lobby and straight ahead the narrow stairs that led up. To the right of the lobby would be the door to the single sitting room, whose broken, cardboard-stuffed windows flanked the door. Between the two was the passage running to the small, filthy kitchen and the door leading to the yard and the outside privy. The sitting room would have a tiny fireplace, for the chimney running up the side of the house still jutted to the weeping sky. Behind the house, Hanley had seen from the side view, was a back yard wide as the width of the house and 25 feet long. The yard was fringed by a 6-foot-high timber plank fence. Inside the yard, so Hanley had been told by those who had peered over the fence, the bare earth was slick with the droppings of the four speckled hens the old man kept in a hutch at the foot of the yard, up against the back fence. And that was it.

The city council had done its best for the old man. There had been offers of rehousing in a bright, clean, new council flat; even a small house of his own somewhere else. There had been social workers, and relief workers, and church workers round to see him. They had reasoned and cajoled; given him deadline after deadline. He had refused to move. The street had come down around him and behind him and in front of him. He would not go. The work had gone on; the car park had been levelled and paved and fenced on three sides of him. Still the old man would not shift.

The local press had had quite a field day with the "Hermit of Mayo Road." So had the local kids, who had pelted the house with rocks and mud balls, breaking most of the windows while the old man, to their intense delight, shouted obscenities at them through the shattered panes.

Finally, the city council had issued its eviction notice,

the magistrate had given permission for forcible removal of the occupant, and the might of the city had ranged itself before the front door on a wet November morning.

The chief housing officer greeted Hanley. "Unpleasant business," he said. "Always is. Hate these evictions."

"Aye," said Hanley, and scanned the group. There were the two bailiffs who would do the job, big, burly men looking embarrassed. Two more from the council, two of Hanley's own policemen, someone from Health and Welfare, a local doctor, an assortment of minor officialdom. Barney Kelleher, the veteran photographer from the local newspaper, was there with a beardless young cub reporter in tow. Hanley had good relations with the local press and a friendly if guarded relationship with its older servants. They both had jobs to do; no need to make a guerrilla war out of it. Barney winked; Hanley nodded back. The cub took this as a sign of intimacy.

"Will you be bringing him out by force?" he asked brightly.

Barney Kelleher shot him a look of venom. Hanley swivelled his grey eyes to the sprog and held the gaze until the young man wished he had not spoken.

"We will be as gentle as we can," he said gravely. The sprog scribbled furiously, more for something to do than because he could not remember such a short sentence.

The magistrate's order specified nine o'clock. It was two minutes past nine. Hanley nodded to the chief housing officer.

"Proceed," he said.

The council officer approached the door of the house and knocked loudly. There was no answer.

"Are you there, Mr. Larkin?" he called. No answer. The official looked back at Hanley. Hanley nodded. Clearing his throat, the official read out the eviction order in a voice loud enough to be heard inside the house.

There was no answer. He stepped back to the group in the road.

"Will we give him five minutes?" he asked.

"Very well," said Hanley. Behind the crush barrier a murmur started among the growing crowd of former dwellers in the Gloucester Diamond. Finally one at the back became bolder.

"Leave him alone," called the voice. "Poor old man."

Hanley strolled leisurely over to the barrier. Without haste he walked down the line of faces, staring into the eyes of each. Most looked away; all fell silent.

"Is it sympathy you'd be giving him?" asked Hanley softly. "Was it sympathy that broke all his windows last winter and himself freezing in there? Was it sympathy that had him pelted with stones and muck?" There was a long silence. "Hold your hour," said Hanley and walked back to the group by the front door. There was silence behind the barrier. Hanley nodded to the two bailiffs who were staring at him.

"On you go," he said.

Both men had crowbars. One walked round the side of the house, between the chain-link fence and the corner of the brickwork. With skilled ease, he pried loose three of the fence planks and entered the back yard. He walked to the back door and rapped at it with his bar. When his colleague at the front heard the sound, he rapped at the front. There was no reply to either. The man at the front inserted the tip of the crowbar between the door and side post and had it open in a trice. The door yielded 3 inches and stopped. There was furniture behind it. The bailiff shook his head sadly and, turning to the other edge of the door, whisked off both hinges. Then he picked up the door and laid it in the front garden. Piece by piece, he removed the pile of chairs and tables in the hallway until the space was clear. Finally he entered the lobby calling,

"Mr. Larkin?" From the back there was a splintering sound as his friend entered through the kitchen.

There was silence in the street while the men searched the ground floor. At the upper bedroom window a pale face appeared. The crowd spotted it.

"There he is," yelled three or four voices from the crowd, like hunt followers spotting the fox before the riders. Just trying to be helpful. One of the bailiffs popped his head round the front doorpost. Hanley nodded upwards towards the bedroom window; the two men clumped up the narrow stairs. The face disappeared. There was no scuffle. In a minute they were coming down, the leader cradling the frail old man in his arms. He emerged into the drizzle and stood undecided. The relief worker hurried forward with a dry blanket. The bailiff set the old man down on his feet and the blanket was wrapped round him. He looked underfed and slightly dazed, but most of all very frightened. Hanley made up his mind. He turned towards his car and beckoned the driver forward. The council could have him later for the old folks home, but first a damn good breakfast and a hot cup of tea was called for.

"Put him in the back," he told the bailiff. When the old man was settled in the warm rear seat of the car, Hanley climbed in beside him.

"Let's get out of here," said Hanley to his driver. "There's a transport café half a mile down here and second left. We'll go there."

As the car moved back through the barrier and past the staring crowd, Hanley gave a glance at his unusual guest. The old man was dressed in grubby slacks and a thin jacket over an unbuttoned shirt. Word had it he had not looked after himself properly for years, and his face was pinched and sallow. He stared silently at the back of the car seat in front of him, not returning Hanley's gaze.

"It had to come sooner or later," said Hanley gently. "You knew that all along."

Despite his size and the capacity, when he wished to use it, to cause hard villians from the dockland to wet their knickers when he faced them, Big Bill Hanley was a much kinder man than his meaty face and twice-broken nose would give reason to think. The old man turned slowly and stared at him, but he said nothing.

"Moving house, I mean," said Hanley. "They'll fix you up in a nice place, warm in winter, and decent food. You'll see."

The car drew up at the café. Hanley descended and turned to his driver.

"Bring him in," he said.

Inside the warm and steamy café Hanley nodded to a vacant corner table. The police driver escorted the old man to the corner and sat him down, back to the wall. The old man said nothing, neither of thanks nor protestation. Hanley glanced at the wall chart behind the counter. The café owner wiped his hands on a damp dishcloth and looked inquiringly.

"Double eggs, bacon, tomatoes, sausage and chips," said Hanley. "In the corner. The old fella. And start with a mug of tea." He placed two pound notes on the counter. "I'll be back for the change," he said.

The driver returned from the corner table to the counter.

"Stay there and keep an eye on him," said Hanley. "I'll be taking the car myself."

The driver thought it was his lucky day; first a warm car, now a warm café. Time for a cup of tea and a smoke.

"Will I sit with him, sir?" he asked. "He smells a bit."

"Keep an eye on him," repeated Hanley. He drove himself back to the demolition site in Mayo Road.

The team had been all ready and prepared and they were not wasting time. A line of contractor's men came in and out of the house, bearing the squalid goods and chattels of the former occupant, which they deposited in the road under the now streaming rain. The council housing officer had his umbrella up and watched. Inside the carpark compound two mechanical shovels on their rubber wheels were waiting to begin on the rear of the house, the back yard and small privy. Behind them waited a line of ten tipper trucks to carry away the rubble of the house. Mains water, electric current and gas had been cut off months ago, and the house was damp and filthy as a result. Sewage there had never been, hence the outside privy which had been served by a buried septic tank, soon to be filled in and concreted over for ever. The council housing officer approached Hanley when he got out of his car again. He gestured towards the open back of a council van.

"I've saved what we could of any sentimental value," he volunteered. "Old photos, coins, some medal ribbons, some clothes, a few personal documents in a cigar box, mostly mouldy. As for the furniture . . ." he indicated the pile of bric-a-brac in the rain, "it's alive; the medical officer has advised us to burn the lot. You wouldn't get tuppence for it."

"Aye," said Hanley. The official was right, but that was his problem. Still, he seemed to want moral support.

"Will he get compensation for this?" asked Hanley.

"Oh, yes," said the official eagerly, anxious to explain that his department was not a heartless beast. "For the house, which was his own title property, and a fair valuation for the furniture, fixtures, fittings and any personal effects lost, damaged or destroyed. And a displacement allowance to cover the inconvenience of moving . . .

though frankly he's cost the council a lot more than the total by refusing to quit for so long."

At this moment, one of the men came from round the side of the house carrying two chickens, head down, in each hand.

"What the hell do I do with these?" he asked no one in particular.

One of his colleagues told him. Barney Kelleher snapped off a photo. Good picture, that, he thought. The last friends of the Hermit of Mayo Road. Nice caption. One of the contractor's men said he too kept chickens and could put them in with his small flock. A cardboard carton was found, the damp birds popped inside and they went in the council van until they could go to the workman's home.

Within an hour, it was over. The small house was gutted. A burly foreman in gleaming yellow oilskins came over to the council official.

"Can we start?" he asked. "The boss wants the car park finished and fenced. If we can concrete by tonight, we can tar it over tomorrow first thing."

The official sighed. "Go ahead," he said. The foreman turned and waved toward a mobile crane from whose arm swung a half-ton iron ball. Gently the crane moved forward to the flank of the house, planted itself and rose with a soft hiss onto its hydraulic feet. The ball began to swing, gently at first, then in bigger arcs. The crowd watched fascinated. They had seen their own houses go down in just this way, but the sight never palled. Finally, the ball thumped into the side of the house, not far from the chimney, splintering a dozen bricks and sending two cracks racing down the wall. The crowd gave a long, low "Aaaaaah." There's nothing like a nice bit of demolition to cheer up a bored crowd. At the fourth crunch, two upper windows popped out from their frames and fell into the car park. A corner of the house detached itself from the rest, waltzed slowly in a half spiral and collapsed into the back yard. Moments later, the chimney stack, a solid column of brick, snapped at the mid-section and the upper portion crashed through the roof and down through the floor to ground level. The old house was coming apart. The crowd loved it. Chief Superintendent Hanley got back into his car and returned to the café.

It was even warmer and more humid than before. His driver sat at the bar counter before a steaming cup of tea. He stubbed out a cigarette as Hanley walked in and slithered from his bar stool. The old man seemed busy in the corner.

"Is he finished yet?" asked Hanley.

"He's taking a powerful long time, sir," said the driver. "And the buttered bread is going down like there was no tomorrow."

Hanley watched as the old man embalmed yet another morsel of greasy fried food in soft, white bread and began to chew.

"The bread'll be extra," said the café owner. "He's had three portions already."

Hanley glanced at his watch. It was past eleven. He sighed and hoisted himself on a stool.

"A mug of tea," he said. He had told the Health and Welfare official to join him in thirty minutes and take the old man into council care. Then he could get back to his office and on with some paperwork. He'd be glad to be shot of the whole business.

Barney Kelleher and his cub reporter came in.

"Buying him breakfast, are you?" asked Barney.

"I'll claim it back," said Hanley. Kelleher knew he wouldn't. "Get some pictures?"

Barney shrugged. "Not bad," he said. "Nice one of the chickens. And the chimney stack coming down. And himself being brought out in a blanket. End of an era. I remember the days when ten thousand people lived in the Diamond. And all of them at work. Poor paid, mind you, but working. It took fifty years to create a slum in those days. Now they can do it in five."

Hanley grunted. "That's progress," he said.

A second police car drew up at the door. One of the young officers who had been at Mayo Road jumped out, saw through the glass that his chief was with the press and halted, irresolute. The cub reporter did not notice. Barney Kelleher pretended not to. Hanley slid off his stool and went to the door. Outside in the rain the policeman told him, "You'd better come back, sir. They've . . . found something."

Hanley beckoned to his driver who came out to the pavement. "I'm going back," said Hanley. "Keep an eye on the old man." He glanced back into the café.

At the far back the old man had stopped eating. He held a fork in one hand, a piece of rolled bread containing half a sausage in the other, perfectly immobile, as he stared silently at the three uniforms on the pavement.

Back at the site, all work had stopped. The demolition men in their oilskins and hard hats stood grouped in a circle in the rubble of the building. The remaining policeman was with them. Hanley strode from his car, picking his way over the shattered piles of brick, to where the circle of men stared downwards. From behind, the remnants of the crowd murmured.

"It's the old man's treasure," whispered someone loudly from the crowd. There was a murmur of agreement. "He had a fortune buried there; that's why he'd never leave."

Hanley arrived at the centre of the group and looked at the area of attention. The short stump of the shattered chimney stack still stood, 5 feet high, surrounded by piles of debris. At the base of the stack, the old black fireplace could still be seen. To one side a couple of feet of outer house wall still stood. At its base, inside the house, was a collection of fallen bricks, from which protruded the shrunken and wizened, but still recognizable leg of a human being. A shred of what looked like a stocking still clung below the kneecap.

"Who found it?" asked Hanley.

The foreman stepped forward. "Tommy here was working on the chimney breast with a pick. He cleared some bricks to get a better swing. He saw it. He called me."

Hanley recognized a good witness when he saw one.

"Was it under the floorboards, then?" asked Hanley.

"No. This whole area was built on a marsh. The builders cemented in the floors."

"Where was it, then?"

The foreman leaned down and pointed to the stump of the fireplace. "From the inside of the sitting room the fireplace looked to be flush with the wall. In fact it wasn't. Originally it jutted out from the house wall. Someone ran up a quick brick wall between the chimney breast and the end of the room, forming a cavity twelve inches deep, right up to the room ceiling. And another on the other side of the fireplace to give symmetry. But the other one was empty. The body was in the cavity between the false wall and the house wall. Even the room was repapered to cover the work. See, the same paper on the front of the chimney breast as on the false wall."

Hanley followed his finger; shreds of the same damp-mottled wallpaper adhered to the front of the chimney breast above the mantelshelf and to the bricks surrounding and part covering the body. It was an old paper with a rosebud pattern on it. But on the inside of the original house wall beside the fireplace, a dingy and even older striped wallpaper could be discerned.

Hanley stood up. "Right," he said. "That's the end of your work for today. You might as well stand the men down and let them go. We'll be taking over from here." The hard hats began to move back off the pile of bricks. Hanley turned to his two policemen.

"Keep the crowd barriers up," he said. "The whole place sealed off. More men will be coming, and more barriers. I want this place unapproached from any of the four sides. I'll get more manpower up here and the forensic boys. Nothing touched until they say so, OK?"

The two men saluted. Hanley heaved himself back into his car and called precinct headquarters. He issued a stream of orders, then had himself patched through to the technical section of the Investigation Bureau, tucked away in a grim old Victorian barracks behind Heuston railway station. He was lucky. Detective Superintendent O'Keefe came on the line, and they had known each other many years. Hanley told him what had been found and what he needed.

"I'll get them up there," O'Keefe's voice crackled down the line. "Do you want the Murder Squad brought in?"

Hanley sniffed. "No thanks. I think we can handle this one at divisional level."

"Do you have a suspect then?" asked O'Keefe.

"Oh, yes, we have one of those all right," said Hanley.

He drove himself back to the café, passing Barney Kelleher who was trying unsuccessfully to get back through the crowd barrier. This time, the patrolman on duty was not being nearly so helpful.

At the café, Hanley found his driver still at the counter. At the rear sat the old man, meal finished, sipping a cup of tea. He stared at Hanley as the giant policeman came over to him.

"We've found her," said Hanley, leaning over the table

and speaking so softly that no one else in the room could hear him.

"We'd better be going, had we not, Mr. Larkin? Down to the station, now? We have to do a little talking, do we not?"

The old man stared back without a word. It occurred to Hanley that so far he had not opened his mouth. Something flickered in the old man's eyes. Fear? Relief? Probably fear. No wonder he had been afraid all these years.

He rose quietly and with Hanley's firm hand on his elbow went out to the police car. The driver followed and climbed behind the wheel. The rain had stopped and a chill wind blew toffee papers like autumn leaves down the street where no trees grew. The car drew away from the kerb. The old man sat hunched, staring ahead, silent.

"Back to the station," said Hanley.

There is no country in the world where a murder investigation is a matter of inspired guesses as television would have it. They are 90 per cent plodding routine, formalities to be gone through, procedures to be fulfilled. And administration, plenty of that.

Big Bill Hanley saw the old man settled into a cell at the back of the charge room; he made no protest, asked for no lawyer. Hanley had no intention of charging him—yet. He could hold him on suspicion for at least twenty-four hours and he wanted more facts first. Then he sat at his desk and started with the telephone.

"By the book, lad, by the book. We're not Sherlock Holmes," his old sergeant used to tell him, years before. Good advice. More cases have been lost in court by procedural screw-ups than have ever been won by intellectual brilliance.

Hanley formally informed the city coroner of the fact of a death, catching the senior civil servant just as he was leaving for his lunch. Then he told the city morgue in

Store Street, just behind the bus terminal, that there would be a complex post-mortem that afternoon. He traced the state pathologist, Professor Tim McCarthy, who listened calmly on a telephone in the hallway of the Kildare Club, sighed at the thought of missing the excellent breast of pheasant that was on the menu, and agreed to come at once.

There were canvas screens to be organized, and men detailed to collect picks and shovels and report to Mayo Road. He summoned the three detectives attached to his precinct from their lunch in the canteen to his office, and made do with two sandwiches and a pint of milk as he worked.

"I know you are busy," he told them. "We all are. That's why I want this one tied up fast. It shouldn't take too long."

He named his detective chief inspector to be scene-of-crime examiner and sent him to Mayo Road without delay. The two young sergeants got separate jobs. One was detailed to check into the house itself; the council official had said the old man owned it, freehold, but the rating office at the City Hall would have details of its past history and ownership. The register of deeds would clinch the final details.

The second detective sergeant got the legwork; trace every former occupant of Mayo Road, most of them now rehoused in the council apartment blocks. Find the neighbours, the gossips, the shopkeepers, the patrolmen who had had the beat including Mayo Road for the past fifteen years before its demolition, the local priest—anybody who had known Mayo Road and the old man for as many years back as possible. And that, said Hanley with emphasis, includes anyone who ever knew Mrs., that is, the late Mrs. Larkin.

He dispatched a uniformed sergeant with a van to repossess all the personal memorabilia from the destroyed house that he had seen in the council van that morning, and to bring the abandoned furniture, fleas and all, into the police station yard.

It was past two in the afternoon when he finally rose and stretched. He instructed that the old man be brought to the interview room, finished his milk and waited five minutes. When he walked into the interview room, the old man was seated at the table, hands clasped in front of him, staring at the wall. A policeman stood near the door.

"Any word from him?" murmured Hanley to the officer.

"No, sir. Not a thing."

Hanley nodded for him to go.

When they were alone, he sat at the table facing the old man. Herbert James Larkin, the council records showed.

"Well, now, Mr. Larkin," said Hanley softly. "Don't you think it would be a sensible thing to tell me about it?"

His experience told him there was no use trying to bully the old man. This was no street villain from the underworld. He'd had three wife-murderers in his time, and all of them mild, meek little fellows who had soon seemed relieved to get rid of the awful details to the big sympathetic man across the table. The old man slowly looked up at him, held his gaze for a few moments, and looked back at the table. Hanley took out a packet of cigarettes and flipped it open.

"Smoke?" he said. The old man didn't move. "Actually I don't use them myself either," said Hanley, but he left the pack invitingly open on the table, a box of matches beside it.

"Not a bad try," he conceded. "Holding on to the house like that, all those months. But the council had to win sooner or later. You knew that, didn't you? Must have been awful, knowing that they'd send the bailiffs for you sooner or later."

He waited for a comment, any hint of communication from the old man. There was none. No matter, he was patient as an ox when he wanted a man to talk. And they all talked sooner or later. It was the relief really. The unburdening. The Church knew all about the relief of confession.

"How many years, Mr. Larkin? How many years of anxiety, of waiting? How many months since the first bulldozers moved into the area, eh? Man, what you must have gone through."

The old man lifted his gaze and met Hanley's eyes, maybe searching for something, a fellow human being after years of self-imposed isolation; a little sympathy perhaps. Hanley felt he was nearly there. The old man's eyes swivelled away, over Hanley's shoulder to the rear wall.

"It's over, Mr. Larkin. All over. It's got to come out, sooner or later. We'll go back through the years, slowly, plodding away, and we'll piece it together. You know that. It was Mrs. Larkin, wasn't it? Why? Another man? Or just an argument? Maybe it was just an accident, eh? So you panicked, and then you were committed; to living like a hermit all your days."

The old man's lower lip moved. He ran his tongue along it.

I'm getting through, thought Hanley. Not long now.

"It must have been bad, these past years," he went on. "Sitting there all alone, no friends like before it happened, just you and the knowledge that she was still there, not far away, bricked away beside the fireplace."

Something flickered in the old man's eyes. Shock at the memory? Perhaps the shock treatment would work better. He blinked twice. I'm nearly there, thought Hanley, I'm nearly there. But when the old man's eyes moved back to meet his own, they were blank again. He said nothing.

Hanley kept it up for another hour, but the old man never uttered a word.

"Please yourself," said Hanley as he rose. "I'll be back, and we'll talk it over then."

When he arrived at Mayo Road, the scene was a hive of activity, the crowd bigger than before, but able to see far less. On all four sides, the ruin of the house was surrounded by canvas screens, whipped by the wind but enough to keep prying eyes from seeing the job going on within. Inside the hollow square that included a portion of the roadway, twenty hefty policemen in heavy boots and rummage gear were pulling the rubble to pieces by hand. Each brick and slate, each shattered timber from the stairs and banisters, each tile and ceiling joist, was carefully plucked out, examined for whatever it might show, which was nothing, and tossed out into the roadway, where the rubble mounted higher and higher. The contents of cupboards were examined, the cupboards themselves ripped out to see if there was anything behind them. All walls were tapped to see if they contained hollow cavities before they were pulled down brick by brick and thrown into the road.

Round the fireplace, two men worked with special care. The rubble on top of the corpse was lifted carefully away until only a thick film of dust covered the body. It was bent into an embryo posture, lying on its side, though in its cavity it had probably sat upright, facing sideways. Professor McCarthy, looking over what was left of the house wall, directed these two men at their work. When it was done to his satisfaction, he entered the cavity among the remaining bricks and with a soft brush, like a careful housewife, began to whisk away the creamy dust of the old mortar.

When he had cleared the major part of the dust, he examined the body more closely, tapped part of the exposed thigh and of the upper arm, and emerged from the cavity.

"It's a mummy," he told Hanley.

"A mummy?"

"Just so. With a brick or concrete floor, a sealed environment on all six sides, and the warmth of the fireplace two feet away, mummification has taken place. Dehydration, but with preservation. The organs may well be intact, but hard as wood. No use trying to cut tonight. I'll need the warm glycerine bath. It'll take time."

"How long?" asked Hanley.

"Twelve hours at least. Maybe more. I've known it take days." The professor glanced at his watch. "It's nearly four. I'll have it immersed by five. Tomorrow morning around nine, I'll look in at the morgue and see if I can start."

"Blast," said Hanley. "I wanted this one sewn up."

"An unfortunate choice of words," said McCarthy. "I'll do the best I can. Actually, I don't think the organs will tell us much. From what I can see there's a ligature round the neck."

"Strangulation, eh?"

"Maybe," said McCarthy. The undertaker who always got the city contracts had his van parked out beyond the screens. Under the state pathologist's supervision, two of his men lifted the rigid corpse, still on its side, onto a bier, covered it with a large blanket and transferred their cargo to the waiting hearse. Followed by the professor, they sped off to Store Street and the city morgue. Hanley walked over to the fingerprint man from the technical section.

"Anything here for you?" he asked.

The man shrugged. "It's all brick and rubble in there, sir. There's not a clean surface in the place."

"How about you?" Hanley asked the photographer from the same office.

"I'll need a bit more, sir. I'll wait until the boys have got it cleared down to the floor, then see if there's anything there. If not, I've got it for tonight."

The gang foreman from the contractor wandered over. He had been kept standing by at Hanley's suggestion, as a technical expert in case of hazard from falling rubble. He grinned.

"That's a lovely job you've done there," he said in his broad Dublin accent. "There'll not be much for my lads left to do."

Hanley gestured to the street where most of the house now lay in a single large mound of brick and timber debris.

"You can start shifting that if you like. We're finished with it," he said.

The foreman glanced at his watch in the gathering gloom. "There's an hour left," he said. "We'll get most of it shifted. Can we start on the rest of the house tomorrow? The boss wants to get that park finished and fenced."

"Check with me at nine tomorrow morning. I'll let you know," he said.

Before leaving he called over his detective chief inspector who had been organizing it all.

"There are portable lights coming," he said. "Have the lads bring it down to floor level and search the floor surface for any signs of interference since it was laid down."

The detective nodded. "So far it's just the one hiding place," he said. "But I'll keep looking till it's clean."

Back at the station, Hanley got the first chance to look at something that might tell him about the old man in the cells. On his desk was the pile of assorted odds and ends that the bailiffs had removed from the house that morning and put into the council van. He went through each document carefully, using a magnifying glass to read the old and faded lettering.

There was a birth certificate, giving the name of the old man, his place of birth as Dublin and his age. He had been born in 1911. There were some old letters, but from people who meant nothing to Hanley, mostly from long ago, and their contents had no seeming bearing on the case. But two things were of interest. One was a faded photograph, mottled and warped, in a cheap frame, but unglassed. It showed a soldier in what looked like British Army uniform, smiling uncertainly into the camera. Hanley recognized a much younger version of the old man in the cells. On his arm was a plump young woman with a posy of flowers; no wedding dress but a neutral-coloured two-piece suit with the high, square shoulders of the mid to late 1940s.

The other item was the cigar box. It contained more letters, also irrelevant to the case, three medal ribbons clipped to a bar with a pin behind it, and a British Army service pay book. Hanley reached for the telephone. It was twenty past five, but he might be lucky. He was. The military attaché at the British Embassy out at Sandyford was still at his desk. Hanley explained his problem. Major Dawkins said he would be glad to help if he could, unofficially, of course. Of course. Official requests have to go through channels. Officially all contact between the Irish police force and Britain goes through channels. Unofficially, contacts are much closer than either side would be prepared to concede to the idle inquirer. Major Dawkins agreed to stop by the police station on his way home, even though it meant quite a detour.

Darkness had long fallen when the first of the two young detectives doing the legwork reported back. He was the man who had been checking the register of deeds and the rating lists. Seated in front of Hanley's desk, he flicked open his notebook and recited.

The house at 38 Mayo Road had been bought, so the records of deeds showed, by Herbert James Larkin in 1954 from the estate of the previous owner, then deceased. He had paid £400 for the property, title freehold. No evidence of a mortgage, so he had had the money available. The rating list showed the house to have been owned since that date by the same Herbert James Larkin and occupied by Mr. Herbert James Larkin and Mrs. Violet Larkin. No record of the wife's decease or departure, but then the rating list would not show a change of occupancy, even in part, unless advised in writing by the continuing occupant, which had not happened. But a search of the death certificates over at the Custom House, going back to 1954, revealed no trace of the death of any Mrs. Violet Larkin, of that address or any other.

Department of Health and Welfare records showed that Larkin drew a state pension for the past two years, never applied for supplementary benefit, and prior to pensionable retirement was apparently a storekeeper and night watchman. One last thing, said the sergeant. His internal PAYE forms, starting in 1954, had shown a previous address in North London, England.

Hanley flicked the Army pay book across the desk.

"So he was in the British Army," said the sergeant.

"Nothing strange in that," said Hanley. "There were fifty thousand Irishmen in the British Armed Forces during the Second World War. Larkin was one of them, it seems."

"Perhaps the wife was English. He came back to Dublin in 1954 with her from North London."

"Likely she was," said Hanley, pushing over the wedding photo. "He married her in uniform."

The internal phone rang to inform him the military attaché from the British Embassy was at the front desk. Hanley nodded at his sergeant, who left. "Show him in, please," said Hanley.

Major Dawkins was Hanley's luckiest find of the day. He crossed his pinstripe-clad legs elegantly, aimed a glittering toe-cap at Hanley across the desk and listened quietly. Then he studied the wedding photograph intently for a while.

Finally he came round the desk and stood by Hanley's shoulder with the magnifying glass in one hand and his gold propelling pencil in the other. With the tip of the pencil, he tapped the cap badge above Larkin's face in the photograph.

"King's Dragoon Guards," he said with certainty.

"How do you know that?" asked Hanley.

Major Dawkins passed Hanley the magnifying glass.

"The double-headed eagle," he said. "Cap badge of the King's Dragoon Guards. Very distinctive. None like it."

"Anything else?" asked Hanley.

Dawkins pointed to the three medals on the chest of the newly-wed.

"The first one is the 1939-1945 Star," he said, "and the third one at the end is the Victory Medal. But the one in the middle is the Africa Star with what looks like the bar clasp of the Eighth Army across it. That makes sense. The King's Dragoon Guards fought against Rommel in North Africa. Armoured cars, actually."

Hanley brought out the three medal ribbons. Those in the photograph were the full ceremonial medals; those on the desk were the smaller version—the miniatures on a bar—for wearing with un-dress uniform.

"Ah, yes," said Major Dawkins, with a glance at them. "The same pattern, see. And the Eighth Army bar."

With the glass, Hanley could make out that the pattern

was the same. He passed Major Dawkins the service pay book. Dawkins' eyes lit up. He flicked through the pages.

"Volunteereed at Liverpool, October 1940," he said, "probably at Burton's."

"Burton's?" asked Hanley.

"Burton, the tailors. It was the recruiting centre at Liverpool during the war. A lot of the Irish volunteers arrived at Liverpool docks and were directed there by the recruiting sergeants. Demobilized January 1946. Honourable discharge. Odd."

"What?" asked Hanley.

"Volunteered in 1940. Fought in action with armoured cars in North Africa. Stayed until 1946. But he stayed a trooper. Never won a stripe on his arm. Never made corporal." He tapped the uniformed arm in the wedding photograph.

"Perhaps he was a bad soldier," suggested Hanley.

"Possibly."

"Can you get me some more details of his war record?" asked Hanley.

"First thing in the morning," said Dawkins. He noted most of the details in the pay book and left.

Hanley had a canteen supper and waited for his second detective sergeant to report back. The man arrived at well past 10:30, tired but triumphant.

"I spoke with fifteen of those who knew Larkin and his wife in Mayo Road," he said, "and three came up trumps. Mrs. Moran, the next-door neighbour. She'd been there for thirty years and remembers the Larkins moving in. The postman, now retired, who served Mayo Road up till last year, and Father Byrne, also retired, now living in a retired priests' home out at Inchicore. I've just got back from there, hence the delay."

Hanley sat back as the detective flicked back to the start of his notebook and began to report.

"Mrs. Moran recalled that in 1954 the widower who had lived there, at Number 38, died and shortly afterwards, a For Sale notice went up on the house. It was only there a fortnight, then it came down. A fortnight later, the Larkins moved in. Larkin was then about forty-five, his wife much younger. She was English, a Londoner, and told Mrs. Moran they had moved from London where her husband had been a store clerk. One summer, Mrs. Larkin disappeared; Mrs. Moran put the year at 1963."

"How is she so certain?" asked Hanley.

"That November Kennedy was killed," said the detective sergeant. "The news came from the lounge bar up the street where there was a television set. Within twenty minutes everyone in Mayo Road was on the pavement discussing it. Mrs. Moran was so excited she burst into Larkin's house next door to tell him. She didn't knock, just walked into the sitting room. Larkin was dozing in a chair. He jumped up in great alarm and couldn't wait to get her out of the house. Mrs. Larkin had left by then. But she was there in the spring and summer; she used to baby-sit for the Morans on a Saturday night; Mrs. Moran's second baby was born in January 1963. So it was the late summer of '63 that Mrs. Larkin disappeared."

"What was the reason given?" asked Hanley.

"Walked out on him," said the detective without hesitation. "No one doubted it. He worked hard, but never wanted to go out in the evening, not even Saturday, hence Mrs. Larkin's availability as a baby-sitter. There were rows about it. Something else; she was flighty, a bit of a flirt. When she packed her bags and left him, no one was surprised. Some of the women reckoned he deserved it for not treating her better. No one suspected anything.

"After that, Larkin kept himself even more to himself.

Hardly ever went out, ceased to care much for himself or the house. People offered to help out, as they do in small communities, but he rejected all offers. Eventually people left him alone. A couple of years later, he lost his job as a storeman and became a night watchman, leaving after dark and returning at sunrise. Kept the door double-locked at night because he was out, by day because he wanted to sleep. So he said. He also started keeping pets. First ferrets, in a shed in the back garden. But they escaped. Then pigeons, but they flew off or were shot elsewhere. Finally chickens, for the past ten years."

The parish priest confirmed much of Mrs. Moran's recollections. Mrs. Larkin had been English, but a Catholic and a churchgoer. She had confessed regularly. Then in August 1963 she had gone off, most people said with a man friend, and Father Byrne had known of no other reason. He would not break the confessional oath, but he would go so far as to say he did not doubt it. He had called at the house several times, but Larkin was not a churchgoer and refused all spiritual comfort. He had called his departed wife a tart.

"It all fits," mused Hanley. "She could well have been about to leave him when he found out and went at her a bit too hard. God knows, it's happened enough times."

The postman had little more to add. He was a local man and used the local bar. Mrs. Larkin had liked to have her noggin on a Saturday night, had even helped out as a barmaid one summer, but her husband soon put a stop to that. He recalled she was much younger than Larkin, bright and bubbly, not averse to a bit of flirting.

"Description?" asked Hanley.

"She was short, about five feet three inches. Rather plump, well-rounded anyway. Curling dark hair. Giggled a lot. Plenty of chest. Postman recalled when she pulled a pint of ale from those old-style beer pumps they used to have, it was worth watching. But Larkin went wild when he found out. Came in and pulled her home. She left him, or disappeared soon afterwards."

Hanley rose and stretched. It was nearly midnight. He clapped a hand on the young detective's shoulder.

"It's late. Get yourself home. Write it all up in the morning."

Hanley's last visitor of the night was his chief inspector, the scene-of-crime investigator.

"It's clean," he told Hanley. "The last brick removed, and not a sign of anything else that might be helpful."

"Then it's up to the poor woman's body to tell us the rest of what we want to know," said Hanley. "Or Larkin himself."

"Has he talked yet?" asked the chief inspector.

"Not yet," said Hanley, "but he will. They all talk in the end."

The chief inspector went home. Hanley called his wife and told her he would be spending the night at the station. Just after midnight he went down to the cells. The old man was awake, sitting on the edge of his bunk, staring at the opposite wall. Hanley jerked his head at the police officer with him and they all trooped up to the interview room. The policeman sat in a corner with his notebook at the ready. Hanley faced the old man and read him the caution:

"Herbert James Larkin, you are not obliged to say anything. But anything you say will be taken down and may be used in evidence."

Then he sat down opposite the old man.

"Fifteen years, Mr. Larkin. That's a long time to live with a thing like that. August of 1963, wasn't it? The neighbours remember it; the priest remembers it; even the postman remembers it. Now, why don't you tell me about it?"

The old man raised his eyes, held Hanley's gaze for a few seconds, then lowered his eyes to the table. He said nothing. Hanley kept it up almost until dawn. Larkin seemed not to tire, although the policeman in the corner yawned repeatedly. Larkin had been a night watchman for years, Hanley recalled. Probably more awake at night now than during the day.

There was a grey light filtering through the frosted-glass window of the interview room when he rose finally.

"Have it your own way," he said. "You may not talk, but your Violet will. Strange that, eh? Talking back from the grave behind the wall, fifteen years later. But she'll talk to the state pathologist, in a few hours now. She'll talk. She'll tell him in his laboratory what happened to her, when it happened, maybe even why it happened. Then we'll come here again, and I'll charge you."

Slow to anger though he was, he was becoming irritated by the silence of the old man. It was not that he said little; he said absolutely nothing. Just stared back at Hanley with that strange look in his eyes. What was that look, Hanley asked himself. Trepidation? Fear of him, Hanley? Remorse? Mockery? No, not mockery. The man's number was up.

Finally he rose, rubbed a large hand round the stubble on his chin and went back to his office. Larkin went back to the cell.

Hanley snatched three hours' sleep in his chair, head tilted back, feet out, snoring loudly. At eight he rose, went to the rest room and washed and shaved. Two startled young police cadets surprised him there at half past eight as they came on duty and went about their business like two dormice in carpet slippers. At nine he was breakfasted and working his way through a mountain of accumulated paperwork. At 9:30 the contractor's foreman at the Mayo Road job came on the line. Hanley considered his request.

"All right," he said at last, "you can fence it in and concrete over."

Twenty minutes later, Professor McCarthy was on the line.

"I've got the limbs straightened out," he said cheerfully. "And the skin is soft enough to take the scalpel. We're draining and drying it off now. I'll begin in an hour."

"When can you give me a report?" asked Hanley.

"Depends what you mean," came the voice down the line. "The official report will take two to three days. Unofficially, I should have something just after lunch. Cause of death at least. We've confirmed the ligature round the neck. It was a stocking, as I suspected yesterday."

The pathologist agreed to come the mile from the Store Street morgue to Hanley's office by 2:30.

The morning was uninterrupted, save by Major Dawkins, who phoned at midday.

"Bit of luck," he said. "Found an old friend of mine in the records office at the War House. He gave me priority."

"Thank you, Major," said Hanley. "I'm taking notes; go ahead."

"There's not too much, but it confirms what we thought yesterday."

What you thought yesterday, Hanley said to himself. This laborious English courtesy.

"Trooper Herbert James Larkin arrived on the Dublin ferry at Liverpool, October 1940 and volunteered for the Army. Basic training at Catterick Camp, Yorkshire. Transferred to the King's Dragoon Guards. Sent by troopship to join the regiment in Egypt in March 1941. Then we come to the reason he never made corporal."

"Which was?"

"He was captured. Taken prisoner by the Germans in Rommel's autumn offensive of that year. Spent the rest of the war as a farm worker at a POW camp in Silesia, eastern end of the Third Reich. Liberated by the Russians, October 1944. Repatriated April 1945, just in time for the end of the war in Europe in May."

"Anything about his marriage?" asked Hanley.

"Certainly," said Major Dawkins. "He was married while a serving soldier, so the Army has that on file, too. Married at St. Mary Saviour's Catholic Church, Edmonton, North London, 14th of November 1945. Bride, Violet Mary Smith, hotel chambermaid. She was seventeen at the time. As you know, he got an honourable discharge in January 1946 and stayed on in Edmonton working as a storekeeper until 1954. That's when the Army has its last address for him."

Hanley thanked Dawkins profusely and hung up. Larkin was thirty-four, turning thirty-five, when he married a young girl of seventeen. She would have been a lively twenty-six when they came to live in Mayo Road, and he a perhaps not so lively forty-three. By the time she died in August 1963, she would have been a still-attractive and possibly sexy thirty-five, while he would have been a perhaps very uninteresting and uninterested fifty-two. Yes, that might have caused problems. He waited with impatience for the visit of Professor McCarthy.

The state pathologist was as good as his word and was seated in the chair facing Hanley by 2:30. He took out his pipe and began leisurely to fill it.

"Can't smoke in the lab," he apologized. "Anyway, the smoke covers the formaldehyde. You should appreciate it."

He puffed contentedly.

"Got what you wanted," said Professor McCarthy eas-

ily. "Murder beyond a doubt. Manual strangulation with
the use of a stocking, causing asphyxiation; coupled with
shock. The hyoid bone here"—pointing to the area between chin and Adam's apple—"was fractured in three
places. Prior to death, a blow to the head was adminis-
tered, causing scalp laceration, but not death. Probably
enough to stun the victim and permit the strangulation to
take place."

Hanley leaned back. "Marvellous," he said. "Anything
on year of death?"

"Ah," said the professor, reaching for his attaché case.
"I have a little present for you." He reached into the
case and produced a polythene bag containing what appeared to be a 6-inch by 4-inch fragment of yellowed and
faded newspaper.

"The scalp wound must have bled a bit. To prevent a
mess on the carpet, our murderer must have wrapped the
area of the scalp wound in newspaper. While he built his
oubliette behind the false wall, no doubt. By good fortune
it's recognizable as a piece of a daily newspaper, with the
date still discernible on it."

Hanley took the polythene bag and through the
transparent material, with the aid of his reading spotlight
and magnifying glass, studied the newsprint fragment.
Then he sat up sharply.

"Of course, this was an old piece of newspaper," he
said.

"Of course it's old," said McCarthy.

"It was an old piece, a back number, when it was used
to wrap the wound in the head," insisted Hanley.

McCarthy shrugged.

"You could be right," he agreed. "With this kind of
mummy, one can't be accurate as to the exact year of
death. But reasonably so."

Hanley relaxed.

"That's what I meant," he said with relief. "Larkin must have grabbed the newspaper lining a drawer, or a cupboard, that had been there for years untouched. That's why the date on the paper goes back to March 13th, 1943."

"So does the corpse," said McCarthy. "I put the death at between 1941 and 1945. Probably within a few weeks of the date of that piece of newspaper."

Hanley glared at him, long and hard. "Mrs. Violet Mary Larkin died during August 1963," he said.

McCarthy stared at him and held the stare while he re-lit his pipe. "I think," he said gently, "we're talking at cross-purposes."

"I'm talking about the body in the morgue," said Hanley.

"So am I," said McCarthy.

"Larkin and his wife arrived from London in 1954," said Hanley slowly. "They bought Number 38, Mayo Road, following the death of the previous owner/occupant. Mrs. Larkin was announced as having run away and left her husband in August 1963. Yesterday, we found her body bricked up behind a false wall while the house was being demolished."

"You didn't tell me how long the Larkins had been at that house," McCarthy pointed out reasonably. "You asked me to do a pathological examination of a virtually mummified body. Which I have done."

"But it was mummified," insisted Hanley. "Surely in those conditions there could be a wide range in the possible year of death?"

"Not twenty years," said McCarthy equably. "There is no way that body was alive after 1945. The tests on the internal organs are beyond much doubt. The stockings can be analysed, of course. And the newsprint. But as you say, both could have been twenty years old at the time of use. But the hair, the nails, the organs—they couldn't."

Hanley felt as though he was living, while awake, his only nightmare. He was bulldozing his way towards the goal line, using his strength to cut a path through the English defenders during that last Triple Crown final match in 1951. He was almost there, and the ball began slipping from his hands. Try as he might, he could not hold on to it . . .

He recovered himself.

"Age apart, what else?" he asked. "The woman was short, about five feet three inches?"

McCarthy shook his head. "Sorry, bones don't alter in length, even after thirty-five years behind a brick wall. She was five feet ten to eleven inches tall, bony and angular."

"Black hair, curly?" asked Hanley.

"Dead straight and ginger in colour. It's still attached to the head."

"She was about thirty-five at the age of death?"

"No," said McCarthy, "she was well over fifty and she had had children, two I'd say, and there had been remedial surgery done, following the second."

"Do you mean to say," asked Hanley, "that from 1954, they—until Violet Larkin walked out, and Larkin alone for the past fifteen years—have been sitting in their living room six feet from a walled-up corpse?"

"Must have done," said McCarthy. "A body in a state of mummification, which itself would occur within a short time in such a warm environment, would emit no odour. By 1954, assuming she was killed, as I think, in 1943, the body would long since have achieved exactly the same state as that in which we found her yesterday. Incidentally, where was your man Larkin in 1943?"

"In a prisoner-of-war camp in Silesia," said Hanley.

"Then," said the professor, rising, "he did not kill that woman and brick her up beside the fireplace. So who did?"

Hanley picked up the internal phone and called the detectives' room. The young sergeant came on the line.

"Who," asked Hanley with deliberation, "was the man who owned and occupied the house in Mayo Road prior to 1954 and died in that year?"

"I don't know, sir," said the young man.

"How long had he been in it?"

"I didn't take notes about that, sir. But I recall the previous occupant had been there for thirty years. He was a widower."

"He certainly was," growled Hanley. "What was his name?"

There was a pause. "I never thought to ask, sir."

The old man was released two hours later, through the back door in case anyone from the press was hanging around the front lobby. This time, there was no police car, no escort. He had the address of a council hostel in his pocket. Without saying a word, he shuffled down the pavement and into the mean streets of the Diamond.

At Mayo Road, the missing section of chain-link fence where the house had once been was in place, closing off the entire car park. Within the area, on the spot where the house and garden had stood, was a sheet of level concrete in the last stages of drying. In the gathering dusk, the foreman was stomping over the concrete with two of his workers.

Every now and then he hacked at the surface with the steel-capped heel of one of his boots.

"Sure it's dry enough," he said. "The boss wants it finished and tarmacked over by tonight."

On the other side of the road, in the rubble field, a bonfire burned up the last of a pile of banisters, stairs, roof joists, ceiling beams, cupboards, window frames and doors, the remnants of the plank fence, the old privy and the chicken house. Even by its light, none of the workers noticed the old figure that stared at them through the chain-link wire.

The foreman finished prowling over the rectangle of new concrete and came to the far end of the plot, up against where the old back fence had been. He looked down at his feet.

"What's this?" he asked. "This isn't new. This is old."

The area he was pointing at was a slab of concrete about 6 feet by 2.

"It was the floor of the old chicken house," said the worker who had spread the ready-mix concrete that morning by hand.

"Did you not put a fresh layer over it?" asked the foreman.

"I did not. It would have raised the level too high at that spot. There'd have been a fierce hump in the tarmac if I had."

"If there's any subsidence here, the boss'll have us do it again, and pay for it," said the foreman darkly. He went a few feet away and came back with a heavy pointed steel bar. Raising it high above his head, he brought it down, point first, on the old concrete slab. The bar bounced back. The foreman grunted.

"All right, it's solid enough," he conceded. Turning towards the waiting bulldozer, he beckoned. "Fill it in, Michael."

The bulldozer blade came down right behind the pile of steaming fresh tarmac and began to push the hot mountain, crumbling like soft, damp sugar, towards the rectangle of concrete. Within minutes, the area had turned from gray to black, the tar raked flat and even, before the mechanical roller, waiting behind the spreaders, finished the job. As the last light faded from the sky, the man left for home and the car park was at last complete.

Beyond the wire, the old man turned and shuffled away. He said nothing, nothing at all. But for the first time, he smiled, a long, happy smile of pure relief.

Privilege

~

The telephone rang just after half past eight, and as it was a Sunday morning Bill Chadwick was still in bed. He tried to ignore it, but it just went on ringing. After ten rings he hauled himself out of bed and down the stairs to the hall.

"Yes?"

"Hello, Bill? Henry."

It was Henry Carpenter from down the road, a man whom he knew socially, but not well.

"Morning, Henry," said Chadwick. "Don't you have a lie-in on a Sunday morning?"

"Er, no," said the voice. "I go for a jog in the park, actually."

Chadwick grunted. He would, he thought. Eager beaver type. He yawned.

"What can I do for you at this hour on a winter's day?" he asked. Down the line, Carpenter seemed diffident.

"Have you started into the morning papers yet?" asked Carpenter. Chadwick glanced towards the hall mat where his usual two lay unopened.

"Nope," he said. "Why?"

"Do you take the *Sunday Courier*?" asked Carpenter.

"Nope," said Chadwick. There was a long pause.

187

"I think you should have a look at it today," said Carpenter. "There's something about you in it."

"Oh," said Chadwick, with rising interest. "What's it say?"

Carpenter was even more diffident. His embarrassment was evident in the tone of voice. Clearly he had thought Chadwick would have seen the article and would be able to discuss it with him.

"Well, you'd better look at it for yourself, old boy," said Carpenter, and put the phone down. Chadwick stared at the buzzing telephone and replaced it. Like all people who hear they have been mentioned in a newspaper article they have not yet seen, he was curious.

He returned to the bedroom with the *Express* and *Telegraph*, handed them to his wife and began to pull trousers and a polo-necked sweater over his pyjamas.

"Where are you going?" his wife asked.

"Just going down the road to get another paper," he told her. "Henry Carpenter says there's something in it about me."

"Oh, fame at last," said his wife. "I'll get the breakfast."

The corner newspaper shop had two copies left of the *Sunday Courier*, a heavy, multi-supplemented newspaper written, in Chadwick's view, by the pretentious for the pretentious. It was cold on the street so he refrained from delving into the numerous sections and supplements there and then, preferring to restrain his curiosity a few minutes more and look at them in the comfort of his own home. By the time he returned his wife had the orange juice and coffee on the kitchen table.

He realized as he started into the paper that Carpenter had not given him a page number, so he began with the general news section. By his second cup of coffee he had finished that, thrown down the arts-and-culture section and similarly discarded the sports section. That left the colour magazine and the business review. Being a self-employed businessman in a small way on the outskirts of London, he tried the business review.

On the third page, a name caught his eye; not his own, but that of a company which had recently collapsed and with which he had had a brief and, as it turned out, costly association. The article was in a column that prided itself on its investigative intent.

As he read the piece, he put his coffee down and his mouth fell open.

"He can't say this sort of thing about me," he whispered. "It's just not true."

"What's the matter, dear?" asked his wife. She was evidently concerned at the stricken expression on her husband's face. Without a word he passed her the paper, folded so she could not miss the article. She read it carefully, emitting a single short gasp when she reached the middle of it.

"That's terrible," she said when she had finished. "This man's implying that you were in some way a part of a fraud."

Bill Chadwick had risen and was pacing the kitchen.

"He's not implying it," he said, his anger taking over from his shock, "he's bloody well saying it. The conclusion is inescapable. Damn it, I was a victim of those people, not a knowing partner. I sold their products in good faith. Their collapse cost me as much as anyone else."

"Could this do you harm, darling?" asked his wife, her face creased with worry.

"Harm? It could bloody ruin me. And it's just not true. I've never even met the man who wrote this. What's his name?"

"Gaylord Brent," said his wife, reading the by-line from the article.

"But I've never even met him. He never bothered to contact me to check. He just can't say those things about me."

He used the same expression when closeted with his solicitor on Monday afternoon. The lawyer had expressed the inevitable distaste for what he had read and listened with sympathy to Chadwick's explanation of what had really happened in the matter of his association with the now-liquidated merchandising company.

"On the basis of what you say there seems no doubt that a prima facie libel of you has been uttered in this article," he said.

"Then they'll damn well have to retract it and apologize," said Chadwick hotly.

"In principle, yes," said the lawyer. "I think as a first step it would be advisable for me to write to the editor on your behalf, explaining that it is our view you have been libelled by the editor's employee and seeking redress in the form of a retraction and an apology, in a suitably prominent position, of course."

This was what was eventually done. For two weeks there was no reply from the editor of the *Sunday Courier*. For two weeks Chadwick had to endure the stares of his small staff and avoid other business associates where he could. Two contracts he had hoped to obtain slid away from him.

The letter from the *Sunday Courier* eventually came to the solicitor. It was signed by a secretary on behalf of the editor and its tone was politely dismissive.

The editor, so it said, had considered the solicitor's letter on behalf of Mr. Chadwick carefully, and was prepared to *consider* publication of a letter from Mr.

Chadwick in the correspondence column, subject of course to the editor's overriding right to edit the letter.

"In other words, cut it to ribbons," said Chadwick as he sat facing his solicitor again. "It's a brush-off, isn't it?"

The solicitor thought this over. He decided to be frank. He had known his client for a number of years.

"Yes," he said, "it is. I have only had dealings with a national newspaper once before on this kind of matter, but that sort of letter is a pretty standard response. They hate to publish a retraction, let alone an apology."

"So what can I do?" asked Chadwick.

The lawyer made a move. "There is the Press Council, of course," he said. "You could complain to them."

"What would they do?"

"Not much. They tend to entertain allegations against newspapers only where it can be shown that distress was caused unnecessarily due to carelessness by the paper in its publication or by blatant inaccuracy on the part of the paper's reporter. They also tend to avoid claims of a clear libel, leaving that to the courts. In any case, they can only issue a rebuke, nothing more."

"The Council cannot insist on a retraction and an apology?"

"No."

"What does that leave?"

The solicitor sighed. "I'm afraid that only leaves litigation. A suit in the High Court for libel, claiming damages. Of course, if a writ were actually issued, the paper might decide it did not wish to proceed, and publish the apology you ask for."

"It might?"

"It might. But it might not."

"But surely they'd have to. It's an open-and-shut case."

"Let me be very frank with you," said the solicitor. "In libel there is no such thing as an open-and-shut case. For one thing, there is in effect no law of libel. Or rather, it comes under common law, a great mass of legal precedents established over centuries. These precedents may be open to differing interpretations, and your case, or any case, will be different from its predecessors in some slight shade or detail.

"Secondly, one is arguing about a state of awareness on your part, a state of mind, of what was in a man's mind at a given time, the existence of knowledge and therefore of intent, as against ignorance and thence of innocence of intent. Do you follow me?"

"Yes, I think so," said Chadwick. "But surely, I don't have to prove my innocence?"

"In effect, yes," said the solicitor. "You see, you would be the plaintiff; the paper, the editor and Mr. Gaylord Brent, the defendants. You would have to prove that you were innocent of any awareness of the unreliability of the now-liquidated company when you were associated with them; only then would it be shown you had been libelled by the suggestion that you were implicated."

"Are you advising me not to sue?" asked Chadwick. "Are you seriously suggesting I should accept being treated to a bunch of lies from a man who never bothered to check his facts before publishing; that I should even accept ruin in my business, and not complain?"

"Mr. Chadwick, let me be frank with you. It is sometimes suggested of us lawyers that we encourage our clients to sue right, left and centre, because such action obviously enables us to earn large fees. Actually, the reverse is usually the case. It is usually the litigant's friends, wife, colleagues and so forth who urge him to go ahead and sue. They, of course, do not have to bear the costs. For the outsider a good court case is all bread and circuses. We in the legal profession are only too well aware of the costs of litigation."

Chadwick thought over the question of the cost of justice, something he had seldom considered before.

"How high could they run?" he asked quietly.

"They could ruin you," said the solicitor.

"I thought in this country all men had equal recourse to the law," said Chadwick.

"In theory, yes. In practice it is often quite different," said the lawyer. "Are you a rich man, Mr. Chadwick?"

"No. I run a small business. In these days that means I have to run on a knife edge of liquidity. I have worked hard all my life, and I get by. I own my own house, my own car, my clothes. A self-employed person's pension scheme, a life-assurance policy, a few thousand of savings. I'm just an ordinary man, obscure."

"That's my point," said the solicitor. "Nowadays only the rich can sue the rich, and never more so than in the field of libel, where a man may win his case but have to pay his own costs. After a long case, not to mention an appeal, these may be ten times the awarded damages.

"Big newspapers, like big publishing houses and others, all carry heavy insurance policies for libel damages awarded against them. They can employ the blue-chip lawyers of the West End, the costliest of Queen's Counsel. So, when faced with—if you will excuse me—a little man, they tend to face him down. With a little dexterity a case can be delayed from coming to court for up to five years, during which the legal costs to both sides mount and mount. The preparation of the case alone can cost thousands and thousands. If it gets to court, the costs rocket as the barristers take a fee and a daily 'refresher.' Then the barrister will have a junior tagging along as well."

"How high could the costs go?" asked Chadwick.

"For a lengthy case, with years of preparation, even excluding a possible appeal, several tens of thousands of pounds," said the lawyer. "Even that's not the end of it."

"What else should I know?" asked Chadwick.

"If you won, got damages and costs awarded against the defendants, that is, the newspaper, you would get the damages clear. But if the judge made no order as to costs, which they only tend to do in the worst of cases, you would have to carry your own costs. If you lost, the judge could even award the defendants' costs against you, in addition to your own. Even if you won, the newspaper could take the case to appeal. For that you could double the costs involved. Even if you won the appeal, without an order as to costs, you would be ruined.

"Then there is the mud-slinging. After two years people have long forgotten the original article in the paper anyway. The court case repeats it all again, with a mass of further material and allegations. Although you would be suing, the paper's counsel would have the task of destroying your reputation as an honest businessman, in the interests of his clients. Sling enough mud, and some will stick. There have been men, too numerous to mention, who have won their cases and emerged with very smeared reputations. In court all allegations can be printed publicly and do not have to be substantiated."

"What about legal aid," asked Chadwick. Like most people he had heard of it, but never investigated it.

"Probably not what you think," said the solicitor. "To get it you have to show you have no assets. That doesn't apply to you. Before you would be eligible, your house, car and savings would have to go."

"So it looks like ruin either way," said Chadwick.

"I'm sorry, truly sorry. I could encourage you to begin a lengthy and costly lawsuit, but I honestly feel the best favour I can do for you is to point out the hazards and pitfalls as they really are. There are many people who hotly entered into litigation and lived to regret it bitterly.

Some never even recovered from the years of strain and the financial worry of it all."

Chadwick rose. "You have been very honest and I thank you," he said.

From his office desk later that day he rang the *Sunday Courier* and asked to speak to the editor. A secretary came on the line. In answer to her query he gave his name.

"What is it you want to speak to Mr. Buxton about?" she asked.

"I would like an appointment to see him personally," said Chadwick.

There was a pause on the line and he heard an internal telephone being used. She came back on the line.

"In what connection did you wish to see Mr. Buxton?" she asked.

Chadwick explained briefly that he wanted to see the editor to explain his side of the suggestion that had been made about him in Gaylord Brent's article of two weeks earlier.

"I'm afraid Mr. Buxton is not able to see people in his office," said the secretary. "Perhaps if you'd be kind enough to write a letter, it will be given consideration."

She put the phone down. The following morning Chadwick took the underground into Central London and presented himself at the front desk of Courier House.

In front of a large uniformed commissionaire he filled out a form, stating his name, address, the person he wished to see and the nature of his business. It was taken away and he sat and waited.

After half an hour the lift doors opened to emit an elegant and slim young man shrouded in an aura of aftershave. He raised an eyebrow at the commissionaire, who nodded towards Bill Chadwick. The young man came over. Chadwick rose.

"I'm Adrian St. Clair," said the young man, pronouncing it Sinclair, "Mr. Buxton's personal assistant. Can I help you?"

Chadwick explained about the article under the by-line of Gaylord Brent and said that he wished to explain to Mr. Buxton personally that what had been said about him was not only untrue but threatened him with ruin in his business. St. Clair was regretful but unimpressed.

"Yes, of course, one sees your concern, Mr. Chadwick. But I'm afraid a personal interview with Mr. Buxton is simply not possible. A very busy man, don't you see. I . . . ah . . . understand a solicitor representing you has already communicated with the editor."

"A letter was written," said Chadwick. "The reply was from a secretary. It said a letter to the correspondence column *might* be considered. Now I am asking for him at least to hear my side of it."

St. Clair smiled briefly. "I have already explained that that is impossible," he said. "The letter on behalf of the editor is as far as we are prepared to go."

"Could I see Mr. Gaylord Brent himself, then?" asked Chadwick.

"I don't think that would be very helpful," said St. Clair. "Of course, if you or your solicitor wished to write again, I am sure the letter would be considered by our legal branch in the usual way. Other than that, I'm afraid I cannot help you."

The commissionaire showed Chadwick out through the swing doors.

He had a sandwich lunch in a coffee bar just off Fleet Street and spent the time it took to eat it lost in thought. In the early afternoon he was seated in one of those reference libraries to be found in Central London which specialize in contemporary archives and newspaper cuttings. His perusal of the file of recent libel cases showed him his solicitor had not been exaggerating.

One case appalled him. A middle-aged man had been badly libelled in a book by a fashionable author. He had sued and won, being awarded £30,000 damages and costs against the publisher. But the publisher had appealed, and the Appeal Court had quashed the damages, making each party pay their own costs. Facing utter financial ruin after four years of litigation, the plaintiff had taken the case to the Lords. Their Lordships had reversed the Appeal Court decision, re-awarding him his damages, but making no order as to costs. He had won his £30,000 damages, but after five years had a legal bill of £45,000. The publishers, with a similar legal bill, had lost £75,000, but were insured for the great bulk of that sum. The plaintiff had won, but was ruined for life. Photographs showed him in the first year of litigation as a sprightly man of sixty. Five years later he was a broken wreck, made haggard by the endless strain and the mounting debts. He had died bankrupt, his reputation restored.

Bill Chadwick determined no such thing was going to happen to him, and took himself to the Westminster Public Library. There he retired to the reading room with a copy of Halsbury's *Laws of England*.

As his solicitor had said, there was no statute law on libel in the same way there was a Road Traffic Act, but there was the Law of Libel Amendment Act of 1888, which gave the generally accepted definition of a libel or defamation as:

A defamatory statement is a statement which tends to lower a person in the estimation of right-thinking members of society generally, or cause him to be shunned or avoided, or to expose him to hatred, contempt or ridicule, or to convey an imputation on him disparaging or injurious to him in his office, profession, calling, trade or business.

Well, that last part applies to me at least, thought
Chadwick.

Something his solicitor had said in his homily about the
courts nagged at his mind. "In court all allegations can be
printed publicly and do not have to be substantiated."
Surely not?

But the lawyer was right. The same Act of 1888 made
that clear. Anything said during the sitting of the court
can be reported and published without reporter or editor,
printer or publisher fearing a suit of libel, provided only
that the report be "fair, contemporaneous and accurate."

That, thought Chadwick, must be to protect the judges,
magistrates, witnesses, police officers, counsel and even
the defendant from fearing to state what they believe to
be true, regardless of the outcome of the case.

This exemption from any reaction by any person, however insulted, slandered, defamed or libelled, providing
only that the allegation was made in the body of the court
during the sitting of the court, and the exemption for anyone accurately reporting, printing and publishing what
was said, was called "absolute privilege."

On the underground back to the outer suburbs, the
germ of an idea began to grow in Bill Chadwick's mind.

Gaylord Brent, when Chadwick finally traced him after
four days of searching, lived in a trendy little street in
Hampstead, and it was there that Chadwick presented
himself the following Sunday morning. He estimated that
no Sunday-paper journalist would be at work on a Sunday, and took pot luck on the Brent family not being away
in the country for the weekend. He mounted the steps and
rang the bell.

After two minutes the door was answered by a
pleasant-looking woman in her mid-thirties.

"Is Mr. Brent in?" asked Chadwick, and added without
pause, "It's about his article in the *Courier*."

It was no lie, but enough to persuade Mrs. Brent that the caller was from the office in Fleet Street. She smiled, turned, called "Gaylord" down the hallway and turned back to Chadwick.

"He'll be here in a minute," she said, and withdrew towards the sounds of small children somewhere in the house, leaving the door open. Chadwick waited.

A minute later Gaylord Brent himself appeared at the door in pastel linen slacks and pink shirt, an elegant man in his mid-forties.

"Yes?" he inquired.

"Mr. Gaylord Brent?" asked Chadwick.

"Yes."

Chadwick opened the cutting he carried in his hand and held it out.

"It's about this article you wrote in the *Sunday Courier*."

Gaylord Brent studied the cutting for several seconds without touching it. His expression was of perplexity touched with petulance.

"This is about four weeks old," he said. "What about it?"

"I'm sorry to disturb you on a Sunday morning," said Chadwick, "but it's a risk it seems we must all take. You see, in this article you libelled me, and did so rather badly. It has hurt me considerably in my business and social life."

The perplexity remained on Brent's face, but shifted to give way to an increased level of irritation.

"Who on earth *are* you?" he demanded.

"Oh, my apologies. The name is William Chadwick."

Enlightenment came at last to Gaylord Brent on hearing the name, and the irritation took over completely.

"Now look here," he said, "you can't just come round

to my house to complain. There are proper channels. You'll have to ask your lawyer to write . . ."

"I did," said Chadwick, "but it did no good at all. I also tried to see the editor, but he wouldn't receive me. So I have come to you."

"This is outrageous," protested Gaylord Brent, making to close the door.

"You see, I have something for you," said Chadwick mildly. Brent's hand on the door jamb paused.

"What?" he asked.

"This," said Chadwick.

On the word, he raised his right hand, fist closed, and dotted Gaylord Brent firmly but not viciously on the tip of his nose. It was not the sort of blow to break the bone, or even damage the septum cartilage, but it caused Gaylord Brent to retreat a pace, emit a loud "Ooooooh" and clap his hand to his nose. Water welled into his eyes and he began to sniff back the first trickle of blood. He stared at Chadwick for a second as if confronting a madman, then slammed the door. Chadwick heard steps running down the hallway.

He found his police constable at the corner of Heath Street, a young man enjoying the peace of the crisp morning, but otherwise somewhat bored.

"Officer," said Chadwick as he came up to him, "you had better come with me. An assault has been committed on a local resident."

The young policeman perked up. "Assault, sir?" he asked. "Whereabouts?"

"Only two streets away," said Chadwick. "Please follow me."

Without waiting to be asked more questions he beckoned the policeman with his forefinger, turned and set off at a brisk walk back the way he had come. Behind him he heard the policeman talking into his lapel radio and the thud of official boots.

The officer of the law caught up with Chadwick at the corner of the street in which the Brent family lived. To forestall more questions, Chadwick kept up his brisk pace, telling the policeman, "Here it is, officer, at Number Thirty-Two."

The door, when they reached it, was still closed. Chadwick gestured to it.

"In there," he said.

After a pause and with a suspicious glance at Chadwick, the constable mounted the steps and rang the bell. Chadwick joined him on the top step. The door opened, carefully. Mrs. Brent appeared. Her eyes widened at the sight of Chadwick. Before the policeman could say anything Chadwick chipped in.

"Mrs. Brent? I wonder if this officer could have a word with your husband?"

Mrs. Brent nodded and fled back into the house. From inside, both callers heard a whispered conversation. The words "police" and "that man" were discernible. After a minute Gaylord Brent appeared at the door. With his left hand he clutched a cold, wet dishcloth to his nose. Behind it he sniffed repeatedly.

"Yed?" he said.

"This is Mr. Gaylord Brent," said Chadwick.

"Are you Mr. Gaylord Brent?" asked the officer.

"Yed," replied Gaylord Brent.

"A few minutes ago," said Chadwick, "Mr. Brent was deliberately punched on the nose."

"Is that true?" the policeman asked Brent.

"Yed," Brent nodded, glaring over his dishcloth at Chadwick.

"I see," said the officer, who plainly did not. "And who did this?"

"I did," said Chadwick at his side.

The policeman turned in disbelief. "I beg your pardon?" he asked.

"I did. I hit him on the nose. That's a common assault, isn't it?"

"Is that true?" the policeman asked Brent.

The face behind the towel nodded.

"May I ask why?" inquired the policeman of Chadwick.

"As to that," said Chadwick, "I'm only prepared to explain it all in a statement at the police station."

The policeman looked nonplussed. At last he said, "Very well, sir, then I must ask you to accompany me to the station."

There was a panda car on Heath Street by this time, summoned by the constable five minutes earlier. He had a brief conversation with the two uniformed policemen inside, and he and Chadwick both climbed into the rear. The car brought them to the local police station inside two minutes. Chadwick was led up to the duty sergeant. He stood silent while the young constable explained to the sergeant what had happened. The sergeant, a middle-aged veteran of world-weary patience, contemplated Chadwick with some interest.

"Who is this man you hit?" he asked at length.

"Mr. Gaylord Brent," said Chadwick.

"Don't like him, do you?" asked the sergeant.

"Not much," said Chadwick.

"Why come up to this officer and tell him you've done it?" asked the sergeant.

Chadwick shrugged. "It's the law, isn't it? An offence in law has been committed; the police should be informed."

"Nice thought," conceded the sergeant. He turned to the constable. "Much damage done to Mr. Brent?"

"Didn't look like it," said the young man. "More like a gentle thump on the hooter."

The sergeant sighed. "Address," he said. The constable gave it to him. "Wait here," said the sergeant.

He withdrew to a back room. Gaylord Brent had an unlisted number, but the sergeant obtained it from Directory Inquiries. Then he rang it. After a while he came back.

"Mr. Gaylord Brent doesn't seem very eager to press charges," he said.

"That's not the point," said Chadwick. "It's not up to Mr. Brent to press charges. This is not America. The fact is, an offence of assault has plainly been committed, against the law of the land, and it is up to the police to decide whether to press charges."

The sergeant eyed him with distaste.

"Know a bit about the law, do you, sir?" he asked.

"I've read some," said Chadwick.

"Haven't they all?" sighed the sergeant. "Well now, the police might decide not to press the case."

"If that is so, I shall have no option but to inform you that if you do not, I'll go back there and do it again," said Chadwick.

The sergeant slowly drew a pad of charge forms towards him.

"That does it," he said. "Name?"

Bill Chadwick gave his name and address and was taken to the charge room. He declined to make a statement, other than to say he wished to explain his action to the magistrate in due course. This was typed out and he signed it. He was formally charged and bailed by the sergeant on his own recognisance of £100 to appear before the North London magistrates the following morning. Then he was allowed to go.

The next day he appeared on remand. The hearing

took two minutes. He declined to enter a plea, knowing that such refusal would have to be interpreted by the court as meaning that in due course he might plead not guilty. He was remanded for two weeks and bail was renewed for the sum of £100. As it was only a remand hearing, Mr. Gaylord Brent was not present in court. The remand was on a charge of common assault and did not make more than one inch in the local newspaper. No one in the district where Bill Chadwick lived ever read that paper, so no one noticed.

In the week before the case came up a number of anonymous phone calls were received by the news editors of the main daily, evening and Sunday newspapers in Fleet Street and its environs.

In each case the caller tipped off the news editor that star *Courier* investigator Gaylord Brent would be appearing in connection with an assault case at the North London magistrates' court on the following Monday, in the matter of *Regina versus Chadwick,* and that it might pay dividends for the editor to send his own staffer rather than rely solely on the Press Association court reporting service.

Most of the editors checked the court list for that court on that day, confirmed the name of Chadwick did indeed appear in the list, and assigned a staffer. No one knew what was afoot, but hoped for the best. As in the trade union movement, the theory of camaraderie in Fleet Street stops well short of practical solidarity.

Bill Chadwick surrendered to his bail on the dot of 10 a.m. and was asked to wait until his case was called. It came at a quarter past eleven. When he entered the dock a quick glance at the press benches confirmed they were full to overflowing. He had noticed that Gaylord Brent, summoned as a witness, was sitting outside the courtroom on one of the benches in the main hall. In British law, no witness may enter the court until he is called to give evidence. Only after giving evidence may he take a seat in the rear of the court and listen to the rest of the case. That caused Chadwick a moment of perplexity. He solved the dilemma by pleading not guilty.

He declined the stipendiary magistrate's suggestion that the case be again adjourned until he had professional legal counsel, and explained he wished to conduct his own defence. The magistrate shrugged but agreed.

Prosecuting counsel outlined the facts of the case, or as many as were known, and caused a few raised eyebrows when he mentioned that it was Chadwick himself who had approached P.C. Clarke in Hampstead that morning with news of the assault. Without further ado he then called P.C. Clarke.

The young officer took the oath and gave evidence of arrest. Chadwick was asked if he wished to cross-examine. He declined. He was urged again. He declined. P.C. Clarke was dismissed and took a seat in the rear. Gaylord Brent was called. He mounted the witness box and took the oath. Chadwick rose in the dock.

"Your worship," he said to the magistrate in a clear voice, "I have been thinking it over, and I wish to change my plea. To one of guilty."

The magistrate stared at him. Prosecuting counsel, who had risen to examine, sat down. In the witness box Gaylord Brent stood silent.

"I see," said the magistrate. "You are sure, Mr. Chadwick?"

"Yes, sir. Absolutely sure."

"Mr. Cargill, have you any objection?" the magistrate asked counsel for the Crown.

"No objection, your honour," said Mr. Cargill. "I must assume the defendant no longer disputes the facts of the case as I have outlined them."

"No dispute at all," said Chadwick from the dock. "They are exactly as they happened."

The magistrate turned to Gaylord Brent. "I am sorry you have been troubled, Mr. Brent," he said, "but it appears you will not now be needed as a witness. You may either leave or take a seat in the rear of the court."

Gaylord Brent nodded and left the box. He exchanged a further nod with the press benches and took a seat at the back, next to the police constable who had already given his evidence. The magistrate addressed Chadwick.

"Mr. Chadwick, you have changed your plea to guilty. That means of course that you admit the assault on Mr. Brent. Do you wish to call any witnesses on your own behalf?"

"No, your worship."

"You may call character witnesses if you wish, or give evidence yourself in mitigation."

"I wish to call no witnesses, sir," said Chadwick. "As to mitigation, I wish to make a statement from the dock."

"This is your privilege and right," said the magistrate.

Chadwick, by now standing to address the bench, produced a folded cutting from his pocket.

"Your worship, six weeks ago Mr. Gaylord Brent published this article in the newspaper for which he works, the *Sunday Courier*. I should be grateful if your worship would glance through it."

An usher rose from the well, took the cutting and approached the bench.

"Is this germane to the case before the court?" asked the magistrate.

"I assure you, sir, it is. Very much so."

"Very well," said the magistrate. He took the proffered cutting from the usher and read it quickly. When he had finished, he put it down and said, "I see."

"In that article," said Chadwick, "Gaylord Brent perpetrated upon me a vicious and immensely damaging libel. You will observe, sir, that the article deals with a company merchandising a product and then going into liquidation, leaving a number of members of the public in forfeit of their deposits. I unfortunately was one of those businessmen who were also taken in by that company, which I, like many others, believed to be a sound company with a reliable product. The fact is, I also lost money by my mistake, but mistake it was. In this article, out of the blue, I was baselessly accused of some ill-defined complicity in the affair, and accused moreover by a slovenly, lazy and incompetent hack who cannot even be bothered to do his homework properly."

There was a gasp from the court, then a pause. After the pause the pencils in the press box flew frantically across pads of lined paper.

Prosecuting counsel rose. "Is this really necessary for mitigation, your worship?" he asked plaintively.

Chadwick cut in. "I assure your worship that I merely seek to explain the background to the case. I simply feel that your worship may be better able to judge the misdemeanour if he understands the reason for it."

The magistrate contemplated Chadwick for a while.

"Defendant has a point," he conceded. "Proceed."

"Thank you, sir," said Chadwick. "Now, had this so-called investigative journalist bothered to contact me before writing this piece of garbage, I could have produced all my files, my accounts and my bank statements to prove to him beyond a doubt that I had been as misled as the purchasers. And had lost substantial sums into the bargain. But he could not even be bothered to contact me, although I am in the phone book and the commercial directory. It seems that behind his veneer of pretentiousness this fearless investigator is more prone to listen to bar gossip than check out his facts . . ."

Gaylord Brent, puce with outrage, rose from the back of the court. "Now look here . . ." he shouted.

"*Silence*," roared the usher, also on his feet. "*Silence in court.*"

"I understand your sense of anger, Mr. Chadwick," said the magistrate gravely, "but I am wondering what this has to do with mitigation."

"Your worship," said Chadwick humbly. "I appeal only to your sense of justice. When a man who has led a peaceable and law-abiding life suddenly strikes another human being, surely it is pertinent to understand his motives for such an uncharacteristic act. This, I submit, must affect the judgement of the man whose duty it is to pass sentence?"

"Very well," said the magistrate, "explain your motives. But please moderate your language."

"Indeed I shall," said Chadwick. "After the appearance of this farrago of lies masquerading as serious journalism, my business was badly affected. It was evident that some of my associates, unaware that Mr. Gaylord Brent's alleged exposés emerge less from slogging investigation than from the bottom of a whisky bottle, were even prepared to believe the libel."

At the back of the court Gaylord Brent was beside himself. He nudged the policeman next to him.

"He can't get away with this, can he?" he hissed.

"Shush," said the policeman.

Brent rose. "Your worship," he called out, "I would just like to say . . ."

"*Silence*," shouted the usher.

"If there are any more disturbances from the body of

the court, I shall cause those responsible for them to be removed," said the magistrate.

"So you see, sir," proceeded Chadwick, "I began to brood. I wondered by what right an ill-informed clown too idle to check out his allegations could hide behind the ramparts of legal and financial resources afforded by a major newspaper and from that vantage point ruin a small man he had never even bothered to meet; a man who had worked hard all his life and as honestly as he could."

"There are other recourses for an alleged libel," observed the magistrate.

"There are indeed, sir," said Chadwick, "but as a man of the law yourself you must be aware that few nowadays can afford the immense burden of trying to take on the might of a national newspaper. So I tried to see the editor to explain, with facts and documents, that his employee had been utterly wrong and had not even made an attempt to be accurate. He refused to see me, then or ever. So I went to see Gaylord Brent personally. As they wouldn't let me see him in the office I went to his home."

"To hit him on the nose?" said the magistrate. "You may have been seriously libelled, but violence can never be the answer."

"Gracious, no, sir," said Chadwick in surprise. "Not to hit him at all. To reason with him. To ask him to examine the evidence, which I believed would show him that what he had written was simply untrue."

"Ah," said the magistrate with interest. "Motive at last. You went to his house to appeal to him?"

"That indeed I did, sir," said Chadwick. He was as aware as prosecuting counsel that, as he had not taken the oath and was speaking from the dock, he could not be cross-examined.

"And why did you not reason with him?" asked the magistrate.

Chadwick's shoulders slumped. "I tried," he said. "But he just treated me with the same dismissive contempt that I had received at the newspaper offices. He knew I was too small a man, a man of no account; that I could not take on the mighty *Courier*."

"Then what happened?" asked the magistrate.

"I confess something inside me snapped," said Chadwick. "I did the unforgivable. I dotted him one on the nose. For just one second in all my life I lost control."

With that he sat down. The magistrate gazed across the court from his bench.

You, my friend, he thought privately, lost control like the Concorde flies on elastic bands. He could not, however, help recalling an incident years earlier when he had been savaged in the press over a judgement he had given in another court; his anger then had been compounded by the knowledge that he had later been proved to be right. Out loud he said, "This is a very serious case. The court must accept that you felt you had been wronged, and even that you did not proceed from your home to Hampstead that morning with violence in mind. Nevertheless, you did hit Mr. Brent, on his own doorstep. As a society, we simply cannot have private citizens feeling able to go around dotting the country's leading journalists on their noses. Fined one hundred pounds with fifty pounds costs."

Bill Chadwick wrote out his cheque as the press benches emptied and the scribes pelted for telephones and taxis. As he came down the steps of the court building he felt himself seized by one arm.

He turned to find himself facing Gaylord Brent, pale with anger and trembling with shock.

"You bastard," said the journalist. "You can't bloody well get away with what you said in there."

"I can, actually," said Chadwick. "Speaking from the dock, yes, I can. It's called absolute privilege."

"But I'm not all those things you called me," said Brent. "You can't call another man things like that."

"Why not?" said Chadwick mildly. "You did."

Duty*

❧

The car's engine had been spluttering for more than two miles and when it finally began to give up the ghost I found myself heading up a steep and winding hill. I prayed to all my Irish saints that it would not pack in at that point and leave me lost amid the wild beauties of the French countryside.

By my side Bernadette darted alarmed glances at me as I hunched over the wheel, pumping the accelerator to try and coax the last gasp of power from the failing machine. Something was evidently amiss beneath the bonnet and I was surely the most ignorant man on earth about such technological mysteries.

The old Triumph Mayflower just made the brow of the hill, and finally coughed into silence at the peak. I shut off the ignition, put on the handbrake and climbed out. Bernadette joined me and we gazed down the other side of the hill where the country road sloped away towards the valley.

It was undeniably beautiful that summer evening in the

---

* It has been pointed out to me that the following story is out of character with the others in this collection and fits into no real category. It is pure idiosyncrasy on my part, but I have decided to include it anyway. It was told to me by an Irish friend and he swore it was absolutely true and had happened to him. For this reason, unlike all the other stories, I have elected to tell it in the first person.   F.F.

early fifties. The area of the Dordogne in those days was completely "undiscovered"—by the smart set at least. It was an area of rural France where little had changed over the centuries. No factory chimneys or electricity pylons jutted to the sky; no motorways carved a scar through the verdant valley. Hamlets nestled beside narrow lanes, drawing their living from the surrounding fields over which the harvest was drawn in creaking wooden carts hauled by pairs of oxen. It was this region that Bernadette and I had decided to explore in our elderly tourer that summer, our first holiday abroad; that is, beyond Ireland and England.

I sought my road map from the car, studied it and pointed to a spot on the northern fringes of the Dordogne valley.

"We are about here—I think," I said.

Bernadette was peering down the road ahead of us. "There's a village down there," she said.

I followed her gaze. "You're right."

The spire of a church could be seen between the trees, then the glimpse of a barn roof. I glanced dubiously at the car and the hill.

"We might make it without the engine," I said, "but no farther."

"It's better than being stranded here all night," said my better half.

We got back into the car. I put the gear in neutral, depressed the clutch to fullest extent and let off the hand-brake. The Mayflower began to roll gently forward, then gathered speed. In an eerie silence we coasted down the hill towards the distant spire.

The pull of gravity brought us to the outskirts of what turned out to be a tiny hamlet of two dozen buildings, and the car's momentum rolled us to the centre of the village street. Then the car stopped. We climbed out again. The dusk was falling.

The street appeared to be wholly empty. By the wall of a great brick barn a lone chicken scratched in the dirt. Two abandoned haywains, shafts in the dust, stood by the roadside but their owners were evidently elsewhere. I had made up my mind to knock at one of the shuttered houses and try with my complete ignorance of the French language to explain my predicament, when a lone figure emerged from behind the church a hundred yards away and came towards us.

As he approached I saw he was the village priest. In those days they still wore the full-length black soutane, cummerbund and wide-brimmed hat. I tried to think of the word in French with which to address him. No use. As he came abreast of us I called out, "Father."

It was enough, anyway. He stopped, approached and smiled inquiringly. I pointed to my car. He beamed and nodded, as if to say "Nice car." How to explain that I was not a proud owner seeking admiration for his vehicle, but a tourist who had broken down?

Latin, I thought. He was elderly, but surely he would remember some Latin from his schooldays. More importantly, could I? I racked my brains. The Christian Brothers had spent years trying to beat some Latin into me, but apart from saying Mass I had never had to use it since, and there is little enough reference in the missal to the problems of broken-down Triumphs.

I pointed to the bonnet of the car.

"*Currus meus fractus est,*" I told him. It actually means "My chariot is broken" but it seemed to do the trick. Enlightenment flooded over his round face.

"*Ah, est fractus currus teus, filius meus?*" he repeated.

"*In veritate, pater meus,*" I told him. He thought for a while, then made signs that we were to wait for him. At

quickened pace he hurried back up the street and entered
a building which I saw, when I passed it later, was the village café and evidently the centre of life. I should have
thought of that.

He emerged in a few minutes accompanied by a big
man who wore the blue canvas trousers and shirt of a typ-
ical French peasant. His rope-soled espadrilles scraped
the dust as he plodded towards us beside the trotting
priest.

When they came abreast of us the abbé broke into
rapid French, gesticulating at the car and pointing up and
down the road. I got the impression he was telling his pa-
rishioner that the car could not stand blocking the road
all night. Without a word the peasant nodded and went
off up the road again. That left the priest, Bernadette and
me standing alone by the car. Bernadette went and sat in
silence by the roadside.

Those who have ever had to spend time waiting for
something unknown to happen, in the presence of someone with whom not a word can be exchanged, will know
what it is like. I nodded and smiled. He nodded and
smiled. We both nodded and smiled. Eventually he broke
the silence.

"Anglais?" he asked, indicating Bernadette and myself.
I shook my head patiently. It is one of the burdens of the
Irish to pass through history being mistaken for the En-
glish.

"Irlandais," I said, hoping I had got it right. His face
cleared.

"Ah, Hollandais," he said. I shook my head again, took
him by the arm to the rear of the car and pointed. The
sticker on the wing bore the capital letters, black on
white, IRL. He smiled as if to a trying child.

"Irlandais?" I nodded and smiled. *"Irlande?"* More
smiling and nodding from me. *"Partie d'Angleterre,"* he

said. I sighed. There are some struggles one cannot win
and this was neither the time nor the place to explain to
the good father that Ireland, thanks in some part to the
sacrifices of Bernadette's father and uncle, was not a part
of England.

At this point the peasant emerged from a narrow alley
between two slab-sided brick barns, atop an aged and
grunting tractor. In a world of horse-drawn carts and
oxen, it may well have been the village's sole tractor and
its engine sounded little better than the Mayflower's just
before it packed up. But it chugged down the street and
stopped just in front of my car.

With a stout rope the blue-clad farmer attached my car
to the towing hook of his tractor and the priest indicated
we should climb into the car. In this fashion, with the
priest walking beside us, we were towed down the road,
round a corner and into a courtyard.

In the gathering dusk I made out a peeling board above
what looked like yet another brick barn. It said *"Garage,"*
and was evidently closed and locked. The peasant
unhooked my car and began to stow his rope. The priest
pointed to his watch and the shuttered garage. He indicated it would open at seven the next morning, at which
time the absent mechanic would see what was wrong.

"What are we supposed to do till then?" Bernadette
whispered to me. I attracted the priest's attention, placed
my two palms together beside one side of my face and
tilted my head in the international gesture of one who
wishes to sleep. The priest understood.

Another rapid conversation began between the priest
and the peasant. I could follow none of it, but the peasant
raised one arm and pointed. I caught the word "Preece"
which meant nothing to me, but saw the priest nod in
agreement. Then he turned to me and indicated we should

take a suitcase from the car and mount the rear step of the tractor, holding fast with our hands.

This we did, and the tractor turned out of the court-yard onto the highway. The kindly priest waved us good-bye and that was the last we saw of him. Feeling utterly foolish, we stood side by side on the rear step of the trac-tor, I with a grip containing our overnight things in one hand, and held on.

Our silent driver went up the road on the farther side of the village, across a small stream and up another hill. Near the brow he turned into the yard of a farm whose surface was a mixture of summer dust and cow-pats. He came to rest near the farm door and indicated we should dismount. The engine was still running and making a fair racket.

The peasant approached the farm door and knocked. A minute later a short, middle-aged woman in an apron ap-peared, framed by the light of a paraffin lamp behind her. The tractor driver conversed with her, pointing at us. She nodded. The driver, satisfied, returned to his tractor and pointed us towards the open door. Then he drove off.

While the two had been talking, I had looked round the farmyard in what remained of the day's light. It was typi-cal of many I had seen so far, a small mixed farm with a bit of this and a bit of that. There was a cow byre, a stable for the horse and the oxen, a wooden trough beside a hand-pump and a large compost heap on which a clus-ter of brown hens pecked a living. All looked weathered and sun-bleached, nothing modern, nothing efficient, but the sort of traditional French small-holding of which hundreds of thousands made up the backbone of the agri-cultural economy.

From somewhere out of sight I heard the rhythmic rise and fall of an axe, the thwack as it bit into timber, and the rending of the split logs as the cutter then tore them apart. Someone was splitting billets for the fires of winter yet to come. The lady in the doorway was beckoning us to enter.

There may have been a living room, sitting room, lounge—call it what you will—but we were led into the kitchen which was evidently the centre of household life, a stone-flagged room containing sink, dining table and two battered easy chairs by an open fire. Another hand-pump near the stone sink indicated water came from the well, and illumination was by paraffin lamp. I set down the case.

Our hostess turned out to be lovely; round, apple-cheeked face with grey hair drawn back in a bun, care-worn hands, long grey dress, white pinafore and a chirpy birdlike smile of welcome. She introduced herself as Madame Preece, and we gave her our names which were for her quite unpronounceable. Conversation would evidently be confined to more nodding and smiling, but I was grateful to have a place to stay at all, considering our predicament on the hill an hour ago.

Madame Preece indicated Bernadette might like to see the room and wash; such niceties were evidently not necessary for me. The two women disappeared upstairs with the handgrip. I walked to the window, which was open to the warm evening air. It gave out onto another yard at the back of the house, where a cart stood among the weeds near a wooden shed. Extending from the shed a paling fence ran a short way, about six feet high. From above the fence the blade of a great axe rose and fell, and the sound of the chopping of timber went on.

Bernadette came down ten minutes later looking fresher, having washed in a china bowl with cold water from a stone crock. The water coming out of the upper window into the yard would have accounted for the odd splash I had heard. I raised my eyebrows.

"It's a nice little room," she said. Madame Preece, who was watching, beamed and bobbed, understanding nothing but the approving tone. "I hope," said Bernadette with the same bright smile, "that there aren't any hoppers."

I feared there might be. My wife has always suffered terribly from fleas and midges, which raise great lumps on her white Celtic skin. Madame Preece gestured for us to sit in the battered armchairs, which we did; and made small talk while she busied herself at the black cast-iron kitchen range at the other end of the room. Something that smelled appetizing was a-cook and the odour made me hungry.

Ten minutes later she bade us come to table, and placed before us china bowls, soup spoons and a long loaf each of delicious fluffy white bread. Finally in the centre she placed a large tureen from which protruded a steel ladle, and indicated we should help ourselves.

I served Bernadette a portion of what turned out to be a thick, nourishing and tasty vegetable broth, mainly of potatoes and very filling, which was just as well. It constituted the meal of the evening, but was so good we both ended up by having three portions. I offered to serve Madame Preece her portion, but she would have none of it. It was obviously not the custom.

"Servez-vous, monsieur, servez-vous," she repeated, so I filled my own bowl to the brim and we tucked in.

Hardly five minutes had passed before the sound of the log-chopping ended, and seconds later the back door was pushed open as the farmer himself entered for his evening meal. I rose to greet him, as Madame chattered an explanation of our presence, but he evinced not the slightest interest in two strangers at his dinner table. So I sat back down again.

He was a huge man, whose head scraped the ceiling of the room. He lumbered rather than walked and one had

the immediate impression—accurate as it turned out—of
enormous strength allied to a very slow intelligence.

He was about sixty, give or take a few years, and his
grey hair was cut short to his head. I noticed he had tiny,
button ears and his eyes, as he looked at us without sign
of greeting, were a guileless, vacant baby-blue.

The giant sat down at his accustomed chair without a
word and his wife at once served him a brimming portion
of the soup. His hands were dark with earth and, for all I
knew, other substances, but he made no move to wash
them. Madame Preece resumed her seat, flashed us another bright smile and a bob of her birdlike head, and we
continued our meal. From the corner of my eye I saw the
farmer was shovelling down spoonfuls of his broth, accompanied by great chunks of bread which he tore without ceremony from his loaf.

No conversation took place between the man and his
wife, but I noticed she darted him affectionate and indul-
gent looks from time to time, though he took not the
slightest bit of notice.

Bernadette and I tried to talk, at least between ourselves. It was more for the relief of breaking the silence
than to convey information.

"I hope the car can be repaired in the morning," I said.
"If it's something serious I might have to go to the
nearest big town for a spare part or a breakdown van."

I shuddered to think what that expense might do to our
tiny postwar tourist budget.

"What is the nearest big town?" asked Bernadette between mouthfuls of soup.

I tried to remember the map in the car. "Bergerac, I
think."

"How far is that?" she asked.

"Oh, about sixty kilometres," I replied.

There was nothing much else to say, so silence fell

again. It had continued for a full minute when out of nowhere a voice suddenly said in English, "Forty-four."

We both had our heads bowed at the time and Bernadette looked up at me. I looked as puzzled as she. I looked at Madame Preece. She smiled happily and went on eating. Bernadette gave an imperceptible nod in the direction of the farmer. I turned to him. He was still wolfing his soup and bread.

"I beg your pardon?" I said.

He gave no sign of having heard, and several more spoonfuls of soup, with more large chunks of bread, went down his gullet. Then twenty seconds after my question, he said quite clearly in English, "Forty-four. To Bergerac. Kilometres. Forty-four."

He did not look at us; he just went on eating. I glanced across at Madame Preece. She flashed a happy smile as if to say, "Oh yes, my husband has linguistic talents." Bernadette and I put down our spoons in amazement.

"You speak English?" I asked the farmer.

More seconds ticked away. Finally he just nodded.

"Were you born in England?" I asked.

The silence lengthened and there was no reply. It came a full fifty seconds after the question.

"Wales," he said, and filled his mouth with another wad of bread.

I should explain here that if I do not, in the telling of this tale, speed up the dialogue somewhat, the reader will die of weariness. But it was not like that at the time. The conversation that slowly developed between us took ages to accomplish because of the inordinately long gaps between my questions and his answers.

At first I thought he might be hard of hearing. But it was not that. He could hear well enough. Then I thought he might be a most cautious, cunning man, thinking out the implications of his answers as a chess player thinks out the consequences of his moves. It was not that. It was simply that he was a man of no guile at all, of such slow thought processes that by the time he had ingested a question, worked out what it meant, devised an answer to it and delivered the same, many seconds, even a full minute, had elapsed.

I should perhaps not have been sufficiently interested to put myself through the tiresomeness of the conversation that occupied the next two hours, but I was curious to know why a man from Wales was farming here in the depths of the French countryside. Very slowly, in dribs and drabs, the reason came out, and it was charming enough to delight Bernadette and myself.

His name was not Preece, but Price, pronounced in the French way as Preece. Evan Price. He was from the Rhondda Valley in South Wales. Nearly forty years earlier he had been a private soldier in a Welsh regiment in the First World War.

As such he had taken part in the second great battle on the Marne that preceded the end of that war. He had been badly shot up and had lain for weeks in a British Army hospital while the Armistice was declared. When the British Army went home he, too ill to be moved, had been transferred to a French hospital.

Here he had been tended by a young nurse, who had fallen in love with him as he lay in his pain. They had married and come south to her parents' small farm in the Dordogne. He had never returned to Wales. After the death of her parents his wife, as their only child, had inherited the farm, and it was here that we now sat.

Madame Preece had sat through the oh-so-slow narration, catching here and there a word she recognized, and smiling brightly whenever she did so. I tried to imagine her as she would have been in 1918, slim then, like a darting active sparrow, dark-eyed, neat, chirpy at her work.

Bernadette too was touched by the image of the little French nurse caring for and falling in love with the huge, helpless, simple-minded overgrown baby in the lazaret in Flanders. She leaned across and touched Price on the arm.

"That's a lovely story, Mr. Price," she said.

He evinced no interest.

"We're from Ireland," I said, as if to offer some information in return.

He remained silent while his wife helped him to his third portion of soup.

"Have you ever been to Ireland?" asked Bernadette.

More seconds ticked away. He grunted and nodded. Bernadette and I glanced at each other in delighted surprise.

"Did you have work there?"

"No."

"How long were you there?"

"Two years."

"And when was that?" asked Bernadette.

"1915 . . . to 1917."

"What were you doing there?" More time elapsed.

"In the Army."

Of course, I should have known. He had not joined up in 1917. He had joined up earlier and been posted to Flanders in 1917. Before that he had been in the British Army garrison in Ireland.

A slight chill came over Bernadette's manner. She comes from a fiercely Republican family. Perhaps I should have let well alone; not probed any more. But my journalist's background forced me to go on asking the questions.

"Where were you based?"

"In Dublin."

"Ah. We come from Dublin. Did you like Dublin?"

"No."

"Oh, I'm sorry to hear that."

We Dubliners tend to be rather proud of the place. We would prefer foreigners, even garrison troops, to appreciate our city's qualities.

The earlier part of ex-Private Price's career came out like the latter part, very, very, slowly. He had been born in the Rhondda in 1897, of very poor parents. Life had been hard and bleak. In 1914, at the age of seventeen, more to secure food, clothing and barracks to live in than out of patriotic fervour, he had joined the Army. He had never gone beyond private soldier.

For twelve months he had been in training camps as others went off to the front in Flanders, and at an army stores depot in Wales. In late 1915 he had been posted to the garrison forces in Ireland, quartered in the chill of barracks at Islandbridge on the south side of the River Liffey in Dublin.

Life, I had to suppose, had been boring enough for him to have said he did not enjoy Dublin. Sparse barrack dormitories, low pay even for those days, and an endless, mindless round of spit and polish, buttons, boots and beds; of guard duty on freezing nights and picquets in the streaming rain. And for leisure . . . not much of that either on a soldier's pay. Beer in the canteen, little or no contact with a Catholic population. He had probably been glad to have been posted away after two years. Or was he ever glad or sad for anything, this lumbering, slow man?

"Did nothing ever happen of interest?" I asked him finally, in some desperation.

"Only once," he replied at last.

"And what was that?"

"An execution," he said, absorbed in his soup.

Bernadette put down her spoon and sat rigid. There

was a chill in the air. Only Madame, who understood not a word, and her husband, who was too insensitive, were oblivious. I should definitely have left well alone.

After all, in those days a lot of people were executed. Common murderers were hanged at Mountjoy. But hanged. By prison warders. Would they need the soldiery for that? And British soldiers would be executed too, for murder and rape, under military regulations after court martial. Would they be hanged or shot? I did not know.

"Do you remember when it was, this execution?" I asked.

Bernadette sat frozen.

Mr. Price raised his limpid blue eyes to mine. Then he shook his head. "Long time ago," he said. I thought he might be lying, but he was not. He had simply forgotten.

"Were you in the firing party?" I asked.

He waited the usual period while he thought. Then he nodded.

I wondered what it must be like to be a member of a firing party; to squint along the sights of a rifle towards another human being, tethered to a post 60 feet away; to pick out the white patch over the heart and hold the fore-sight steady on that living man; on the word of command to squeeze the trigger, hear the bang, feel the thud of recoil; to see the bound figure beneath the chalk-white face jerk and slump in the ropes. Then go back to barracks, clean the rifle and have breakfast. Thank God I had never known nor ever would.

"Try to remember when it was," I urged him.

He did try. He really did. You could almost feel the effort. Eventually he said, "1916. In the summer I think."

I leaned forward and touched his forearm. He raised his eyes to mine. There was no deviousness in them, just patient inquiry.

"Do you remember . . . try to remember . . . who was the man you shot?"

But it was too much. However he tried, he could not recall. He shook his head at last.

"Long time ago," he said.

Bernadette rose abruptly. She flashed a strained, polite smile at Madame.

"I'm going to bed," she told me. "Don't be long."

I went up twenty minutes later. Mr. Price was in his armchair by the fire, not smoking, not reading. Staring at the flames. Quite content.

The room was in darkness and I was not going to fiddle with the paraffin lamp. I undressed by the light of the moon through the window and got into bed.

Bernadette was lying quiet but I knew she was awake. And what she was thinking. The same as me. Of that bright spring of 1916 when on Easter Sunday a group of men dedicated to the then unpopular notion that Ireland should be independent of Britain had stormed the Post Office and several other large buildings.

Of the hundreds of troops being brought in to flush them out with rifle and artillery fire—but not Private Price in his boring Islandbridge barracks, or he would have mentioned the occasion. Of the smoke and the noise, the rubble in the streets, the dead and the dying, Irish and British. And of the rebels being finally led out of the Post Office defeated and disowned. Of the strange green-orange-white tricolour they had hoisted atop the building being contemptuously hauled down to be replaced again by the Union Jack of Britain.

They do not teach it now in schools of course, for it forms no part of the necessary myths, but it is a fact for all that; when the rebels were marched in chains to Dublin docks en route to jail in Liverpool across the water, the Dubliners, and most among them the Catholic poor, threw refuse and curses at them for bringing so much trouble upon Dublin's head.

It would probably have ended there but for the stupid, crazy decision of the British authorities to execute the six-teen leaders of the rising between 3 and 12 May at Kil-mainham Jail. Within a year the whole mood had changed; in the election of 1918 the independence party swept the country. After two years of guerrilla war, inde-pendence was finally granted.

Bernadette stirred beside me. She was rigid, in the grip of her thoughts. I knew what they would be. They would be of those chill May mornings when the nail-studded boots of the firing parties rang out as they marched from the barracks to the jail in the darkness before dawn. Of the soldiers waiting patiently in the great courtyard of the jail until the prisoner was led out to the post up against the far wall.

And of her uncle. She would be thinking of him in the warm night. Her father's elder brother, worshipped but dead before she was born, refusing to speak English to the jailers, talking only in Irish to the court martial, head high, chin up, staring down the barrels as the sun tipped the horizon. And of the others . . . O'Connell, Clarke, MacDonough, and Padraig Pearse. Of course, Pearse.

I grunted with exasperation at my own foolishness. All this was nonsense. There were others, rapists, looters, murderers, deserters from the British Army, also shot af-ter court martial. It was like that in those days. There was a whole range of crimes for which the death penalty was mandatory. And there was a war on, making more death penalties.

"In the summer," Price had said. That was a long period. From May to late September. Those were great events in the history of a small nation, those of the spring of 1916. Dumb privates have no part to play in great events. I banished the thoughts and went to sleep.

Our waking was early, for the sun streamed through the window shortly after dawn and the farmyard fowl made enough noise to rouse the dead. We both washed, and I shaved as best I could, in the water from the ewer, and threw the residue out of the window into the yard. It would ease the parched earth. We dressed in our clothes of yesterday and descended.

Madame Price had bowls of steaming milky coffee on the kitchen table for each of us, with bread and white butter, which went down very well. Of her husband there was no sign. I had hardly finished my coffee when Madame Price beckoned me through to the front of the farmhouse. There in the cow-patted front yard off the road stood my Triumph and a man who turned out to be the garage owner. I thought Mr. Price might help me with the translations, but he was nowhere to be seen.

The mechanic was voluble in his explanations, of which I understood not a word but one; "*carburateur*" he kept repeating, then blew as through a tube to remove a particle of muck. So that was it; so simple. I vowed to take a course in basic motor mechanics. He asked a thousand francs, which in those days before de Gaulle invented the new franc was about a pound sterling. He handed me the car keys and bade me goodbye.

I settled up with Madame Price, another thousand francs (you really could take a holiday abroad for little money in those days) and summoned Bernadette. We stowed the grip and climbed aboard. The engine started at once. With a final wave Madame disappeared inside her house. I backed the car once and turned for the highway running past the entrance.

I had just reached the road when I was stopped by a roaring shout. Through the open window of the driver's

side I saw Mr. Price running towards us across the yard,
twirling his great axe around his head like a toothpick.

My jaw dropped, for I thought he was about to attack
us. He could have chopped the car in bits, had he a mind
to. Then I saw his face was alight with elation. The shout
and the waving axe were to attract our attention before
we drove off.

Panting, he arrived at the window and his great moon
face appeared in the aperture.

"I've remembered," he said, "I've remembered."

I was taken aback. He was beaming like a child who
has done something very special to please his parents.

"Remembered?" I asked.

He nodded. "Remembered," he repeated. "Who it was
I shot that morning. It was a poet called Pearse."

Bernadette and I sat stunned, immobile, expressionless,
staring at him without reaction. The elation drained from
his face. He had tried so hard to please, and had failed.
He had taken my question very seriously, and had
wracked his poor brain all night for some piece of information that was for him utterly meaningless anyway.
Ten seconds earlier it had finally come to him after so
much effort. He had caught us just in time and we were
staring at him with neither expression nor words.

His shoulders slumped. He stood upright, turned and
went back to his billets of firewood behind the shed. Soon
I heard the cadence of thuds resume.

Bernadette sat staring out through the front windscreen. She was sheet-white, lips tight. I had a mental
image of a big, lumbering boy from the Rhondda Valley
drawing one rifle and a single round of live ball from the
quartermaster in a barracks at Islandbridge all those years
ago.

Bernadette spoke. "A monster," she said.

I glanced across the yard to where the axe rose and

fell, held by a man who with a single shot had started a war and a nation on its road to independence.

"No, girl," I said, "no monster. Just a soldier doing his duty."

I let in the clutch and we started down the road to Bergerac.

A Careful Man

❧

Timothy Hanson was a man who approached the problems of life with a calm and measured tread. He prided himself that this habitual approach, of calm analysis followed by the selection of the most favourable option and finally the determined pursuit of that choice, had brought him in the prime of middle age to the wealth and standing that he now enjoyed.

That crisp April morning he stood on the top step of the house in Devonshire Street, heartland of London's medical elite, and considered himself as the gleaming black door closed deferentially behind him.

The consultant physician, an old friend who had been his personal doctor for years, would have been a model of concern and regret even with a stranger. With a friend it had been even harder for him. His anguish had evidently been greater than that of his patient.

"Timothy, only three times in my career have I had to impart news like this," he had said, his flattened hands resting on the folder of X-rays and reports before him. "I ask you to believe me when I say it is the most dreadful experience in any medical man's life."

Hanson had indicated that he did indeed believe him.

"Had you been a man different from that which I know

231

you to be, I might have been tempted to lie to you," said the doctor.

Hanson had thanked him for the compliment and the candour.

The consultant had escorted him personally to the threshold of the consulting room. "If there is anything . . . I know it sounds banal . . . but you know what I mean . . . anything . . ."

Hanson had gripped the doctor's upper arm and given his friend a smile. It had been enough and all that was needed.

The white-coated receptionist had brought him to the door and ushered him through it. Hanson now stood there and drew a deep breath. It was cold, clean air. The northeast wind had scoured the city during the night. From the top steps he looked down at the street of discreet and elegant houses, now mostly the offices of financial consultants, chambers of expensive lawyers and surgeries of private practitioners.

Along the pavement a young woman in high heels walked briskly towards Marylebone High Street. She looked pretty and fresh, eyes alight, a pink flush on her chilled cheeks. Hanson caught her eye and on an impulse gave her a smile and an inclination of grey head. She looked surprised, then realized she did not know him, nor he her. It was a flirt she had received, not a greeting. She flashed a smile back and trotted on, swinging her hips a mite more. Richards, the chauffeur, pretended not to notice, but he had seen it all and looked approving. He was standing by the rear of the Rolls, waiting.

Hanson descended the steps and Richards pulled open the door. Hanson climbed in and relaxed in the interior warmth. He removed his coat, folded it carefully, placed it on the seat beside him and put his black hat on top. Richards took his place behind the wheel.

"The office, Mr. Hanson?" he asked.

"Kent," said Hanson.

The Silver Wraith had turned south into Great Portland Street, heading for the river, when Richards ventured a question.

"Nothing wrong with the old ticker, sir?"

"No," said Hanson. "Still pumping away."

There was indeed nothing wrong with his heart. In that sense he was as strong as an ox. But this was not the time or the place to discuss with his chauffeur the mad, insatiable cells eating away in his bowel. The Rolls swept past the statue of Eros in Piccadilly Circus and joined the traffic stream down the Haymarket.

Hanson leaned back and stared at the upholstery of the roof. Six months must seem an age, he mused, if you have just been sentenced to prison, or sent to hospital with two broken legs. But when that is all that is left to you it does not look so long. Not so long at all.

There would have to be hospitalization during the last month, of course, the physician had told him. Of course; when things got very bad. And they would. But there were anodynes, new drugs, very powerful . . .

The limousine pulled left into Westminster Bridge Road and then onto the bridge itself. Across the Thames Hanson watched the cream bulk of County Hall moving towards him.

He was, he reminded himself, a man of no small substance despite the penal taxation levels introduced by the new socialist regime. There was his City dealership in rare and precious coins; well established, respected in the trade and owning the freehold on the building in which it was housed. And it was wholly owned by him, with no partners and no shares.

The Rolls had passed the Elephant and Castle roundabout, heading for the Old Kent Road. The studied ele-

gance of Marylebone was long past now, as also the
mercantile wealth of Oxford Street and the twin seats of
power in Whitehall and County Hall, straddling the river
at Westminster Bridge. From the Elephant onwards the
landscape was poorer, deprived, part of the swathe of in-
ner-city problem areas between the wealth and the
power of the centre and the trim complacency of the commuter suburbs.

Hanson watched the tired old buildings pass, cocooned
in a £50,000 motor on a £1,000,000-a-mile highway.
He thought with fondness of the lovely Kentish manor
house to which he was heading, set in twenty acres of
clipped parkland beset with oaks, beeches and limes. He
wondered what would happen to it. Then there was the
large apartment in Mayfair where he occasionally spent
weekday nights rather than face the drive to Kent, and
where he could entertain foreign buyers in an atmosphere
less formal than that of a hotel, and usually more condu-
cive to relaxation and therefore to a beneficial business
deal.

Apart from the business and the two properties there
was his private coin collection, built up with loving care
over so many years; and the portfolio of stocks and
shares, not to mention the deposit accounts in various
banks, and even the car in which he now rode.

The last-mentioned came to a sudden stop at a
pedestrian crossing in one of the poorer sections of the
Old Kent Road. Richards let out a clucking noise of exasperation. Hanson looked out of the window. A crocodile
of small children was crossing the road under the
guidance of four nuns. Two were in the lead, the others
bringing up the rear. At the end of the queue a small boy
had stopped in the middle of the crossing and was staring
with undisguised interest at the Rolls Royce.

He had a round and pugnacious face with a snub nose;

his tousled hair was surmounted by a cap set askew with the initials "St. B" on it; one stocking was rumpled in creases around his ankle, its elastic garter no doubt performing a more important service somewhere else as a vital component of a catapult. He looked up and caught sight of the distinguished silver head staring at him from behind the tinted window. Without hesitation the urchin wrinkled his face into a grimace, placed the thumb of his right hand to his nose and waggled the remaining fingers in defiance.

Without a change of expression, Timothy Hanson placed the thumb of his own right hand against the tip of his nose and made the identical gesture back at the boy. In the rear view mirror Richards probably caught sight of the gesture but after the flicker of one eyebrow stared straight ahead through the windscreen. The boy on the crossing looked stunned. He dropped his hand, then grinned from ear to ear. In a second he was whisked off the crossing by a flustered young nun. The crocodile had now re-formed and was marching towards a large grey building set back from the road behind railings. Freed of its impertinent obstacle, the Rolls purred forward on the road to Kent.

Thirty minutes later the last of the sprawling suburbs were behind them and the great sweep of the M20 motorway opened up, the chalky North Downs dropped away and they entered the rolling hills and vales of the garden of England. Hanson's thoughts strayed back to his wife, now dead these ten years. It had been a happy marriage, indeed very happy, but there had been no children. Perhaps they should have adopted; they had thought about it enough. She had been an only child and her parents were also long dead. On his own side of the family there remained his sister, whom he heartily disliked, a sentiment only matched by that he bore towards her ghastly husband and their equally unpleasant son.

Just south of Maidstone the motorway finally ran out and a few miles later, at Harrietsham, Richards pulled off the main road and cut south towards that box of unspoiled orchards, fields, woods and hop gardens that is called the Weald. It was in this tract of lovely countryside that Timothy Hanson had his country house.

Then there was the Chancellor of the Exchequer, master of his country's finances. He would want his share, thought Hanson, and a substantial share it would be. For there was no doubt about it. One way and another, after years of delay, he was going to have to make a will.

"Mr. Pound will see you now, sir," said the secretary.

Timothy Hanson rose and entered the office of Martin Pound, senior partner in the law firm of Pound, Gogarty.

The lawyer rose from behind his desk to greet him. "My dear Timothy, how good to see you again."

Like many wealthy men in middle age, Hanson had long established a personal friendship with his four most valued advisers, lawyer, broker, accountant and doctor, and was on first-name terms with them all. Both men seated themselves.

"What can I do for you?" asked Pound.

"For some time now, Martin, you have been urging me to make a will," said Hanson.

"Certainly," replied the lawyer, "a very wise precaution, and one long overlooked."

Hanson reached into his attaché case and brought out a bulky manilla envelope, sealed with a large blob of red wax. He handed it over the desk to the surprised solicitor.

"There it is," he said.

Pound handled the package with a frown of perplexity

on his usually smooth face. "Timothy, I do hope . . . in the case of an estate as large as yours . . ."

"Don't worry," said Hanson. "It was indeed prepared by a lawyer. Duly signed and witnessed. There are no ambiguities; nothing to provide any ground to contest it."

"I see," said Pound.

"Don't be put out, old friend. I know you wonder why I did not ask you to prepare it, but went instead to a provincial firm. I had my reasons. Trust me, please."

"Of course," said Pound hastily. "No question of it. Do you wish me to put it in safekeeping?"

"Yes, I do. There is one last thing. In it I have asked you to be the sole executor. I have no doubt you would prefer to have seen it. I give you my word there is nothing in the executor's duties that could possibly trouble your conscience, either professional or personal. Will you accept?"

Pound weighed the heavy package in his hands.

"Yes," he said. "You have my word on it. In any case, I've no doubt we are talking about many years to come. You're looking marvellous. Let's face it, you'll probably outlive me. Then what will you do?"

Hanson accepted the banter in the spirit in which it was made. Ten minutes later he stepped out into the early May sunshine of Gray's Inn Road.

Until the middle of September Timothy Hanson was as busy as he had been for many years. He travelled several times to the Continent and even more frequently to the City of London. Few men who die before their time have the opportunity to put their many and complex affairs in order, and Hanson had every intention of ensuring that his were exactly as he would wish them to be.

On 15 September he asked Richards to come into the

house and see him. The chauffeur-cum-handyman who, with his wife, had looked after Hanson for a dozen years found his employer in the library.

"I have a piece of news for you," said Hanson. "At the end of the year I intend to retire."

Richards was surprised, but gave no sign of it. He reasoned there was more to come.

"I also intend to emigrate," said Hanson, "and spend my retirement in a much smaller residence, somewhere in the sun."

So that was it, thought Richards. Still, it was good of the old boy to let him have over three months' forewarning. But the way the labour market was, he would still have to start looking at once. It was not just the job; it was also the handsome little cottage that went with it.

Hanson took a thick envelope from the mantelpiece. He extended it to Richards, who took it without comprehension.

"I'm afraid," said Hanson, "that unless the future occupants of the Manor wish to continue to employ you, and even Mrs. Richards, it will mean looking for another post."

"Yes, sir," said Richards.

"I shall of course provide the most favourable references before I depart," said Hanson. "I would, however, for business reasons, be most grateful if you would not mention this in the village, or indeed to anyone at all until it becomes necessary. I would also be happy if you would not seek further employment until, say, November the 1st. In short, I do not wish news of my impending departure to get about just yet."

"Very well, sir," said Richards. He was still holding the thick envelope.

"Which brings me," said Hanson, "to the last matter.

The envelope. You and Mrs. Richards have been good and loyal to me these past twelve years. I want you to know I appreciate it. Always have."

"Thank you, sir."

"I would be very grateful if you were to remain as loyal to my memory after my departure abroad. I realize that asking you to seek no further employment for another six weeks may impose hardship. That apart, I would like to help you in some way in your future life. That envelope contains, in used and untraceable twenty-pound notes, the sum of ten thousand pounds."

Richards' self-control broke at last. His eyebrows went up.

"Thank you, sir," he said.

"Please don't mention it," said Hanson. "I have put it in the unusual form of cash because, like most of us, I have an aversion to handing over large chunks of my earned money to the tax people."

"Too right," said Richards with feeling. He could sense the thick wads of paper through the envelope.

"As such a sum would attract a large forfeit in gift tax, payable by you, I would suggest you don't bank it, but keep it in a safe place. And spend it in amounts not large enough to attract attention. It is designed to help you both in your new life in a few months' time."

"Don't worry, sir," said Richards. "I know the score. Everyone's at it nowadays. And thank you very much, on behalf of both of us."

Richards crossed the gravel yard to continue polishing the new Rolls Royce in a happy frame of mind. His salary had always been generous, and with the free cottage he had been able to save quite a bit. With his new windfall there would perhaps be no need to go back to the ever-shrinking labour market. There was that small boarding house at Porthcawl in his native Wales that he and Megan had spotted that very summer . . .

On the morning of 1 October Timothy Hanson came down from his bedroom before the sun had fully cleared the horizon. It would be a full hour before Mrs. Richards came across to prepare his breakfast and start the cleaning.

It had been another terrible night and the pills he kept in his locked bedside drawer were steadily losing their battle against the shafts of pain that tore through his lower stomach. He looked grey and drawn, older than his years at last. He realized there was nothing more he could do. It was time.

He spent ten minutes writing a short note to Richards apologizing for the white lie of a fortnight earlier and asking that Martin Pound be telephoned at his home immediately. The letter he laid ostentatiously on the floor at the threshold of the library where it stood out against the dark parquet. Then he rang Richards and told the sleepy voice that answered that he would not need Mrs. Richards for an early breakfast, but that he would need the chauffeur, in the library, in thirty minutes.

When he had finished he took from his locked bureau the shotgun from whose barrel he had sawn ten inches of metal to render it more easily manageable. Into the breech he loaded two heavy-gauge cartridges and retired to the library.

Meticulous to the last, he covered his favourite button-back-leather winged chair with a heavy horse blanket, mindful that it now belonged to someone else. He sat in the chair cradling the gun. He took one last look round, at his rows of beloved books and the cabinets that had once housed his cherished collection of rare coins. Then he turned the barrels against his chest, fumbled for the triggers, took a deep breath, and shot himself through the heart.

Mr. Martin Pound closed the door to the conference room adjacent to his office and took his place at the head of the long table. Halfway down the table to his right sat Mrs. Armitage, sister of his client and friend, and of whom he had heard. Next to her sat her husband. Both were dressed in black. Across the table, seeming bored and indolent, sat their son, Tarquin, a young man in his early twenties who appeared to have an inordinate interest in the contents of his oversized nose. Mr. Pound adjusted his spectacles and addressed the trio.

"You will understand that the late Timothy Hanson asked me to act as sole executor of his will. In the normal course of events I would, in this capacity, have opened the will immediately upon learning of his death, in order to ascertain whether there were any instructions of immediate importance concerning, for example, preparations for the burial."

"Didn't you write it anyway?" asked Armitage senior.

"No, I did not," replied Pound.

"So you don't know what is in it either?" asked Armitage junior.

"No, I do not," said Pound. "In fact the late Mr. Hanson pre-empted such an opening of the will by leaving me a personal letter on the mantelpiece of the room in which he died. In it he made a number of things plain, which I am now able to impart to you."

"Let's get on with the will," said Armitage junior.

Mr. Pound stared at him coldly without speaking.

"Quiet, Tarquin," said Mrs. Armitage mildly.

Pound resumed. "In the first place, Timothy Hanson did not kill himself while the balance of mind was disturbed. He was in fact in the last stages of terminal cancer, and had known this since the previous April."

"Poor bugger," said Armitage senior.

"I later showed this letter to the Kent county coroner and it was confirmed by his personal physician and the autopsy. This enabled the formalities of death certificate, inquest and permission for burial to be hurried through in only a fortnight. Secondly, he made plain he did not wish the will to be opened and read until these formalities had been completed. Finally, he made plain he wished for a formal reading, rather than any correspondence by mail, in the presence of his only surviving relative, his sister Mrs. Armitage, her husband and son."

The other three in the room looked round with mounting and less than grief-stricken surprise.

"But there's only us here," said Armitage junior.

"Precisely," said Pound.

"Then we must be the only beneficiaries," said his father.

"Not necessarily," said Pound. "The attendance here today was simply according to my late client's letter."

"If he's playing some kind of joke on us . . ." said Mrs. Armitage darkly. Her mouth adopted, as of much-practised ease, a thin straight line.

"Shall we proceed with the will?" suggested Pound.

"Right," said Armitage junior.

Martin Pound took a slim letter opener and carefully slit the end of the fat envelope in his hands. From it he withdrew another bulky envelope and a three-page document, bound along the left-hand margin with narrow green tape. Pound placed the fat envelope to one side and opened out the folded sheets. He began to read.

"This is the last will of me, Timothy John Hanson, of . . ."

"We know all that," said Armitage senior.

"Get on with it," said Mrs. Armitage.

Pound glanced at each with some distaste over the top of his glasses. He continued. "I declare that this my will is to be construed in accordance with English law. Two, I hereby revoke all former wills and testamentary dispositions made by me . . ."

Armitage junior gave vent to the noisy sigh of one whose patience has been too long tried.

"Three, I appoint as executor the following gentleman, a solicitor, and ask that he administer my estate, and pay any duty payable thereon, and execute the provisions of this my will, namely: Martin Pound of Pound, Gogarty. Four, I ask my executor at this point of the reading to open the enclosed envelope wherein he will find a sum of money to be used for the expenses of my burial, and for the settlement of his professional fees, and of any other disbursements incurred in the execution of my wishes. And in the event that there be any monies remaining from the enclosed sum, then do I direct that he donate such monies to any charity of his own choice."

Mr. Pound laid down the will and took up again his letter knife. From the unopened envelope he extracted five wads of £20 notes, all new and each encircled by a brown paper band indicating that the sum in each wad amounted to £1000. There was silence in the room. Armitage junior ceased exploring one of his cavities and stared at the pile of money with the indifference of a satyr observing a virgin. Martin Pound picked up the will again.

"Five, I ask my sole executor, in deference to our long friendship, that he assume his executive functions upon the day following my burial."

Mr. Pound glanced again over the top of his glasses.

"In the normal course of events I would have already visited Mr. Hanson's business in the city, and his other known assets, to ensure that they were being well and properly run and maintained, and that no financial damage would accrue to the beneficiaries by neglect of the assets," he said. "However, I have only just formally learned of my appointment as sole executor, so I have not been able to do so. Now it appears I cannot begin until the day after the funeral."

"Here," said Armitage senior, "this neglect, it wouldn't diminish the value of the estate, would it?"

"I cannot say," replied Pound. "I doubt it. Mr. Hanson had excellent assistants in his City dealership and I have no doubt he trusted in their loyalty to keep things running well."

"Still, hadn't you better get weaving?" asked Armitage.

"The day after the funeral," said Pound.

"Well then, let's get the funeral over with as soon as possible," said Mrs. Armitage.

"As you wish," replied Pound. "You *are* his next of kin." He resumed reading. "Six, I give to . . ."

Here Martin Pound paused and blinked as if he had trouble reading what he read. He swallowed. "I give to my dear and loving sister the rest and residue of my estate absolutely, in the confidence that she will share her good fortune with her lovable husband Norman and their attractive son Tarquin. The same being subject to the conditions of paragraph seven."

There was a stunned silence. Mrs. Armitage dabbed delicately at her eyes with a cambric handkerchief, less to wipe away a tear than cover the smile that twitched at the corner of her mouth. When she removed the handkerchief she glanced at her husband and son with the air of an over-age hen who has just lifted one buttock to find a solid gold egg reposing beneath. The two male Armitages sat with open mouths.

"How much was he worth?" demanded the senior one at last.

"I really couldn't say," said Pound.

"Come on, you must know," said the son. "Roughly. You handled all his affairs."

Pound thought of the unknown solicitor who had drawn up the will in his hand. "Almost all," he said.

"Well . . . ?"

Pound bit on the bullet. However unpleasant he found the Armitages, they were the sole beneficiaries of his late friend's will. "I should have thought, at current market prices, assuming all the estate is called in and realized, between two and a half and three million pounds."

"Bloody hell," said Armitage senior. He began to have mental images. "How much will death duties come to?"

"Quite a large amount, I'm afraid."

"How much?"

"With such a sizable estate, the bulk will be adjusted at the highest rate, seventy-five per cent. Overall, I suppose something like sixty-five per cent."

"Leaving a million clear?" asked the son.

"It's a very rough estimate, you understand," said Pound helplessly. He thought back to his friend Hanson as he had been: cultured, humorous, fastidious. Why, Timothy, for heaven's sake why? "There is paragraph seven," he pointed out.

"What's it say?" demanded Mrs. Armitage, breaking off from her own reverie concerning her social take-off.

Pound began to read again. "I have, all my life, been possessed by a great horror of one day being consumed beneath the ground by worms and other forms of parasites," he read. "I have therefore caused to be constructed a lead-lined coffin which now reposes in the funeral parlour of Bennett and Gaines, in the town of Ashford. And it is in this that I wish to be committed to my last resting place. Secondly, I have never wished that one day I might be dug up by an excavator or anything else. In consequence of this I direct that I shall be buried at sea, specifically twenty miles due south of the coast of Devon where I once served as a naval officer. Finally, I direct that it shall be my sister and brother-in-law who shall, out of respect for their lifelong love for me, be the ones who impel my coffin towards the ocean. And to my executor I direct that should any of these wishes not be fulfilled, or any impediment be placed before the arrangements by my beneficiaries, then shall all that has gone before be null and void, and I direct that then my entire estate be bequeathed to the Chancellor of the Exchequer."

Martin Pound looked up. Privately he was surprised to learn of his late friend's fears and fancies, but he gave no sign of it.

"Now, Mrs. Armitage, I have to ask you formally; do you object to the wishes of your late brother as expressed in paragraph seven?"

"It's stupid," she replied, "burial at sea, indeed. I didn't even know it was allowed."

"It is extremely rare, but not illegal," replied Pound. "I have known of one case before."

"It'll be expensive," said her son, "much more than a cemetery burial. And why not cremation anyway?"

"The cost of the funeral will not affect the inheritance," said Pound testily. "The expenses will come out of this." He tapped the £5000 at his elbow. "Now, do you object?"

"Well, I don't know . . ."

"I have to point out to you that if you do, the inheritance is null and void."

"What does that mean?"

"The state gets the lot," snapped her husband.

"Precisely," said Pound.

"No objection," said Mrs. Armitage. "Though I think it's ridiculous."

"Then as next of kin will you authorize me to make the arrangements?" asked Pound.

Mrs. Armitage nodded abruptly.

"The sooner the better," said her husband. "Then we can get on with the probate and the inheritance."

Martin Pound stood up quickly. He had had enough.

"That constitutes the final paragraph of the will. It is duly signed and witnessed twice on every page. I think therefore there is nothing more to discuss. I shall make the necessary arrangements and contact you in respect of time and place. Good day to you."

The middle of the English Channel is no place to be on a mid-October day unless you are an enthusiast. Mr. and Mrs. Armitage contrived to make perfectly plain before they had cleared the harbour mole that they were definitely not.

Mr. Pound sighed as he stood in the wind on the after-deck so as not to have to join them in the cabin. It had taken him a week to make the arrangements and he had settled on a vessel out of Brixham in Devon. The three fishermen who ran the inshore trawler had taken the unusual job once they were satisfied over the price and assured they were breaking no law. Fishing the Channel provided slim pickings these days.

It had taken a block and tackle to load the half-ton coffin from the rear yard of the Kentish undertakers onto an open-backed one-ton van, which the black limousine had followed throughout the long haul down to the southwest coast that morning. The Armitages had complained throughout. At Brixham the van had drawn up on the quayside and the trawler's own davits had brought the

coffin aboard. It stood now athwart two beams of timber
on the wide afterdeck, waxed oak and polished brass
gleaming under the autumn sky.

Tarquin Armitage had accompanied the party in the
limousine as far as Brixham, but after one look at the sea
had elected to stay within the warm confines of a hostelry
in town. He was not needed for the burial at sea in any
case. The retired Royal Navy chaplain whom Pound had
traced through the chaplaincy department of the Admi-
ralty had been happy enough to accept a generous stipend
for his services and now sat in the small cabin also, his
surplice covered by a thick overcoat.

The skipper of the trawler rolled down the deck to
where Pound stood. He produced a sea chart which
flapped in the breeze, and pointed with a forefinger at a
spot twenty miles south of start point. He raised an eyebrow. Pound nodded.

"Deep water," said the skipper. He nodded at the coffin. "You knew him?"

"Very well," said Pound.

The skipper grunted. He ran the small trawler with his
brother and a cousin; like most of these fishermen, they
were all related. The three were tough Devonians, with
nut-brown hands and faces, the sort whose ancestors had
been fishing these tricky waters since Drake was learning
the difference between main and mizzen.

"Be there in an hour," he said, and stumped back forward.

When they reached the spot, the captain held the vessel
with her bow into the weather, holding station with an
idling engine. The cousin took a long piece of timber,
three planks bolted together with crosspieces on the un-
derside and 3 feet wide, and laid it across the starboard
rail, smooth side up. The chipped timber rail took the
plank almost at the mid-section, like the fulcrum of a see-

saw. One half of the planks lay towards the deck, the other jutted out over the heaving sea. As the captain's brother manned the davit motor, the cousin slipped hooks under the coffin's four brass handles.

The engine revved and the davits took the strain. The great coffin lifted off the deck. The winchman held it at a height of 3 feet and the cousin manoeuvred the oaken casket onto the plank. He pointed it headfirst towards the sea and nodded. The winchman let it down so it came to rest directly above the supporting rail. He slackened off and the coffin creaked into position, half in and half out of the trawler. While the cousin held it steady, the winchman descended, cleared away the shackles and helped lift the inboard edge of the planks to the horizontal. There was little weight on them now, for the coffin was evenly balanced. One of the men looked to Pound for guidance and he summoned the chaplain and the Armitages from their shelter.

The six people stood in silence under the lower clouds, occasionally dusted by a misty spray blown from the crest of a passing wave, steadying themselves against the heave and pitch of the deck. To be fair to him, the chaplain kept it as short as decently possible, as well he might, for his white hair and surplice flayed about him in the breeze. Norman Armitage was also bare-headed, looking sick as a parrot and chilled to the bone. What he thought of his late relative, now lying a few feet from him encased in layers of camphor, lead and oak, could only be surmised. Of Mrs. Armitage nothing could be seen between fur coat, fur hat and woollen scarf save a pointed, freezing nose.

Martin Pound stared at the sky as the priest droned on. A single gull wheeled on the wind, impervious to wet, cold, and nausea, unknowing of taxes, wills and relatives, self-sufficient in its aerodynamic perfection, independent,

free. The solicitor looked back at the coffin and beyond it
the ocean. Not bad, he thought, if you are sentimental
about such things. Personally he had never been caring
about what happened to him after death, and had not
known that Hanson had been so concerned. But if you did
care, not a bad place to lie. He saw the oak beaded with
spray that could not enter. Well, they'll never disturb you
here, Timothy old friend, he thought.

". . . commend this our brother Timothy John Hanson
to Thy everlasting care, through Jesus Christ, Our Lord,
Amen."

With a start Pound realized it was over. The chaplain
was looking at him expectantly. He nodded to the Armitages. One went round each of the fishermen holding the
planks steady and placed a hand on the rear of the coffin.
Pound nodded to the men. Slowly they eased their end of
the planks upwards. The other end dipped to the sea. At
last the coffin moved. Both Armitages gave a shove. It
scraped once, then slid fast off the other end. The boat
rocked. The coffin hit the side of a wave with more of a
thud than a splash. And it was gone. Instantly. Pound
caught the eye of the skipper in the wheelhouse above.
The man raised a hand and pointed back towards the way
they had come. Pound nodded again. The engine note
rose. The large plank was already inboard and stowed.
The Armitages and the chaplain were hurrying for cover.
The wind was rising.

It was almost dark when they rounded the corner of
the mole at Brixham and the first lights were flickering in
the houses behind the quay. The chaplain had his own
small car parked nearby and was soon gone. Pound
settled with the skipper, who was happy to make as much
in an afternoon as in a week after mackerel. The undertaker's men waited with the limousine and a worse-for-
wear Tarquin Armitage. Pound elected to let them have

the car. He preferred to return to London by train and keep his own company.

"You'll get on with the calculation of the estate immediately," insisted Mrs. Armitage shrilly. "And the filing of probate. We've had enough of all this play-acting."

"You may be confident I shall waste no time," said Pound coldly. "I shall be in touch." He raised his hat and walked towards the station. It would not, he surmised, be a long business. He knew already the extent and details of Timothy Hanson's estate. It was bound to be in perfect order. Hanson had been such a very careful man.

It was not until mid-November that Mr. Pound felt able to communicate with the Armitages again. Although as sole beneficiary it was only Mrs. Armitage who was invited to his office off Gray's Inn Road, she turned up with husband and son none the less.

"I find myself in something of a quandary," he told her.

"What about?"

"Your late brother's estate, Mrs. Armitage. Let me explain. As Mr. Hanson's solicitor, I already knew the extent and location of the various assets comprising his estate, so I was able to examine each of them without delay."

"What are they?" she asked brusquely.

Pound refused to be hurried or harried. "In effect he had seven major areas that constituted his estate. Together they would account for ninety-nine per cent of what he owned. First there was the rare and precious coin dealership in the City. You may know it was a wholly-owned private company with himself as sole proprietor. He founded and built it up himself. He also owned, through the company, the building in which it is situated.

He bought this, with a mortgage, shortly after the war when prices were low. The mortgage was long since paid off; the company owned the freehold and he owned the company."

"What value would all this have?" asked Armitage senior.

"No problem there," said Pound. "With the building, the dealership, the stock, the goodwill and the unexpired portions of the leases of the other three tenant companies in the building, exactly one and a quarter million pounds."

Armitage junior whistled through his teeth and grinned.

"How do you know so exactly?" asked Armitage.

"Because he sold it for that sum."

"He what . . . ?"

"Three months before he died, after brief negotiations, he sold the company lock, stock and barrel to a rich Dutch dealer who had wanted it for years. The sum paid was what I have mentioned."

"But he was working there almost until he died," objected Mrs. Armitage. "Who else knew about this?"

"No one," said Pound. "Not even the staff. In the sale deal the conveyancing of the building was performed by a provincial lawyer who quite properly said no more about it. The remaining part of the sale was a private treaty between him and the Dutch purchaser. There were conditions. The staff of five keep their jobs; and he personally was to remain on as sole manager until the end of this year or his death, whichever should be the sooner. Of course, the buyer thought this was a mere formality."

"You have seen this man?" asked Mrs. Armitage.

"Mr. de Jong? Yes, a reputable Amsterdam dealer in coins. And I have seen the paperwork. It is all perfectly in order, absolutely legal."

"So what did he do with the money?" asked Armitage senior.

"He banked it."

"Well, then, no problem," said the son.

"His next asset was his manor in Kent, a lovely property, set in twenty acres of parkland. Last June he took out a ninety-five per cent mortgage on the property. At the time of his death he had only paid off one quarterly instalment. On his death the building society became a primary creditor and now has taken possession of the title deeds. Again, perfectly legal and proper."

"How much did he get for it, the manor?" asked Mrs. Armitage.

"Two hundred and ten thousand pounds," said Pound.

"Which he banked?"

"Yes. Then there was his apartment in Mayfair. He sold this by private treaty about the same time, employing yet another lawyer for the deed of sale, for a hundred and fifty thousand. This too was banked."

"That makes three assets. What else?" demanded the son.

"Apart from the three properties he had a valuable private coin collection. This was sold piecemeal, through the company, for just over half a million pounds, over a period of several months. But the invoices were kept quite separate and were found in his safe at the manor house. Perfectly legitimate and every sale carefully noted. He banked each sum of money following each sale. His broker, on instruction, realized his entire portfolio of stocks and shares before the first day of August. Last but one, there was his Rolls Royce. He sold it for forty-eight thousand and leased another one instead. The leasing company has repossessed this vehicle. Finally he had various deposit accounts in various banks. His total estate as I have been able to trace it, and I am convinced there is nothing missing, amounts to a shade over three million pounds."

"You mean," said Armitage senior, "that before he died he called in and realized every single asset he possessed, converted it to cash and banked it, without telling a soul or raising any suspicions in those who knew him or worked for him?"

"I couldn't have put it better myself," conceded Pound.

"Well, we wouldn't have wanted all that junk anyway," said Armitage junior. "We'd have wanted it realized. So he spent his last months doing your job for you. Tot it all up, settle the debts, assess the revenue and let's have the money."

"I'm afraid I can't," said Mr. Pound.

"Why not?" There was a shrill edge of anger in Mrs. Armitage's tone.

"The money he deposited for all these assets . . ."

"What about it?"

"He withdrew it?"

"He *what* . . . ?"

"He put it in. And he took it all back out again. From a score of banks, in tranches, over a period of many weeks. But he got it out all right. In cash."

"You can't withdraw three million pounds in cash," said Armitage senior in disbelief.

"Oh, yes, you can," said Pound mildly. "Not all at once of course, but in sums up to fifty thousand pounds from major banks, with prior notice. Quite a lot of businesses operate with large floats of cash. Casinos, betting shops for example. And dealers in the second-hand market of almost anything . . ."

He was cut off by the growing hubbub. Mrs. Armitage was pounding the table with a plump fist; her son was on his feet waving a forefinger down the table; her husband was seeking to adopt the posture of a judge about to de-

liver a particularly severe sentence. They were all shouting at once.

"He couldn't get away with this . . . he must have put
it somewhere . . . you had just better find it . . . you two
were in this together . . ."

It was the last remark that finally snapped Martin
Pound's patience.

"*Silence* . . ." he roared, and the outburst was so unexpected that the three fell silent. Pound pointed a finger
directly at young Armitage. "You, sir, will retract that last
remark immediately. Do I make myself plain?"

Armitage junior shuffled in his seat. He glanced at his
parents who were glaring at him. "Sorry," he said.

"Now," resumed Pound, "this particular ploy has been
used before, usually to avoid payment of taxes. I am surprised at Timothy Hanson. It seldom ever works. One
may withdraw a large amount of cash, but disposing of it
is entirely a different matter. He might have banked it on
deposit with a foreign bank, but knowing he was going to
die, this does not make sense. He had no desire to enrich
already rich bankers. No, he must have put it somewhere,
or bought something with it. It may take time, but the
result is always the same. If it has been deposited, it will
be found. If some other asset has been acquired, that too
will be traced. Apart from anything else, there are capital
gains tax and estate duties payable on the sales of assets
and on the estate itself. So the Inland Revenue will wish
to be informed."

"What can you do personally?" asked Armitage senior
at last.

"So far I have contacted every major bank and merchant bank in the United Kingdom, empowered as I am
by the terms of his own will. Everything is computerized
nowadays. But no deposit at all in the name of Hanson
has turned up. Also I have advertised in the nation's ma-

jor newspapers for information but there has been no response. I have been to visit his former chauffeur and
valet, Mr. Richards, now retired to South Wales, but he
cannot help. No large quantities—and believe me they
would have to be *very* large quantities and volumes—of
notes has he seen anywhere. Now, the question is: what
more would you wish me to do now?"

There was silence as the three of them pondered the issue.

Privately, Martin Pound was saddened by what his
friend had evidently tried to do. How could you think to
get away with it? he asked the departed spirit. Had you so
little respect for the Inland Revenue? It was never these
greedy, shallow people you had to fear, Timothy. It was
always the tax men. They are inexorable, untiring. They
never stop. They never run out of funds. However well
hidden it is, they will, when we have given up and their
turn comes, seek it. So long as they do not know where it
is, they will go on and on with the hunt, and until they
know, they will never, never cease. Only when they do
know, even if it is outside Britain and beyond their juris-
diction, will they close the file.

"Couldn't you go on looking?" asked Armitage senior
with a degree more courtesy than he had yet shown.

"For a while, yes," agreed Pound. "But I have done
my best. I have a practice to run. I cannot devote my
whole time to the search."

"What do you advise?" asked Armitage.

"There is always the Inland Revenue," said Pound
mildly. "Sooner or later, and probably sooner, I shall
have to inform them of what has happened."

"You think they will trace it?" asked Mrs. Armitage
eagerly. "After all, they are beneficiaries too, in a sense."

"I am sure they will," said Pound. "They will want

their cut. And they have all the resources of the state at their disposal."

"How long would they take?" asked Armitage.

"Ah," said Pound, "that's another matter. My experience is that they are usually in no hurry. Like the mills of God, they grind slowly."

"Months?" asked Armitage junior.

"More likely years. They will never call off the hunt. But they will not hurry."

"We can't wait that long," shrilled Mrs. Armitage. Her social take-off was beginning to look like a cold start. "There must be a quicker way."

"Hey, what about a private detective?" suggested Armitage junior.

"Could you employ a private detective?" asked Mrs. Armitage.

"I prefer the term private inquiry agent," said Pound. "So do they. Yes, it is possible. I have in the past had occasion to use a very respected such agent in tracing missing beneficiaries. Now it appears the beneficiaries are present but the estate is missing. Still . . ."

"Well, then get on to him," snapped Mrs. Armitage. "Tell him to find where the damned man put all his money."

Greed, thought Pound. If only Hanson could have guessed how greedy they would turn out to be.

"Very well. There is however the question of his fee. I have to tell you that of the five thousand pounds that was allocated for all expenses, rather little remains. The outgoings have been heavier than usual . . . And his services are not inexpensive. But then, he *is* the best . . ."

Mrs. Armitage looked at her husband. "Norman."

Armitage senior swallowed hard. He had mental images of his car and the planned summer holiday being forfeit. He nodded. "I'll . . . er . . . take care of his fees when the remaining money from the five thousand pounds is exhausted," he said.

"Very well, then," said Pound rising. "I shall engage the services of Mr. Eustace Miller and him alone. I have no doubt he will trace the missing fortune. He has never failed me yet."

With that he showed them out and retired to his office to ring Eustace Miller, private inquiry agent.

For four weeks there was silence from Mr. Miller, but not from the Armitages, who bombarded Martin Pound with their ceaseless clamours for a quick location of the missing fortune to which they were entitled. At last Miller reported to Martin Pound to say that he had reached a watershed in his inquiries and felt he should report his progress to date.

Pound was by this time almost as curious as the Armitages, so he arranged a meeting at his office.

If the Armitage family had expected to confront a figure in the mould of Philip Marlowe or any other popular conception of a tough private eye, they were doomed to disappointment. Eustace Miller was short, round and benign, with tufts of white hair round an otherwise bald head, and half-moon glasses. He wore a sober suit with a gold watch chain across the waistcoat, and he rose to his not very great height to present his report.

"I began this inquiry," he said, surveying them all in turn over the top of his half-moons, "with three assumptions in mind. One was that the late Mr. Hanson had gone through this extraordinary performance in the months before he died with complete deliberation and a firm purpose. Secondly, I believed, and still do, that Mr. Hanson's purpose was to deny his apparent inheritors and the Commissioners of Inland Revenue any access to his fortune after his death . . ."

"The old bastard," snapped Armitage junior.

"He need not have left it to you in the first place," interposed Pound mildly. "Do proceed, Mr. Miller."

"Thank you. Thirdly, I presumed that Mr. Hanson had neither burned the money nor undertaken the considerable risks of trying to smuggle it abroad, bearing in mind the enormous volume that such a large sum would occupy in cash form. In short, I came to the view that he had bought something with it."

"Gold? Diamonds?" asked Armitage senior.

"No, I examined all these possibilities and after intensive inquiries ruled them out. Then I found myself thinking of another kind of commodity of great value but relatively small bulk. I consulted the firm of Johnson Matthey, dealers in precious metals. And I found it."

"The money?" chorused the three Armitages together.

"The answer," said Miller. Enjoying his moment he drew from his attaché case a wad of pieces of paper. "These constitute sales documents for the purchase by Mr. Hanson from Johnson Matthey of two hundred and fifty fifty-ounce ingots of high-grade 99.95 per cent pure platinum."

There was a stunned silence round the table.

"It was not, frankly, a very clever ruse," said Mr. Miller with some regret. "The buyer may have destroyed all record of his purchases, but obviously the vendor would not destroy *his* records of the sales. And here they are."

"Why platinum?" queried Pound faintly.

"That's interesting. Under the present Labour government you need a licence to purchase and hold gold. Diamonds are instantly identifiable within the trade and not nearly as easy to dispose of as one would gather from some ill-informed thriller fiction. Platinum does not need a licence, is presently about the same value as gold, and apart from rhodium is one of the most valuable metals in the world. When he bought the metal he paid the free market price of five hundred American dollars per fine ounce."

"How much did he spend?" asked Mrs. Armitage.

"Nigh on the whole three million pounds he had secured for all his worldly goods," said Miller. "In U.S. dollars—and this market is always calculated in U.S. dollars —six and a quarter million dollars; twelve and a half thousand ounces in all. Or, as I said, two hundred and fifty ingots each of fifty fine ounces weight."

"Where did he take them all?" Armitage senior demanded.

"To his manor in Kent," said Miller. He was enjoying his moment and was aware with anticipatory pleasure that he had more to reveal.

"But I have been there," protested Pound.

"With a lawyer's eye Mine is that of an investigator," said Miller. "And I knew what I was looking for. So I did not start with the house, but with the outbuildings. Are you aware that Mr. Hanson had an extremely well-equipped carpentry workshop in a former barn behind the stables?"

"Certainly," said Pound. "It was his hobby."

"Precisely," said Miller. "And it was here I concentrated my efforts. The place had been scrupulously cleaned; vacuum-cleaned."

"Possibly by Richards, the chauffeur/handyman," said Pound.

"Possibly, but probably not. Despite the cleaning, I observed stains on the floorboards and had some splinters analysed. Diesel fuel. Pursuing a hunch, I thought of some kind of machine, an engine perhaps. It's a small enough market and I found the answer within a week.

Last May Mr. Hanson bought a powerful diesel-fuelled electric generator and installed it in his workshop. He disposed of it for scrap just before he died."

"To operate his power tools, no doubt," said Pound.

"No, the ring main was strong enough for that. To operate something else. Something that needed enormous power. In another week I had traced that too. A small, modern and very efficient furnace. It too is long gone, and I have no doubt the ladles, asbestos gloves and tongs have been dumped at the bottom of some lake or river. But, I think I may say I was a little more thorough than Mr. Hanson. Between two floorboards, jammed out of sight and covered by compacted sawdust, no doubt just where it had fallen during his operations, I discovered this."

It was his *pièce de résistance* and he drew out the moment. From his case he took a white tissue and slowly unwrapped it. From inside he held up a thin sliver of congealed metal that glittered in the light, the sort of sliver that must have dribbled down the side of a ladle, coagulated and dropped off. Miller waited while all stared at it.

"I have had it analysed of course. It is high-grade 99.95 per cent pure platinum."

"You have traced the rest?" whispered Mrs. Armitage.

"Not yet, madam, but I shall. Have no fear. You see Mr. Hanson made one great mistake in selecting platinum. It has one property that he must have underestimated and yet which is quite unique. Its weight. Now at least we know what we are looking for. A wooden crate of some kind, apparently innocent to look at, but—and this is the point—weighing just under half a ton . . ."

Mrs. Armitage threw back her head and uttered a strange raucous cry like the howl of a wounded animal. Miller jumped a foot. Mr. Armitage dropped his head forward into his hands. Tarquin Armitage rose to his feet, his spotty complexion brick red with rage, and screamed, "That bloody bastard."

Martin Pound stared unbelievingly at the startled private investigator. "Good Lord," he said. "Oh, my goodness me. He actually took it with him."

Two days later Mr. Pound informed the Inland Revenue of the full facts of the case. They checked the facts and, albeit with an ill grace, declined to pursue.

Barney Smee walked happily and with a brisk pace towards his bank, confident he would just get there before they closed for the Christmas holiday. The reason for his pleasure was tucked inside his breast pocket: a cheque for a quite substantial sum, but only the last of a series of such cheques that over the past few months had ensured him a much higher income than he had ever managed to earn in twenty years in the risky business of dealing in scrap metals for the jewellery industry.

He had been right, he congratulated himself, to take the risk, and it had undeniably been a high one. Still, everyone was in the tax-dodging business nowadays and who was he to condemn the source of his good fortune simply because the man had wished to deal only in cash? Barney Smee had no difficulty in understanding the silver-haired investor who called himself Richards and had a driving licence to prove it. The man evidently had bought his 50-ounce ingots years before, when they were cheap. To have sold them on the open market through Johnson Matthey would beyond doubt have secured him a higher price, but at what cost in capital gains tax? Only he could have known and Barney Smee was not one to probe.

In any case, the whole trade was rife with cash deals. The ingots had been genuine; they even bore the original assay mark of Johnson Matthey, from whom they had once come. Only the serial number had been blazed out. That had cost the old man a lot, because without the serial number Smee could not offer him anything near fair market price. He could only offer scrap price, or producer's price, about 440 U.S. dollars an ounce. But then, the serial numbers would have identified the owner to the Inland Revenue, so maybe the old man knew his onions after all.

Barney Smee had got rid of all fifty eventually, through the trade, and had made a cool ten dollars an ounce for himself. The cheque in his pocket was for the sale of the last of the deal, the ultimate two ingots. He was blissfully unaware that in other parts of Britain another four like himself had also spent the autumn filtering fifty 50-ounce ingots each back into the market through the second-hand trade, and had bought them for cash from a silver-haired seller. He swung out of the side street and into the Old Kent Road. As he did so he collided with a man descending from a taxi. Both men apologized to each other and wished each other a merry Christmas. Barney Smee passed on his contented way.

The other man, a solicitor from Guernsey, peered up at the building where he had been dropped, adjusted his hat and made for the entrance. Ten minutes later he was closeted with a somewhat mystified Mother Superior.

"May I ask, Mother Superior, whether Saint Benedict's Orphanage qualifies as a registered charity under the Charities Act?"

"Yes," said the Mother Superior. "It does."

"Good," said the lawyer. "Then no infringement has taken place and there will be no application in your case of the capital transfer tax."

"The what?" she asked.

"Better known as the 'gift tax,'" said the lawyer with a smile. "I am happy to tell you that a donor whose identity

I cannot reveal, under the rules of confidentiality govern-
ing business between client and lawyer, has seen fit to donate a substantial sum to your establishment."

He waited for a reaction, but the grey-haired old nun
was staring at him in bewilderment.

"My client, whose name you will never know, instructed me quite specifically to present myself to you here on
this day, Christmas Eve, and present you with this envelope."

He took an envelope of thick cartridge paper from his
briefcase and held it out to the Mother Superior. She took
it but made no move to open it.

"I understand it contains a certified bank cheque, purchased from a reputable merchant bank incorporated in
Guernsey, drawn on that bank and made out in favour of
Saint Benedict's Orphanage. I have not seen the contents,
but those were my instructions."

"No gift tax?" she queried, holding the envelope, irresolute. Charitable donations were few and far between,
and usually hard fought for.

"In the Channel Islands we have a different fiscal system to that of the United Kingdom mainland," said the
lawyer patiently. "We have no capital transfer tax. We
also practise bank confidentiality. A donation within
Guernsey or the Islands attracts no tax. If the recipient is
domiciled or resident within the UK mainland, then he or
she would be liable under mainland tax law. Unless already exempted. Such as by the Charities Act. And now,
if you will sign a receipt for one envelope, contents unknown, I will have discharged my duty. My fee is already
settled and I would like to get home to my family."

Two minutes later the Mother Superior was alone.
Slowly she ran a letter knife along the envelope and ex-
tracted the contents. It was a single certified cheque.
When she saw the figure on it she scrabbled for her ro-

sary and began telling it rapidly. When she had regained some of her composure she went to the prie-dieu against the wall and knelt for half an hour in prayer.

Back at her desk, still feeling weak, she stared again at the cheque for over two and a half million pounds. Who in the world ever had such money? She tried to think what she should do with so much. An endowment, she thought. A trust fund, perhaps. There was enough to endow the orphanage for ever. Certainly enough to fulfil the ambition of her lifetime: to get the orphanage out of the slums of London and establish it in the fresh air of the open countryside. She could double the number of children. She could . . .

Too many thoughts flooding in, and one trying to get to the front. What was it? Yes, the Sunday newspaper the week before last. Something had caught her eye, caused a pang of longing. That was it, that was where they would go. And enough money in her hands to buy it and endow it for always. A dream come true. An advert in the property columns. For sale, a manor house in Kent with twenty acres of parkland . . .

Sharp Practice

❧

Judge Comyn settled himself comfortably into the corner seat of his first-class compartment, unfolded his day's copy of the *Irish Times*, glanced at the headlines, and laid it on his lap.

There would be plenty of time for the newspaper during the slow four-hour trundle down to Tralee. He gazed idly out of the window at the bustle of Kingsbridge station in the last minutes before the departure of the Dublin–Tralee locomotive which would haul him sedately to his duties in the principal township of County Kerry. He hoped vaguely he would have the compartment to himself so that he could deal with his paperwork.

It was not to be. Hardly had the thought crossed his mind when the compartment door opened and someone stepped in. He forbore to look. The door rolled shut and the newcomer tossed a handgrip onto the luggage rack. Then the man sat down opposite him, across the gleaming walnut table.

Judge Comyn gave him a glance. His companion was a small, wispy man, with a puckish quiff of sandy hair standing up from his forehead and a pair of the saddest, most apologetic brown eyes. His suit was of a whiskery thornproof with a matching weskit and knitted tie. The

266

judge assessed him as someone associated with horses, or a clerk perhaps, and resumed his gaze out of the window.

He heard the call of the guard outside to the driver of the old steam engine puffing away somewhere down the line, and then the shrill blast of the guard's whistle. Even as the engine emitted its first great chuff and the carriage began to lurch forward, a large running figure dressed entirely in black scurried past the window. The judge heard the crash of the carriage door opening a few feet away and the thud of a body landing in the corridor. Seconds later, to the accompaniment of a wheezing and puffing, the black figure appeared in the compartment's doorway and subsided with relief into the far corner.

Judge Comyn glanced again. The newcomer was a florid-faced priest. The judge looked again out of the window; he did not wish to start a conversation, having been schooled in England.

"By the saints, ye nearly didn't make it, Father," he heard the wispy one say.

There was more puffing from the man of the cloth. "It was a sight too close for comfort, my son," the priest replied.

After that they mercifully lapsed into silence. Judge Comyn observed Kingsbridge station slide out of sight, to be replaced by the unedifying rows of smoke-grimed houses that in those days made up the western suburbs of Dublin. The loco of the Great Southern Railway Company took the strain and the clickety-clack tempo of the wheels over the rails increased. Judge Comyn picked up his paper.

The headline and leading news item concerned the premier, Eamon de Valera, who the previous day in the Dail had given his full support to his agriculture minister in the matter of the price of potatoes. Far down at the bottom was a two-inch mention that a certain Mr. Hitler had taken over Austria. The editor was a man who had his priorities right, thought Judge Comyn. There was little more to interest him in the paper, and after five minutes he folded it, took a batch of legal papers from his briefcase and began to peruse them. The green fields of Kildare slid by the windows soon after they cleared the city of Dublin.

"Sir," said a timid voice from opposite him. Oh dear, he thought, he wants to talk. He raised his gaze to the pleading spaniel eyes of the man opposite.

"Would you mind if I used a part of the table?" asked the man.

"Not at all," said the judge.

"Thank you sir," said the man, with a detectable brogue from the southwest of the country.

The judge resumed his study of the papers relating to the settlement of a complex civil issue he would have to adjudicate on his return to Dublin from Tralee. The visit to Kerry as circuit court judge to preside over the quarterly hearings there would, he trusted, offer no such complexities. These rural circuit courts, in his experience, offered only the simplest of issues to be decided by local juries who as often as not produced verdicts of bewildering illogicality.

He did not bother to look up when the wispy man produced a pack of none-too-clean playing cards from his pocket and proceeded to set some of them out in columns to play patience. His attention was only drawn some seconds later to a clucking sound. He looked up again.

The wispy man had his tongue between his teeth in an effort of great concentration—this was producing the clucking sound—and was staring at the exposed cards at the foot of each column. Judge Comyn observed at a glance that a red nine had not been placed upon a black ten, even though both cards were clearly visible. The wispy man, failing to see the match, began to deal three more cards. Judge Comyn choked back his irritation and returned to his papers. Nothing to do with me, he told himself.

But there is something mesmeric about a man playing patience, and never more so than when he is playing it badly. Within five minutes the judge's concentration had been completely broken in the matter of the civil lawsuit, and he was staring at the exposed cards. Finally he could bear it no longer. There was an empty column on the right, yet an exposed king on column three that ought to go into the vacant space. He coughed. The wispy one looked up in alarm.

"The king," said the judge gently, "it should go up into the space."

The cardplayer looked down, spotted the opportunity and moved the king. The card now able to be turned over proved to be a queen, and she went to the king. Before he had finished he had legitimately made seven moves. The column that began with the king now ended with a ten.

"And the red nine," said the judge. "It can go across now."

The red nine and its dependent six cards moved over to the nine. Another card could be exposed; an ace, which went up above the game.

"I do believe you will get it out," said the judge.

"Ah, not me, sir," said the wispy man, shaking his head with its sad spaniel eyes. "Sure I've never got one out yet in all me life."

"Play on, play on," said Judge Comyn with rising interest. With his help the game did indeed come out. The wispy man gazed at the resolved puzzle in wonderment.

"There you are, you see; you've done it," said the judge.

"Ah, but not without your honour's help," said the sad-eyed one. "It's a fine mind ye have for the cards, sir."

Judge Comyn wondered if the cardplayer could possibly know he was a judge, but concluded the man was simply using a common form of address in Ireland in those days towards one worthy of some respect.

Even the priest had laid down his collection of the sermons of the late, great Cardinal Newman and was looking at the cards.

"Oh," said the judge, who played a little bridge and poker with his cronies at the Kildare Street Club, "not really."

Privately he was rather proud of his theory that a good legal mind, with its trained observation, practised powers of deduction and keen memory, could always play a good game of cards.

The wispy man ceased playing and began idly dealing five-card hands, which he then examined before returning the cards to the pack. Finally he put the deck down. He sighed.

"It's a long way to Tralee," he said wistfully.

With hindsight Judge Comyn never could recall who exactly had mentioned the word poker, but he suspected it might have been himself. Anyway, he took over the pack and dealt a few hands for himself. One of them, he was pleased to notice, was a full house, jacks on tens.

With a half-smile, as if amazed at his boldness, the wispy man took up one hand and held it in front of him.

"I will bet you, sir, one imaginary penny that you cannot deal yourself a better hand than this one."

"Done," said the judge, and dealt a second hand, which he held up in front of him. It was not a full house, but contained a pair of nines.

"Ready?" asked Judge Comyn. The wispy man

nodded. They put their cards down. The wispy man had three fives.

"Ah," said the judge, "but I did not draw any fresh cards, as was my right. Again, my dear fellow."

They did it again. This time the wispy man drew three fresh cards, the judge two. The judge had the better hand.

"I win my imaginary penny back," said the judge.

"That you do, sir," said the other. "That was a fine hand. You have the knack of the cards. I have seen it, though not having it myself. Yes, sir. The knack it is."

"Nothing but clear deduction and the calculated risk," corrected Judge Comyn.

At this point they exchanged names, only surnames as was the practice in those days. The judge omitted his title, giving his name simply as Comyn, and the other revealed he was O'Connor. Five minutes later, between Sallins and Kildare, they attempted a little friendly poker. Five-card draw seemed the appropriate form and went without saying. There was, of course, no money involved.

"The trouble is," said O'Connor after the third hand, "I cannot remember who has wagered what. Your honour has his fine memory to help him."

"I have it," said Judge Comyn, and triumphantly foraged in his briefcase for a large box of matches. He enjoyed a cigar after his breakfast and another after dinner, and would never have used a petrol lighter on a good fourpenny Havana.

" 'Tis the very thing," said O'Connor in wonderment as the judge dealt out twenty matchsticks each.

They played a dozen hands, with some enjoyment, and honours were about even. But it is hard to play two-handed poker, for if one party, having a poor hand, wants to "fold," the other party is finished also. Just past Kildare town O'Connor asked the priest, "Father, would you not care to join us?"

"Oh, I fear not," said the rubicund priest with a laugh, "for I am no hand with the cards. Though," he added, "I did once play a little whist with the lads in the seminary."

"It's the same principle, Father," said the judge. "Once learned, never forgotten. You are simply dealt a hand of five cards; you can draw fresh ones up to five if you are not happy with the deal. Then you assess whether the hand you hold is good or bad. If it is good, you wager it is better than ours, if not, you decline to wager, and fold your hand."

"I'm not certain about wagering," said the priest doubtfully.

" 'Tis only matchsticks, Father," said O'Connor.

"Does one try to take tricks?" asked the priest.

O'Connor raised his eyebrows. Judge Comyn laughed a trifle patronizingly.

"No taking of tricks," he said. "The hand you hold is evaluated according to a precise scale of values. Look . . ."

He rummaged in his briefcase and produced a sheet of white lined paper. From his inner pocket a rolled-gold propelling pencil. He began to write on the sheet. The priest peered to see.

"Top of the list," said the judge, "is the royal flush. That means five cards, all in the same suit, all in sequence and beginning with the ace. Since they must be in sequence that means, of course, that the others must be king, queen, jack and ten."

"I suppose so," said the priest warily.

"Then comes four of a kind," said the judge, writing the words in below the royal flush. "That means exactly what it says. Four aces, four kings, four queens and so forth down to four twos. Never mind the fifth card. And, of course, four aces is better than four kings or anything else. All right?"

The priest nodded.

"Then comes the full house," said O'Connor.

"Not quite," corrected Judge Comyn. "The straight flush comes next, my friend."

O'Connor clapped his forehead in the manner of one who admits he is a fool. "Of course, that's true," he said. "You see, Father, the straight flush is like the royal, save only that it is not led off by an ace. But the five cards must be of the same suit and in sequence."

The judge wrote this description under the words "four of a kind" on the sheet of paper.

"Now comes Mr. O'Connor's full house, which means three of a kind and two of another kind, making up the full five cards. If the three cards are tens and the other two queens, this is called a full house, tens on queens."

The priest nodded again.

The judge went down the list, explaining each hand, through "flush," "straight," "threes," "two pairs," "one pair" and "ace high."

"Now," he said when he had finished, "obviously one pair, or ace high, or a mixed hand, which is called a bag of nails, would be so poor you really wouldn't wager on them."

The father gazed at the list. "Could I refer to this?" he asked.

"Of course," said Judge Comyn, "keep it by you, Father, by all means."

"Well, seeing as it's only for matchsticks . . ." said the priest, and was dealt in. Friendly games of chance, after all, are not a sin. Not for matchsticks. They divided the sticks into three even piles and began to play.

For the first two hands the priest folded early, watching the others bid. The judge won four matchsticks. On the third hand the priest's face lit up.

"Is that not good?" he asked, displaying his hand to the

other two. It *was* good; a full house, jacks on kings. The judge folded his own hand in exasperation.

"Yes, it's very good, Father," said O'Connor patiently, "but you are not supposed to show us, don't you see? For if we know what you have, we will not wager anything if our hand is not as good as yours. Your own hand should be . . . well now, like the confessional."

That made sense to the priest. "Like the confessional," he repeated. "Yes, I see. Not a word to anyone, eh?"

He apologized and they started again. For sixty minutes up to Thurles they played fifteen hands, and the judge's pile of matchsticks mounted. The priest was almost cleaned out and sad-eyed O'Connor had only half his pile left. He made too many lapses; the good father seemed half at sea; only the judge played hard, calculating poker, assessing the options and odds with his legally trained mind. The game was a vindication of his theory of mind over luck. Just after Thurles O'Connor's mind seemed to wander. The judge had to call him to the game twice.

"I fear it's not very interesting, playing with matchsticks," he confessed after the second time. "Shall we not end it here?"

"Oh, I confess I'm rather enjoying it," said the judge. Most winners enjoy the game.

"Or we could make it more interesting," said O'Connor apologetically. "I'm not by nature a betting man, but a few shillings would do no harm."

"If you wish," said the judge, "though I observe that you have lost a few matches."

"Ah, your honour, my luck must change soon," said O'Connor with his elfin smile.

"Then I must retire," said the priest with finality. "For I fear I have but three pounds in my purse, and that to last me through my holiday with my mother at Dingle."

"But, Father," said O'Connor, "without you we could not play. And a few shillings . . ."

"Even a few shillings, my son, are too much for me," said the priest. "The Holy Mother Church is no place for men who want to have money jingling in their pockets."

"Wait," said the judge, "I have it. You and I, O'Connor, will divide the matchsticks between us. We will each then lend the good Father an equal amount of sticks, the sticks by now having a value. If he loses, we will not claim our debt. If he wins, he will repay us the sticks we loaned him, and benefit by the balance."

" 'Tis a genius you are, your honour," said O'Connor in wonderment.

"But I could not gamble for money," protested the priest.

There was a gloomy silence for a while.

"Unless any winnings went to a Church charity?" suggested O'Connor. "Surely the Lord would not object to that?"

"It's the Bishop who would object," said the priest, "and I may well meet him first. Still . . . there *is* the orphanage at Dingle. My mother prepares the meals there, and the poor wains are fierce cold in winter, with the price of turf being what it is . . ."

"A donation," cried the judge in triumph. He turned to his bewildered companions. "Anything the father wins, over and above the stake we lend him, is our joint donation to the orphanage. What do you say?"

"I suppose even our Bishop could not object to a donation to the orphanage . . ." said the priest.

"And the donation will be our gift in return for your company at a game of cards," said O'Connor. " 'Tis perfect."

The priest agreed and they started again. The judge and O'Connor split the sticks into two piles. O'Connor pointed out that with under fifty sticks they might run out of tokens. Judge Comyn solved that one too. They broke the sticks in halves; those halves with a sulphur head were worth twice those without.

O'Connor averred that he was carrying his personal holiday money of over £30 on him, and to this limit would play the game. There was no question of either party refusing Comyn's cheque; he was so obviously a gentleman.

This done, they loaned the priest ten matches with heads and four without, half from each of them.

"Now," said Judge Comyn as he shuffled the cards, "what about the stakes?"

O'Connor held up half a matchstick without any head on it.

"Ten shillings?" he said. That shook the judge a bit. The forty matchsticks he had emptied from his box were now in eighty halves, representing £60 sterling, a sizable sum in 1938. The priest had £12 in front of him, the other two men £24 each at those values. He heard the priest sigh.

"In for a penny, in for a pound. Lord help me," said the priest.

The judge nodded abruptly. He need not have worried. He took the first two hands and nearly £10 with it. In the third hand O'Connor folded early, losing his 10s. playing stake yet again. The priest put down four of his £1 matchsticks. Judge Comyn looked at his hand; he had a full house, jacks on sevens. It had to be better. The priest only had £7 left.

"I'll cover your four pounds, Father," he said pushing his matches to the centre, "and I'll raise you five pounds."

"Oh dear," he said, "I'm nearly out. What can I do?"

"Only one thing," said O'Connor, "if you don't want

Mr. Comyn to raise you again to a sum you cannot cover. Push five pounds forward and ask to see the cards."

"I'll see the cards," said the priest, as if reciting a ritual as he pushed five headed matchsticks forward. The judge put down his full house and waited. The priest laid out four tens. He got his £9 back, plus another £9 from the judge, plus the 30s. table stakes. With his £2 still in hand, he had £21 10s.

In this manner they arrived at Limerick Junction which, as is proper for an Irish railway system, is nowhere near Limerick but just outside Tipperary. Here the train went past the main platform, then backed up to it, since the platform could not be reached on the down line. A few people got on and off, but no one disturbed the game or entered the compartment.

By Charleville the priest had taken £10 off O'Connor, who was looking worried, and the game slowed up. O'Connor tended to fold quickly, and too many hands ended with another player electing to fold as well. Just before Mallow, by agreement, they eliminated all the small cards, keeping sevens and up, and making a thirty-two-card deck. Then the game speeded up again.

By Headford poor O'Connor was down £12 and the judge £20, both to the priest.

"Would it not be a good idea if I paid back now the twelve pounds I started with?" asked the priest.

Both the others agreed it would. They got their £6 loans back. The priest still had £32 to play with. O'Connor continued to play cautiously, only once wagering high and winning £10 back with a full house that beat two pairs and a flush. The lakes of Killarney drifted by the window unadmired.

Out of Farranfore the judge knew he had the hand he had been waiting for. After drawing three cards he gazed in delight at four queens and a seven of clubs in his hand.

O'Connor must have thought he had a good hand too, for he went along when the judge covered the priest's £5 and raised him £5. When the priest responded by covering the £5 and raising £10, O'Connor lost his nerve and folded. Once again he was £12 down on where he had started playing.

The judge bit his thumbnail. Then he covered the priest's £10 and raised him £10.

"Five minutes to Tralee," said the guard, poking his head round the compartment door. The priest stared in dismay at the matchsticks in the centre of the table and at his own small pile representing £12.

"I don't know." he said. "Oh, Lord, I don't know."

"Father." said O'Connor. "you can't raise any more; you'll have to cover it and ask to see."

"I suppose so," said the priest sadly, pushing £10 in matchsticks into the centre of the table and leaving himself with £2. "And I was doing so well. I should have given the orphanage the thirty-two pounds while I had it. And now I have only two pounds for them."

"I'll make it up to five pounds, Father," said Judge Comyn. "There. Four ladies."

O'Connor whistled. The priest looked at the spread-out queens and then at his own hand.

"Are not kings above queens?" he asked in puzzlement.

"They are if you have four of them," said the judge.

The priest laid his cards on the table.

"But I do." he said. And he did. "Lord save us," he breathed, "but I thought all was lost. I thought you must have the royal thing there."

They cleared the cards and matches away as they rolled into Tralee. O'Connor got his cards back. The judge put the broken matches in the ashtray. O'Connor counted out twelve single pound notes from his pocket and handed them over to the priest.

"God bless you, my son," said the priest.

Judge Comyn regretfully got out his cheque book. "Fifty pounds exactly, I believe, Father," he said.

"If you say so," said the priest, "sure and I have forgotten what we even started with."

"I assure you I owe the orphanage fifty pounds," said the judge. He prepared to write. "You said the Dingle Orphanage? Is that what I should write?"

The priest appeared perplexed.

"You know, I do not believe they even have a bank account, so small is the place," said the Father.

"Then I had better make it out to you personally," said the judge. waiting for the name.

"But I do not even have a bank account myself," said the priest in bewilderment. "I have never handled money."

"There is a way round it," said the judge urbanely. He wrote rapidly, tore out the cheque and offered it to the priest. "This is made payable to bearer. The Bank of Ireland in Tralee will cash it and we are just in time. They close in thirty minutes."

"You mean they will give me money at the bank for this?" asked the priest, holding the cheque carefully.

"Certainly," said the judge, "but be careful not to lose it. It is payable to the bearer, so anyone in possession of it would be able to cash it. Well now, O'Connor, Father, it has been a most interesting, albeit expensive trip. I must wish you good day."

"And for me," said O'Connor sadly. "The Lord must have been dealing you the cards, Father. I've seldom seen such a hand. It'll be a lesson to me. No more playing cards on trains, least of all with the Church."

"And I'll see the money is in the most deserving of orphanages before the sun sets," said the priest.

They parted on Tralee station platform and Judge

Comyn proceeded to his hotel. He wished for an early night before the start of the court hearings on the morrow.

The first two cases of the morning were very straightforward, being pleas of guilty for minor offences and he awarded fines in both cases. The empanelled jurors of Tralee sat in enforced idleness.

Judge Comyn had his head bowed over his papers when the third defendant was called. Only the top of his judge's wig was visible to the court below.

"Put up Ronan Quirk O'Connor," boomed the clerk to the court.

There was a scuffling of steps. The judge went on writing.

"You are Ronan Quirk O'Connor?" asked the clerk of the new defendant.

"I am," said a voice.

"Ronan Quirk O'Connor," said the clerk, "you are charged with cheating at cards, contrary to Section 17 of the Gaming Act of 1845. In that you, Ronan Quirk O'Connor, on the 13th day of May of this year, in the County of Kerry, by fraud or unlawful device or ill-practice in playing at, or with, cards, won a sum of money from one Lurgan Keane to yourself. And thereby obtained the said sum of money from the said Lurgan Keane by false pretences. How say you to the charge? Guilty or not guilty?"

During this recitation Judge Comyn laid down his pen with unusual care, stared for a few more seconds at his papers as if wishing he could conduct the entire trial in this manner, and finally raised his eyes.

The wispy little man with the spaniel eyes stared back at him across the court in dumb amazement. Judge Comyn stared at the defendant in equal horror.

"Not guilty," whispered O'Connor.

"One moment," said the judge. The court sat in silence, staring at him as he sat impassive on his bench. Behind the mask of his face, his thoughts were in a turmoil. He could have stopped the case at once, claiming that he had an acquaintance with the defendant.

Then the thought occurred to him that this would have meant a retrial, since the defendant had now been formally charged, with all the extra costs to the taxpayer involved in that procedure. It came down, he told himself, to one question: could he trust himself to conduct the court fairly and well, and to give a true and fair summing up to the jury? He decided that he could.

"Swear in the jury, if you please," he said.

This the clerk did, then inquired of O'Connor if he had legal representation. O'Connor said he did not, and wished to conduct his own defence. Judge Comyn swore to himself. Fairness would now demand that he bend over backwards to take the defendant's part against prosecuting counsel.

This gentleman now rose to present the facts which, he said, were simple enough. On 13 May last, a grocer from Tralee, one Lurgan Keane, had boarded the Dublin to Tralee train in Dublin to return home. He happened perchance to be carrying a quantity of cash upon his person, to wit, £71.

During the course of the journey he had entered into a game of chance with the defendant and another party, using a pack of cards produced by the defendant. So remarkable had been the losses he had incurred that he became suspicious. At Farranfore, one stop before Tralee, he had descended from the train on an excuse, approached a servant of the railway company and asked that the police at Tralee be present upon the platform.

His first witness was a police sergeant of the Tralee

force, a large, solid man who gave evidence of arrest. He swore that, acting on information received, he had been present at Tralee station on 13 May last, when the Dublin train rolled in. There he had been approached by a man he later knew to be Mr. Lurgan Keane, who had pointed out to him the defendant.

He had asked the defendant to accompany him to Tralee police station, which the man did. There he was required to turn out his pockets. Among the contents was a pack of cards which Mr. Keane identified as those that had been used in a game of poker upon the train.

These, he said, had been sent to Dublin for examination and upon receipt of the report from Dublin the accused O'Connor had been charged with the offence.

So far, so clear. The next witness was from the Fraud Squad of the Garda in Dublin. He had evidently been on the train of yesterday, mused the judge, but travelling third class.

The detective constable swore that upon close examination the deck of cards had been seen to be a marked deck. The prosecuting counsel held up a deck of cards and the detective identified it by his own mark. The deck was passed to him. In what way were the cards marked, inquired counsel.

"In two manners, my lord," the detective told the judge. "By what is called 'shading' and 'trimming.' Each of the four suits is indicated on the back of the cards by trimming the edges at different places, on each end of the card so that it does not matter which way up the card is held. In the trimming, the white border between the edge of the pattern and the edge of the card is caused to vary in width. This variation, though very slight, can be observed from across the table, thus indicating to the cheat what suits his opponent is holding. If that is clear?"

"A model of lucidity," said Judge Comyn, staring at O'Connor.

"The high cards, from ace down to ten, were distinguished from each other by shading, that is, using a chemical preparation to cause slight darkening or lightening of tiny areas of the pattern on the backs of the cards. The areas so affected are extremely small, sometimes no larger than the tip of one whorl in the complex pattern. But enough to be spotted by the cardsharp from across the table, because he knows exactly what he is looking for."

"Would it be necessary for the cardsharp to deal dishonestly as well?" asked counsel. He was aware the jury was riveted. It made such a change from stealing horses.

"A crooked deal might be included," conceded the detective from the Fraud Squad, "but it would not be necessary."

"Would it be possible to win against such a player?" asked counsel.

"Quite impossible, sir," the witness told the bench. "The cardsharp would simply decline to wager when he knew his opponent had a better hand, and place high bets when he knew his own was better."

"No further questions," said counsel. For the second time O'Connor declined to cross-examine.

"You have the right to ask the witness any questions you may wish, concerning his evidence," Judge Comyn told the accused.

"Thank you, my lord," said O'Connor, but kept his peace.

Counsel's third, last and star witness was the Tralee grocer, Lurgan Keane, who entered the witness box as a bull to the arena and glared at O'Connor.

Prompted by the prosecuting counsel, he told his story. He had concluded a business deal in Dublin that day, which accounted for the large amount of cash he had been carrying. In the train, he had been inveigled into a game of poker, at which he thought he was a skilled player, and before Farranfore had been relieved of £62. He had become suspicious because, however promising the hand he held, he had always been bettered by another and had lost money.

At Farranfore he had descended from the train, convinced he had been cheated, and had asked for the police to be present at Tralee.

"And I was right," he roared to the jury, "your man was playing with marked cards."

The twelve good men and true nodded solemnly.

This time O'Connor rose, looking sadder than ever and as harmless as a calf in the byre, to cross-examine. Mr. Keane glowered at him.

"You say that I produced the pack of cards?" he asked sorrowfully.

"You did," said Keane.

"In what manner?" asked O'Connor.

Keane looked puzzled. "From your pocket," he said.

"Yes," agreed O'Connor, "from my pocket. But what did I do with the cards?"

Keane thought for a moment. "You began to play patience," he said.

Judge Comyn, who had almost begun to believe in the possibility of the law of remarkable coincidence, got that sinking feeling again.

"And did I speak first to you," asked the accused, "or did you speak first to me?"

The burly grocer looked crestfallen. "I spoke to you," he said, then turning to the jury he added, "but your man was playing so badly I could not help it. There were blacks on reds and reds on blacks that he couldn't see, so I pointed a couple out to him."

"But when it came to the poker," persisted O'Connor, "did I suggest a friendly game of poker or did you?"

"You did," said Keane heatedly, "and you suggested we make it interesting with a little wagering. Wagering indeed. Sixty-two pounds is a lot of money."

The jury nodded again. It was indeed. Enough to keep a working man for almost a year.

"I put it to you," said O'Connor to Keane, "that it was *you* who suggested the poker, and *you* who proposed the wager. Before that we were playing with matchsticks?"

The grocer thought hard. The honesty shone from his face. Something stirred in his memory. He would not lie.

"It may have been me," he conceded, then a new thought came to him. He turned to the jury. "But isn't that the whole skill of it? Isn't that just what the cardsharp does? He *inveigles* his victim into a game."

He was obviously in love with the word "inveigle" which the judge thought was new to his vocabulary. The jurymen nodded. Quite obviously they too would hate to be inveigled.

"One last point," said O'Connor sadly, "when we settled up, how much did you pay me?"

"Sixty-two pounds," said Keane angrily. "Hard-earned money."

"No," said O'Connor from the dock, "how much did you lose to *me*, personally."

The grocer from Tralee thought hard. His face dropped. "Not to you," he said. "Nothing. It was the farmer who won."

"And did I win from him?" asked O'Connor, by now looking on the edge of tears.

"No," said the witness. "You lost about eight pounds."

"No further questions," said O'Connor.

Mr. Keane was about to step down when the judge's voice recalled him. "One moment, Mr. Keane. You say 'the farmer won'? Who exactly was this farmer?"

"The other man in the compartment, my lord. He was a farmer from Wexford. Not a good player, but he had the devil's own luck."

"Did you manage to get his name?" asked Judge Comyn.

Mr. Keane looked perplexed. "I did not," he said. "It was the accused who had the cards. He was trying to cheat me all right."

The prosecution case ended and O'Connor took the stand on his own behalf. He was sworn in. His story was as simple as it was plaintive. He bought and sold horses for a living; there was no crime in that. He enjoyed a friendly game of cards, but was no dab hand at it. A week before the train journey of 13 May he had been having a quiet stout in a Dublin public house when he felt a hard lump on the wooden pew near his thigh.

It was a pack of cards, apparently abandoned by a previous occupant of the booth, and certainly not new. He thought of handing them in to the barman, but realized such a time-worn pack would have no value anyway. He had kept them, and amused himself with patience on his long journeys seeking a foal or mare to buy for clients.

If the cards were marked, he was totally ignorant of it. He knew nothing of this shading and trimming the detective had talked about. He would not even know what to look for on the backs of his pack of cards, found on a pub seat.

As for cheating, didn't cheats win? he asked the jury. He had lost £8 10s. on that journey, to a complete stranger. He was a fool to himself, for the farmer had had all the run of the good hands. If Mr. Keane had wagered and lost more than he, that was perhaps because Mr. Keane was a more rash man than he. But as to cheating, he would have no part of it, and certainly he would not have lost so much of his own hard-earned money.

In cross-examination prosecuting counsel sought to break his story. But the wispy little man stuck to it with apologetic and self-deprecating tenacity. Finally counsel had to sit down.

O'Connor returned to the dock and awaited the summing up. Judge Comyn gazed at him across the court. You're a poor specimen, O'Connor, he thought. Either your story is true, in which case you are a truly unlucky cardplayer. Or it is not, in which case you must be the world's most incompetent cardsharp. Either way, you have twice lost, using your own cards, to strangers in railway trains.

On the matter of the summing-up, however, he could allow no such choice. He pointed out to the jury that the accused had claimed he had found the cards in a Dublin pub and was completely unaware that they were a marked deck. The jury might privately wish to believe that story or not; the fact was the prosecution had not disproved it, and in Irish law the burden of proof was upon them.

Secondly, the accused had claimed that it was not he but Mr. Keane who had proposed both the poker and the wagering, and Mr. Keane had conceded that this might be true.

But much more importantly, the prosecution case was that the accused had won money by false pretences from the witness Lurgan Keane. Whatever the pretences, true or false, witness Keane had conceded on oath that the accused had won no money from him. Both he, the witness, and the accused had lost money, albeit widely differing sums. On that issue the case must fail. It was his duty to direct the jury to acquit the defendant. Knowing his court, he also pointed out that it lacked fifteen minutes to the hour of luncheon.

It takes a case of weighty jurisprudence to keep a Kerry jury from its lunch, and the twelve good men were back in ten minutes with a verdict of not guilty. O'Connor was discharged and left the dock.

Judge Comyn disrobed behind the court in the robing room, hung his wig on a peg and left the building to seek his own lunch. Without robes, ruffle or wig, he passed through the throng on the pavement before the court house quite unrecognized.

He was about to cross the road to the town's principal hotel where, he knew, a fine Shannon salmon awaited his attention, when he saw coming out of the hotel yard a handsome and gleaming limousine of noted marque. At the wheel was O'Connor.

"Do you see your man?" asked a wondering voice by his side. He glanced to his right and found the Tralee grocer standing beside him.

"I do," he said.

The limousine swept out of the hotel yard. Sitting beside O'Connor was a passenger dressed all in black.

"Do you see who's sitting beside him?" asked Keane in wonderment.

The car swished towards them. The cleric with a concern to help the orphans of Dingle bestowed a benign smile and raised two stiff fingers towards the men on the sidewalk. Then the car was heading down the street.

"Was that an ecclesiastical blessing?" asked the grocer.

"It might have been," conceded Judge Comyn, "though I doubt it."

"And what was he dressed in those clothes for?" asked Lurgan Keane.

"Because he's a priest of the Holy Church," said the judge.

"He never is," said the grocer hotly, "he's a farmer from Wexford."

FREDERICK FORSYTH, who lives outside London, is the author of seven bestselling novels. *The Deceiver, The Day of the Jackal, The Devil's Alternative, The Dogs of War, The Fourth Protocol, The Negotiator,* and *The Odessa File*. His other works include *The Biafra Story. The Shepherd,* and an acclaimed collection of short fiction, *No Comebacks*.

CLASSIC SUSPENSE FROM
A MASTER OF INTRIGUE!

THE DAY OF THE JACKAL, Frederick Forsyth's first novel, soared onto international bestseller lists and made publishing history by reinventing the thriller. THE ODESSA FILE, THE DOGS OF WAR, and THE DEVIL'S ALTERNATIVE, forever placed him in the front ranks of bestselling suspense novelists. THE FOURTH PROTOCOL, THE NEGOTIATOR, and THE DECEIVER have made him a publishing legend.

THE DAY OF THE JACKAL

The Jackal: a killer at the top of his profession, a man unknown to any Secret Service in the world, an assassin with a contract to kill the world's most heavily guarded man. That marked man is Charles de Gaulle, and after six attempts on de Gaulle's life, the Jackal has the assignment of a lifetime.

"Since you have read the files available, I will not bore you with the motivations behind our organisation, which you have accurately summed up as idealism. We believe France is now ruled by a dictator who has polluted our country and prostituted its honour. We believe his regime can only fall and France be restored to Frenchmen if he first dies. Out of six attempts by our supporters to eliminate him, three were exposed in the early planning stages, one was betrayed the day before the attempt, and two took place but misfired.

"We are considering, but at this stage only considering, engaging the services of a professional to do the job. However, we do not wish to waste our money. The first thing we would like to know is if it is possible."

Rodin had played his cards shrewdly. The last sentence, to which he already knew the answer, brought a flicker of expression to the grey eyes.

"There is no man in the world who is proof against an assassin's bullet," said the Englishman. "de Gaulle's exposure rate is very high. Of course, it's possible to kill him. The point is that the chances of escape would not be too high. A fanatic prepared to die himself in the attempt is always the most certain method of eliminating a dictator who exposes himself to the public. I notice," he added with a touch of malice, "that despite your idealism you have not yet been able to produce such a man. Both Pont-de-Seine and Petit-Clamart failed because no one was prepared to risk his own life to make absolutely certain."

"There are patriotic Frenchmen prepared even now—" began Casson hotly, but Rodin silenced him with a gesture. The Englishman did not even glance at him.

"And as regards a professional?"—prompted Rodin.

"A professional does not act out of fervour and is therefore more calm and less likely to make elementary errors. Not being idealistic, he is not likely to have second thoughts at the last minute about who else might get hurt in the explosion, or whatever method, and being a professional he has calculated the risks to the last contingency. So his chances of success on schedule are surer than anyone else's, but he will not even enter into operation until he has devised a plan that will enable him not only to complete the mission, but to escape unharmed."

"Do you estimate that such a plan could be worked out to permit a professional to kill Grand Zohra and escape?"

The Englishman smoked quietly for a few minutes and stared out of the window. "In principle, yes," he replied at length. "In principle, it is always possible with enough time and planning. But in this case it would be extremely difficult. More so than with most other targets."

"Why more than other?" asked Montclair.

"Because de Gaulle is forewarned—not about the specific attempt but about the general intention. All big men have bodyguards and security men, but over a period of years without any serious attempt on the life of the big man, the checks become formal, the routines mechanical, and the degree of watchfulness is lowered. The single bullet that finishes the target is wholly unexpected and therefore provokes panic. Under cover of this the assassin escapes. In this case there will be no lowering of the level of watchfulness, no mechanical routines, and if the bullet were to get to the target, there would be many who would not panic but would go for the assassin. It could be done, but it would be one of the hardest jobs in the world at this moment. You see, gentlemen, your own efforts have not only failed but have queered the pitch for everyone else."

"In the event that we decide to employ a professional assassin to do this job—" began Rodin.

"You have to employ a professional," cut in the Englishman quietly.

"And why, pray? There are many men still who would be prepared to do the job out of purely patriotic motives."

"Yes, there are still Watin and Curutchet," replied the blond man. "And doubtless there are more Degueldres and Bastien-

Thirys around somewhere. But you three men did not call me here for a chat in general terms about the theory of political assassination, nor because you have a sudden shortage of trigger-fingers. You called me here because you have belatedly come to the conclusion that your organisation is so infiltrated by the French Secret Service agents that little you decide remains secret for long, and also because the faces of every one of you are imprinted on the memory of every cop in France. Therefore you need an outsider. And you are right. If the job is to be done, an outsider has to do it. The only questions that remain are who, and for how much. Now, gentlemen, I think you have had long enough to examine the merchandise, don't you?''

Robin looked sideways at Montclair and raised an eyebrow. Montclair nodded. Casson followed suit. The Englishman gazed out of the window without a shred of interest.

"Will you assassinate de Gaulle?" asked Rodin at last. The voice was quiet, but the question filled the room. The Englishman's glance came back to him, and the eyes were blank again.

"Yes, but it will cost a lot of money."

THE DAY OF THE JACKAL Copyright © 1971 by Frederick Forsyth

THE ODESSA FILE

A secret organization, ODESSA, is exposed following the suicide of a German Jew, Eduard Roschmann, and journalist Peter Miller is suddenly thrust into a desperate search for a fugitive known as the "Butcher of Riga." Yet no matter where his journey takes him, all indications are that Roschmann is long dead.

"You wanted to see me?" Miller asked.

The man sprang to his feet. "Herr Miller?"

"Yes."

"Herr Peter Miller?"

"Yes."

The man inclined his head in the short, jerky bow of old-fashioned Germans. "My name is Schmidt. Doctor Schmidt."

"What can I do for you?"

Dr. Schmidt smiled deprecatingly and gazed out of the windows where the black, bleak mass of the Rhine flowed under the fairy lights of the deserted terrace.

"I am told you are a journalist. Yes? A freelance journalist. A very good one." He smiled brightly. "You have a reputation for being very thorough, very tenacious."

Miller remained silent, waiting for him to get to the point.

"Some friends of mine heard you are presently engaged on an inquiry into events that happened—well, let us say, a long time ago. A very long time ago."

Miller stiffened and his mind raced, trying to work out who the "friends" were and who could have told them. Then he realized he had been asking questions about Roschmann all over the country.

"An inquiry about a certain Eduard Roschmann." And he said tersely, "So?"

"Ah yes, about Captain Roschmann. I just thought I might be able to help you." The man swiveled his eyes back from the river and fixed them kindly on Miller. "Captain Roschmann is dead."

"Indeed?" said Miller, "I didn't know."

Dr. Schmidt seemed delighted. "Of course not. There's no reason why you should. But it is true nevertheless. Really, you are wasting your time."

Miller looked disappointed. "Can you tell me when he died?" he asked the doctor.

"You have not discovered the circumstances of his death?" the man asked.

"No. The last trace of him I can find was in late April nineteen forty-five. He was seen alive then."

"Ah yes, of course." Dr. Schmidt seemed happy to oblige. "He was killed, you know, shortly after that. He returned to his native Austria and was killed fighting against the Americans in early nineteen forty-five. His body was identified by several people who had known him in life."

"He must have been a remarkable man," said Miller.

Dr. Schmidt nodded in agreement. "Well, yes, some thought so. Yes indeed, some of us thought so."

"I mean," continued Miller as if the interruption had not occurred, "he must have been remarkable to be the first man since Jesus Christ to have risen from the dead. He was captured alive by the British on December twentieth, nineteen forty-seven, at Graz in Austria."

The doctor's eyes reflected the glittering snow along the balustrade outside the window. "Miller, you are being very foolish. Very foolish indeed. Permit me to give you a word of advice, from an older man to a much, much younger one. Drop this inquiry."

Miller eyed him. "I suppose I ought to thank you," he said without gratitude.

"If you will take my advice, perhaps you ought," said the doctor.

"You misunderstand me again," said Miller. "Roschmann was also seen alive in mid-October this year in Hamburg. The second sighting was not confirmed. Now it is. You just confirmed it."

"I repeat, you are being very foolish if you do not drop this inquiry." The doctor's eyes were as cold as ever, but there was a hint of anxiety in them. There had been a time when people did not reject his orders, and he had never quite got used to the change.

Miller began to get angry, a slow glow of anger worked up from his collar to his face. "You make me sick. *Herr Doktor*," he told the older man. "You and your kind, your whole stinking gang. You have a respectable façade, but you are filth on the face of my country. So far as I am concerned, I'll go on asking questions till I find him."

He turned to go, but the elder man grabbed his arm. They stared at each other from a range of two inches.

"You're not Jewish, Miller, You're Aryan. You're one of us. What did we ever do to you, for God's sake, what did we ever do to you?"

Miller jerked his arm free. "If you don't know yet, *Herr Doktor*, you'll never understand."

"*Ach*, you people of the younger generation, you're all the same. Why can you never do what you're told?"

"Because that's the way we are. Or at least it's the way *I* am."

The older man stared at him with narrowed eyes. "You're not stupid, Miller. But you're behaving as if you were. As if you were one of these ridiculous creatures constantly governed by what they call their conscience. But I'm beginning to doubt that. It's almost as if you had something personal in this matter."

Miller turned to go. "Perhaps I have," he said and walked away across the lobby.

THE DOGS OF WAR

In a remote corner of Zangaro, Africa, lies Crystal Mountain, which contains ten billion dollars of the world's most valuable mineral; platinum. Only one man, Sir James Manson, has this knowledge, but his problem is how to get hold of it. His plan is as dangerous as it is ingenious. With untold wealth the reward, Sir James has unleashed the dogs of war . . .

Sir James Manson stared out of the window for some time. Finally he said, "Get Martin Thorpe up here." While Thorpe was being summoned, Manson walked to the window and gazed down, as he usually did when he wanted to think hard.

He bade them sit down and, remaining standing with his back to the window, he told them, "I want you two to think this one over very carefully, then give me your reply. How far would you be prepared to go to be assured of a personal fortune in a Swiss bank of five million pounds each?"

The hum of the traffic ten floors down was like a buzzing bee, accentuating the silence in the room.

Endean stared back at his chief and nodded slowly. "A very, very long way," he said softly.

Thorpe made no reply. He knew this was what he had come to the City for, joined Manson for, absorbed his encyclopedic knowledge of company business for. The big one, the once-in-a-decade grand slam. He nodded assent.

"How?" whispered Endean. For answer Manson walked to his wall safe and extracted two reports. The third, Shannon's, lay on his desk as he seated himself behind it.

Manson talked steadily for an hour. He started at the beginning and soon read the final six paragraphs of Dr. Chalmers's report on the samples from the Crystal Mountain.

Thorpe whistled softly and muttered, "Jesus."

"If it is to work at all, it must be a question of mounting two parallel, highly secret operations," Manson said finally. "In one, Shannon, stage-managed throughout by Simon, mounts a project to take and destroy that palace and all its contents, and for Bobi, accompanied by Simon, to take over the powers of state the following morning and become the new president. In the other, Martin would have to buy a shell company without revealing who had gained control or why."

Endean furrowed his brow. "I can see the first operation, but why the second?" he asked.

"Tell him, Martin," said Manson.

Thorpe was grinning, for his astute mind had caught Manson's drift. "A shell company, Simon, is a company, usually very old and without assets worth talking about, which has virtually ceased trading and whose shares are very cheap—say, a shilling each."

"So why buy one?" asked Endean, still puzzled.

"Say Sir James has control of a company, bought secretly through unnamed nominees, hiding behind a Swiss bank, all nice and legal, and the company has a million shares valued at one shilling each. Unknown to the other shareholders or the board of directors or the Stock Exchange, Sir James, via the Swiss bank, owns six hundred thousand of these million shares. Then Colonel—beg his pardon—President Bobi sells that company an exclusive ten-year mining franchise for an area of land in the hinterland of Zangaro. A new mining survey team from a highly reputable company specializing in mining goes out and discovers the Crystal Mountain. What happens to the shares of Company X when the news hits the stock market?"

Endean got the message. "They go up," he said with a grin.

"Right up," said Thorpe. "With a bit of help they go from a shilling to well over a hundred pounds a share. Now do your arithmetic. Six hundred thousand shares at a shilling each cost thirty thousand pounds to buy. Sell six hundred thousand shares at a hundred pounds each—and that's the minimum you'd get—and what do you bring home? A cool sixty million pounds, in a Swiss bank. Right, Sir James?"

"That's right." Manson nodded grimly. "Of course, if you sold half the shares in small packets to a wide variety of people, the control of the company owning the concession would stay in the same hands as before. But a bigger company might put in a bid for the whole block of six hundred thousand shares in one flat deal."

Thorpe nodded thoughtfully. "Yes, control of such a company bought at sixty million pounds would be a good market deal. But whose bid would you accept?"

"My own," said Manson.

Thorpe's mouth opened. "Your own?"

"ManCon's bid would be the only acceptable one. That way the concession would remain firmly British, and ManCon would have gained a fine asset."

"But," queried Endean, "surely you would be paying yourself sixty million quid?"

"No," said Thorpe quietly. "ManCon's shareholders would be paying Sir James sixty million quid, without knowing it."

"What's that called—in financial terms, of course?" asked Endean.

"There is a word for it on the Stock Exchange," Thorpe admitted.

Sir James Manson tendered them each a glass of whisky. He reached round and took his own. "Are you on, gentlemen?" he asked quietly.

Both younger man looked at each other and nodded.

"Then here's to the Crystal Mountain."

They drank.

"Report to me here tomorrow morning at nine sharp," Manson told them, and they rose to go.

At the door to the back stairs Thorpe turned. "You know, Sir James, it's going to be bloody dangerous. If one word gets out . . ."

Sir James Manson stood again with his back to the window, the westering sun slanting onto the carpet by his side. His legs were apart, his fists on his hips.

"Knocking off a bank or an armored truck," he said, "is

merely crude. Knocking off an entire republic has, I feel, a certain style.''

THE DEVIL'S ALTERNATIVE

Intrigue, terror, suspense. Russia faces famine, and is forced to pin its hopes for survival on the U.S. Yet the rescue of a Ukrainian "freedom fighter" from the Black Sea unleashes a savagery that endangers peace between the superpowers—and brings the world to the brink of nuclear destruction . . .

"These figures," asked President Matthews, "they represent the final aggregate grain crop the Soviet Union brought in a month ago?"

He glanced across at the four men seated in front of his desk. At the far end of the room a log fire crackled in the marble fireplace, adding a touch of visual warmth to the already high temperature assured by the central heating system. Beyond the bulletproof south windows, the sweeping lawns held their first dusting of November morning frost. Being from the South, William Matthews appreciated warmth.

Robert Benson and Dr. Myron Fletcher nodded in unison. David Lawrence and Stanislaw Poklewski studied the figures.

"All our sources have been called on for these figures, Mr. President, and all our information has been correlated extremely carefully," said Benson. "We could be out by five percent either way, no more."

"And according to the Nightingale, even the Politburo agrees with us," interposed the Secretary of State.

"One hundred million tons, total," mused the President. "It will last them till the end of March, with a lot of belt tightening."

"They'll be slaughtering the cattle by January," said Poklewski. "They have to start making sweeping concessions at Castletown next month if they want to survive."

The President laid down the Soviet grain report and picked up the presidential briefing prepared by Ben Kahn and presented by his Director of Central Intelligence. It had been read by all four in the room, as well as himself. Benson and Lawrence had agreed with it; Dr. Fletcher was not called upon for an opinion; the hawkish Poklewski dissented.

"We know—and they know—they are in desperate straits," said Matthews. "The question is, how far do we push them?"

"As you said weeks ago, Mr. President," said Lawrence, "if we don't push hard enough, we don't get the best deal we can for America and the free world. Push too hard and we force Rudin to abort the talks to save himself from his own hawks. It's a question of balance. At this point, I feel we should make them a gesture."

"Wheat?"

"Animal feed to help them keep some of their herds alive?" suggested Benson.

"Dr. Fletcher?" asked the President.

The man from the Agriculture Department shrugged.

"We have the feed available, Mr. President," he said. "The Soviets have a large proportion of their own merchant fleet, Sovfracht, standing by. We know that because with their subsidized freight rates they could all be busy, but they're not. They're positioned all over the warm-water ports of the Black Sea and down the Soviet Pacific coast. They'll sail for the United States if they're given the word from Moscow."

"What's the latest we need to give a decision on this one?" asked President Matthews.

"New Year's Day," said Benson. "If they know a respite is coming, they can hold off slaughtering the herds."

"I urge you not to ease up on them," pleaded Poklewski. "By March they'll be desperate."

"Desperate enough to concede enough disarmament to assure peace for a decade, or desperate enough to go to war?" asked Matthews rhetorically. "Gentlemen, you'll have my decision by Christmas Day. Unlike you, I have to take five chairmen of Senate subcommittees with me on this one: Defense, Agriculture, Foreign Relations, Trade, and Appropriations. And I can't tell them about the Nightingale, can I, Bob?"

The chief of the CIA shook his head.

"No, Mr. President. Not about the Nightingale. There are too many Senate aides, too many leaks. The effect of a leak of what we really know at this juncture could be disastrous."

"Very well, then. Christmas Day it is."

NO COMEBACKS

In this surprising volume are ten suspenseful, serpentine stories of betrayal, blackmail, murder, and revenge—all culminating in shocking twists of fate that only Frederick Forsyth could devise.

He bent back the two covers and held them together with an elastic band. The intervening 400 pages he secured as a block to the edge of the kitchen table with two carpenter's clamps.

Onto this block of paper he began to work with the thin, razor-sharp scalpel acquired the same afternoon. He sliced away for almost an hour until a square, set 1½ inches into the area of the page from each edge, had been cut out, forming a box 7 inches by 6 inches and 3 inches deep. The insides of this hollow square he daubed thickly with a tacky glue, and smoked two cigarettes while waiting for the glue to dry. When it was hard the 400 pages would never open again.

A cushion of foam rubber, cut to size, went into the hollow to replace the 1½ pounds of paper which had been cut out and which he had weighed on the kitchen scales. He dismantled the slim Browning 9-mm automatic he had acquired on a trip into Belgium two months earlier when he had used and thrown into the Albert Canal his previous gun, a Colt .38. He was a careful man, and never used the same shooter twice. The Browning had had the tip of its barrel exposed to half an inch, and the barrel's end tooled to take a silencer.

A silencer on an automatic is never truly quiet, despite the efforts of the sound-effects men in television thrillers to pretend it is. Automatics, unlike revolvers, do not have a closed breech. As the bullet leaves the barrel the automatic's jacket is forced backwards to expel the spent cartridge and inject a fresh one. That is why they are called automatics. But in that split second as the breech opens to expel the used shell, half the noise of the explosion comes out through the open breech, making a silencer on the end of the barrel only 50 percent effective. Calvi would have preferred a revolver with its breech closed during firing, but he needed a flat gun to go into the cavity in the book.

The silencer he laid beside the parts of the Browning was the largest component, 6½ inches long. As a professional he knew the champagne-cork-sized silencers shown on television are as much use as a hand-held fire extinguisher to put out Mount Vesuvius.

Arranged side by side on top of the rubber cushion, the five parts, including silencer and magazine, would not quite fit, so he smacked the magazine into the automatic's handle to save space. He marked out the beds of the four components with a felt-nib pen and began to cut into the foam rubber with a fresh scalpel. My midnight the parts of the gun lay peacefully in their foam beds, the long silencer vertical, parallel to the book's spine, the barrel, butt and jacket breech in three horizontal rows from top to bottom of the page.

He covered the assembly with a thin sheet of foam rubber, daubed the insides of the front and back covers with more glue and closed the book. After an hour pressed between the floor and an upturned table, the book was a solid block that would need a knife to prise it open. He weighed it again. It was just half an ounce heavier than the original.

Finally he slid the history of Spain into an open-ended envelope of strong polythene, such as publishers of high-quality books use to protect the dust covers from dirt and scratching. It fitted snugly, and he bonded the open end of the envelope together with the blade of his switchknife, heated over the gas stove. Should his parcel be opened, he hoped and expected the examiner would be content to assure himself through the transparent polythene that the contents were indeed a harmless book, and reseal the parcel.

The following morning he mailed the letter by air and the package by surface post, which meant the train and a ten-day delay.

THE FOURTH PROTOCOL

The wheels are in motion, the pawns are in place, and the countdown has begun toward an "accident" that could trigger the collapse of the Western Alliance. Only British agent John Preston's desperate investigation stands any chance of breaching the conspiracy . . . yet his every move is blocked by deceit and treachery, and by the most deadly enemy of all . . . time.

The General Secretary seemed lost in meditation, which no one was about to disturb. The hooded eyes brooded behind the glittering glasses for five minutes. At length he raised his head.

"There are no notes, no tape recordings, no shreds of this plan outside this room?"

"None," agreed the four committeemen.

"Gather up the files and folders and pass them to me," said the General Secretary. When this was done, he went on, in his habitual monotone.

"It is reckless, crazy, adventurist, and dangerous beyond belief," he intoned. "The Committee is disbanded. You are to return to your professions and never mention either the Albion Committee or Plan Aurora again."

He was still sitting there, staring at the table, when the four subdued and humbled men trooped out. They put on their coats and hats in silence, hardly meeting one another's eyes, and were led downstairs to their cars.

In the courtyard, each climbed into his own car. In his Volga, Philby waited for Gregoriev to start the engine, but the man just sat there. The three other limousines swept out of the square, under the arch, and into the boulevard. There was a tap on Philby's window. He wound it down to see the face of Major Pavlov.

"Would you come with me, please, Comrade Colonel?"

Philby's heart sank. He understood now that he knew too much; he was the one foreigner in the group. The General Secretary had a reputation for tying up loose ends rather permanently. He followed Major Pavlov back into the building. Two minutes later he was shown into the General Secretary's sitting room. The old man was still in his wheelchair at the low coffee table. He gestured Philby to a seat. In trepidation the British traitor took it.

"What did you really think of it?" asked the General Secretary softly.

Philby swallowed hard. "Ingenious, audacious, hazardous, but, if it worked, effective," he said.

"It's brilliant," murmured the General Secretary. "And it is going ahead. But under my personal auspices. This is to be no one else's operation, just mine. And you will be closely involved in it."

"May I ask one thing?" Philby ventured. "Why me? I am a foreigner. Even though I have served the Soviet Union all my life and have lived here for a third of it, I am still a foreigner."

"Precisely," replied the General Secretary, "and you have no patronage except mine. You could not begin to conspire against me.

"You will take leave of your wife and family and dismiss your driver. You will take up residence in the guest suite at my dacha at Usovo. There you will put together the team that will undertake Plan Aurora. You will have any authority you need— it will come from my office at the Central Committee. You, personally, will not show yourself." He pressed a buzzer under the table. "You will work at all times under the eye of this man. I believe you already know him."

The door had opened. In it stood the impassive, cold Major Pavlov.

"He is highly intelligent and extremely suspicious," said the General Secretary with approval. "He is also totally loyal. He happens to be my nephew."

As Philby rose to accompany the major, the General Secretary held out a slip of paper to him. It was a flimsy note from the First Chief Directorate marked for the personal attention of the General Secretary of the CPSU. Philby read it with disbelief.

"Yes," said the General Secretary, "it reached me yesterday. You will not have General Marchenko's ten to sixteen months. It appears that Mrs. Thatcher is going to make her move in June. We must make ours one week before that."

Philby let out his breath slowly. In 1917 it had taken ten days to complete the Russian Revolution. Britain's greatest turncoat of them all was being given just ninety days to guarantee the British one.

THE FOURTH PROTOCOL Copyright © 1984 by Frederick Forsyth

THE NEGOTIATOR

The terror begins as an Oxford student is kidnapped, and the President of the United States, bent on signing a sweeping disarmament treaty, is rendered distraught and helpless. Enter Quinn, the Negotiator. Yet ransom is not the objective and in an act of terrorism beyond compare, the future of the free world is pushed to the brink . . .

The street he had been told to walk down was narrow, dirty, and empty. To one side, derelict tea warehouses, ripe for development, fronted the river. To the other, abandoned factories and steel sheds. He knew he was being watched from somewhere. He walked along the center of the street. The steel hangar with the faded painted name of Babbidge above one door was at the end. He turned inside.

Two hundred feet long, eighty wide. Rusted chains hung from roof girders; the floor was concrete, fouled by the windswept detritus of years of abandonment. The door he had entered by would take a pedestrian but not a vehicle; the one at the far end was wide enough and high enough to take a truck. He walked to the middle of the floor and stopped. He took off the phony eyeglasses and tweed hat and stuffed them in his pocket. He would not need them again. Either he walked out of here with a deal for Simon Cormack, or he would need a police escort anyway.

He waited an hour, quite immobile. At eleven o'clock the big Volvo appeared at the far end of the hangar and drove slowly toward him, coming to a stop with its engine running forty feet away. There were two men in the front, both masked so that only their eyes showed through the slits.

He sensed more than heard the scuffle of running shoes on concrete behind him and threw a casual glance over his shoulder. A third man stood there; black track suit without insignia, ski mask covering the head. He was alert, poised on the balls of his feet, with the submachine carbine held easily, at the port but ready for use if need be.

The passenger door of the Volvo opened and a man got out. Medium height, medium build.

He called: "Quinn?"

Zack's voice. Unmistakable.

"You got the diamonds?"

"Right here."

"Hand them over."

"You got the kid, Zack?"

"Don't be a fool. Trade him for a sack of glass pebbles? We examine the stones first. Takes time. One piece of glass, one piece of paste—you've blown it. If they're okay, then you get the boy."

"That's what I figured. Won't work."

"Don't play games with me, Quinn."

"No games, Zack. I have to see the kid. You could get pieces of glass—you won't, but you want to be sure. I could get a corpse."

"You won't."

"I need to be sure. That's why I have to go with you."

Behind the mask Zack stared at Quinn in disbelief. He gave a grating laugh.

"See that man behind you? One word and he blows you away. Then we take the stones anyway."

"You could try," admitted Quinn. "Ever seen one of these?"

He opened his raincoat all the way down, took something that hung free from near his waist and held it up.

Zack studied Quinn and the assembly strapped to his chest over his shirt, and swore softly but violently.

From below his sternum to his waist, Quinn's front was occupied by the flat wooden box that had once contained liqueur chocolates. The bonbons were gone, along with the box's lid. The tray of the box formed a flat container strapped with surgical tape across his chest.

In the center was the velour package of diamonds, framed on each side by a half-pound block of tacky beige substance. Jammed into one of the blocks was a bright-green electrical wire, the other end of which ran to one of the spring-controlled jaws of the wooden clothespin Quinn held aloft in his left hand. It went through a tiny hole bored in the wood, to emerge inside the jaws of the peg.

Also in the chocolate box was a PP3 nine-volt battery, wired to another bright-green cord. In one direction the green cord linked both blocks of beige substance to the battery; in the other direction the wire ran to the opposite jaw of the clothespin. The jaws of the pin were held apart by a stub of pencil. Quinn flexed the fingers of his hand; the stub of pencil fell to the floor.

"Phony," said Zack without conviction. "That's not real."

With his right hand Quinn twisted off a blob of the light-brown substance, rolled it into a ball, and tossed it across the floor to Zack. The criminal stooped, picked it up, and sniffed. The odor of marzipan filled his nostrils.

"Semtex," he said.

"That's Czech," said Quinn. "I prefer RDX."

Zack knew enough to know all explosive gelatins both look

and smell like the harmless confection marzipan. There the difference ends. If his man opened fire now they would all die. There was enough plastic explosive in that box to clear the floor of the warehouse clean, lift off the roof, and scatter the diamonds on the other side of the Thames.

"Knew you were a bastard," said Zack. "What do you want?"

"I pick up the pencil, put it back, climb into the trunk of the car, and you drive me to see the boy. No one followed me. No one will. I can't recognize you, now or ever. You're safe enough. When I see the kid alive, I dismantle this and give you the stones. You check them through; when you're satisfied, you leave. The kid and I stay imprisoned. Twenty-four hours later you make an anonymous phone call. The fuzz comes to release us. It's clean, it's simple, and you get away."

THE NEGOTIATOR Copyright © 1989 by Frederick Forsyth

THE DECEIVER

Forsyth's latest hero is Sam McCready, known also as The Deceiver. Sam served as chief of covert operations for years, but what with the end of the cold war, he is now being forced into retirement. The only thing that could save him is his past— a twisted past of violence down the secret corridors of espionage . . .

The Russian colonel stepped out of the shadows slowly and carefully, even though he had seen and recognized the signal. All meetings with his British controller were dangerous and to be avoided if possible. But this one he had asked for himself. He had things to say, to demand, that could not be put in a message in a dead-letter box. A loose sheet of metal on the roof of a shed down the railway line flapped and creaked in a puff of predawn May wind of that year, 1983. He turned, established the source of the noise, and stared again at the patch of darkness near the locomotive turntable.

"Sam?" he called softly.

Sam McCready had also been watching. He had been there for an hour in the darkness of the abandoned railway yard in the outer suburbs of East Berlin. He had seen, or rather heard, the Russian arrive, and still he had waited to ensure that no other feet were moving amidst the dust and the rubble. However many times you did it, the knotted ball in the base of your stomach never went away.

At the appointed hour, satisfied they were alone and unaccompanied, he had flicked the match with his thumbnail, so that it had flared once, briefly, and died away. The Russian had seen it and emerged from behind the old maintenance hut. Both men had reason to prefer the gloom, for one was a traitor and the other a spy.

McCready moved out of the darkness to let the Russian see him, paused to establish that he too was alone, and went forward.

"Yevgeni. It's been a long time, my friend."

At five paces they could see each other clearly, establish that there had been no substitution, no trickery. That was always the danger in a face-to-face. The Russian might have been taken and then broken in the interrogation rooms, allowing the KGB and the East German SSD to set up a trap for a top British intelligence officer. Or the Russian's message might have been intercepted, and it might be he was moving into the trap, thence to the long dark night of the interrogators and the final bullet in the nape of the neck. Mother Russia had no mercy for her traitorous elite.

McCready did not embrace or even shake hands. Some assets needed that: the personal touch, the comfort of contact. But Yevgeni Pankratin, Colonel of the Red Army, on attachment to the GSFG, was a cold one: aloof, self-contained, confident in his arrogance.

He had first been spotted in Moscow in 1980 by a sharp-eyed attaché at the British Embassy. It was a diplomatic function—polite, banal conversation, then the sudden tart remark by the Russian about his own society. The diplomat had given no sign, said nothing. But he had noted and reported. A possible. Two months later a first tentative approach had been made. Colonel Pankratin had been noncommital but had not rebuffed it. That ranked as positive. Then he had been posted to Potsdam, to the Group of Soviet Forces Germany, the GSFG, the 330,000-man, twenty-two-division army that kept the East Germans in thrall, the puppet Honecker in power, the West Berliners in fear, and NATO on the alert for a crushing breakout across the Central German Plain.

McCready had taken over; it was his patch. In 1981 he made his own approach, and Pankratin was recruited. No fuss, no outpourings of inner feelings to be listened to and agreed with— just a straight demand for money.

THE DECEIVER Copyright © 1991 by F.S.S. Partnership